RELEASED

by S. J. Pajonas

Onigiri Press
U.S.A.

Cover design by Najla Qamber Designs

Book design and production by S. J. Pajonas (Stephanie J. Pajonas).

To my love, Keith, for supporting me through all my craziness.

RELEASED

Chapter One

Mark Sakai, you are a dead man.

I'm still so angry despite living in this house for fourteen days now. With no one else to calm me down, no one to talk to, and no place to go, all I can do is sit and stew or pace and let my anger bubble over. Yesterday, I spent so much time screaming at the view out the window, my voice was hoarse after. I let the desert, the dunes, and the blue sky have it, gave the outside world all of my anger and frustration. My voice is gone today. It doesn't get much use otherwise. I haven't seen anyone in weeks.

After the fight at the theater, after I cut Tadao Matsuda's head off and passed out, I was unconscious until I awoke in the hospital. Sakai was there to tell me everything that happened — everything I want to forget but can't. I tried to get away but couldn't rip the IVs out of my arms fast enough. Then I ended up here. When I checked the tablet after reading Sakai's message, it had been almost two weeks since the fight at the theater. Now it's been a month. It's late April. How much longer will I be here?

Pace, back and forth. I've worn a path on the floor boards between the couch in the living room, the door to the kitchen, and the locked door that I suppose leads outside. I'm not sure because the door won't open no matter how many times I kick it or throw the chair at it. That chair is permanently mangled, but pummeling it against the door was the best exercise I've had in weeks.

When I'm sitting on the floor, which is often, I can see my footprints all over the section on which I pace. The floor was buffed and shiny when I first arrived, but now that area is dull and lifeless.

Koichi is dead. Jiro's father is dead, killed during a fight in which people were coming to kill me. Me! I still can't wrap my head around it.

The four days I spent with Jiro in our apartment right after I found out I'm a direct descendent of the emperor of Old Japan were amazing and confusing. My whole life transformed, and I kept trying to deal with the change, be okay with it. I went from being an engineer, to watching all the clan leaders in Nishikyō, to having to lead them all in the space of a few months. I fell in love, which is something I never thought would happen again. I miss Jiro, my aunts, Miko, and Helena. I even miss Sakai, though I want to beat the crap out of him.

I miss Mariko, Jiro's mother, too, and I wonder how she's doing with Koichi gone. I can close my eyes and remember the way they walked away from the okiya together after our big dinner, her head on his shoulder, his arm around her waist, still so in love after so much time. Will she hate me now? I did this. It's my fault.

My feet aren't moving anymore. I've come to a standstill in the middle of the living room, tears from my face running down my nose and off my cheeks straight to the floor. My gaze falls on my body, and I cringe. I've neglected myself since I've been here. The bruising on my back is almost gone, my arms finally clear of the IV marks, but I've been bad about feeding myself. I'm only eating once or twice per day, sleeping twelve to fourteen hours otherwise, and when I'm awake I do nothing but pace.

Pace and think. Contemplate my mistakes. What if I had stayed with Jiro instead of running for the door? What if we both had stayed in the theatre box instead of climbing out? Would we have been able to defend Koichi? Would we be alive or dead? Would Tadao Matsuda still be alive? That's the only thing I don't regret. He deserved to die. This is his fault, too. He sold me to Tomio Miura, head of Taira clan. My life was worth something to him. In the end, his life was worth something to me.

Once the tears start, I can't stop them. I've avoided crying since I've been here and focused on being angry, furious, and destructive instead. Koichi is dead. Jiro chose to go with me at the theater. He chose to climb out of that box with me instead of staying and defending his family. I want to scream at him now too.

How could you do that, Jiro? How could you choose me over your own family?

I know he loved me, but we were so new when this happened. He must hate me now.

And I can't even ask him. I can't see Jiro's face and know he still loves me or regrets ever having met me because Sakai has sent me away.

Mark Sakai, you are a dead man.

Day 32. My food is lasting a long time. I'm sure I should have eaten a lot more by now, but if I keep up eating only one or two meals per day, I can make them last almost three months instead of just the one. I'm afraid that could be the case since I've heard nothing from Sakai.

It's late morning. I think I slept for fourteen hours last night, and, if I don't eat now, I'll pass out. When I first arrived here, I was worried some of the provided food would go bad, but the fridge is brand new. It can keep food fresh almost indefinitely if you don't open the door too many times. Every shelf was stocked with packages of prepared meals and basic vegetables, mock chicken, tofu, mock fish, hand-pulled noodles, and countless other things like pickles and condiments. The freezer was also packed to the brim with frozen meals and vegetables of every kind, and a small container of soy ice cream. I don't remember the last time I had a dessert. Not even on my birthday.

My options are getting slim, so I pull one of the last refrigerated prepared meals from the fridge (a vegetable curry) and slip the container into the oven to heat up. With rice in the cooker, I sit down at the table and stare out the window. The blue sky used to terrify me, but now the fear is merely a tickle in the back of my brain. We'll see how I feel standing underneath the sky with nothing to shield me from being sucked away into space. The view, though, is my only form of entertainment besides the books Sakai left me on the tablet. He loaded it up with classics, but I am not a fan of Dickens.

"It was the best of times, it was the worst of times." You can say that again.

But I did find one book worth reading in my current situation: *The Art of War.* I'm going to have it memorized in no time.

My reflection in the mirror this morning surprised me. My face is thin with barely a trace of my baby fat left, and dark circles float under my eyes even with sleeping so much it's practically become my job. Professional sleeper.

I think my hair is growing. Funny that once my hair is long it seems to grow slower but now that it's short it grows faster. When I cut off my hair to save myself from Matsuda, it was in a ponytail and now I sport the strangest style I have ever seen. Longer, wispy strands hang down around my face, and the back of my head has hair that can't be longer than two centimeters, then it gets longer further down my head close to my neck.

I remember tying my hair up at the dōjō with Jiro and complaining about how I needed to get it cut. *"Don't. It suits you,"* he said. I can't even fix it. There are no scissors in this gods forsaken house. I've taken to tucking the front behind my ears and sometimes I can pretend it's in a ponytail as long as I don't reach up and touch my head. It's stupid, but I miss my hair.

The rice cooker chimes, signaling the cooking cycle is done, but I ignore it and let it sit.

What's going on at home? What is Sakai going to do with Taira clan? What can he accomplish over this month he was never able to do in the past? Maybe all of those dead bodies I was dragged past are finally the catalyst he needed to get them into prison. How is he going to subdue them? How is he going to keep them away from me long enough for us to get to Yūsei? Maybe he put me here to get rid of me. Would he do something like that?

What's Jiro doing? Do I even want to know? Forget about Jiro. How are my aunts? I never saw their new apartment so I imagine what it looks like. I think about Helena living in Ku 6 now. Has she seen any more of Usagi? Miko must be planning her wedding. I probably missed Koichi's funeral, which makes me think of Mariko, of Jiro, of Beni, and I wince. I'll most likely be left here because my very presence destroyed all of their lives.

Oh no.

I've been too busy thinking about how angry I am at Sakai and my situation that I haven't stopped to think about how everyone at home must feel about what happened, about me. I am the cause of all their lives falling apart.

I think I need to stay away from everyone. I have to distance myself, protect them all by staying out of their lives as much as possible.

Yes. I can do that. I'll be strong, and I'll do that. I had two relationships before Jiro without being loved in return. It'll be hard to go back to a loveless life, but I'd rather not have anyone hurt or killed because of me.

So it's decided then. If I ever get out of here, if I ever make it home, I'm going to ask Jiro to move out. He should have the opportunity to grow old and have kids with someone he can marry, and our relationship will be just business. I know he's next in line to head Sakai clan but maybe by the time that happens, he'll have a family, and we'll be two totally different people.

My appetite has vanished as quickly as a whirlwind on the dunes outside, my anger faded so fast to be almost nonexistent. Darkness settles on my shoulders, pushing them low, defeating my somewhat positive attitude I've had since I arrived here. A week ago, I hoped someone would come, let me out, and bring me home, and I could try to pick up where we all left off, try to reassemble my life.

That doesn't seem possible anymore.

Going to the kitchen, I make sure the rice cooker is on the warm setting and go back to bed without eating or showering like I normally do.

Sleep. Sleep will make it all go faster.

Chapter Two

Day 42. The eighth of May. My anger has not returned. I think I've been angry enough for an entire lifetime. Now I sit and imagine the conversations I'm going to have with everyone when I get back to Nishikyō. I imagine telling Sakai how I want to live somewhere else, how I want to slip back into anonymity. Surely I'm not that important, and he must be able to arrange this. And then maybe I can go to Miko's wedding and the izakaya without seeing Jiro. The conversation I'll have with Jiro about how we can't continue to be together will be hard. The imagined scenario always makes me cry so I try not to think about breaking up with him, but yet my brain doesn't listen, and I keep coming back to it. It's sadistic. I know I'm obsessive but even this borders on extreme.

Tonight, I do my usual evening routine of pacing and thinking then force myself to eat leftover rice from my lunch while I stargaze. Usually, I wait until I can see the stars slowly coming out as the sun dips low on the horizon and progresses from yellow, to orange, to blazing red before dying away completely. Then I stand and stare with my face pressed against the window.

Besides using the tablet to read Sakai's message over and over again, I checked the localization settings and found I'm somewhere in Middle Africa, probably Kenya or Tanzania since the tablet is pointed to three timezones ahead of Greenwich Mean Time. I'm also sure I'm between the Tropic of Cancer and the Tropic of Capricorn based on the fact the sun is directly overhead at noon every day. The Dead Belt. This used to be the only region on Earth in which coffee would grow. Now nothing grows or lives here anymore.

But the Dead Belt is the perfect place to put a space elevator. The space elevator has been here and working for the last fifty years. I've managed to catch sight of the shuttles that go to and from the top of the elevator to the space station at the North Pole. Watching them flit back and forth all night long is fascinating. I'm going to be up there someday. In space! It doesn't seem possible.

Past midnight, my legs can't hold me up anymore, and I sink to the floor in front of the picture window. Sleep. I can't even get myself to bed.

I dream about Jiro. He's standing over me as I lay on the mats at the dōjō. With his hair fallen down across his face, he says to me, "Do you miss me, Sanaa?" The dream feels so real, the mats soft underneath me, his feet sunken in next to me, the happy glint in his eyes when I smile at him and reach out to grab his foot.

I wake up on the floor, my hand stretched out to my side, grasping at the air. He's not here. Regardless of how much it hurts to think of Jiro, I go back to sleep hoping I'll dream of him again.

Day 48. Something's not right. I managed to shower the last few days and eat my required one meal and sleep in the bed, but I wake up this morning and wind is whipping across the desert, sand blasting the side of the house. The horizon is fuzzy, smudged with an orange haze. I blink my eyes, and the dimness doesn't go away.

A sandstorm is coming. How long do these things last? A day? Several? A week?

Forty-eight days ago, I awoke in the house. It's possible I was here two or three days before that, so I've been here maybe fifty days. Sakai said he'd left enough food for a month, and he'd come for me before the month was up. That hasn't happened, obviously. I was worried I'd have to spend more time here than what he planned on, but I hoped I was wrong. I really hoped I was wrong. This is one instance where I don't want to be right!

I pick up the tablet and re-check the date. Yes, it's the fourteenth of May now. The fight at the theater was at the end of March. I've been gone so long. What if this sandstorm keeps them away? What if they've forgotten about me here?

The sight of the growing sandstorm has me transfixed and panicking, and despite my fear of the sky, I've grown to tolerate the dunes and my view. In another hour or two, the desert will be completely gone. The cloud of sand is expanding, the amount of blue above lessening in width every moment.

"No! No! Stay away!"

Slamming my hands against the glass, I burst into tears, my voice cracking from disuse. A coughing fit doubles me over and brings up the tears even harder. I wish the door to the outside wasn't locked. I would get out. I would run. I'd take my chances with the blue sky and the radiation.

But it's too late. Specks of sand are already slapping against the window, a steady, high-pitched hiss replacing the desert silence. I back up from the window and sit at the table. I had never been ready to give up, not until now.

Damn you, Mark Sakai. How could you bring me all the way out here and leave me? How could you?

I sit and watch, numb, as the sky is swallowed and everything turns orange.

Chapter Three

Day 51. The storm is still raging outside, but I think it might be tapering off. The wind has quieted, hollow and low. Good. Maybe this will all be over soon.

Once the storm started, I decided the time was right to stop meting out the food. Sakai said he'd be back for me in a month. I figured I could last three months if I went down to one meal per day. But now that he's blown past his deadline, I had better live every day like it's my last, and I don't think I can handle three months of almost starvation. I'm constantly light-headed and dizzy, and I don't like it at all. I'm tired of starving, so I'll eat now, not starve, and worry about what happens later when the food runs out. I've lost a lot of weight since coming here, but three days of eating two to three meals a day is making me feel better physically, if not emotionally. Between the injuries and the fact that I just don't like feeding myself, I'm the skinniest I've ever been.

I'm having trouble getting out of bed. Bed is nice. Bed with Jiro was even nicer, but I don't think about that. I can't. The one dream I had of him was enough to shake me for days. Jiro. I love him. How can I tell him what I need to tell him if I never see him again?

Instead of sitting on the couch in the living room where the view is blotted out by orange during the day, I've been spending time in the bedroom sleeping or hanging out in the bed. I ate dinner in here yesterday and left my bowl on the floor. I should put it away. I'm not a slovenly person, even in this state.

It's late morning. I don't want to get up. Willing myself to go back to sleep, I roll over and face the wall. Maybe this time I'll dream of Nishikyō and the people I love. It'll make me cry, but I miss them too much not to dream of them.

Amongst the howl of the wind outside, a bump echoes through the house, soft and metallic. Other houses and infrastructure must be near here, and I wonder if something has fallen over in the storm. No matter. I can't get out to do anything about it anyway.

Go to sleep.

"Did you miss me, Sanaa?"

The dream of Jiro and the dōjō starts up immediately. It's so real, I can feel his hand on my neck, on my back. "Sanaa?"

I don't want to open my eyes and have him go away. "Jiro, don't go away."

"I'm right here."

My mind is playing tricks on me.

"Sanaa, wake up. I'm worried about you."

Wait.

Wait.

I roll over, and he's here. He's wearing a black, knit hat pulled down over his head and a black shirt that's up his neck to his chin. Sand is caught on his eyebrows, his eyelashes, and a small line of beard along his jaw.

"Jiro?"

"Yes, love. I've come for you."

But I don't believe it. Orange light streams in the window, coloring everything around me.

His hands come to my face. The warmth of his fingers caress my cheeks, and I can't stop the tears that jump into my eyes when the bed creaks, his knees coming down on either side of me, and his soft kiss is on my lips.

Every thought I had about freezing him out of my life to protect him flies straight out of my head. I can taste him. It's Jiro. It's Jiro's kiss. The kiss is hot and dry and tastes vaguely like dirt, but it's him.

He pulls back and his eyes search my face. This must be a dream — the most real and cruel dream I have ever dreamt — and the thought that he's not really here makes me burst into a sob.

"Oh, don't cry." Jiro leans in and kisses me again, his hands on either side of my face press in and make me moan with happiness.

"You're really here?"

"I am."

I reach up and remove the hat from his head, sand falling on me. His hair is messy and long, and I tuck it behind his ears.

"But the storm?"

"It's almost over. They dropped me outside, and I came in through the back. I couldn't leave you here anymore. Watching you fight against the storm?" He shakes his head, tears in his eyes. "I just couldn't bear to see you like that."

I sit up and wrap my arms around him. "Jiro, you're really here! I've missed you so much."

His hands cradle the back of my head, and his chest shakes as he catches his breath. Jiro's long fingers move from my head, down my back, probing along my ribs and my hips. "My gods, what happened to you? You're so thin."

This makes me cry even more, and I squeeze him harder still. How do I tell him I starved myself to survive longer because I didn't think he'd ever come for me?

"How? What? Talk to me, please. I've barely said five words aloud since I got here."

"Just a minute..."

He gets up from the bed, brushes himself off, and turns on the lights. I haven't turned on the lights in weeks, and the artificial glare explodes in my brain.

Sand is scattered on the bed, gritty sand sinking into the creases in the sheets. Sand has settled on Jiro's boots in between the straps. Sand leads out the bedroom door behind him.

Shakily, I stand up from the bed, and he lunges forward to grab my arms before I fall over. I'm only wearing an undershirt and underwear, and my bony arms and legs are jutting out from me at all angles.

"Sanaa, I'm so sorry," Jiro says as he leans back and scans me from the top of my head all the way down to my toes. He touches my hair, and I'm so embarrassed a blush bursts onto my cheeks. "You need to get this taken care of. This style does not suit you at all."

I haven't laughed in weeks, and it is the best feeling to laugh now at Jiro, but the joy tires me quickly. I wrap my arms around him before I fall over.

"How's your back? Is it healed?" He lifts up my undershirt in the back.

"Yes. The bruise is almost gone now though it's still a little tender."

"And your head?"

"Fine. I had a headache for a few days. Mark never left me coffee."

"Ouch," he says, shaking his head. Then a smile creeps up. "You're going to kill him, aren't you?"

"He deserves it."

"Damn right he does. I fought with him for days for not telling me he was taking you here." He smiles and shakes his head at me, and I step back and hug my chest with my thin arms. Why am I torturing myself by holding him? His smile falls, his eyes narrowing and searching mine, but I direct my gaze at my feet.

"Why didn't Mark come?" I ask.

"Are you unhappy to see me?" His voice breaks, and my insides crumble.

"No. Good gods, no. I'm… I've missed you so much, but I've had a lot to think about while I've been here, and…" Rip off the bandage. Get this over with as soon as possible. "It's not fair to you, to have to be stuck with me. Your father is dead because of me. How could you possibly still love me or want to be with me after everything that's happened?"

Silence stretches between us, and I'm so weak I can't stand up anymore, so I sit on the bed and wring my hands. Deep breath, Sanaa. Don't cry. I told myself I wouldn't cry when I did this, but it's much harder with him standing right next to me, and I'm so desperate for love and attention having been alone for seven weeks straight.

"You think this is your fault?" He sits down next to me on the bed and puts his hand on my back. I nod my head but don't say anything. My voice is too shaky. "Sanaa, none of what's happened is your fault. Nothing."

"Miura's men were coming for me. Me. They wanted to kill me and instead they killed so many others including your father. I don't even know how you could come here. You must hate me. Your mother must hate me." Moaning, I put my face in my hands and cry. I'm ashamed with myself for being so weak. "When we get back to Nishikyō, I'll find someplace else to live, and you can have the apartment and be close to your family. I'm sorry. So, so sorry."

"Whoa. Stop. There's no way that's going to happen. Look at me." I shake my head, the tears flying off my face and all over my arms. "I mean it, Sanaa. I want to see your face."

Smearing the tears from my cheeks, I blow out a breath and look at him, and he's horrified, his eyes wide and concerned.

"I love you. I showed you my scary and screwed-up life, and you didn't even blink." His hand moves from my back and cradles my elbow before sliding down my inner arm and holding my hand. "I gave you my heart, and you're the only person I want to be with. Once I give my heart, you can't give it back. You didn't know when you snared me, but you're mine forever."

Goosebumps erupt all over my neck. Forever.

I shake my head at him, trying one more time to make the point I've been convinced of for weeks.

"You've been gone from me for so long now. These last two months have felt like an eternity, sleeping in our bed every night alone, surrounded by your belongings. I refuse to let this go on any longer. It physically hurt to come home every day and not find you in our apartment. I never want that to happen again."

What was I thinking? That Jiro would just up and say okay? I've been attracted to him from the start because he's intense and commanding. Being apart from him made me forget how assertive he is.

"And those men came because, sure, they wanted to kill you, but do you have any idea how many times Miura has tried to kill Sakai?"

I shake my head again. I don't know much about their history.

"Numerous times. They've been adversaries their entire lives. And Matsuda and my parents..." Jiro closes his eyes for a moment. "That grudge has been going on forever, too. I don't hate you. My mother certainly doesn't hate you. No one does. We've been frantic and lonely without you."

"But..." I want to argue with him, get him to see reason.

"No. Just no. Do you have any idea how many days, weeks, I've been fighting with Sakai to come and get you from here? I've been watching you waste away little by little, and it's been torture."

"Watching me? You've been watching me? How?"

Jiro tilts his head up to each corner of the room and narrows his eyes. "Huh. Wow. They are a lot smaller here than I thought they would be. Just a moment."

He leaves the room. I have to stop myself from screaming at him to come back, but he quickly returns with a chair from the table in the living area. Placing it in the corner, he stands on the chair and inspects a small section of the wall at the corner.

"Well, damn, it's right here, though the camera can't be larger than a pin prick. No wonder you didn't know."

"How long have you been watching me?"

"About twenty days." He jumps down from the chair and comes

back to me at the bed. "Let me back up. After I fought off the men at the theater, I ran down the stairs to try and find you. I walked into that hallway with all of our dead men, and I was certain I was going to find you dead there, too. Instead, I found Matsuda but his head was far from his body, and your hair was on the floor next to him."

"He tried to take me, and I fought him as hard as I could, but he gave me a concussion, and my brain kept spinning, and... I was so sick. I had the chance to get away once, and he kicked me right in the kidney. Then he grabbed me by my hair and tried to drag me off to Miura. Once he let go of my arms, I used the knife you gave me to cut myself free and stabbed him in the stomach."

"Did you really cut his head off?"

My bottom lip trembles. This is the first time I've regretted doing something so rash, but I know Jiro will understand. I'm not sorry. "I did. He asked me for mercy, and I gave it to him."

He holds and squeezes my hands. "Are you okay?"

"With killing him?" The surprise must be all over my face because he laughs. "Yes, I'm okay with it! I wish I had killed him sooner. The only thing I'm not okay with is being left here all alone. Never leave me alone like this ever again, Jiro. Swear it."

"I swear it on our unborn children." He leans in and kisses me below my ear, and I close my eyes.

"I've missed you so much."

"I've missed you, too." He takes a deep breath. "I missed you at my father's funeral. I wish you had been there."

"Me too." The tears still come, and he wipes them away with his thumb.

"I came to the hospital several times before you regained consciousness. Sakai was with you when you finally woke up, and you became so upset they sedated you again. Two days later, someone tried to poison you while you were in the hospital."

"What?"

"Yes, but Usagi caught him. He would not leave your side. The man was a hired assassin posing as a nurse."

My life was in danger in the hospital and not from my injuries.

"Sakai went to Coen-sama right afterward and arranged this house for you. He did it as quickly as possible, and you were gone from the hospital the next time I came to see you. He even kept your location a secret from me because he knew how upset I was going to be." He nods his head and looks at me. "I decked him, Sanaa."

"Really? No."

"He was lucky I wasn't armed at the time, though I have a good right hook."

Hugging Jiro's arm, I lean my head on his shoulder.

"About a month after you were gone, I was in the surveillance room in the dōjō thinking of my father. I've missed him a lot." I squeeze him again, and we both keep a moment of silence between us. "I was watching all of our video feeds of our territory and found a menu that was password protected. I tried my father's old password, and the video feeds for this house came up. There you were. Sakai must have been checking in on you periodically. I know he was in the surveillance room in between every meeting.

"But every time I came to watch you, you were sleeping. It took me a few days to figure out you were sleeping because you were on the other side of the world, and my day was your night. So I started coming to watch you at night instead. I hardly ever saw you eat. You looked thin and so depressed. You yelled at the window, and wow, you were right about your temper. All the pacing. And then the storm came." His voice catches and his head dips low. "My mother had been watching you, too, for weeks and hadn't told me, and I'll never forget the look on her face when you started eating again after the storm hit."

"I didn't think anyone would come for me. It had been so long, and I didn't want to spend my last days starving to death." I never thought about what I would do once the food ran out. Hang myself? Starve? I doubt I could commit suicide. I was only dividing up my food in the first place to last as long as possible.

"You were breaking my heart. I couldn't let you stay here. I knew if I didn't persuade Sakai to let me come and get you, you would die before too long. I couldn't lose my father *and* you all at the same time."

"Jiro, I... I thought you had forgotten about me. I was desperately alone and so far from everyone I loved."

"How could you think I forgot about you? I could never forget about you. You're the only thing I've thought of for weeks," he says, putting his arm around me and squeezing. "It was completely unfair and wrong, but Sakai did keep you alive. He had his reasons even if they weren't very good. The good news is Taira clan is handled now and you can come home."

"How?"

"He's brilliant, really. I wish I had come up with it. Sakai managed to arrest every Taira boss and Miura himself. Then, instead of putting them in prison, he offered Miura a choice: die or be put in hibernation for Yūsei now. Miura had to promise everyone in his ranks would never lay a hand on you again. If anyone tries anything, we will cut the power to his hibernation chambers and he and the rest of his crew, and family — they are asleep too — will die."

"Die? Why not prison?"

Jiro laughs. "The same laws that make you an empress also protect you. Treason is punishable by death."

I close my eyes against this crazy reasoning. Treason. Miura. His family. Yes, he has a wife and two daughters. I know I would do anything to protect my family. I can only hope this is the one thing Miura and I would agree upon.

"Where are they now?"

"Asleep on their ship. Sakai went up with them about two days ago. He'll be back for us in five days, and we can go home."

"Home." I cannot wait.

"Yes. In the meantime, I brought more food, sake, coffee..." My eyes light up, I'm sure. "Coffee concentrate only, Sanaa."

"Ah, it's better than no coffee."

"I brought your tablet and a few other things. But mostly, I brought myself, and I'm going to make sure you eat and get happy again." He stands up, pulls me to my feet, and puts his arms around me. He's warm and solid. I'm immediately relieved being against his chest.

"Did you really just try to break up with me?" He laughs so self-assuredly, I want to hit him, but I squeeze him tight.

"Yes, but it was for your own good."

"Nice try, and as soon as you have a good meal or two in you, I'm taking you to bed and there will be no objections about it."

Music to my ears. No objections.

Chapter Four

Jiro escorts me to the bathroom, turns on the shower, and orders me to get in. He's not taking no for an answer today which I find both stupidly sweet and frustrating all at the same time.

When I'm done, I make my way out to the couch instead of going back to the bedroom. The door to the outside is closed again, Jiro's sandy boots next to it, but I don't think about opening the door because he's standing in the kitchen. While I was in the shower, he changed into Nishikyō grays and combed out his hair. It's so long now, longer than mine. And the thin line of beard he has along his jaw is so handsome. I can't believe I just tried to break up with him. I must be crazy.

I sit on the couch, pull my legs up to my chest, and hug them. I've slept so much and yet I'm still so tired I could put my head down and go back to sleep right now.

"Here. Let's eat." He hands me a bowl with noodles, mushrooms, and spinach. Much better than the frozen meals I've been eating.

"Did Oyama make this?"

"Yes. He cooked for an entire day when he heard I was coming. I made it here on one of the shuttles in only eight hours, but they couldn't drop me off outside until this morning. I had to fight with them to let me because of the storm. I've been fighting with everyone lately." He smiles at me. "This is my first time out of the city limits."

"Exciting, ne?"

"Very. How are you doing with that?" He points his chopsticks at the window, and I don't look. "I saw you yelling at it. I also saw what you did to the chair." His eyes move to the chair in the corner, one of the four legs broken off and the back bent.

"I told you I have a temper, and I was angry for weeks." I was certain I actually became a dragon, instead of just having one in my chest, during some of my more insanely infuriating moments.

"I know. I like your temper. Watching you beat up the door was enthralling."

"I bet." Slipping my feet under Jiro's legs, I heave a sigh. "The storm scares me more than the outdoors. I was starting to get used to the view when it came."

"Well, it's progress. Maybe this house hasn't been one hundred percent bad for you. Only about ninety-five percent."

These noodles taste delicious right now. I wish I could cook for myself the way Oyama cooks for me. I eat my meal fast until I'm over half-way through, but I stop and put my chopsticks down askew in the bowl.

"What's up?" he asks.

"Nothing. I just... I just want to look at you for a few seconds." My heart has picked up pace in my chest. I'm so close to him now, and when the storm started, I thought I would never see him again. "When did you get this?" I reach over the tops of my knees and stroke the line of hair now along his jawline. His eyes close, and he leans in lightly to my touch.

"Well, I didn't take good care of myself either while you were gone. I didn't sleep much, and once I figured out I could see you, I barely ever left that surveillance room. Beni came and brought me food, and my mother slept a few nights on the cot in there. I showered at the dōjō and forgot to shave. It was only when I found out I'd see you soon that I cleaned myself up."

"Were you busy helping Mark?"

He nods. "I hunted down several people myself. I finally got to see that theater you spent so much time in in Ku 1. I couldn't believe how many data gathering jobs you had set up. Hundreds, Sanaa."

"I spent a lot of time in 3B before we started training and still a lot after."

"I found all of your jobs on Miura and his top people. It was a little eerie seeing the data on Matsuda stop one day."

I ended his life so swiftly. No regrets.

"I actually miss that place. I miss all of Nishikyō." I pick up my bowl of noodles and continue eating.

"You'll be home soon. When Beni heard I was coming here to get you, she started cleaning up our apartment. I'm afraid I left the place a disaster."

"You? But you're always so neat!"

"Well, I wasn't concentrating on anything but you."

I'm so, so lucky.

"How is Beni? I miss her, and I wish she had been here with me."

Sadness washes over Jiro's face, and I immediately begin to dread whatever news he's about to deliver. "Beni lost both her parents in the earthquake. Her side of the family is completely devastated. My whole family is devastated, Sanaa. I lost my father. My mother lost her husband and cousins. They're gone, just like that."

He lets out a sob so heartbreaking I'm frozen for a minute in shock. My strong, fearless, compassionate Jiro is crying, and I think a piece of my soul just withered and died.

I quickly grab my bowl and his and set them down on the floor. Placing my hand on his chest, he clutches it with both of his. I stay silent since I don't know what I can say to make this awful situation better.

"You cannot do that to me again, Sanaa. You cannot waste away and not take care of yourself. What would I have done if I had lost you, too?"

The control I thought I had on my tears disappears, and they roll from my eyes and land on the couch between us.

"I'm sorry, Jiro. So sorry."

When I think of how Sakai lost my mother, my aunt, and his only daughter all in one day and how he almost died from the grief, I remember he had no one but his brother and sister-in-law to get him through it. Now I will have to be strong for Jiro. He has his family but needs me, too.

I settle myself on his lap, wrap his arms around me, and hold his head to my chest. He's a silent crier, no blubbering or moaning, but his breath is short, and his back shakes. I run my hand lightly down his spine until he calms, and when he looks up at me, I wipe the tears from his face and kiss him.

"I never want to be away from you again, Jiro. This has been the hardest seven weeks of my life, and it was hard because I wasn't with you."

"No one is going to separate us again. No one."

I believe him.

Jiro nods and presses his cheek against me, inhaling deeply before letting the sadness out with a big huff. I'll get him to talk more about his father, Koichi, later when he's feeling less emotional.

"Your hair's getting long. It's almost at your chin."

I love playing with his hair. It's getting so long his white streak is buried under the rest of it. I run the streak through my fingers for a minute before tucking his hair behind his ears.

He smiles at me. It's a relief to see his smile again. "I know. I was going to get it cut but there was no time."

"Don't. I love it even though it's longer than mine now."

I turn away before the blush starts. I never realized how much my hair meant to me until it was gone. Standing up, I remove myself from his lap and give us both back our bowls before sitting next to him again. Best to eat and move on.

"No worries, Sanaa. You're still the most beautiful girl I've ever seen."

My heart stops for a moment, and I catch my breath to start it beating again. I'm still not used to getting compliments from Jiro. Miko and Helena were always complimenting me as friends do but it's a different experience when it comes from him.

"Hmmm, maybe you should talk to Manami. Get the back all cut short and the front dyed a wild color."

"Are you crazy? What would the rest of the clan leaders say when I came in front of them again?"

Jiro looks at me seriously, his eyebrows drawn together. "When have you cared about what other people thought of you, except for your family and close friends? You know, if this fight and the stay here to recuperate has changed you that much, I'll kill Sakai myself."

How many times have I said no one tells me what I can or cannot do? Sure, I've taken a lot of direction in the past few months concerning my long-term life plans, but I've always been adamant about doing it my way. If I want to change anything about myself then that's my prerogative, not anyone else's. I make the decisions that affect my life.

Jiro's right. I need to turn my attitude around. I need to start now, and when I get home, I need to start training again and learn new things. Sword fighting boosted my confidence in ways I never dreamed were possible. Now it's time to step it up.

"No, no. I get the next shot at Mark. You already got to hit him. It's my turn."

He reaches over and pinches my cheek. "That's my girl. I'm sorry for crying on you."

"Please." I hold his hand, so warm and strong. I missed this. "I love that you share with me. You know I want to spend the rest of my life with you. I'm sure we'll have lots of emotions to go through before we're old and gray."

"You're so very right." He leans forward and kisses me under my ear again. My favorite spot. "Ice cream?"

"Yes, okay." He jumps up off the couch and comes back with chocolate soy ice cream and two spoons. We share it all, and I fall asleep on the couch with my head in his lap.

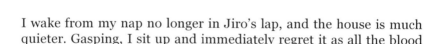

I wake from my nap no longer in Jiro's lap, and the house is much quieter. Gasping, I sit up and immediately regret it as all the blood leaves my head.

"Are you okay?" Jiro sits at the table, facing me, his back to the window which is no longer orange. The blue sky and desert have returned while I was sleeping. The sun is starting to make its way down from the zenith to the horizon. It's past mid-afternoon.

"Yes. Yes, I'm fine. It was so quiet, I thought you were gone. What time is it?"

"3:23. You slept for a long time."

I peel myself from the couch and stretch, my arms reaching high up and all of my muscles lengthening. Jiro eyes me with a small smile, his eyes running over me, and I think he finds me attractive even in this state.

"How long did I sleep on you?" I ask, walking to his side and taking in the view at the window before sitting down. I have a short moment of panic seeing the sky again, but tell myself I'm inside. I'm inside. "I'm inside" is my mantra when I'm here.

"I got up after thirty minutes. I moved us into the second bedroom. Start fresh?" He reaches out and holds my hand, and I nod.

"Will you get me something to eat? I'm hungry again."

"Of course," he says with a relieved smile. "Any requests?"

"No. Just put food in front of me. I'll eat whatever you bring."

Setting his tablet down, Jiro goes into the kitchen, and I glance over to his tablet to see what he's doing. He's drawing the room. How does he get the perspective so perfectly? He started with me asleep on the couch, my legs and arms curled underneath me. I wonder if I always sleep like that.

He returns to the table with three onigiri rice balls wrapped in nori. "Here, eat these. You know rice balls never taste fresh by the second day."

"Normally, you'd be right, but the refrigerator here is a new design. It keeps food good for a very long time. That's the reason why I stopped eating three meals a day and went to one. I knew the food would last if I had to wait longer than expected."

"You plan too much... And you didn't trust Sakai's note?"

I shrug my shoulders. "I couldn't ask him. Couldn't communicate with anyone. I trust you all, but I felt abandoned." Another tear leaks from my eye. I've cried enough for two lifetimes today. "I want to go home."

Jiro squeezes my hand and nods. "Soon. Eat."

The rice balls, filled with soy salmon, taste delicious, like they were just made. "Mmmm, delicious." I love technology.

"Really? Can I try?" I hold out the onigiri to him and then snatch it back with a laugh. "Sanaa, you must learn to share." He quickly grabs one off the plate before I can stop him. "Be careful, Miss Itami. I know your ticklish spot."

"Miss Itami. You're the first person to call me that since I decided I wanted to change my name." It makes me smile and blush. I like my new name a lot.

"Actually, that's what Coen-sama calls you, and that's how Sakai refers to you when he talks to her."

"Have you met her?" I've always wanted to meet the Chief Administrator. I watched the news cast about Yūsei enough times to have her voice and face memorized.

Jiro bites into his onigiri and hitches a sly grin. "I have. I suspect you will too before long."

"What? What's with the smile?"

"Um, you'll see. I'm not going to say anything else until you get home. Oh, I almost forgot." He jumps up from the table, runs to the bathroom then comes back, a pair of scissors in his hand. "Look what I found in my kit. Do you trust me?"

Way too many questionable activities in the world have started off with that phrase, but I hate my hair the way it is.

In the bathroom, I hold all of the longer hair on the crown of my head forward while he cuts everything in back to the same short length.

"It's a good thing I cut my own hair on occasion," he says from behind me. "I know basically what I'm doing."

"Basically? You can't be more confident than 'basically?'"

"I'll do a good job. I promise. Here, I'm all done in back. Let go of the top."

I do as I'm told and glance at myself in the mirror. My hair is already looking better.

"Turn towards me." He combs my hair forward with his fingers and cuts the length to just over my ears in back but longer in front. He even clips all the ends around my face where it was looking particularly ragged because I needed two swipes to cut my hair off instead of one clean one.

"I never thought I'd let my boyfriend cut my hair."

"Well, there's a first time for everything. No worries. When we get back, I'll treat you to the real thing."

"Make the front a little shorter on one side so I can sweep it over and tuck it behind my ear or get some hair clips."

I'm so different when I look in the mirror. My hair is short in back and a bit longer on the right side of my head, but from my part all the way over to the left my hair is long, almost to my chin, and when I tuck it back, it actually looks kind of cute.

"Kawaii. Definitely," Jiro says and laughs. "I can't believe I just cut my future empress's hair."

"Stop," I say, smacking him on the chest. "Never call me that in private. If you have to in public, so be it, but never here between us."

I turn my head from side-to-side in the mirror while Jiro watches me.

"I love you, Sanaa."

He is so still, watching me intently, serious again. I turn and put my arms around his neck.

"I love you, Jiro."

I want to kiss him but little bits of hair are all over me and my face. Instead, I pull him close to me. My libido is kicking back up again. I was wondering how buried it was but, apparently, not too deep. I'd give anything to feel our bodies pressed against each other right now.

"I want to sleep with you, too," Jiro whispers in my ear, and I can't help but laugh. In this, I am so predictable. "But let's get you cleaned up and have another meal together. I want to make sure you're on the road to recovery before I spend every waking moment in bed with you."

I hug him even tighter and let my body go limp so he has to hold me close to him. I'm happy again.

Chapter Five

I clean myself up and join Jiro in my old bedroom. He's standing on the chair in the corner again.

"What are you doing?"

"Covering up the cameras. You don't care, but I do, especially when I'm sure my mother is probably sitting in the surveillance room back home."

"I hope you waved to her before you did it."

Jiro dips his finger into a container of plastic putty and pushes the gray goop into the wall over the camera he pointed out to me earlier. He seriously thought of everything before he left.

"I did wave and smile. I may not want my mother to know anything about my private life, but I still love her. Anyway, I'm just covering up the ones in the bedrooms, hallway, and bathroom next. I think they'd panic back at home if I covered them all."

He finishes and jumps down. "I brought your tablet for you. It's not hooked up to NishikyōNet here but you could access your files if you want to. It's in my bag."

"Okay." I would like a distraction, and I have tons of downloaded files I can read on my tablet including everything Aunt Kimie gave me having to do with my parents and the storage space.

In the bedroom, I crouch down next to Jiro's bag and open it. On top of my tablet is a small, flat, rectangular wrapped package with my name printed on it in katakana. I haven't seen my name written in katakana in forever.

"What's this, Jiro? Is this for me, too?"

He comes in from the hallway. "Oh yeah, that's from my mother. She slipped it in my bag while I was packing."

I open the package and reveal a framed photo of Mariko and my mother from when they were around my age, both smiling and wearing yukata at a street festival. Another photo to cherish.

Jiro peeks over my shoulder and puts his arm around me, leaning his head against mine.

"Wow. You do look like your mother."

"So do you," I say, pointing at Mariko. Jiro has the same eyes, nose, and smile. He has his father's bone structure, though. "Your mother is sweet. They were good friends."

"What does your father look like?"

"Here, Jiro." I grab my tablet with one hand and pull him to sit on the bed with me. "I have some photos."

I show him all the pictures I flip through every New Year's Day, and it's strange seeing them again with someone else. This was always a tradition I kept to myself. But I want to make Jiro a permanent part of my family. He should see all of this.

He looks from the tablet to me and back again. "Well, believe it or not, I do see some of your father in you, too. In the shape of your face and your eyes. And it's possible your freckles stand out because you have his fair skin." Whenever he mentions my freckles, I always blush.

He closes the photos and points to the video in the same folder. "Is this the video your mother made for you? Can I watch it?"

I hesitate and only because I wonder if seeing my mother again right now will make me cry. "Of course. I should skip through the beginning because she's all emotional. She recorded this only a few days after she gave birth to me."

"You don't have to."

Jiro has an eagerness about him I've not seen before. He wants to be a part of my life, and it reminds me that if we spend the rest of our lives together, he will never have met my parents or known them — just my aunts. I'm glad I got to meet and spend time with Koichi before he died, even if I didn't know him very well.

Jiro watches the whole video, his eyes never leaving the screen. When it's over, he plays it again and watches it just as intently as the first time.

"Sanaa," he says, setting the tablet aside, "I now completely understand why you accepted Sakai's help so willingly. Your mother was very convincing, very intense."

"After watching this, I knew there was no other alternative for me. She was so into this path, so persuasive. It scares me, Jiro. If she were alive today, I'd have no choice. This would be how I was raised. I hate not having a choice."

"Wasn't Helena's advice to accept it?" I nod in response. Caring and devoted Helena. She wants me to be happy. "Helena's a smart girl. You should take her advice." He punctuates his statement with a smile and butts his shoulder up against mine before becoming serious again. "This video also gives me concerns about your safety."

"I remember watching it the first time and being thankful for all of the sword training you've given me. I miss Kazenoho."

"I'm sorry I couldn't bring it with me, but I'm not sure if a sword is going to be enough."

With all of what I saw during the fight, reading *Art of War* which is a treatise on spying and understanding your enemies, and remembering what Aunt Kimie told me about my life being in danger, I know what to do.

"I've been thinking a lot about this, and when we get home, I want you to teach me everything. And I'm sure you know a whole lot more than sword fighting."

His face becomes passive, a trick both he and Sakai use to keep me from reading them. "What do you mean?"

"Don't play dumb with me. I saw the way you fought, the way you climbed in the theater, the way you jump through the air like gravity means nothing to you. You move so quietly I can't even hear you."

Slowly, his face loses passivity. He shakes his head. "I should have known I would never be able to hide any of that from you."

"And you shouldn't! I want to learn."

"Are you serious?"

"Yes! Everything. I want to learn to fight with different weapons and to climb like you do. I want to know where the most vulnerable points are on another human being and how to take advantage of them... to move around in stealth. Everything. I'm not going to be some empress that sits back and doesn't take her own safety into account. I refuse to live my life in isolation. I'll be out and about amongst the people, and I need to learn to defend myself in every possible way."

"You can't do that."

"Jiro..." I don't want to die, but I don't want to be caged up either.

"No way. Not now at least. Sakai says there are still grumblings in the minor clans. You'll be killed."

"But..."

Jiro's look of shock stops me dead. He knows this world better than I do. Maybe I *should* be scared?

"How do you know about any of this?" He actually sounds angry, like I've figured out a secret only a few people are aware of. "I've never met a girl who could even think this way, much less want to learn and use those kinds of skills."

"Am I crazy?"

"Yes. Yes, absolutely you're crazy."

"Good. Crazy and unexpected. That's exactly the kind of leader I want to be."

He laughs, takes my face in his hands, and kisses me hard, aggressive. I couldn't move my head even if I wanted to because he's pinned to my lips, taking control of me as if I'm a runaway train speeding towards an inevitable crash. Just as I'm about to get up and sit on his lap, though, he stops and pulls away from me.

"If I had any doubts about whether or not you were perfect for me, they're all gone now. Of course, I'll teach you. I'll teach you everything. And we'll persuade Sakai to teach you as well."

"Mark? Why?"

He shakes his head and laughs. "The fact you don't already know tells me Sakai is the most skilled deceiver I have ever met. You are so observant, just like me, and have spent so much time with him."

"What are you talking about?"

"Sakai has spent his whole life learning everything you want to know, the *shinobi* way. I had a feeling you didn't know when you handed him Kazenoho at the theater, and the look on his face told me he didn't want you to know. But if you're going to learn how to be a ninja, you'll learn from both him and me."

Mark Sakai. A ninja. When I think of the way he easily changed his personality in front of people, the way he moves from one job to another, or how he was always entering and leaving rooms and I never heard him, everything starts to make sense. Sakai has kept his skills hidden from me, always guarded, and, most times, difficult to read. Did my mother know about his ninja training? I suspect she did. She told me to go to him first about all of this, didn't she? She trusted him. He loved her. I doubt he would have kept this a secret from her.

I must learn everything they can teach me, know it all.

Obsessing. I'm already obsessing over it.

"Jiro, teach me. I want you to."

Together, we sit down and eat dinner at the table at dusk. My spirits are much better already. One day with Jiro here, real food and conversation, has changed me significantly. Even if Sakai had left someone here, anyone here with me, it would have been better than no one. I would have even been okay with Risa. Well, maybe not Risa.

We eat slowly and talk mainly of Nishikyō. Jiro fills me in on Aunt Kimie and Lomo. They miss me but understood Sakai stashed me away someplace else until they could secure Ku 6. Jiro visited them both while I was gone and told them about the fight and my hospital stay but wasn't too specific with details. Helena's building was damaged in the earthquake. She moved in late but now she's living only two blocks away from me. Izakaya Tanaka is fine as usual. A few tables and chairs fell over and some customers were hurt, but the whole block faired well.

The total loss of life for the whole city after the earthquake was 1,809 people. Several water mains broke again and people drowned in the sudden floods. Four buildings collapsed, and over three hundred people were killed in an accident on the transitway. An explosion occurred in Ku 10, the Farming Ward, but luckily it didn't affect the food supply. Ku 2, the Medical Services Ward, was overcome with injuries for weeks, including my own. I owe Usagi for standing by my hospital bed in the chaos. I have to think about how I'm going to thank him when I get home.

When the sun goes down, the stars come out, and Jiro and I stand at the window for over an hour together, holding hands and staring. He points out several constellations, and I'm surprised a few of the brightest stars are actually other planets in the solar system, Venus and Mercury. The moon rises, enormous and glowing brightly. I'm in love with it.

"Yūsei has two moons. I wonder what they'll look like. Will they be bigger or smaller?" I press my forehead to the glass and stare as long as I can at the moon without blinking. It's amazing the way it hangs there.

"Are you feeling better?"

"I am," I say, turning to him. Mmmm. His eyes are full of lust.

"Much better. More like my old self than I have in weeks."

"I have to admit I like this new hair style on you. It makes you look even smaller and cuter."

Jiro's compliments are making me lightheaded with want.

"I've been dying to sleep with you all day. Don't make me wait any longer."

He smiles, leans forward and kisses me, a consuming kiss, his lips pressed tightly to mine, his hands pulling my face and body into him. I will never get tired of this. Our slow and steady starts always grow and grow until I'm ready to burst. I inhale sharply through my nose, wrapping my arms around his chest, and parting my lips, his tongue slips down over mine. My head swims, and I can't stop the moan that bubbles straight up from my belly. He pulls away and guides me to the bedroom.

"I love that you always tell me what you want. Never stop that."

"Take off all of your clothes and get into bed with me. I want to feel your body on me." So many things in life embarrass me but talking to Jiro like this does not.

He smiles at me. "That's what I like to hear."

The first thing I do is peel his shirt off. I'm so happy to touch Jiro's tattoos again, his broad chest, his flat stomach. He said he let himself go while I was gone, but I don't see it here. He must have kept training. I trail kisses along his shoulders to his neck as he pulls at my pants. Once my shirt is off, Jiro is careful to lightly caress my body, not dipping his fingers in between each rib along my side. They're pronounced now, but neither of us want to be reminded of why.

We slip into bed naked. I want him on top of me, in me, as close to me as possible. I craved personal closeness so badly when I was all alone, and Jiro's presence is a drug calming every fear but exciting every nerve I possess. I was content for so long with my familial love, the love I had for my aunts and my friends. I tried to find love with Joshua and Chad but never succeeded. Now that I have this passionate love, this romantic love with Jiro, I can never go without it again. I tried to convince myself I'd be fine without, but with Jiro kissing across my belly to my breasts, I'm sure I can't. When I think about the loneliness, the ache makes me hold him even tighter. I run my fingers through his hair and grab on.

It's the best sex we've had yet because, for once, we have no place to be, nobody can hear us, nobody is waiting on us. We're gentle with each other, like it's the first time. It may as well be. Seven weeks is a long time to be apart, and I had already forgotten about the dip in muscle where his abs meet his hips and the scar on his elbow. He runs his hands down the length of my body, cupping my backside, and lifting me up against him. I let my kisses linger on his lips, catching his breath with mine. Reaching down, I wrap my fingers around him and stroke gently until he's hard. This is what I love, how responsive he is to me. No man has ever been so turned on by me. He presses his forehead into mine and moans, and the sound rushes all the blood to my abdomen.

With his body warm and hovering over mine, he massages me close to a climax, then eases back, which makes me whimper and him smile. I never realized what a tease he could be.

"Don't be cruel to me."

He starts back up again with a smile. "I could never be cruel to you. I'll give you whatever you want."

He's watching me closely, his gaze so intense it brings chills to my body even though the room is warm and Jiro is hot. My brain buzzes, my vision light, and I can hardly breathe I'm so close.

When I can't take anymore without a release, I pull him into me as far as I can, and the contact between us sends us both right over the edge. It didn't take long this time, but I'm sure this won't be our last time tonight. We have a lot of catching up to do.

"Mmmm, Sanaa. I missed you." Jiro's eyes are closed, his breathing slowing.

Without separating us, I hold his face over me so I can see him, so I can watch his eyes, his smile. I rub my thumbs along the soft hair at his jaw and bring his forehead to mine.

"Jiro, what did you wish for on New Year's Eve?"

"I asked the gods to bring me love, to bring me you, and they answered me."

Chapter Six

At noon on our fifth day together, Jiro and I sit down to have our last meal at the house. I'm happy with how the time has gone by since Jiro arrived. We spent our stolen holiday laughing, talking, and making love whenever we wanted. I barely got dressed, just wanting to lie in bed and hold Jiro's warm body to me or listen to his breathing and beating heart. This time was freedom, freedom I have never had. Freedom from work, from life, from my family except my love. I treasured every moment because I doubt we'll ever have this again.

Jiro opens the freezer and decides to defrost the last two curry dishes so I load up the rice cooker to go along with it. While we're sitting and eating, a low, soft hum builds to a high-pitched whine. Looking out the window, though, I see nothing but desert.

"I think Sakai is here. The airbase is on the other side of this cliff."

"The space elevator is over there, too?"

"Yes. It's wonderful. I can't wait for you to see it."

The whine outside fades, and a metallic thump similar to the one I heard on the morning Jiro arrived here echoes outside the door.

Soft footsteps approach from the other side. I set down my chopsticks, get up and run to the door, pull it open, and Sakai is standing in front of me. His hair is pulled back but tousled up by the wind, he's dressed in Nishikyō grays, and a smile is on his face. Oh gods, I missed him. I throw my arms around his neck, my feet leaving the ground as he picks me up and hugs me back.

"Mark, I missed you."

I did, I really did, even though anger quickly replaces everything.

Pulling back from him, I smack him hard right across the face. My hand stings, and his eyes are closed, his cheek blossoming bright red. "You're lucky I'm not armed."

"I missed you, too, Sanaa-chan." Sakai gently touches his cheek, his eyes shining with the smallest of tears, probably brought on by my slap. He deserved it. I step back to him and hug him again around his chest.

"Don't ever leave me like that again. Ever."

He hesitates only a moment and hugs me back. "I'm sorry. I have good reasons for leaving you here alone."

"I'm sorry I hit you. I'm sorry." We release from the hug at the same time, and I wipe my tears away and glance over at Jiro. He didn't move from the table. I wonder how mad at Sakai he still is.

"Jiro," Sakai says, stiffly

"Sakai-san," Jiro responds, his face like stone.

Uh, oh. I think they *both* might be mad at each other.

"Mark, come and eat with us."

I cannot have the two most important men in my life angry with each other. Sakai takes off the bag he's wearing, and I put my hand on his back and lightly push him to the table. I sit him across from Jiro, and while they're staring at each other in silence, I grab lunch for Sakai. Slipping into the chair next to Jiro at the window, I place my hand on his knee and squeeze.

"You can't be angry with each other forever," I say, breaking their silence. "I love you both. Your relationship with each other is as important as your relationship with me, and you'll forgive each other because I forgive you."

They both soften a little, so I continue. "You took care of me when I was injured, and I couldn't take care of myself. But I know Jiro feels guilty for making me leave him during the fight, and Mark, you feel guilty for bringing me here and not telling Jiro until I was already gone. And I'm angry for being left so utterly alone. But it's done, and everyone is still alive, so let's just put this situation behind us, ne?"

Sakai, with his passive face, examines me for a moment before sighing. "I'm sorry, Sanaa. I'm sorry, Jiro."

I squeeze Jiro's knee a little more. Give in, Jiro. You're so stubborn sometimes.

"Okay, I'm sorry, Sakai-san. I shouldn't have punched you."

I clap my hands once and smile. "Great. Everyone's forgiven. Itadakimasu." They both smirk at me identically, mirror twins of each other twenty years apart.

I start eating, and they each hesitate before picking up their chopsticks.

"The shuttle will be back for us in an hour, and we have a lot to talk about before they arrive. Sanaa, did you cut your hair yourself?" A small smile plays across his lips.

"No, Jiro cut it." I'll never forget that. It was one of the sweetest things anyone has ever done for me.

"You look different, but I like it." Sakai wants a little small talk before he leads into whatever big issues he needs to discuss. "You've lost a lot of weight, though. Oyama will not be happy."

"He can cook me four meals a day if he wants when we get home." And I know Oyama will stand over me as I eat each one. I no longer care. I'll be happy to have him there.

"Good. He and Usagi can't wait to have you back." He sighs and puts his chopsticks down. "I'm assuming Jiro filled you in on Taira and what happened with Beni?" Jiro and I both nod. "It was a devastating few weeks for everyone, and I had to act fast. Obviously, Miura was prepared to strike at the theater. He had many men armed and ready and the ninjas... but only family knew you were going to be there."

"I've been thinking the same thing since the fight, Sakai-san." Jiro and Sakai examine each other with their passive faces. How in gods' names do they read each other, ever?

"Is someone a... spy?" I ask, my world rapidly shrinking. I never suspected anyone close to me. Who?

"Yes." Sakai nods, his eyes focused past me. "I have my suspicions, but I'm not sure yet. I'm sorry, Sanaa. I had to move you fast and not tell anyone you were gone until I dropped you off here. I had to make sure you were absolutely safe. I wanted to leave Beni with you, and if she hadn't lost what was left of her family, she would've been here. I figured she'd be the only person besides Jiro or me that could handle your wrath at being so far from Nishikyō."

All three of us turn to the broken chair in the corner. Never before has there been concrete evidence of my temper like that chair.

"We need to be cautious. Now that we've subdued Taira clan, I'm wondering how many other free agents like Matsuda are out there. It's not just you I'm worried about now. I'm worried about my whole family especially Mariko's side that has all become Sakai clan in the last forty years. Taira held a grudge and others do too since we're so connected to your line. Now that Koichi is gone..." Both he and Jiro hang their heads and tears spring to my eyes. "Mariko is even more my responsibility."

He stops and eats for a minute while we all sit in silence. Many responsibilities exist for all of us right now.

"Sanaa, before I left, Yoshinori Minamoto requested that, once you are recovered, you meet with him to discuss his family's support."

I expect a smile on Sakai's face but none appears.

"You don't seem pleased at all. This is good news, right?" Neither Sakai nor Jiro reassure me. They sit in silence, Jiro's knee rubbing against mine under the table. "Or... wait, there must be a price for his support?"

"Most likely. He has a son who is twenty-two. I suspect he's hoping you'll take him as a consort."

"No." Both Jiro and I say at the same time. I shakily take his hand, and he squeezes my fingers tight.

Sakai smiles at me. "I thought you'd say that. It's only a guess, but I believe I'm right. Still, if we go into this meeting with him, we can't say no and walk away. He'll want some sort of compromise. You need to think about what you could offer instead."

I have no idea what I could possibly offer Minamoto, but I nod anyway. "You haven't heard at all from Maeda?" Noboru Maeda, the head of Nishikyō's largest yakuza clan, was the last to bow to me. I don't expect him to come around easily.

"No. Not yet."

I bet Maeda thinks he can ignore me, and I'll just go away. What does he think of me? What has he learned about me from other sources?

"Sakai-san..." Jiro starts, but Sakai raises his hand.

"Wait." He takes a big breath and sighs. "You should start calling me Mark, too. At the very least, here, with family. You're my family, Sanaa's my family, you two are... well, I have no doubt you'd be on your way to marriage if that law wasn't in the way. It makes no sense for us to be so formal amongst each other."

This is a huge peace offering, and Jiro's face cracks and softens even more. Sakai has been his teacher, his uncle, and the head of his family. Now with Koichi gone, they'll be even closer. I concentrate on my hand in Jiro's. Though I'm supposed to be family, I feel like a stranger in this moment.

"Mark, Sanaa and I have concerns over her safety going forward. I'm aware it's late in Sanaa's life to be learning brand-new skills but she picked up the sword fighting so fast. I think she's ready to move on to more important training."

"'Important' as in?" Sakai lifts an eyebrow at Jiro.

I lean forward and make eye contact. "It's no use trying to hide from me anymore. I know about your *ninjutsu* training, and I want those skills for myself."

Sakai's head swivels from me to Jiro to me and back to Jiro again before muttering "the death of me" under his breath.

"Fine!" He throws his hands up in the air. "You want to be a ninja *and* an empress? Go for it. It sounds like an excellent idea." It sounds like he thinks it's the worst idea I've ever come up with, but I'll show him I can do it. I will.

"Will you teach me?" I ask, barely able to stop from bouncing in my seat.

"Yes, of course I will," he says with a sigh. "If you're going to do this, you'll do it right, and you'll do it exceptionally well, or you won't do it at all. Understood?"

"Yes," I say with the biggest, widest smile I have.

Jiro laughs and shakes his head. I'm sure I resemble an eager child hoping for dessert.

"I'll teach you all the mental skills, and Jiro can teach you all the physical ones. Please do not end up in the hospital again."

It's time to go. Sakai opens the door and in front of us is a twenty meter long hallway-like tunnel carved into the rock of the cliff this house is embedded into. At the end of the tunnel, a metal ladder leads up to a heavy metal door.

"I'll go first. Sanaa, you follow me, and Jiro will bring up the rear. Can you do this, Sanaa-chan?"

I nod at him and swallow through a throat parched and dry. I will no longer be inside. I can do this. I can do this. "I can do this" is my new mantra.

As Sakai starts to climb, I turn and whisper to Jiro. "When we get up there, put your arm around me please and make sure I don't faint and hit my head again." I'm not sure how many more traumas my head can take.

He smiles and kisses me on the cheek. "Okay. Be brave."

Sakai spins the wheel and pushes the door open. Beyond his shoulder, blue sky stretches to infinity. Look down, Sanaa, and climb.

I place one hand over the other, grabbing and pulling myself up with each cold metal rung of the ladder, and, before I know it, I'm hit dead in the face with the hottest air I have ever felt. It must be at least 50°C out here! I close my eyes for a brief moment.

I can't do this.

"Come on." Jiro reaches up and squeezes my shin. "Sakai's waiting out there."

Move your legs, Sanaa. Get off the ladder and on the ground.

My body listens to my brain, and I climb out of the airlock, my feet hitting sandy, gravel covered ground.

Sakai steps up to my side, grabs my hand, and I turn my face into his arm, opening one eye to take in my surroundings. We're on a mountain cliff stretching several kilometers in the middle of the desert. In the distance, six other airlocks are jutting out of the ground. The houses were embedded in the cliff to keep out even more ambient radiation than the man-made materials could protect against. Pretty smart.

Closing my one open eye, I turn my head and look out the other side. A small, six-person shuttle is waiting for us about twenty meters away, and, off on the other side of the cliff, the desert flattens into the gray pavement and buildings of an airbase.

But what really catches my attention is the space elevator in the distance. A large, squat building sits on the ground with a ribbon stretching out of the roof way up into the sky. Someday soon, I'll be loaded into a ribbon carriage and climb into orbit for the long trip to Yūsei.

Jiro comes up next to me, slips his arm over my shoulder and under my other arm. "Did you see it?" he asks as I turn my face from Sakai with my eyes closed.

"Yes, Jiro. Let's go." I don't want to sound disappointed because Jiro's so excited, but I'm barely staying conscious. Between the heat and my impending anxiety attack, I can't breathe. I direct my sight down and follow Sakai's feet. If I just pretend I'm indoors, I can walk. I concentrate on each step, one foot in front of the other, closer and closer to my way back to Nishikyō.

We make it to the shuttle, the doors close, and I breathe a huge sigh of relief. I can't believe I was outside that long and didn't pass out. I'm improving. A young woman attendant sits us down, adjusts our seat belts, communicates with the pilot, and we're off.

The whole process from the short-range shuttle to the airbase then through security and onto the long-range shuttle is confusing and annoying. I stand and wait while Sakai sorts everything out. I let my hand be scanned and occasionally glance out the window when I get up the nerve.

Jiro purchases bento boxes for each of us from the cafeteria, and we sit and eat in the waiting area until it's time to depart. Eventually, we board with about fifty other people, slowly inching down the jetway with baggage and a grumble or two about the wait. Once I'm in my seat, I lay my head on Jiro's shoulder and fall asleep for the duration of the flight.

Chapter Seven

Walking back into Sakai building, I immediately feel like I'm back at home. Home. This place was only my home for four days before I was swept away, but it's now more familiar to me than my old apartment in Ku 9 I shared with my aunts. The lobby is quiet, only one guard at the long rounded desk to the right, and another guard enjoying a cup of tea while sitting on the plush black couches in the open atrium to the left. They both stand and bow, and I do my best to smile and nod back.

We arrived here via a hired car from the airbase outside of Ku 10. I had never been to the airbase before, never even been on the transitway branch that services the base. Air travel is restricted based on your occupation. Most people live in Nishikyō their entire lives without going anywhere.

Sakai leaves me and Jiro at the door to our apartment. Ahhh, I missed this place so much. I walk in and am overcome by the smell of home. The house in the desert smelled sterile, as if no one had ever lived or breathed in the rooms. This place smells like me, my aunts, Jiro.

Jiro heads straight for the bedroom to unpack his bag, and I walk around the main space and get a sense of it again: Jiro's drawing on the wall, my blanket on the couch, a glass left out on the coffee table, the small, square ceramic salt and pepper shakers my aunts gifted me when I moved here sitting on the kitchen table, my coffeemaker on the counter, Jiro's jar of tea. In the bedroom, I find him lying on the bed with his arm flung across his face.

"Tired?" It's four o'clock in the afternoon, but my body thinks it's one in the morning. I slept on the flight, so I'm in fairly good shape, but my internal clock is going to be confused for a few days. Jiro is down for the count, though.

"Yes, very."

"You should take a nap, get up and have dinner, and then we'll both go back to bed." I pull the blanket out from beneath him and cover him up. "Go to sleep. I'll wake you in two hours."

I turn out the lights in the bedroom and make my way to the couch after pouring a glass of water and grabbing some salted soy beans from the fridge. First off, I get caught up on messages from Miko, Helena, my aunts, Chad, and a few other co-workers wondering why I had suddenly dropped off the map after the earthquake. I ignore the ones from my family because Jiro handled them while I was away, but I open a new message to Chad. I let him know I'm fine but was injured during the earthquake. I leave it at that, though, because I'm pretty sure I can't lie to him anymore.

I read through all of my favorite fiction updates online until it's time to wake up Jiro. He was so exhausted I have to pull him from the bed. Out in the kitchen, I make him tea while he yawns and scratches his head. In the refrigerator, a container of tofu teriyaki sits with a little note from Oyama, "*Okaeri nasai.*" Welcome home.

"You must have authorized someone else on this apartment's occupancy list while we were gone?" I ask, setting a plate of food in front of Jiro.

"Beni. Of course, I trust Oyama and Usagi but Beni said she'd take care of the place for us."

"Good. I trust them all, too, but Beni is my jihi. I have to put my whole trust in her like I do you."

Jiro nods, bobbing his head from side to side. "Tomorrow we need to start training again. It's already late May, and you should learn as much as possible before the end of the year. I had the luxury of training while you were away, though it wasn't half as much fun without you." He smiles at me across the table. "We'll stick with sword fighting for a week or two until you build up some stamina again — I'm sure it'll come back to you quickly — then we'll work on the ninjutsu."

A small squeal escapes me, and I jig a little dance in my chair that makes him laugh. I am stupidly excited about learning how to be a ninja.

Jiro must have been hungry because he eats half of his dinner all at once. "Now, I know you said you wanted to learn everything..."

I nod my head vigorously at him, and he laughs again. He's coming out of his sleep stupor.

"But, in general, that's not how training works. Each ninja learns techniques that will make him into the perfect spy. By teaching each ninja differently, no two are alike and therefore they are unpredictable. So ninjutsu schooling is not rigid like sword fighting is."

"Okay, so no *kata.*"

"No kata. No forms. No set lesson plan. Each person is evaluated to see what his natural strengths are and then those strengths are enhanced. Certainly, a ninja may learn several different skills but rarely does any one person know them all." He takes a sip of tea, and I wait anxiously, barely able to sit still. "I, obviously, have trained in many fighting techniques, stealth, climbing, and disguise. Sakai... um, Mark, has trained also in stealth and fighting, but his main strength is deception which I think you will have to learn even if you think you'll never be good at it."

"Deception? In what way?" I set my chopsticks down and lean forward.

"Yes, for example, when Mark was younger, he was always the one that eavesdropped on meetings or gathered information from people. He was an adept spy. He was good at changing his personality (still is) and disguising himself so he could infiltrate the other clans. He used to do this to Taira and Minamoto and a few other families until he came of age to re-form Sakai clan. Before Mark, Sakai clan had no standing, Now he uses his skills to negotiate and handle disputes between the clans and our own family."

I'm imagining Sakai as a young man, much like Jiro, doing all of these things while studying hydroponics and going out on dates. How the hell did he do all of that and not get caught?

"What do you think my strengths are?"

"Well, I've been thinking about our previous training sessions," he says, pushing his empty bowl away from him and taking another sip of tea, "and it's safe to say you're excellent at handling a weapon."

Looking over at Kazenoho and Oninoten on the couch, I have an incredible amount of love for two inanimate objects. Besides the faith Jiro, Sakai, and the countless new people in my life have shown me, my sword has given me confidence I didn't know I was capable of. And to think Kazenoho was sitting in storage all of those years just waiting for me to come and get it.

Jiro follows my eyes to our swords and smiles at me. I think he feels the same way about Oninoten.

"But as an empress, you will not be able to carry Kazenoho at all public appearances. When we're out in small groups, at meetings, and so forth, you can have it on you. If you cannot carry your sword, I can for you. For safety's sake, I think you will need to learn another weapon as well. One not as noticeable that you can have on you at all times. You have a wakizashi as well, and we'll use that more too. As a short sword, the blade can be wedged in cracks of buildings or walls to give you a foothold or slipped into windows or doors to pry them open. You're so small, Sanaa, I think you'd be an excellent climber. I'll also teach you how to walk or step in different situations so you make no noise, but we'll probably save those skills for Yūsei."

My heart pounds in my chest I'm so excited. A blush is rising up to my cheeks, and Jiro is smiling at it.

"I love your blush response but you will need to work with Sakai on repressing that. It completely gives you away."

"Hmph. But I never want to stop blushing when you compliment me." The heat moves straight up my face.

"You're so damned adorable sometimes it hurts."

If anyone is adorable, it's him with his sleepy hair and rumpled shirt. I rub my feet up against his under the table and sigh. I think if Jiro is going to be training me all day and talking to me about these exciting things then we should probably have more people around to keep us cool.

I rise from the table to pour us each some water and find a bottle of sake in the fridge. Even better. I set the sake on the table with two cups and Jiro doesn't object. Being tired and jet-lagged, we'll need to sleep the whole night if we're to get back on schedule by tomorrow. A little sake will help.

"When we were in your storage area in Ku 9, I noticed other weapons in the same bin with the katanas we should retrieve. There were *shuriken* and other short knives I think you could work with, and I wonder how well you'd do with a *shinobijō*. So we'll get you one of those too but someone else will have to teach you. In fact —"

"Jiro…" I pour us each more sake. "What's a shinobijō?"

He laughs as he lifts his cup. "Sorry, Sanaa. I sometimes forget you didn't grow up in this world. It's a stick or a staff. They come in two lengths, short or long, 1.3 meters or 1.8 meters. I think the shorter version would be best for you. The shinobi version has weapons built into each end. On one end is a blade and the other has this ball and chain, but they're made in several different fashions now. You can use the staff to fight and disarm people, use it to climb. The newer ones are hollow and have some bend to it. I've never been very good with the staff, but maybe you would be."

Hmmm, sounds dangerous. I'm intrigued.

"Sanaa, this meeting with Minamoto you're going to have soon..." His voice trails off, and he taps his fingers on the table before draining his sake.

"Shhh —" I stop a swear. "I completely forgot. What should I do, Jiro? I have no idea what I could offer Minamoto instead of bringing his son in as a consort. You knew this was going to happen."

The time we were out back of Izakaya Tanaka right before Matsuda interrupted us, Jiro told me I would be wanted once the clans knew who I was. I really didn't believe him. At the time, I barely believed he wanted me. Reaching across the table, our hands meet, and I place my head down on my arm. This is such a ridiculous decision, and I'm going to be put in this situation over and over again. I'm sure of it.

"Well, I know Kentaro Minamoto. We grew up together."

"Really? I never saw Kentaro Minamoto on surveillance, and I certainly never saw you two together."

"Well, there's a good reason for that. Minamoto's desire for Kentaro to be your consort will die once Kentaro gets a good look at you. He likes blondes. I hate to admit it, but he stole the girl I proposed to, not that I care about that now."

I pull my hand away from Jiro, press my forehead into the table, and groan.

"I forgot about the fiancée, and she was a blonde. She must have been tall and gorgeous, too."

"Sanaa, we were never engaged. She didn't accept my proposal because she was sleeping with Kentaro behind my back."

I chance to look up, and Jiro is focused on the cup on the table.

"I'm sorry." I don't like to see him hurting, for any reason, even this.

"Don't apologize," he says, his head snapping to me. "Never apologize for my stupid mistakes. Ever. Obviously, she wasn't the right girl for me. Kentaro did me a favor."

"Well..." I pull my confidence back in. So what if she was blonde and gorgeous like I imagine her being? She cheated on him? What a mistake. "You're mine now."

He smiles at me again, the sadness and tension melted away. "You have no idea how happy I am to hear that." With a huge breath of relief, he looks at me steadily for a moment. "I think you should offer to take Kentaro into your entourage."

I blink at him, dumbfounded. "Jiro..."

"You don't have to, but if you brought him into the clan, let him stay close to you, Minamoto would consider that advantageous. Kentaro would be privy to information, a somewhat insider spy. We could choose what he would know or not know. He could even relay false information back to Minamoto."

This seems like an idea Sakai would approve of, but the situation is complicated by this history between Jiro and Kentaro. Will they be openly hostile to each other? Will Jiro worry about losing me to Kentaro? Kentaro's presence will disrupt a delicate balance we're trying to keep around here.

"I see your point, but I don't want some strange guy around here all the time. How could you even want that?"

"I don't. In fact, I want you all to myself. I don't even want to share you with Mark or Miko or your aunts, but I do because I know it's what I have to do. I have your heart."

"You do. It's yours."

"And you have mine."

My heart is breaking into tiny pieces. I want to claim Jiro, and for him to claim me, putting to rest anyone else's ideas on my availability. When I found out all of this imperial nonsense, I felt it didn't matter I couldn't get married, but now I want to.

Chapter Eight

6:10am. I can't sleep anymore. Jiro is passed out next to me. What to do, what to do.

Lying in bed for another fifteen minutes, I try and force myself back to sleep like I did at the house, but all I can do is stare at Jiro's chest rising and falling peacefully. I want that kind of peace. My mind, though, wants to be awake and thinking, planning strategies, and researching.

I wonder if Sakai is up. Now is the time for me to visit him the way he visited me before the concert. Perhaps he's always an early riser.

I get dressed, brush my hair and clip the long strands back over my ear with some pins Aunt Lomo left in the makeup bag she gifted me. Slipping on my shoes, I send Jiro a note on my tablet and close the apartment door quietly behind me.

Two flights up the stairs is Mariko's apartment and Sakai said he was in the penthouse above her. Mmmm, the heady scent of onions and garlic cooking is getting stronger, so I climb the stairs even faster. When I reach the landing, two large caucasian men stand on either side of the only door in the hallway.

"Can we help you, miss?" asks the man on the right.

"Ummm, I'm here to see Mark Sakai. Who are you?"

The one on the left reaches into his bag sitting on the floor and pulls out his tablet. "Please scan your hand, miss."

I examine them both before stepping up to his tablet and placing my hand on the screen. Is this some new security Sakai has hired? The man examines my credentials and puts his tablet away. "You're cleared. You may scan your hand at the door to request entrance."

The man to the right of the door steps to the side. I watch both warily as I palm the scanner, and the chimes ring inside.

Maybe I should have thought to message Sakai before I came up? The door opens, and he stands shirtless with his hair down. It's about time I got to see those tattoos of his, but I have to admit I'm a little embarrassed by his informality.

"Sanaa-chan, jet lagged?"

"Yes, sorry. Jiro is still sleeping."

"Come in." He doesn't acknowledge the men standing on either side of the door, and they don't acknowledge him. "Are you hungry? We were about to eat breakfast."

"Yeah, sure. I could eat. What's with the guys, Mark?"

His apartment is huge. A loft-style design with lots of open space and high ceilings sprawls out in front of me. His bedroom door is ajar on the right, and another door to a large bathroom is open next to it. The living room area is immediately to my left, and on the couch is a woman's bag and jacket. Did he just say "*we*" were about to have breakfast?

"They're security. Why don't you come in and sit down at the kitchen table with us? I'd like you to meet Lucy."

Shit. I've intruded on some private time Sakai is having with a lady friend, or girlfriend, or something. I doubt he would have let me in if he didn't want me here, but I'm frozen in place and don't want to step farther into his apartment and ruin his lovely morning.

He sighs and pushes me out of the way so he can close the door. Turning to walk to the opposite side of the apartment, his tattoos face me, and all over his back and up over his shoulders to his neck is a large samurai warrior entangled with a dragon. Damn, that's hot.

Just as the embarrassed blush rises to my cheeks for thinking anything about Sakai is hot, I'm stopped by the sight of a woman seated at the kitchen table. She's in her late thirties, fair-skinned, bright green eyes, her red hair messy and pulled into a quick knot at the back of her head.

Oh my gods, it's Coen-sama. *The* Lucinda Coen, Chief Administrator of Nishikyō. The woman I've watched on video countless times inform Nishikyō of our plans for Yūsei. I don't believe it.

She smiles, sets down her mug, and stands up. "Hello, Miss Itami. It's so nice to meet you."

I don't know what else to do but laugh. Laugh and bow, that is. Yes, I should definitely bow.

"Coen-sama, mōshiwake gozaimasen. I'm so sorry to interrupt your morning. I didn't know you were here."

"How could you? And stop bowing," Sakai says to me. "Lucy,

this is Sanaa. Sanaa, Lucy."

Lucinda Coen stretches out her hand to me, and I shake her slim fingers, forcing some strength into my limp-with-shock hand.

Mark Sakai, you certainly do prefer redheads.

"Breakfast, ladies? Sanaa, I have coffee. Lucy drinks it. Want some?"

"Yes, yes, I'll have some. Thanks."

Wow, this is uncomfortable. Sakai is sleeping with Coen, I mean, *Lucy.* So those men outside are here for her, not Sakai. Now I'm remembering Jiro's sly smile at the house when he mentioned Coen, and said, "You'll see." I wonder how long he's known about this relationship. I wonder how long this relationship has been going on! Sakai and Coen *have* spent a whole lot of time together. I remember once, back in theater 3B, I questioned Sakai about meeting with Coen, and he froze up like a statue. I think they've been dating for a while.

Sakai pulls out a chair at the table for me, and I sit down. His kitchen is part of the loft, and on the island stove, he is sautéing tofu scramble with onion and fake bacon, and toast sits on a plate to the side. A wholly un-Japanese breakfast. His hair is tucked behind his ears, and he must still exercise because he doesn't look like he's let himself go at all. There are so many things I don't know about Sakai. I'm learning more each day. He turns off the stove and pours coffee, delivering the large, white ceramic mug to the table.

"Here. I'll be right back." He walks to the bedroom, and I watch him go becoming increasingly nervous about being left alone with Lucy.

"You're up early this morning," Lucy says, blowing on her coffee cradled in her hands. "You just got back in the city yesterday."

"Uh, yeah, but I slept most of the flight and most of my time away so I wasn't too tired." I pick up the mug and hold it in both hands like her, grateful it exists so I don't fidget.

"What did you think of our colonization houses in the desert?"

"They were... well-built and functional... And escape-proof."

Lucy huffs a small laugh. "We rarely have to lock people up there. You weren't the first. I doubt you'll be the last."

My scalp prickles and goosebumps rain down my spine. I never think about my government having to lock people up. I set down my mug and wrap my arms around my chest while Lucy peers through me with her bright green eyes. We're dancing around the fact that Sakai is sleeping with the most supreme administrator of Nishikyō. I've seen her photo in the news every day since I was a kid, and now I'm sitting and having coffee with her in Sakai's apartment. Did I switch into some alternate reality when I returned here yesterday?

I stay silent even though I'm so uncomfortable I'm starting to sweat, but after a minute, I can't help myself. "How long have you two been...?"

"Me and Mark? Two years."

"Two years? You've kept that rather hidden."

She smiles at me. "I have, for obvious reasons, but that's not really necessary anymore."

Sakai returns from the bedroom, his hair pulled back, a shirt on. I'm immediately relieved.

"Why?" I ask.

"Have you caught up on news that happened while you were gone?"

"No, I, um..." I cough, too embarrassed to admit I read fiction instead of checking the news. I just wanted things to be normal for a little longer. "What happened?"

She smiles at Sakai, and he smiles back. Sakai's usually passive face is happy when he looks at her.

"Lucy stepped down as Chief Administrator three weeks ago," Sakai explains, grabbing three plates from a cabinet. "One of your old bosses is now in her place as interim Chief until elections can be held. Robert Starr."

"Robert Starr is running all of Nishikyō? That seems... unsuitable." He doesn't have the same experience Lucy does.

"He's my best candidate right now. Emiko Matsuda stepped down as the Colonization chairwoman when Nishikyō News Service reported her husband was involved in a kidnapping attempt and no longer had his head anymore." I look away from her stare. Technically, I'm a murderer now, but she's not jumping up and calling for my arrest. "Don't worry, Sanaa. Only we know you killed him. Everyone else thinks he died in the quake. But Emiko is now 'mourning' at home, so I asked Robert to step up to interim Chief. No one is running the Colonization Committee, but it can pretty much run itself now. Robert does both jobs."

"Why did you resign? You've been an exemplary leader." My

statement is not just flattery. I'm sure most in the city would agree with me.

Sakai has been listening to our conversation from the stove, and he steps around the counter island with two plates of food, then reaches back for a third and sits down.

"It was time. I've been Chief Administrator for ages now..." She waves her hand and makes a *phsaw* noise before rolling her eyes. Wow, Lucinda Coen is joking about her job like it's just any other job. I'm in awe. "I have other important matters that require my attention. And now Mark has asked me to marry him, and I've said yes."

"Really?" Tears fill my eyes as they each confirm with head nods. "I'm so happy for you both." I wipe the tears from my face quickly before I become too emotional. "Omedetō gozaimasu."

Mark Sakai, married. Finally. No more regrets.

"Thank you. We're very happy. It's nice to be out in the open after all this time." She reaches over, and Sakai holds her hand. Seeing Sakai intimate with someone right in front of me is going to take getting used to. Something about the night of the earthquake and attack must have prompted him to propose to her. That night certainly made me feel like life is too short.

"So now that Lucy is retired from being head of Nishikyō, she's going to help you, Sanaa-chan. You know nothing about politics, government, and ruling, and you're going to need that knowledge for Yūsei."

She nods her head. "I hope that's okay with you."

Lucy has been in charge of Nishikyō for as long as I can remember, and meeting her like this, at Sakai's table? I'm pleased that, in private, she's just as personable, smart, and diplomatic as I thought she was. She's more than qualified to be my advisor, but maybe this is what she wants right now, a quiet married life helping someone else make the decisions, not making them herself.

"It's more than okay; your offer is extremely generous." I bow forward to her in my seat to show my respect.

"I've been aware of your situation for years now, and I think I can be of help to you. Feel free to ask me anything."

As Sakai has a big forkful of food lifted to his mouth, the door chimes, and he sighs, putting it down. "I bet I know who this is."

It's Jiro, of course. I probably disturbed his sleep when I got out of bed.

Jiro comes to the table, kisses me, then Lucy on the cheek. As he passes behind Lucy, he smiles and raises his eyebrows at me twice which causes me to laugh. Sakai goes back into the kitchen to make up another plate, and we sit down and eat together like there's nothing odd about this at all.

Chapter Nine

After a week of training in the Itō dōjō, eating four fatty meals per day with Oyama by my side, and getting caught up with all my family and friends, Sakai stops by the morning of the first of June. My life is about to become stressful again. I've had my rehabilitation, though I'm still weak and underweight, and now it's time to get back to work.

"Minamoto's spies have seen you around town so now he knows you're home. He'd like to meet later today."

"Jiro and I have talked about this..." I let my voice fall away. I think Jiro's been giving me time to ponder the idea of letting Kentaro Minamoto into my life, even at arms-length, but I'm still not sure. I wish I could know what Kentaro is like before I make a decision. I've never met him, never even tried to search for his photo online. I saw him once from far away at the concert right before the earthquake, but I don't remember if he's short, tall, skinny, or overweight. Nothing. And now I know he and Jiro have a rocky history.

"Kentaro is a good fighter," Jiro interjects where I leave off, "and he's exceptional with the shinobijō. He's an excellent climber, too. Maybe if you can win him over with your charm and your wit, he'll teach you as well. Just don't flirt with him, or I may have to kill him."

Sakai laughs and sips tea.

"Jiro," I say, leaning back in my chair and examining my nails, "if it even looks like I'm flirting with someone else, you should know it's just an act to lure some weak and unsuspecting person into my trap."

"Gods, help us all," Sakai says, lifting his eyes to the ceiling. "I'll set the meeting up for afternoon tea at the *Ame* Okiya. Sanaa-chan, you will have to pretend to like tea. Sorry." I shrug my shoulders. It's the least I can do. "How's the dōjō?"

"Sanaa's the most confident I've ever seen her. We spar all the time now. I haven't introduced her to any other weapons though Beni's been to the storage area and brought back a few items we can start with."

Beni has been so helpful and attentive. I only met her four days before I left, yet during those four days, she left an indelible mark on me. I think we were destined to be thrown together. When we were reunited, I was sure to tell her I'm sorry for her loss and thank her for taking care of Jiro while I was gone. Jiro was missing me, in addition to mourning Koichi. He needed the extra attention that she gave him.

"Also," Jiro continues, "I asked Usagi yesterday to go pick up Sanaa's brand-new shinobijō. I ordered one of a specific design. It was fun picking it out." I may not get a ring from Jiro ever but weapons? Yes, indeed.

The thought makes me laugh. "You're so romantic." He shrugs his shoulders, and Sakai rolls his eyes. "Speaking of romance, we have two weddings coming up?"

"Um, no," Sakai replies, and my face falls. "Miko and Yoichi will have their small wedding and a party after. Lucy and I are getting the permit and then that's it. She doesn't want anything big because of the attention it will bring, and I agree. I don't think Sakai family can afford that kind of attention, either."

"Ah, well, we should still go out for dinner or something." Sakai fades into his passive expression, and Jiro smiles. Jiro is aware I'm needling Sakai because I've grown to love Lucy this week. She's been spending a lot of time with me. Sometimes Lucy just sits and listens to us, but other times she could chat for hours. She's even come to the dōjō to watch us practice. She's gathering information on me, my personality, and the way I handle things so she can better advise me. Having her around so casually at first was strange, but now it's like she's always been a part of our lives.

"Fine. We'll all go out to dinner. Immediate family only. Mariko's been asking me for more to do. She can plan it."

Mariko's staying busy to stop herself from thinking about Koichi, too. She's been helping Miko plan their wedding, and now she'll have another event to plan. When Mariko is done with Yoichi, Miko, Sakai, and Lucy, who will she move onto next?

I really want to get along with Mariko. Without my aunts close by, I'd like to be closer to her, but when I first arrived home, I went to hug her, she turned from me and walked away. I don't think anyone noticed her rebuff, but I've been thinking of it ever since. She's so motherly with Jiro, her soft hands smoothing out his hair and grazing his cheeks. He probably reminds her of Koichi. It's most likely too soon for me to show affection to her. I'll try again later.

"Sanaa-chan, I'm here to talk about your new training. Starting tomorrow, you'll be with Jiro in the mornings for training in weapons, climbing, and stealth. In the afternoons, you will either train with me and we will work on... your poker face, or you will meet with Lucy to discuss social and political studies. Days when neither of us can meet with you, you're free to do as you please. My only suggestion for those days off is that you go back to Ku 1 with an escort to gather information on Maeda. As head of the biggest yakuza family here in Nishikyō, he's going to be incredibly powerful once we reach Yūsei. His support means the difference between success and failure."

Way to put the pressure on, Sakai. Looks like my leisurely days with Jiro are coming to an end.

"And I have one last piece of news to deliver. We must make as much progress as possible before the year is out. November twentieth will be your last day in Nishikyō. All of our last days. You, your aunts, your friends, and all of Sakai clan will be on the first wave of ships for Yūsei. We get loaded up for hibernation, the crew boards, and we leave orbit in January."

This is it. This is the news I've been dreading and yet hoping for for months now. When I found out I was the next ruler of New Japan on Yūsei, I suspected I'd be going in the first wave, but no one said anything. Everything in my life has come to a head now that Lucy has been added to the family. It turns out Sakai is influential but even more so with her support.

Jiro, a small, sad smile on his face, puts his hands on my shoulders, and I slip my fingers under one of them. "What are the flight estimates?" I ask.

"Six to eight years of hibernation. We will age half that."

I will go to sleep before I turn twenty-one and wake up a twenty-five-year-old woman. I will lose precious years of my life making this trip, and so will everyone I love. I hope it's worth it.

Chapter Ten

"Itami-sama, I'm glad to see you're feeling better. Sakai-san tells me you were injured during the earthquake. How unfortunate."

What a supremely cunning liar Minamoto is. I'm sure he knows everything about the fight, my injuries, my recovery, and my near death again in the hospital at the hands of an assassin. He has spies. We have spies. If only we all just told each other everything, but instead we do this dance. To men like Minamoto, the dance is everything, and if I don't want to offend him, I will have to step lightly.

"I am quite well now, thank you, Minamoto-san." I rise from seiza to lean forward and lift my cup of tea from the table between us. Jiro sits silently to my left, Usagi standing behind me, and Sakai is on my right.

I sit back on my heels and take the time to sum up Kentaro Minamoto. He's twenty-two, the same age as Jiro. He's lean, fit, and possibly a little wiry under his gray kimono. He has a thin face, long forehead, and short spiky hair. If I had seen him out and about, I definitely would have thought, "Not my type." He has yet to utter a word, but he is watching me while I watch him.

"Minamoto-san, you said you had business to discuss," Sakai says, setting his tea cup down and placing his hands on his upper thighs. I continue to sip at the *genmaicha*. Hmmm, this tea is not as bad as I remember it being.

Kentaro lightly shakes his head at Minamoto. Violence flashes over Minamoto's eyes as Kentaro turns towards me.

"Itami-sama, before the earthquake, I was prepared to get back to you about my support. I am willing to throw the full weight of my house behind you, but I ask one thing in return."

I keep my face as passive as possible. Here it comes.

"You currently have no consort. You are twenty and of the age that such things are permissible. It would be advantageous for both our families if you were to take my son, Kentaro."

Kentaro's eyes close, his breath becoming measured and audible, obviously quelling his anger. I admire his reserve though

I'm secretly wishing he would blow up. There is never enough drama in these meetings for my taste. I wonder if he's like this with everyone or just with his father.

"Your request is very generous, but I do currently have a consort, and I will only ever have the one."

I let the silence brew for a minute while Jiro and Sakai sit still on either side of me. I wanted drama and now I have it. I bet they didn't expect me to come right on out and say I'm already attached, but it's true, and I'm not going to let any one else think I can be bought in this way. I can't legally marry so I must be firm. Kentaro and Jiro grew up together. I wonder what each of them are thinking right now about the other one.

Minamoto is processing this new information, watching me without blinking and drumming his fingers on his knee. His spies have probably told him I've been spending a lot of time with Jiro and now he's certain I've linked myself indefinitely with Sakai clan. He won't be happy about that, I can tell, but he'll have to deal. They will all have to deal with my decisions. I won't let them boss me around about my private life.

In the meantime, Minamoto will have to take my alternate offer if he stands to gain anything in our relationship.

"But I'm thinking Kentaro may be quite useful so I have another suggestion." Kentaro's eyes snap to me, terror behind them. "I'd like to take him into the family fold as an advisor. He will live in the Sakai building, and his services may be required night or day. He may feel free to do as he pleases outside of working for us. I won't restrict his... social life, as long as it does not interfere with business. Does this sound agreeable to you?"

While Minamoto and Kentaro whisper in each other's ears, I sip more tea and wait. I glance at Jiro, and he looks back at me. I love getting dressed up for these meetings. Whenever Jiro wears his black kimono, the sight of him makes me nostalgic for our first meeting on New Year's Eve. Jiro raises his eyebrows a little at me, and I have to turn away before a blush starts to form.

"Itami-sama, your offer is most hospitable. We accept."

Kentaro pales like he's heading to a death sentence. Oh Kentaro, don't be so down. I'll be nice. I promise.

"Great. I'm pleased. Sakai-san will be in charge of our future relationship. Kentaro, your services will be expected immediately. Please be ready for Sakai's men who will come for you and your belongings in two hours."

I stand up, Sakai and Jiro follow suit, and Minamoto and Kentaro bow, touching their foreheads to the tatami. Jiro cocks his head and examines them, then me. I wonder how he must feel about the respect I command now. When the small smile hits his lips, I relax. He's amused, not threatened. I shrug my shoulders at him with a wink.

Usagi opens the door, and we all follow him out. Reaching over, I lace my fingers with Jiro's as we walk down the hallway. Now the news will spread that I'm monogamous, but I can be swayed in other ways. Jiro squeezes my hand and nods. He approves.

At dinnertime, I decide I can sit in this apartment building no longer.

"Jiro, let's go to Izakaya Tanaka for dinner and drinks. I want to get out."

We've been sitting on the couch and reading for the past hour while listening to the sound of people in the hallways and stairs, moving Kentaro into the apartment above us. I wish he were in an apartment farther away. Now another person can listen to Jiro and me whenever he wants. Usagi and Oyama were fine. Kentaro? Not so much.

"Okay."

"What? No objections?"

"No. We should definitely go out, and we should do it as often as we can. November's going to come quickly."

"Oh gods, you're right. It's only a matter of time before we're cold and alone and sleeping for years." I was looking forward to the trip to Yūsei for most of my life and now I don't want hibernation to come. It'll be the end of my life here, the end of so much I was beginning to get used to.

"No worries, Sanaa. We still have many months together before then. We'll make them count. I'll go and talk to Usagi and Oyama. Why don't you get dressed?"

"Okay. We should invite Kentaro, ne?"

Jiro stops at the door and heaves a sigh. "Yes, I suppose we should."

I get up from the couch and go to him. "Do you already regret this? I could send him away. We could put him in another building and never call on him for anything. I'm sure Minamoto would eventually catch on though."

"No," he says, his head bowed.

"Jiro, look at me." I smile at him when he lifts his head to meet my eyes. I step straight up to him, wrap my arms around him, and hug him, lifting my face to his. "Are you jealous? You have no reason to be."

"It's just another adjustment to make, one of millions lately. I want things to be easier for us. And yes, I'm jealous. I don't want to share you, especially with him."

Jiro's heart is in the right place. "You'll have to share me with the whole world soon enough, but you'll always have my love. I promise. Kiss me, Jiro." He leans forward, and we share a kiss that makes me melt. They always do. "I wish I could do something to let you know you never need to be jealous."

"Just give me time. I'll get used to it."

"Okay. Now, go talk to Usagi and Oyama, I'll get dressed and message Miko and Helena. On our way out, we'll surprise Kentaro and make him come with us. Keep him on his toes."

He lets out a laugh while he's slipping his shoes on. "You're a little evil sometimes."

"I know, but you like it that way. Don't deny it."

"I won't."

I don't want to dress up so I put on a black shirt and pants then grab my maroon and white haori coat after messaging Miko and Helena. Jiro comes back, changes into a black shirt and pants, and suddenly this night reminds me of our first date, the one I walked out on.

"Here. Don't forget Kazenoho." Jiro breaks into my thoughts, and I slip the sword over my left shoulder before grabbing my bag.

Oyama, Usagi, Jiro, and I climb the stairs, and I scan my hand at Kentaro's door. The chimes ring inside, and a moment later Kentaro stands before us in Nishikyō grays. Yes, he is wiry. He's got to be at least twelve or thirteen kilos lighter than Jiro but he's taller. Maybe he's one of those guys who eats and eats and never gains weight. He looks strong, though, ribbons of muscle winding up his arms. I bet he spends a lot of time working out and training like we do. I have to get him into the dōjō with us.

"What do you want?"

Kentaro does not seem pleased to see me, so I roll on a huge smile.

"He speaks!" He narrows his eyes at me, but yeah, sorry, Kentaro. Those looks of disdain will not intimidate me. "Get dressed. We're going out for dinner."

"No, thanks," he says, trying to close the door.

"No. The correct answer is, 'Yes, Itami-sama.' You're coming or shall we forget our bargain right now? I know how much this partnership means to your father." I'm sure the two hours Kentaro had to pack were spent with his father going over all the specific information Minamoto wants to gather on me and Sakai clan.

"Fine."

He tries again to shut the door on us, but I stick my boot out and stop it.

"Go on then." I wave him away from the doorway. "Go get dressed. You have five minutes while we all wait for you. Do you regularly carry a sword, Kentaro?"

"No," he says, glancing from mine to Jiro's and Usagi's. Oyama only seems to carry his sword when he's wearing official kimono. "Should I be armed? Do you expect trouble?"

"I always expect trouble, but you don't have to carry."

He walks away from us to the bedroom without responding, and I turn from the door but keep my foot wedged in the jamb so it doesn't close.

"Evil, Sanaa. I swear." Jiro lets out a chuckle, shaking his head.

"Is this how you're always going to treat Ken-chan, miss?" Usagi asks, his eyebrows raised.

"Don't worry. I'm just having a little fun. Kentaro has a lot to learn, and the first thing is I'm not to be ignored."

We wait another minute, and Kentaro returns dressed in dark pants and a gray shirt with a faded print on the front that reads, "*Baka na Boy,*" in katakana. *Idiot boy.* Ironic.

I roll my eyes. "Let's go."

Chapter Eleven

Ugh, I think I made a big mistake by bringing Kentaro into the fold. Here we are having a fantastic time at Izakaya Tanaka, and Kentaro is playing silent but drinking a whole ton of sake. Idiot boy, indeed. I want to tear that shirt from him and tell him to get a better attitude.

And now I sound like his mother.

At this point, I'm afraid for him if he opens his mouth. He's been eyeing Helena all night, and Usagi is showing a lot more affection to her than usual. They are now firmly a couple. Usagi came straight to Helena after the quake and professed his love to her. Who knew he was so romantic? I think I heard them next door the other night laughing and having sex. I try not to imagine what they're doing in there, just like I'm sure poor Usagi and Oyama try not to imagine what Jiro and I do in our apartment late at night.

Jiro leans over with his arm around my waist and whispers, "I told you he likes blondes," into my ear. I wonder if we'll have to break up a fight tonight.

After this, I may keep Kentaro back at the building, unless I can get him to open up somehow.

"Did I see you moving into our building today, Ken-chan?" Miko asks. Oh, Miko, I love you, and I'm so grateful that you had the afternoon off.

Kentaro sits back and crosses his arms across his chest. Come on, Kentaro. Even you cannot be immune to Miko's charm.

"I did. I'm now living one floor above Itami-sama and Jiro-san."

Miko mouths, "Itami-sama?" at me and I roll my eyes. "Kentaro, you can call me Sanaa-san or -chan when we're out like this. We've had enough sake for it, ne?" I reach around and refill everyone's cups. We all blazed through dinner so quickly I don't even remember what I ordered. It was a blur of chopsticks and muttered conversation.

"So you'll be working for Sanaa-chan then?" Miko is doing her damnedest to get Kentaro to talk.

"Yes, it appears so. I'm not sure what she'll have me do though."

I glance sideways at Jiro, and he shrugs his shoulders a little.

"What would you like to do, Kentaro?" I ask him.

"Nothing."

"Nothing? There's not anything, not *one thing,* you'd like to do as an occupation, especially for me? What did you study in school?"

Kentaro slams back another cup of sake, and I don't move to pour for him. He's teetering on the edge of being sent home by Usagi.

"I didn't specialize. I work for the family." His arms are recrossed over his chest.

Wow, this guy is tough. He does not want to open up at all. I'm glad Jiro grew up with him, though, because I know a little more about him than he thinks I do.

"Jiro tells me that you can fight. What is your preferred weapon?"

Wait. A smile lightens the corner of his lips.

"Jiro told you, ne?"

The two of them stare icily across the table at one another. I inwardly sigh. Men and their pissing contests.

"So, weapon, which one?" I ask Kentaro again while placing my hand on Jiro's under the table. His fingers are clenched into a ball and unwilling to relax.

"The staff, long or short."

"Good. You see, Jiro just bought me this fine shinobijō the other day, and I was thinking about finding someone to show me how to use it."

Both Miko and Helena burst into laughter. I must seem completely different to them than six months ago.

"Gods, Sanaa-chan," Helena says with a sigh. "Another weapon? The sword wasn't enough?"

"Shhh. You know how I love to try new things." I turn from her to Kentaro but not before winking at her. Drinking sake makes me flirt, even with my best girl friends, but certainly not with the Idiot Boy.

"How about you teach me? You can come to the dōjō a couple of times per week and train with us, then you could have the rest of the time to yourself."

Kentaro sits and quietly analyzes me. "I don't believe you can fight."

He's antagonistic, I'll give him that.

"I can." I put on the sweetest, most innocent girl face I have, batting my eyelashes at him. "Little ol' me."

Jiro laughs and points to me, finally relaxing. "Don't let her deceive you."

"Did you really buy her a shinobijō?"

"I did," Jiro says, turning his smile on me. He's proud, I can tell. "Brand new design from my cousin on the Suzuki side. It's a super light and sturdy composite that has a bend to it. Collapses into two pieces and uses this conductive current charge to expel the weapons from each end. I was hesitant to buy it, but it practically screamed at me, 'This is for Sanaa!'"

"You went and saw Masa?" Yoichi asks.

"Yeah, he's got a whole range of long and short staffs he's been working on. This one is his pride and joy. Sanaa is a lucky girl."

Kentaro is warming up. His eyes sparkle with interest. Miko and Helena must think that we're all crazy.

"I've heard of this design but haven't seen one for myself. Still, I'm not sure I want to teach Sanaa-san anything."

What a brat.

"Okay, Kentaro," I say, leaning forward and pushing my sake cup aside. "I'll give you this option. You play Rock Paper Scissors with me, best two out of three. I win, you train me. You win, you can hang out in your apartment all day, come to big meetings or not, or press your ear to the floor when you want some good gossip. I don't care. It'll be up to you."

He narrows his eyes at me for a moment. He probably thinks I can't possibly lure him into losing at Rock Paper Scissors. It's a game of chance, right?

"Fine." He pours his own sake and tips back the cup, throwing the alcohol straight down his throat.

Jiro leans into my ear. "Rock Paper Scissors? Are you serious?"

I lean back and whisper, "I am completely serious. Wait till you see what your mother taught me."

"Okay, ready?" He nods. "*Ichi, ni, san.*"

I throw: paper. Kentaro: rock. Predictable. Men tend to always lead with rock.

"One for me." I have another drink, and Yoichi and Jiro lean in a little. "Ichi, ni, san."

I throw: scissors. Kentaro: rock. Again. A repeat. He won't repeat again, though, because that will mean he's *too* predictable.

"One for you. Ichi, ni, san."

I throw: scissors. Kentaro: paper.

"I win."

He was either going to throw paper or scissors. We could have tied, and I would have had to guess the next move, but I got lucky. I'm just one hell of a lucky girl.

Kentaro rubs his face with both his hands. He's been silent and arrogant tonight, but I think he's holding back a big personality. I enjoy winning over big personalities, Kentaro, and I will not stop until you love me.

Jiro's hand makes his way around my waist as he and Yoichi smile at each other across the table.

"You've been talking to Mariko," Miko says, signaling the waiter for more sake.

Mariko gave me her whole strategy on Rock Paper Scissors at our lunch months ago before the earthquake. Her secret is now in my arsenal of weapons like everything else I possess: my wit, my silly sense of humor, my wild side, and my instincts which tell me I'm in for a treat now that Kentaro will be in the dōjō all the time.

"To my new sensei! Kanpai!" Everyone clicks cups and drinks. Even Kentaro. He still hasn't smiled yet but given time, I'm sure he'll come around.

Chapter Twelve

Jiro and I pick up Usagi and then Kentaro at 9:55 the next morning, and he is dressed and waiting for us. Good. He grabs two staff weapons from behind the door and follows us out.

At the dōjō, Kentaro walks the room and looks at everything: the rack of wooden swords and towels, the door to the surveillance room in the back, the windows (he lifts each window covering and peers out), and bounces on the mats a few times.

Jiro and Usagi head to the surveillance room while Kentaro and I silently assess each other.

"So this is where you train? With Jiro?"

"Yes, almost every day. Before he died, Koichi was here with us some days, too."

He stops for a brief moment and nods his head, sadness rounding his shoulders. If he and Jiro were friends, Kentaro's relationship with Koichi might have been strong in the past. I don't know enough about the history here to guess accurately.

"Do you know any other martial arts than iaido?"

"I'm a brown belt in karate as well but it's been at least six months since I've actively practiced."

"But still, a brown belt? Good." He nods his head and lifts his chin, gazing down at me over the length of his nose. "Fighting with the staff is not all that different from fighting with your hands. In fact, *bōjutsu*, fighting with the *bō*," he holds out the longer of the two staff weapons, "is considered the next step for advanced karate students. Usually black belt and higher.

"The *jō*," he points to the shorter of the two, "uses many of the same techniques but, because of its smaller size, is better for close fighting. With time, you could learn how to fight someone attacking you with a sword and disarm them before you come to harm. Is that the sort of training you're looking for, Sanaa-san?"

"I think that's the kind of training I need. I won't always be able to carry Kazenoho..."

"Kazenoho?"

"Sorry, my sword."

"Where did you get it?" He tilts his chin up, his eyebrows drawn together. I'm a puzzle to him.

"It was with all of my family's belongings."

He shakes his head at me. "You're *really* descended from the last emperor of Japan?" His voice is pitched higher, sounding incredulous and unbelieving, and I sigh. I'll be hearing this question for the rest of my life.

"Yes. Really."

"Shouldn't you consider a consort from a... better family?"

I turn my hardest stare on him. "Better? Better than the people who have taken care of me and my family for ages? Do you think your family is better? I hate all of the judgement passed around by the clans. It's stupid and only gets you all in trouble. You will not speak of this again with me."

Kentaro must think his family is better because they were one of the original noble clans in Old Japan along with Taira, Fujiwara, and Tachibana, but it's a family's actions that make them stand out. Sakai clan is more noble and reliable in my eyes than any of the others.

The surveillance room door opens and out comes Jiro with my shiny new weapon. Just in time. Kentaro is not going to apologize for prying into my private life, and I don't feel like making him right now.

"Here it is, Sanaa. You're very own shinobijō with Masa's blessings. He's invited us for dinner soon, by the way."

I love meeting all of Jiro's family. Miko and Yoichi's wedding next week will be small, and I won't get to meet the second cousins like Masa. Jiro's family tree is so wide — the branches stretch on and on forever — and yet Sakai said his family was one of the smaller ones.

I smile at him before taking the shinobijō. The name is the biggest clue to what this is: shinobi (ninja) and jō (short staff). Right now, the weapon is collapsed into two connected segments, about eight centimeters wide and less than a meter long. The shinobijō is lightweight, can't be more than a half a kilo. If I need to carry it with me, I could have it against my back under my obi bow, and it wouldn't be too conspicuous.

"So, here's how it works," Jiro says, taking the collapsed

shinobijō back from me. "Snap the ends up like this…" He points to where the hinge is on the joining point and brings up the ends to meet. "Twist until you feel the two pieces catch." I hear a faint click. "To undo it, you pull in opposite directions and twist. Your body's current makes the mechanisms inside work, so you need to remember that in order to assemble or disassemble it, there should be bare skin contact. Once it's together though you can wear gloves if you ever need to be hidden."

He twirls the staff around, over his head, behind his back and to the side, and the way the shinobijō travels from one side of his body to the other seems effortless. Didn't he say he wasn't any good with the staff? Jiro is too modest sometimes.

"Each end contains weapons." Jiro unhinges the shinobijō into two pieces again and shows me a small button inside. "When this button is flush with the surface, they're on. When it's up, they're off." He turns them off. "You should have them off for practice, obviously. One end is a super sharp knife and the other is an electric weapon, delivers a shock to victims that paralyzes them for a short time. Do not test it out on anything, Sanaa."

I roll my eyes at him. "Please, Jiro. Do I look like I want to play around with it?"

"Yes, you do."

"Okay, I do, but how do they even come out? The ends are solid."

He smiles, opens the shinobijō back up, and presses the button. "This is a composite material. I don't know how it works but with the electrical current applied to the surface it reshapes and opens up. Even works if the thing gets wet. There's this depression here," he points to two places on either side of the joint, "that you run your thumb up while applying pressure, and…" A knife pops out of one end startling me. That was quick! Jiro rubs his thumb down the depression, and the knife recedes back in with a swift zing. I can't tell it was ever there. Jiro flicks his thumb along the other impression and an electrical weapon on the other end comes out sparking and causes both Kentaro and me to back away.

"Wow. Yeah, I will not be trying that out on anyone. Jiro, this shinobijō really screamed at you to buy it for me?"

He smiles and bobs his head back and forth. "Well, it certainly is crazy and unpredictable just like you."

Kentaro laughs, a wide smile splitting his face in two handsome pieces. It's the first time he has shown any other emotion than hatred. "I get the feeling training you is not going to be what I was expecting."

I take the shinobijō from Jiro, open it, and turn off the weapons. There. I feel a little safer now.

Jiro clasps Kentaro on the shoulder. "Good luck, Ken-chan."

I smirk at them both. Jiro is neglecting to tell Kentaro I'm a model student.

"So, Sanaa-san, what do you hope to learn from me? Do you want to concentrate on defense, offense, or both?"

"I think defense first. The only reason I'm learning a new weapon is to protect myself in public situations because I refuse to sit inside all day. I'm not going to be one of those people. I want to be out and about, but I can't always have my sword so this —" I heft the shinobijō in my hands "— is my next line of defense."

Jiro narrows his eyes at me. "Sanaa —"

"What?" I turn my temper on him. "I cannot spend the rest of my days in Sakai building..."

"Just..." He sighs, internally struggling with keeping me safe and keeping me happy. "Later. Once we get the minor clans all aligned, and you should always be with an escort."

Do I keep arguing in front of Kentaro? Jiro doesn't seem angry, just anxious and worried, and my anger backs down, my temperamental dragon sitting back on its haunches and huffing. I shouldn't give him a hard time about this, but I'm already tired of being cooped up.

Kentaro crosses his arms, measuring his breathing while thinking. I wish I could read minds because I must be debunking a stereotype in his head. What did he think of me before he even met me? Taira didn't care and wanted me dead outright. I offended Maeda during our first face-to-face meeting and haven't heard from him since. He's probably been listening to a whole host of lies about me already from someone who wants to do me harm. Minamoto was the first to come around.

"Okay, defense first," Kentaro says, grabbing the short staff and laying the longer one on the floor against the wall, "defense against an unarmed assailant and defense against someone carrying a sword. Then we'll move onto offensive strikes to disable an assailant so that you can get away. Let's warm up."

Kentaro's not going to give anything away. Not today.

Jiro picks up his bag, moves to the wall, and sits down with his tablet. He's going to watch and make sure Kentaro won't try to hurt me though I think his presence will be unnecessary. Kentaro did smile and laugh so maybe he doesn't completely dislike me. I don't know what transpired between him and his father that got Kentaro into this situation, but the solution doesn't seem to be mutually agreed upon.

Taking off my outer shirt and leaving on only my undershirt, I toss it off the mats next to Jiro. Kentaro peeks around my back and takes a good look at my tattoos, but I ignore him and walk to the center of the mats awaiting his instruction. There will be no more witty banter today, Kentaro.

To start, he shows me how to stretch my arms, chest, and back using the staff, and how to stand at rest with it out in front of me. After we're warmed up, he demonstrates three different ways to hold the staff and corrects my grip when I try to hold it too much like a sword. Many of the stances are similar to the ones I've learned in karate, so Kentaro demonstrates the upper, mid-level, and low postures next, how to hold the jō high above my head, at my mid-section, and down around my hips.

He walks around me and nods his head. "I don't think it's going to take you long to learn this, especially all of the different strikes which are similar to sword fighting. Let's try some now."

Kentaro instructs me on how to strike from the front, how to strike across the diagonal, and to sweep up from below, and I follow all of his movements exactly.

"Good, Sanaa-san. You're a quick learner."

He is generous with the compliments, so different from Jiro who held back a long time before complimenting me. Looking over at him now, his eyes are narrowed at Kentaro. Aw, it's okay, Jiro. I'll keep it business.

"Arigatō, Ken-chan. What else is there to learn?"

"Well, we'll continue practicing striking, then we can get Jiro involved with the wooden sword, and I can show you how to block and strike at his hands, arms, legs, head, et cetera until he's disarmed. Then you can learn more sweeps and thrusts in combination. It'll all be basic, but I think you'll do well as long as you're not up against someone who has spent his whole life learning to fight with the staff."

"And then?"

"I would hope you have back-up."

Jiro and I both laugh at this. He turns off his tablet and stands up. "Sanaa, it's almost 12:30. We have to get going. I'll fetch Usagi."

"Is this really all you want from me? To train you?" Kentaro pulls his hand through his short spiky hair already glistening with sweat. The dōjō is never cool.

"What did you think you would be doing when your father accepted this arrangement?"

"I don't know. I had no idea what to expect."

"I'm not going to keep you from your life. Go out, see your friends, come here to the dōjō and practice when we're not using it, get yourself a girlfriend, a boyfriend, or whatever..." I laugh and he smiles lightly. He's warming up. "Keep your tablet on you, and I'll let you know if you're needed. If you want to attend meetings or hang out and listen in, fine. *Advise* me. I don't know what your father wants back from me, but I want his support."

Kentaro nods his head at me. I fold up the shinobijō like Jiro taught me and toss it in my bag. Fits nicely.

"I'll message you when we go out, and you can come along or not. I won't order you again. Know this, Helena is taken." I poke him in the chest with my index finger and make my face as stern as possible. I'm not very menacing since he's at least fifteen centimeters taller than me, but he gets the picture. "You do not want to mess with Usagi or me."

He rolls his eyes, but I almost made him laugh again. I can feel it. "I get it."

"Stay and practice, if you like." I wave as I walk off to meet Jiro and Usagi at the door. They ignored my conversation with Kentaro as they walked past us, though I'm sure Usagi's eyes snapped to me briefly when I mentioned Helena's name.

At the door, we stop to watch Kentaro. He's pretty impressive with the jō. The weapon is a blur as he swipes, flicks, and twirls it around over his head, behind his back, across his shoulders and neck. He is swift and sure, confident like Jiro and I are with our swords. He's fascinating to watch but the jō doesn't thrill me the way my sword does.

"He's good with *nunchaku*, too," Jiro says as I close the door.

"One session at the dōjō with the staff, and I already miss my sword."

Jiro puts his arm around my shoulder and squeezes, pulling me with him down the hall after Usagi. "Aw. You may not love the staff as much as the sword but I can already tell you'll be happy you learned."

"I hope so. I really do."

Chapter Thirteen

Back at our building, while Jiro and Usagi grab our lunch from Oyama, I stop at Beni and Risa's apartment and scan my palm at the door. The door opens, and it's Risa, her hair perfectly curled and falling down around her shoulders, her lips pink, and nails freshly painted. She's always completely put together.

"Risa, I haven't seen you since I got back. How are you?" I ask, putting as much enthusiasm into my greeting as possible.

"Can I help you with something, Sanaa-san?" Risa's hand rests on her hip, her heart-shaped mouth twisting into a grimace, turning her pretty face wicked with enmity. I'm not welcome here.

"Yes, you can. May I come in?" I step in the door anyway, and she sighs, moving out of the way. I don't think friendship is possible between us, but I'll be damned if I'm going to let her treat me poorly. I don't care who she is.

She lets me into the apartment, and though the space is fairly spartan, they have a lot of art up on the wall. Hanging in the corner are strings of hundreds of origami cranes, each string a different color or paper pattern. They're so fun and bright, they immediately make me smile.

"I love the paper cranes, Risa. Are they yours?"

"Yes, Sanaa-san. I fold a few every night before bed."

"I folded a hundred for Miko during the first weeks I was home, for her wedding day." I turn back to smile at her but freeze under Risa's cold stare.

"Are you here to see Beni?" she asks through a clenched jaw.

"Yeah, is she at home?"

Walking along the length of their walls, I examine a line of photos opposite the kitchen. The first few are of Risa with other people, some her age and one with an older man and woman who must be her parents. The next photo in the line is one of Beni and her parents, and my heart clenches. She's a few years younger, and they're all happy together. I have to turn from the photo before it makes me cry.

"Beni is at Mariko's. She hasn't been here much."

Oh no. Maybe she's not doing as well as I originally thought.

"Okay. Well, I guess I'll have to go and find her there. Is everything going well with Miko and the wedding?"

"Yes, Sanaa-san. I'm glad to be of help."

Risa taps her foot and pushes the cuticles back on her left hand, bored of me and our conversation already. She doesn't want to chat, and I can't blame her. We haven't had the best of relationships so far. I chose Beni over Risa for my jihi, dressed her down in front of Beni, and she probably thinks I stole her best chance at marriage and rule over Sakai clan.

"Thank you, Risa. I'm glad you can. I'm sorry to come and go so quickly, but I have to meet Sakai-san in an hour, and I don't want to keep you from your lunch." I gesture to the sushi and steaming cup of hot tea on the kitchen table as I step past her to the door. Risa doesn't even say good-bye. She pushes the door closed behind me, and I hear her groan inside once it's closed and say, "Stupid bitch." Her high-pitched voice echoes in the hallway.

The guard at the top of the stairs remains stony-faced though I'm sure he heard Risa. My head is starting to ache from all the drama this morning. First Kentaro, now Risa.

I rub the spot between my eyes and climb up two flights to Mariko's apartment. When the door opens, my heart sinks and a shock of pain rips through my temples. Mariko's eyes are red and wet with tears.

"Sanaa-chan, I'm sorry you've caught me crying."

Without waiting for an invitation, I wrap my arms around Mariko's shoulders and hug her. I haven't tried to be intimately close with her since she turned me away a few weeks ago. She's stiff for a long moment, and I think maybe I should pull away. Is it still too soon? Before Koichi died, Mariko said they were happy I was with Jiro. I remember how sweet and kind she was to me when Jiro moved in, how she wanted to plan for our wedding as well. Now I wonder if her feelings have changed.

Many moments pass, her body finally softens in my embrace, and she cries into my shoulder. Her sobs are so sad, tears start to brew in my eyes too, but I push them back down. I have to be strong for her, for everyone. They need all the love and support I can give right now, and I want to show Mariko she can depend on me.

After a few more sobs, she blows out a big breath and pulls away from me, stiffening back up into formality again.

"Beni is here, and we've been talking about her parents... and I'm afraid the two of us are just making it worse for each other."

I nod my head at her and squeeze her shoulders. Beni's parents were Mariko's second cousins. Mariko must feel this pain over and over.

"I came to visit with you and Beni."

"Good. We could use the company."

Before letting go, I give her another quick hug and hand her a handkerchief I find on the kitchen table. I wish my schedule weren't so hectic because I'd like to be here every day. I'm going to be here more often, I promise myself. I want to be the best almost-daughter-in-law I can be.

Mariko dabs at her eyes and wipes her cheeks before taking a big breath. "Beni's in the bedroom. Can you go talk to her, please?"

In the bedroom, Beni is sitting on the bed, slumped over and staring at her hands, and my heart aches again.

"Oh, Beni," I say, going straight to her. Gods, all of our lives were destroyed the day of the earthquake. How will it ever be the same again?

"I miss my parents so much. We were so close and now they're just gone."

I don't know what to say, so I take her hand and let her cry. I miss my parents, too. They've been gone for a long time, but I still hurt when I think of them. Beni will hurt for a long time.

"I'm sorry I haven't been around for you, Beni, especially right after the earthquake when I should have been here for you, and Mariko, and Jiro. I've been angry with Sakai for sending me away. I thought about you all night and day."

"Don't be sorry. It was the right thing to do, to put you someplace safe. This place was crazy after the earthquake."

"I just talked with Risa a moment ago. She said you haven't been home much."

She nods her head and looks at me. Her face is red, her eyes swollen. Poor Beni.

"Before you came back, I was at my parents' apartment. I was sleeping there and packing their belongings with Mariko's help. Then when I came back here, I was too sad to stay in the apartment with Risa. She was always gone, so I've been staying here with

Mariko."

The front door squeaks open in the other room. Must be Jiro. He found me.

"Well, I think you staying here might be good for both of you," I say, squeezing her hand. "Mariko's your, what? Second cousin, once removed, or something?"

Beni laughs, tears bouncing off her chin to her lap. I've done some digging into the Sakai family tree, memorizing people and where everyone fits into the puzzle. I have an irrational urge to know every single one of them.

I squeeze her hand again. "I'm glad you have blood family to help keep you from being alone, but you're my family now, too. And I want to make sure that you can be happy again. I have some things I could use your help with. Do you want to stay busy or do you need the time to work through this?"

"No," Beni says, wiping the tears from her face. Unfortunately, that does not make her look any better. Poor Beni. "I would like to be busy, Sanaa-san. What do you need?"

"A haircut," I say with a laugh. "Jiro's handiwork can only go so far."

From the door, Jiro huffs a laugh, and I turn to find him watching us.

"And I wonder if you'll go shopping with me to get Miko and Yoichi's wedding present?"

"Yes, Sanaa-san. I can help you with both." She blows out a shaky breath, smoothing back her hair and replacing the clip to the side.

"I think I'd like a new yukata for the wedding too." Beni nods at me. "Beni, we're going to the temple tomorrow morning to burn incense for Koichi. You should come with us. We'll pay our respects to your parents as well, okay?"

Beni nods again, and I give her a weak smile and pat her on the back. Hopefully, she can come around when some more time has passed. Time does make the hurt seem less intense.

"Jiro brought lunch. Let's go eat."

Jiro puts his hand on her shoulder as she walks by, but then his hand comes to my face. "You've been so good for us. I don't know what we'd do without you."

I sigh and pull my chin from his hand. I don't want him to see how hard it is for me to be strong when everyone else is so sad.

But he must instinctively know. "It's okay to be sad. No one wants you to be happy and fake. We just want you to be a part of our lives."

I swallow my sadness, though. Two crying women in one apartment is enough.

"I'll cry later."

"Here. I made you some *genmaicha* since you drank it at the okiya the other day," Sakai says, passing me a hot and steamy mug.

Sakai is relentless about the tea. After the day I've had already, I'd like to tell him to take his tea and shove it up his ass, but I'm swallowing my temper before I explode and ruin our entire afternoon together.

Instead, I take the cup and look around. His apartment is pretty spotless, much like the morning I was here. A painted scroll of bright orange koi fish takes up most of one wall. Behind the couch, in a small alcove, a few pieces of beautiful black and red lacquerware sit next to a vase holding an arrangement of dried flowered twigs. They're really quite pretty for being so dead. I don't identify anything I would associate with Lucy, though.

Sakai sits to my right on the chair after getting his own tea.

"When is Lucy moving in?"

"After Yoichi's wedding. It'll be the first time we're seen in public together. Then we'll announce our engagement, and she'll move in."

"Seems like a lot of work for something so simple. And I thought *I* was going to have it hard in the relationship area." I try to laugh off my situation, my hands instinctively rising to my head to sweep my hair over my shoulder. I stop them halfway and rest my hands in my lap. The only thing I can do is tuck the long strand over my ear, and it's already clipped back.

"You can see why I never said anything before." Sakai takes a sip of tea. I always knew he was keeping secrets from me. "How was training with Kentaro this morning?"

"He was fairly respectful and didn't try to injure me. A

blessing." I turn the mug around on the table and sit back with it, letting the heat warm my cold hands. "Mark, am I a murderer now that I've killed two people?"

The events of the past few months feel like they happened to an entirely different person, and I am so detached from them. Did I really kill two men?

Sakai brings his legs up onto the chair and crosses them. "Do you think you're a murderer?"

"Oddly enough, no. I'm wondering if I should feel more guilty than I do, if there's something wrong with me because I don't."

"You're not a murderer, Sanaa-chan. You didn't set out that night to kill people. Tadao did. Miura did. They're the murderers here. You defended yourself and your family. There's a big difference between defending yourself and murdering."

"I know this, I think." My line of sight falls down on my tea, and I swirl the dark liquid around to mix up the leaves floating at the bottom. "But I wonder what my parents would think of me, if they were here."

I try not to be woeful when it comes to my parents. In fact, before Sakai came along, I only thought hard about them every New Year's Day. They died so long ago, I have no concrete memories of them. Now I find myself thinking about them all the time, comparing the stories I've been told over the years with what I hear now from Sakai and Mariko.

"Your mother struggled with life and death." Sakai's voice is soft, and his eyes unfocused, looking way back in time to when they were all young. "She agonized over every decision, and the anxiety made her sick, made Max depressed, and Kimie angry. She'd probably think she was to blame for all of this." He pulls back to the present and puts his hand on my knee. "I've been worried that you would either be anxious and obsessive like your mother or depressed like your father, but I think you have Kimie's fire and temper, actually."

He laughs and I shake my head. Once Kimie gets upset, there's no stopping her. We're a lot alike. I press my lips together and keep silent. I don't want to tell Sakai about my obsessive tendencies or how, sometimes, I'm depressed about my situation.

"I've seen you anxious, though, and the pacing helps?" I nod. It does. Physical exercise always helps. "Then keep doing that. Nothing ever helped your mother."

We take a moment to be quiet and think, and I bet we're both thinking of my mother.

"Anyway, business," he says, nodding and moving on. "We should talk about ways in which spies learn to control themselves so they don't get caught doing their jobs."

"My poker face?"

"Or lack thereof. We have to work on that and your blush response."

I have yet to control my blush response. Every time I have told it to go away, the blush comes on even stronger.

"In my head, I call what you do your 'passive face.' You become like a statue and impossible to read when you do it. Jiro does it, too."

"Good," he says, clapping his hands with a laugh. "That's the intention. I've never taught anyone else how to do it so no one else has commented on it before."

"You didn't teach Jiro?"

"No. He learned that on his own, probably by watching me."

Why am I not surprised?

"Do you do that to Lucy, too?" I ask. I wonder how unguarded Sakai and Lucy are in private.

"Of course. She's a politician. She's just as skilled at it as I am. Sanaa, this is a learned skill and will take a lot of practice. One of the core tenants to being a ninja is to rid yourself of your own ego. You must become impartial and free of your emotions, even when you are angry, even when you are devastatingly sad, even when you are head over heels in love. You cannot perform your duties if you are overcome with your own feelings. When I put on my 'passive face,' I'm not covering up my emotions, I'm ridding myself of them so I can concentrate on the emotions I'm interpreting from others."

"Wow. How do you do that?" How does anyone control themselves so fully?

"Me, personally? I become passive by thinking as logically as possible. When a situation presents itself, instead of reacting, I step back in my head and think through all options. This will probably work for you, too, since you're already very logical, but..." Sakai's eyes immediately go to my neck which has started to blush. "We have to do something about your blush. Try putting on the passive face now. Look me in the eye."

I sit up and look him straight in the eye. His face softens, his cheeks drop and relax, and his mouth comes into a straight line across his face. I think about those areas of my face and instruct the muscles there to conform to the same expression. I rid my brain of thoughts of my parents, Jiro, Mariko, or the men I killed and think as bleak and blank as possible. Blank like the dunes stretching for kilometers from the house. Blank like the deep blue sky of early morning I glimpsed while sleeping under the window.

"Good, Sanaa. That was quick! I've never seen you control your own blush response."

I grab my cup of tea and take a sip. "Sometimes I don't want to. Other times it annoys me and gets worse."

"You're bad at taking compliments," he says, and this alone is enough for the blush to start up again.

Dunes. Deep, blue sky. Passive face.

He nods his head at me. "Good, good. Now I'd like to see you stop a blush when Jiro says something."

"You know me too well." I sit back on the couch and bring my feet and knees up. I'm comfortable here in his apartment. "Do you go into meetings and negotiations already having rid yourself of emotions? Is it not sometimes better to go in and be passionate about whatever it is that you want or need?"

"I always go in dispassionate and void of emotions and always get my way. It works every time."

Even the time that I hit him in the dōjō and he apologized, he still managed to not tell me anything. This is a skill that makes him stronger than anyone else I know, and one I'll need to rule, to spy, or to keep on living. This emotionless state of mind, this passivity, is another thing I must have and will obsess over until it's mine.

Chapter Fourteen

"Do you want to talk about it?"

Jiro has been watching me pick at the leftovers of my dinner for the last ten minutes and not saying anything. I can't stop thinking of my mother and father, my aunts, my entire family, what little of it there is.

"It's nothing. Can we do something tonight? Watch an old movie?" Old movies are good distraction material for Jiro, but he's not biting.

"Come on. What's going on with you? You should talk to me. I'm not just another pretty face, you know." He winks at me with a smile, and I can't help but laugh.

"You have a very high opinion of yourself."

"Tell me it's not true." He cocks his head to the side and strokes his beard. It's totally true.

"I... I miss my parents is all." Jiro's face falls, his shoulders going straight with it. "I'm doing all of this stuff now I should have been doing with them. And seeing you with your family, with your mother and Beni, and with Yoichi and Miko's wedding coming up? I just feel left out. Sorry."

"Don't be sorry. I know how you feel." Yes, I'm sure he misses his father, too. "Is this what you talked about with Mark?" I nod, not talking. Talking will lead to my voice shaking and then the crying. I told myself I'd cry later. I'd rather not.

"He's like a father to you. If I can't help you, I always hope he can."

It's a good thing he's not jealous of Sakai. I sometimes worry about that.

"It's not that you can't help me, because I do tell you everything. It's just Mark knew my parents." He knew my mother well enough to know her obsessive and anxious habits and knew my father well enough to know he was depressed. I close my eyes and try to picture them all together, out drinking or hanging out in their apartments. And I always forget my Aunt Charlotte was there too, a fiery redhead Sakai eventually fell in love with and had a baby with.

"What about the rest of your family? Your mother's sister?"

How does he read my mind like that? It's eerie.

"My Aunt Sharon? Ehhh, I'm not sure that's a good idea. I haven't seen her in ages. I invited her to my graduation, but she never came. Last time I saw her, she walked out of my tenth birthday party, drunk and belligerent."

"What about your grandparents? I have one grandmother left. She can't wait to meet you."

I try to smile back at him, but it fails miserably.

"I haven't seen my grandparents since I was eight. Twelve years is a long time to go without seeing your only granddaughter. I don't know what I did to keep them away. I'm not sure I'll ever know."

"I'm sure it's not your fault. Ugh," he says, raking his hands through his hair. "These people make me angry. Thank the gods for your aunts. Do you think your grandparents would change their minds?" he asks, a hopeful lilt to his voice.

"Maybe. Maybe not. If there's a chance for us to be a family again, should I take it?" I'm unsure but Jiro is nodding his head. "Especially before hibernation. I'm not sure if there's a chance, honestly, Jiro. You don't know my family."

"Let's ask Mark about it next time we see him." He gets up from the table, grabs his bowl and mine, and leans over to give me a kiss on the cheek. It's a burst of warmth on my icy face. Talking about my family always makes me cold and regretful. "What did you work on today with him?"

"My poker face."

"You have one?"

"Ha, ha." Everyone's a comedian when it comes to my lack of self-control. "I'm working on it. What did you do?"

"I sat with my mother and Beni for a while, and Yoichi came by, and we talked about the wedding next week. He and Miko are going to come to the temple tomorrow morning, too."

"Okay."

"So, let's stay busy tonight. I have an excellent idea for what we can do."

He walks to the bedroom. I hear a lot of shuffling around, a drawer opening and closing, and out comes Jiro with an armful of paper.

"What are you doing? Paper?"

"Yes, paper," he says, laying sheets of used paper all over the floor. The two of us are pretty neat, and we have a lot of open floor space for such a tiny apartment. He pushes the coffee table up against the couch and lays more paper on the floor there too. I get up from the table and stand at the edge. When he's done, he stands next to me, and we both look at it. What a mess. I want to clean it right up.

"You think I'm crazy and unpredictable? When you said, 'stay busy,' I had another activity in mind."

"I know you did. I can read your thoughts." He looks at me and smiles. My mind is always on sex with him. "But you wanted to learn stealth walking and now's as good a time as any. We should get our socks though." He skirts the edge of the paper floor and retrieves two pairs of socks from the bedroom. Once he has his on, he walks from me to the other side of the room normally over the paper, and the sheets rustle and crack with each step.

"Hear how much noise I make with my casual walk? Now watch."

Jiro's right foot comes out in front of him, heel down on the paper, and he slowly steps across the length of his foot to the toes. His body is upright and back, his knees bent, and once his foot is all the way down, he shifts his upper body weight forward. That one step made absolutely no noise. He repeats this same procedure with his left foot: foot out in front, heel down first then through to his toes, his body upright and back until his foot is solidly down, then he shifts his body's weight forward.

"The keys to stealth walking are: heel to toe, bent knees, and keeping your body's weight back not forward. In normal situations, when you just want to be quiet but not silent, walking heel to toe will suffice. I walk like that normally."

"You and Mark."

He nods. They do this on purpose. I can only imagine how many conversations Jiro has listened to because no one can hear him coming.

"Here in Nishikyō, we never have to worry about walking through grass, water, or leaves, but methods exist for those as well. Maybe someday when we're on Yūsei, and you can travel outside, we can try them."

"We can hope." I close my eyes for a brief moment and imagine trees, sunlight, and a breeze, but the picture in my head is fuzzy and clouded. I have no idea what to expect of a green planet. Hot desert? Sure. I've seen plenty of sand and scorching sun.

"The most you and I will have to contend with," Jiro continues, "is creaking fire escapes, ladders, and composite floorboards. In Old Japan, to keep assassins away, wealthy warlords had special wooden floors constructed that made noise when you walked across them. Only the most skilled ninjas were sent to kill them. Now, you try."

I stick my foot out and down, trying to replicate Jiro's movements, but my weight is too far forward, and I rush through my first step, the paper crackling beneath me.

"Try bending your knees a little more. It'll help keep your weight back."

I couldn't do this for too long. This style of walking requires a lot of quad strength, and I'm only gaining those muscles back now. But my second step is quieter than my first. Third step, silent. Fourth, the same. Jiro's face is all smiles when I step up next to him.

"Excellent. If you were stepping through the woods, this would be useful. By keeping your weight back, you can stop your step if you come across a twig or dead leaves, or whatever else one finds in woods." He shrugs his shoulders and motions to me. "Together."

We walk across the paper side-by-side, making very little noise. Any noise is surely coming from me.

"As I suspected, you'll be a master in no time. Let's add some sake and see if it improves you."

"Are you kidding?" Nope, he's heading straight for the fridge. I love when we hang out and drink together, just the two of us. I never used to drink as much as I do now, but I also used to have a lot more freedom. Oh well. At least we always have a good time.

We each get a cup, and on either side of the floor, we fill back up, drink, and try the stealth walk again. After thirty straight minutes of walking and drinking, I'm making nothing but noise, and Jiro's steps are still silent.

"Jiro! How do you do that?"

"I have a stronger tolerance for alcohol than you do."

A fit of giggles comes over me when I get to one side and am now staggering instead. I set down my cup and jump on Jiro's back. He stumbles to the right, and I clutch on tight and laugh.

"How about a challenge? If you can carry me across without making any noise, I'll take you to bed right now, and I'll be on top and do that thing with my hips you love so much."

For the first time ever, Jiro blushes. That just made my year.

He clears his throat. "You are such a tease."

"I'm only a tease if I'm not going to do it. So you better walk lightly."

"What if I don't make it across silently?"

"Where's your confidence? Okay, if you lose, then, um..." A major blush is rising, and I'm not going to stop it. "I get to come first." I bury my head in the back of his neck so he can't peek over and see me.

"Deal. Because this seems like a win-win situation to me."

He hoists me up higher on his back, and, slowly and deliberately, he steps across the paper without making a noise. Damn, he's good.

"Mmmm, I win, but I have alternate plans for the rest of this evening."

"If you insist." I kiss his neck as he carries me to the bedroom. He kicks the paper in front of us, and the sheets fly up through the air as he charges through them.

Turning around, he dumps me on the bed, and I squeal with delight. He's the only person I've ever let throw me around because I trust him to not hurt me. Trust. I place so much trust in Jiro.

"Off with the pants." In one swift movement, he drags his hands up the sides of my legs, grabs the waistband of both my pants and underwear and yanks them off. I've had way too much sake way too quickly, and all I can do is giggle.

"That's right," Jiro says, pulling my shirt off, up over my head. "Naked. Just the way I like you."

"It's not fair." I pull him forward towards me by his shirt. "You need to lose the clothes."

"Nope." He smiles, his face close to mine. He drags his nose up my cheek and seals his lips over mine, a blinding kiss that makes my head swim. The sake pumps through my blood as our mouths open, and he pushes his tongue deep down. I wrap my arms around his neck and pull myself up on my knees on the bed when he grabs my ass.

Jiro pulls away and steps back from the bed, leaving me

unsteady on my knees. A chill zips up my body, my nipples harden, and all the blood settling between my legs brings an ache so powerful I groan.

"Turn around and get on all fours, Sanaa."

I actually start to shake with anticipation as I position myself. "Jiro..." I begin in a warning tone, but I stop when I hear him stripping down.

"I won the bet," he says, his right hand sweeping up across my behind, grazing the length of my lower back and coming to rest on my shoulder. The bed sinks as he climbs up behind me, and the warmth of his chest presses down on my back. "And I've decided to take you however I want." Cupping his left hand on my breast and propping himself up with his right, he kisses along my tattoos, and my vision starts to fade. I could probably come from this alone.

Jiro's hair sweeps forward across my right cheek, his beard tickling my ear before his lips are there. My whole body is shaking, so he pulls me up close to him, my back against his chest. "I've been watching you, Sanaa. You stay strong and make hard decisions, but you're going to crumble if you don't let go. Here, in our bed, I want to take control, for you. I want to give you a break from everything. I want to give you everything."

"Yes, Jiro." Tears form in my eyes though I'm dying for the release of an orgasm.

"Let me take the lead, and I'll never leave you unsatisfied."

His offer is so tempting as his fingers move south across my stomach and settle into the wetness inside of me. His touch is too much for me to handle, especially in this broken state. I've been strong for everyone. I have to keep being strong, but I'm losing my mind if I think I can control the clans, my destiny, and Jiro too.

"Yes. Please. Please," I beg, a whine tinging my voice, and the tears fall from my face. I have only ever once asked for what I wanted in bed, and that encounter with Chad ended so terribly. No man has ever cared if I was satisfied or not. This is still very new for me, a trusting relationship, not just being a person available for a quick fuck. Jiro presses his fingers up against my G-spot, and I tumble forward into an orgasm that decimates every last brick of wall I had built up to protect me from destructive lovers. I push my face into the bed and cry into the covers in ecstasy and relief.

"You needed that," Jiro whispers as he gently rolls me over and presses his warm body down on mine. He pushes into me, and my eyes roll back into my head. "And I need to do this for you, my love. Let me love you and take care of you, so you can take care of everyone else."

I dig the tips of my fingers into his back and pull him into me even farther until he shakes and lets loose with a low moan.

This is what I've been asking for for years. A man I love who loves me back and would do anything for me. He found me broken in the desert and wants to put me back together because he loves me.

As he kisses along my forehead and rests his face in the hollow of my shoulder, I believe he can give me what I need.

Okay, Jiro. We'll try it your way.

Chapter Fifteen

The next morning, Jiro and I walk to the temple together with Beni, Mariko, and Sakai out in front of us, Usagi in back a little, and Miko and Yoichi behind us by about a block. We all chose to dress in yukata because today it's going to be blistering hot in Nishikyō. Most people will lie low on a day like this when the heat under the domes will hit the mid-thirties, and summer is only beginning.

After prayers at the temple, we'll go out for ramen together. Oyama will be waiting for us at the restaurant across the street from our building.

Jiro holds my hand and gives the palm a kiss. "Feeling better today?"

"Yes. Thank you." I let Jiro take care of me all night. After our first sex, we drank more sake and ate chocolate cake in bed while talking. Then before we slept, we had passionate, emotional, loving sex that made me regret my bloodline and my inability to make a legal lifelong commitment to Jiro.

I need to stop obsessing over marriage. I thought the inability to marry was no big deal and Sakai was being overly dramatic about it. Now I realize he was being truthful, especially with the wedding of my best friend less than a week away. I'm jealous, and I never get jealous.

Try not to think about it, Sanaa.

I'm visiting more of Ku 6 the longer I live here even though I spend an inordinate amount of time in Sakai's building. This temple we're approaching is where we'll be for Miko and Yoichi's wedding in a few days. The complex is at the end of a block with a bright red *torii* gate over the entrance to a wide courtyard bordered on three sides by buildings. The courtyard is one of those random places in Nishikyō where you can look up and see a long expanse of dome above instead of just the tops of buildings.

The main building directly ahead of us has its large paper shōji doors open. Looking in, a few people are kneeling in seiza and praying on tatami mats, and the strong bitter smell of incense is in the air. Usually temples like this are not open for everyday worship. Instead, they hold most of their events out in the courtyard and keep the religious icons behind closed doors. This temple is keeping its main room open since the earthquake because so many people from this neighborhood were lost. A steady stream of mourners flows through here each day.

We step in, setting our shoes off to the side. Jiro and Yoichi meet Sakai off to the left to get incense, light the stick, and stand it up in a trough of sand while I join everyone on the mats. This building is part of the buddhist temple, so the iconography in the main room is all Buddha-related. My family switches back and forth between Buddhism and Shintoism which is typical for most Japanese in Nishikyō. I pray to the Shinto gods because they remind me of nature and where we all came from, but all of our family traditions surrounding birth and death are Buddhist. Most wedding ceremonies are Shinto. In Nishikyō, as in Old Japan, Shinto and Buddhist practices share the same temples.

I debate where to sit for a moment but drop into seiza next to Mariko, squeezing her stiff shoulder before clasping my hands in my lap and meditating. Closing my eyes, I think about Koichi and what a good, kind, and funny man he was. He and Mariko obviously loved one another a lot. They had been together for a long time, often joked and laughed with each other, and never refrained from showing affection even in public. They had two great sons who loved them both. I'm sorry he'll never see his grandchildren or Yūsei. Mariko saved his ashes at home and will bring them with her on the long voyage. He wanted to walk outside on the new world, but instead, his ashes will be spread there.

I remember pushing Mariko to the railing at the theater and how she refused to go when I told her to. Koichi looked at her sadly and the two of them had this moment across the room like no one else was around, like it was just the two of them. And that was the last time Mariko saw him alive.

I didn't come here today intending to cry, but I am.

A warm hand brushes my neck, and I look up to see Jiro standing over me. I don't know how long I've been sitting with my eyes closed, but my legs are numb, so I shift onto my hips and let the blood flow back down my body again. Jiro helps me up, but I push him into my spot next to his mother and motion for him to sit.

Slipping on my shoes, I wipe the tears from my face and leave the room. Out in the courtyard, Sakai stands and stares off into a zen garden between two of the buildings. The small, white rocks are perfectly raked in waves radiating out from two dark stones off-set from the center. The priest who last tended this garden stood his rakes up against the wall next to a bucket.

Sakai is very still, and I slowly walk up to him — heel toe, heel toe — as quiet as I can in my flip-flops. When I get close, I slip my arm under his. He doesn't flinch.

"You're getting better, Sanaa-chan, but I still heard you coming."

"How did you know I was practicing? Jiro only showed me last night."

"You've been sitting seiza for over an hour. Jiro and I were just out here talking."

"My legs are aching. I should have gotten up a long time ago." I hug his arm and rest my head against him. Gone are the days when I was afraid of him or wary of showing him any affection. It feels good to have another man in my life I can be this way with.

"Only a few more days until the wedding. I think that's what upsets me most about Koichi being gone. He always wanted to see his kids get married."

Ouch, my heart. Kids. Not just one child, but both.

"After I asked Jiro to move in with me and Mariko came to visit the first time, I was so worried I had done the wrong thing."

"Why? You know they love you. Koichi was always impressed with you."

"Mark, I worry..." I pause and hug his arm tighter. "I worry that I can't marry Jiro, and it will ruin their dreams of a big, interconnected family. I don't want them to regret letting me into their lives."

"It doesn't matter that you can't legally marry and forever link your family tree with ours. If you and Jiro have children, we'll always have that dotted line between us." He smiles down at me.

I want to believe him, but I remember his face in Ku 1 when he told me I'd never be able to marry.

"It mattered to you, though," I say, and he sighs. "Don't try to deny it. You wanted to marry and couldn't, until now. And you say it doesn't matter, but it does, after all of this time. This is why everyone is allowed to marry regardless of sex, race, or religion. We even let sixteen year olds marry with permission."

"We lost a lot. We killed off our population. We fought. We lost almost all of our technology, all of our planet. Now that we've built most of that back up here in Nishikyō, we've come back to our roots, to our families. Marriage is still tied to family."

I think about all of the dotted lines on my tree, the same dotted line that connects me to my father's side of the family and countless other families going way back in the line. I followed the majority of them, and I have a few very distant third or fourth cousins but most of the families on the outskirts of my tree are dead and gone.

"Do you know much about my Aunt Sharon? She's living in Ku 4 now, but I haven't seen her in a long time. I wonder what she's doing... If she misses me, at all."

Sakai is suddenly still. Either he knows a lot about my aunt or very little.

"She wasn't at your graduation, Sanaa-chan."

"Yes, I know... Wait. How do you know that?"

"Because I was there. I came by myself to support you, even though you didn't know me."

Jiro sidles up next to us, his eyes wide with surprise. He's probably been listening to our entire conversation.

"I've watched after you since you were a baby without letting anyone know." Sakai pats my hand and turns to face us both. "I haven't kept in touch with Sharon either. She pushed me out of her life a long time ago."

"I was thinking of going to her now. Is it safe?" I'm ambivalent about what I'll find if I pry into this, but I need to understand what happened. I may never reconnect with my family, but I won't know till I try.

"Usagi and I could make it work, Mark. We could put a couple of people on Sharon, watch her for a week, and learn her schedule. Then we could escort Sanaa when Sharon is at home and alone."

Sakai sighs. "Okay, but after the wedding, please. We're already stretched thin working on security for that because we'll all be there and Lucy, too. After the wedding is over, things will be calmer."

I turn to head back inside. Mariko stands at the door watching Jiro and me together, her face a blank slate, cold and unhappy, and I'm chilled to my very core. She doesn't soften for my meek smile as she turns and shuffles back to the mats.

Chapter Sixteen

Another evening with Jiro gone. Since we've been back, Jiro has been attending many meetings and dinners with Sakai and Lucy, shouldering more responsibility in Sakai clan and on my behalf. It's sweet, and I'm glad he's been taking care of me in this way, but I miss him especially after submitting to him the other night. I've never done anything like that before, handing myself over to my lover completely. I may not have been satisfied with Joshua or Chad, but I always controlled when they saw me or not.

Now I have no control over anything. I can't go to all these meetings because of security issues, and I have little to do at home. Regardless, I know Jiro has work to do, and I don't want to be the nagging girlfriend wondering why he's not home all the time. That's not the kind of person I am. I trust him, but I'm bored.

What to do, what to do.

It's only seven in the evening and way too early to go to bed. I wonder if anyone is around.

I open the door to our apartment, entering the silent hallway, and scan my hand at Miko's door. Waiting while the chimes ring inside, I tap my feet on the floor, toe heel, toe heel, over and over again. Hmmm, what can I persuade Miko to do if she's at home? Drinking? Card games? But the chimes cycle through again and no one answers the door. Too bad. She's probably working or out with Yoichi.

Perhaps Usagi is home, and we could go out for dinner and a drink. I turn around and move down one door. Scan hand, chimes, tap toes, tap toes. No answer. Okay, I'll try Mariko and Beni next, and if they're not home, I'll message Usagi.

Sprinting down the hall, I wave to the security guard and climb up the stairs two flights. I don't know Kentaro all that well yet, so I won't bother him by stopping on his floor.

I arrive at Mariko's door and proceed with the dance. Scan hand, chimes, tap toes, and, when I look down, light spills across my feet from under the door. Yay! Maybe she's home. I promised myself I would come here more often, and I'm excited I'm getting the chance.

But I wait and wait, and no one answers the door. Aw, that's disappointing. I was having dreams of hanging out with her in our pajamas, eating chocolate, and watching a movie together. This is something we've never done together, but I bet would be fun. Jiro often tells me stories of how Mariko introduced him to classic films. I would love to learn more from her. My aunts are readers and hardly ever watch movies.

Stepping away from the door, I examine the light again, and it's weak. She probably left one lamp on in her bedroom while she was gone.

Anyway, I know Sakai and Lucy are out with Jiro so I won't climb up to their apartment. I take the stairs at a rush, descending quickly to our floor. I have a lot of energy tonight.

I kick off my shoes inside the apartment and pick up my tablet, tapping out a message to Usagi.

"Are you around tonight? Want to get dinner and a drink?"

He's not online so I'll have to wait for the message to hit his inbox and his response. If I'm going to go out tonight, I should think about what's clean and, if there's nothing, do a quick load of laundry in the auto-hamper. It'll only take a few minutes.

Ping! My tablet rings with a new message while I'm digging through my dirty clothes pile.

"Hi! I'm out with Helena, and we're about to go to a movie. Do you want to come? We could go to a later show."

No, I don't want to be the third wheel on their date. I'm imagining Helena looking at the message over Usagi's shoulder and her thinking, "Don't come. Don't come. Don't come." Usagi would have to come all the way back to the building to get me, and it would surely ruin their date. This is Helena's first real, long-term boyfriend. I should let them enjoy their time together.

"No worries! You two enjoy your date. Some other night. Sanaa." I smile when I look at my message. No worries. That's Jiro's phrase.

I set the tablet down and survey my empty apartment. I want to get out. Why can't I just walk out the door and explore my neighborhood tonight? Yes, that's what I'll do. Maybe I can find a little spot to sit and watch people or read. I used to do that all the time for fun. I dress in black pants and a gray top with flowers embroidered along the hems, grab my bag and sword, and walk out the apartment door.

When I reach the bottom of the stairs in the lobby, several guards snap to attention, their heads swiveling around to me and past me, up the stairs. One man steps in front of the door and places his hand in front of him, halting me.

"Good evening, Itami-sama. Where is your escort?" I've seen this man a few times, and I search my brain for his name as fast as I can.

"I'm going out for a little while, Tomo-san. I'll be back in two hours?" I try to step around him, but his hand lands on my arm. I look from him to the two men who approach me from behind. "Please release your hand from my arm, Tomo-san." I laugh lightly, trying to show I'm unfazed by their serious demeanor. He gently lets go, and I step back from him.

"Sakai-san and Jiro-san have given me strict instructions not to let you leave the building without an escort. If you require one, someone can accompany you on your trip once we have analyzed the local surveillance cameras."

"Are you serious?" I roll my eyes in annoyance and tap my foot. "This is ridiculous. I just want to go out for a little while, and no one is home to escort me. And really, I can take care of myself. I don't need anyone to accompany me."

"Akira," Tomo says, gesturing to one of the men behind me, "would be glad to escort you."

Akira nods, but his Adam's apple bobs in his throat. His brow breaks into a sweat, and his face turns a shade of pale I haven't seen in months.

"Please have a seat while we look over local surveillance. It could take as long as thirty minutes or more." Tomo's hand guides my shoulder away from the door and the other men glance at each other, tension ricocheting between them.

These men twice my size are afraid to escort me into the streets around my home. Jiro's shocked face from the house in the desert pops back into my head, and my stomach seizes up. "No, wait. I... I changed my mind." My scalp prickles with the realization I'm in much more danger than I ever believed I was. "Please don't bother. I'll stay in tonight."

Tomo's shoulders fall in relief, but he makes eye contact with me. "Are you sure, Itami-sama? We would be honored to help."

"No. No." I wave my hand at him and back away towards the stairs. "I understand the situation completely. Please don't mention this happened to anyone. Good night."

I run up the stairs two at a time, not stopping to breathe until the door to my apartment closes behind me. I can't believe I almost walked out of my own building without anyone with me. The fear shared between the security guards downstairs was so thick I could swim in it. Here, in my space, in this building at least, I'm safe. I'm safe. "I'm safe" is my mantra for today.

I kick off my shoes, dump my bag next to them, and place Kazenoho in the corner next to Oninoten. The couch welcomes my body, enfolding me in soft fabric and the smell of my loved one. I tip my face into the cushions and breathe deep, a smoky, citrus scent I've seen in the bathroom. I always thought it was his soap until we lived together, but the scent comes from some kind of oil. I miss him, but his familiar scents and items around the room calm my rapidly beating heart.

Since I can't go out, I'll spend the night right here, but doing what? I've already read a ton of fiction. Do I watch a movie? Oyama dropped off a basket of food earlier before going out to play cards. I guess I'll eat and watch an old film.

I grab my tablet to browse the NishikyōNet movie archives when I see Chad online. I haven't talked to him in a long time, and my finger hovers over the screen involuntarily. Do I dare start this up again? Jiro is a jealous guy, and I got the feeling he was happy I had left Chad behind. How would he feel about me reconnecting with Chad, even if it's just as friends?

Dammit. No one is around, and I want to talk to someone.

"Hi Chad!" I write and wait.

"Sanaa! I'm sorry I haven't been in touch. I've been an awful friend." Chad was always a nice guy, not strong or commanding the way I like my men but still good.

"It's fine. I haven't been around either. Work and life have been busy." Lies, mostly. Sigh. But if I want to keep him as my friend, I can't tell him everything.

"I didn't want to bother you. I know you've been busy since you moved to Ku 6. I have so much to tell you."

"Me too. First and foremost, I'm living with someone. Someone I really love. His name is Jiro."

Hold breath and wait. I'm going to be upfront with him about this at the very least.

"Wow, really? That makes my news easy to give. I've also met someone."

Relief washes over me, and my tense shoulders relax. This is fantastic news. Chad and I were always excellent as platonic friends, and we completely flunked at anything else.

I smile and settle back on the couch. "Tell me all about her."

Chapter Seventeen

Beni booked me a salon appointment in a posh and modern place only a few blocks from our building, and we're enjoying a girls' afternoon together. She seems a little happier after our trip to the temple, almost relieved. Maybe Beni feels like she's properly said goodbye to her parents and can start the process of moving on. I was so young when I lost my parents, I don't even remember what I did. It's probably fortunate I don't.

Everyone else is busy today. Jiro is doing something with Yoichi this afternoon and evening. What? I have no idea. Guy stuff that's done before a wedding. I told him I didn't want to know, though I suspect they'll both come stumbling home late together.

Jiro and I trained this morning, and in a weird turn of events, Kentaro sat in the dōjō and watched us the entire time. At first I was annoyed, but he didn't interrupt or make comments of any kind. He just sat and studied us. I'm not sure what he was expecting, but he might be wondering about my relationship with Jiro. Kentaro did steal his last girlfriend.

"What do you want to do with your hair, Sanaa-san?" Beni asks standing behind me with her hair freshly done.

Beni's stylist, Haruna, is next to her. "You really did this to yourself?" Haruna crosses her arms and tilts her head to look at the hair pinned over my ear.

I laugh, especially when Beni smacks her on the arm. "Yes. You should have seen my hair before this happened."

Haruna takes out the pins and brushes the last couple of long pieces out with her fingers. "Your hair was obviously long before *this* happened. Do you want to grow it out again?"

"I do. I'll be on my way to Yūsei soon, and I hear your hair still grows while you sleep. So maybe we should make it really short?"

"So it grows out even, yeah. How about a little longer on top with some bangs, and we put red streaks in it?"

"Okay. Beni, will you let Usagi know we're going to be a while, and could you get him something to drink? I feel bad for making him wait so long."

Haruna doesn't take long to cut my hair since I didn't have much to begin with. Still the amount of hair hitting the floor is alarming. I have to tell myself several times my hair will grow back. It'll grow back. "It'll grow back" is my mantra for today. I did this all to save my life. I need to be thankful for my hair and for my quick thinking. Without either of them, I wouldn't be alive.

When she's done, my hair is the shortest it's ever been, about three centimeters long everywhere, except for on top where the length is a little longer. She takes out a razor, thins out the hair that falls down on my forehead, and slips a tub of hair goop into my bag.

"And now a thick chunk of red. Right here," she says grabbing a wide swath of hair just past my bangs. "We'll have to bleach the section first, but it's fast. Should be all done in about an hour and a half."

I sit patiently through the whole process, drink cold barley tea (it's the only tea I've ever liked because technically it's not even real tea), and, two hours later, we're walking home again.

When we get back, I send Usagi away with strict instructions to go meet Jiro and Yoichi and everyone else wherever it is they are all going tonight. Beni comes home with me, we eat together, and I open up and tell Beni everything about my life.

"I always hoped Jiro would find someone compatible to be with. He had hard luck with girls before you."

Beni has Jiro gossip! Why did I never think to ask Beni about this?

"He said he proposed to a non-Japanese girl, a blonde, last year."

"Almost two years ago," Beni says with a nod. "Her name was Melanie. She cheated on Jiro with Kentaro, and it ripped them both apart. They were angry with each other for ages. Before Melanie, Jiro and Kentaro were practically inseparable. It was hard to see a girl come between them."

"Oh." I take a sip of water and frown.

"But that was definitely for the best because she panicked every time Jiro needed to carry his sword anywhere, and Mariko practically hated her. Before her, he dated a girl in school for a little bit but she was just a passing thing."

"But he had another girlfriend, right? He dated three girls before me." During our time alone at the house in the desert, Jiro and I confessed to each other about every relationship we've had. I want more details.

Beni's cheeks flush. "Yes, a girl who his parents tried to set him up with. Eriko. She was the younger sister of a friend of mine, and they met at a party. She expressed an interest in the sword fighting but didn't get further than one session with Jiro." Beni lets out a hearty laugh. It's nice to see her happy. "Jiro-kun can be very intimidating even when he doesn't mean to be."

"This is true, but I love him for it." I look away from Beni and smile to cover up a blush.

"I got the feeling Koichi and Mariko wanted to test the girl out as quickly as possible. They always talked about how Jiro would need to marry someone who could take care of the whole family someday like Mariko does..."

Beni falters and stops, and my heart flutters and dies in my chest. I'm going to have to take care of a whole country. How am I going to take care of my family, too? Oh no. This is another thing I completely forgot about, what it means to be the matriarch of this family.

I start to wring my hands in my lap, but it's not enough to keep the anxiety away. I can't do this job, and I'm not even sure if Mariko likes me. The image of her cold, hard expression at the temple fills my mind, and, for the first time in weeks, I need to get up and pace. Rising from my chair, I walk the room back and forth while Beni's face progresses from sad to slightly horrified.

"I'm so sorry, Sanaa-san. I didn't mean to imply you shouldn't be with Jiro because you can't marry."

But her implication is true. Who will run Sakai clan when Mariko and Sakai himself are ready to hand the family over to Jiro? Who will he call on? Could I take care of the family, too? Miko will be a part of the family, but I'm not sure she realizes the extent of what Sakai clan does. At least not yet. Maybe this is why Yoichi was never groomed to lead Sakai clan because he wants nothing to do with the business. He's probably happy with the financials and a wife who runs an izakaya, and they will have their little family, and that will be it.

"Beni, Beni, Beni. This is no good. I can't marry Jiro though I want to. I can't run the family. I have to do so much more, and Jiro will need someone he trusts which should be me but can't be me."

This is the exact situation that killed the relationship between Sakai and my mother. I know it. Except my mother was more committed to the imperial business than I could ever be. I'd rather be married and have the family, live in relative anonymity.

I can't stop my feet. My body wants to run, disconnect from my brain that just cannot stop thinking.

"Sanaa-san, you must calm yourself. There will always be Mariko. She would run the family if you asked her to until the day she died. This family means everything to her."

If this family means everything to her, why haven't I been welcomed with open arms? It's been weeks since I've been back, and I've barely seen her. No calls, no visits, and no invitations to eat or meet other members of the family, even though I've tried contacting her several times. Again, her cold stare at the temple pops into my brain, and I want to cry.

"Beni..." I stop my pacing and run to her, grabbing her hands. "I don't think Mariko likes me. At all. I can't ask this of her. She'll think I'm shirking my responsibilities."

"That's nonsense. Mariko loves you."

I look deep into Beni's eyes and find nothing but honesty. Am I imagining things? I'm going crazy with doubts.

"Honestly. She adores you."

"Maybe you're right." I let go of her hands and turn away. Even if she's wrong, I can't talk to Beni about this. She and Mariko are too close. "I would much rather take care of my whole family and all of Sakai clan than a whole new nation that will threaten to go to war as soon as we land. There are days when I don't want to be an empress. I really don't. In fact, there are days when I completely forget it's what I am." I throw myself onto the couch and bury my face in my hands.

"I think you'll find it's not going to be as bad as you think it'll be. The emperor was a figurehead. There were only a few times in Japanese history when he actually ruled the country. You will just have to work with Lucy and Sakai-san to coordinate things and sit politely at big events and have lots of children with Jiro. It's very apparent the two of you are capable of such a thing." She smiles wryly when our eyes meet.

"You can't...?"

"I'm sorry. You and Jiro are very loud. I'm sure people three blocks away can hear you."

My neck heats with a blush, and I put on my passive face,

thinking about dunes and deep, blue sky. This explains why some nights Jiro puts his hand over my mouth. It's a wonder no one has said anything before now, and Kentaro banging on the floor doesn't count. The blush stays down but the fact that Beni is still smiling at me makes me laugh.

The door across the hall to Miko and Yoichi's place opens and closes, and the sound cools me off. Miko must be home from having dinner with her parents, and in a few minutes, she'll come across to drink with us until the boys come home. Originally, I told Miko to go out tonight, to take Helena and have a good time with our old schoolmates and the girls who work in the businesses around Izakaya Tanaka. As I've already found out, I can't leave the building without an escort so I'm stuck here this evening again.

But Miko refused to do anything without me and insisted she's tired of going out. So she's coming over after she gets changed, and Helena will be here after her shift. It'll be nice to see them before life gets hectic tomorrow.

"Don't worry. Nothing makes me happier than seeing you and Jiro-kun happy." She picks up our dishes and loads them into the auto-washer. "And as for the family business, just go to Mariko and ask her to continue as the head. I'm sure she'll be pleased to hear how much you care."

I will. I'll do this next week. I have to make good on this issue because I have twinges of guilt each day about my relationship with Jiro and his family, and this will be how I can win Mariko over.

The door chimes, and Miko's name pops up on the read-out. I open the door, and she walks straight in past me.

"Thank the gods dinner with my parents is over because if I hear one more time how disappointed they are that I can't have children before we leave, I'm going to kill them. Hi Beni. Are you staying? I brought sake."

Miko changed into matching pink pajamas before coming over. It's a grown-up pajama party kind of night.

"I'll stay for a little bit, but I'm planning on being up early tomorrow to help Risa before the rehearsal dinner at the izakaya."

Miko and Beni hug. "Thank you, Beni. You've been a big help." She plunks the bottle on the kitchen table and sets her tablet next to mine before turning around and looking at me again. "Good gods, Sanaa, I walked straight past you and didn't even see your hair. I love it! The red is hot."

"Hot is good," I say, relieved. I was wondering what everyone would think. "Thanks. I hoped you'd like it."

"It's lovely. Your aunts RSVP'd that they'd be coming to the rehearsal dinner tomorrow but won't be at the wedding, but we already knew that, ne?"

"Yes we did." The wedding and reception will all be in Ku 6. Aunt Kimie and Lomo will not be attending.

The door chimes again, and this time it's Helena. "I brought sake." She holds up a bottle as she comes barreling into the apartment. "Sanaa-chan! Your hair! I love it short. You have the perfect face for this style. I wish I could pull off short hair like that."

Maybe I should keep my hair short. I've never received so many compliments on my hair in one day. Beni pulls cups for each of us out of the cabinet, and, just as we're about to sit down, the door chimes again. Who could this be?

Oyama fills my doorway.

"Sanaa-san, I brought some cake for you and your guests." He hands me a pastry box with *Café les pivoines* stamped on the top and bows. "Have a nice night."

"Wait." I place my hand on his chest, tug his shirt till he leans over, and kiss him on the cheek. "Arigatō."

"*Dō itashimashite,*" he says with a smile and turns to head back to his apartment. Once the door is closed, I peek inside the box and a lovely, ornate chocolate cake sits in pastry paper. Oyama is too good to me.

"Cake from Oyama." I place the box on the table.

Both Helena and Miko let out "Ooohs" and open the box.

"It's a good thing I don't have to squeeze into a western dress for my wedding in two days. I'm happy to be wearing a kimono for once."

"I'm always happy to wear kimono," says Helena. "What are you wearing, Beni?"

I smile as my friends talk amongst themselves. Today, I feel very lucky again.

Cake, sake, laughing, talking, sake, more cake, leftovers from my fridge, laughing, talking, and then Beni's had enough, and she excuses herself around midnight. This is about the time Miko, Helena, and I start searching NishikyōNet for our old classmates from Ku 5 — seeing who got married to whom, who's had kids already, who's single (not many) — until I'm so tired and riddled with sake I can't focus on my tablet anymore. I need to go to bed now or I'm in danger of passing out on the couch.

"It's 2am, and I am sleeping *right here*," Helena says as she takes my blanket and a pillow from the chair and stretches her long legs out on the couch. Well, that settles that, I'm going to have to sleep in my own bed for sure.

Miko picks up both bottles of sake from the table, peering into each, one at a time, with one eye closed. "Empty, empty. That's my cue to go home."

"Can you make the long trip across the hall on your own?" I'm barely forming complete sentences, but it's mostly from fatigue even though Jiro seems to think my alcohol tolerance is weak. Pfft. What does he know?

"Yes. I can manage it."

I see her out, and we both wave to each other before our doors simultaneously click closed. I stumble my way to the kitchen and pour a glass of water for Helena that I leave on the coffee table. Her eyes are already shut, and she's breathing deeply. That was quick. I get myself a glass of water, leave the light on in the kitchen, brush my teeth, and go straight to bed.

4:35am. The front door opens breaking into my deep, dreamless sleep. I left the bedroom door open so, when my eyes part, I see Jiro and Usagi standing with their arms crossed looking at Helena on the couch.

"Hmmm," Jiro says. "I guess you could leave her there."

"No, she's a lot lighter than she looks. I got her." Usagi leaves my line of sight but only for a moment because he appears again with Helena in his arms. Jiro opens the door for Usagi, and I roll over.

A few minutes go by, and he slips in bed next to me. All I can do is grunt, "'Llo."

"You are wearing a lot more clothes to bed than usual."

"Mmmhmm."

"And your hair is so short."

"Mmmhmm."

"Remind me to tell you of my night tomorrow."

"Mmmhmm."

10:05am. One thing's for sure about our bedroom, having no window means the room is pitch black even when the lamps are up, and Nishikyō is going about its regular business. The darkness makes it easy to sleep in and eliminate your hangover.

11:15am. Okay, now we really have to get up. I roll over and slip my arm over Jiro to rouse him. He looks at the clock and sighs, his hand settling on my head, playing with my short hair.

"At least we got about seven hours of sleep before today," he says, yawning.

"We're going to need it. You wanted me to remind you to tell me of your night."

"Huh?"

"4am. 'Remind me to tell you of my night.' Does that ring a bell?"

"Wow. You have a good memory." He sits up and drinks the water I left out last night. His hair is all messed up, and, looking at him now, he shaved off the little beard he had going. Damn, I loved that. He probably did it before he went out yesterday. Well, we do have a big event coming up tomorrow, and photos will be taken.

"I have an excellent memory even when I've been drinking, and I'm half asleep. Do I really want to know what you were up to last night?"

"Yes, we were all good, I swear. We did go to the casino and play poker all night, though."

"Did you win or lose?"

"I broke even, but that's not what I want to tell you about. I made sure we went to Maeda's main casino."

This is interesting. "And?"

"Word has already spread from Minamoto that you and I are... linked, and Maeda asked about you."

Everyone is beginning to hear Jiro is my consort which makes me smile. I wonder sometimes how he feels about that term.

"Really? He's never once spoken to Mark about me."

"Probably because Mark doesn't go out and gamble. But anyway, we had a discussion. He was polite enough to steer clear of any truly personal questions but pumped me for information he knew I would give willingly, and I did."

"How... Wait, did you do this on purpose?"

He smiles at me. "The time I was in the Ku 1 theater was not just spent looking at Miura and all the Taira men. I watched Maeda for a bit too because I knew you would have to deal with him eventually. I memorized his schedule and knew he would be at his main casino, Akaboshi, last night. I think if you came and visited him at the casino, it would make an impression."

I never once suspected Jiro would be out trying to gain me a tactical advantage while I was eating cake and drinking sake with my best friends. Of course, I'm sure he was having a great time — they did stay out past 4am — but still.

"What did you tell Maeda?"

"That you're smart. That you're coming into this position only to keep the peace. That keeping the peace means business can continue as normal on Yūsei. And most definitely, that you understand his businesses are important."

"Ah. I knew I was missing something." Maeda is a business man. Casinos, restaurants, and love hotels are his passion. His whole life revolves around them, keeping each running and making money. Business is his number one priority. I wonder if I can assure him somehow he could be the first on the ground to run these same establishments on Yūsei. "I'm going to have to talk to Mark and Lucy about this." I close my eyes and smile.

"I thought this would make you happy."

"It does."

"I know it's crazy for me to do something like that but..."

"I love crazy and unpredictable."

"Right." He leans over and kisses me on my cheek. "I'm going to go next door and ask Oyama to make us hot pot udon even though the temp is going to be in the mid-thirties again today. Soup will be good for our hangovers. I'll be back in a few minutes with water."

He gets up, and I roll over onto his side of the bed, the light from the living room spilling across my head.

"Sanaa, is your hair red?"

"It is. Just right there."

He laughs. "Yesterday I was crazy, and you were, apparently, unpredictable."

"Made for each other," I say, pulling up the covers and falling back to sleep until lunch time.

Chapter Eighteen

Miko is a little green. I honestly thought she was going to go into this wedding with no qualms or cold feet, but no, it's not looking that way at all.

I had every reason to suspect she was fine. She was a brilliant hostess at the rehearsal dinner last night. She laughed and talked to everyone, and she held Yoichi's hand whenever he was next to her. Jiro and I did our best to concentrate only on them throughout the entire evening. If this were more of a western wedding, Jiro would be Yoichi's best man, and Helena and I would be Miko's bridesmaids, so both brothers spent time entertaining family members. We girls handled the rest of the guests.

I sat with Aunt Kimie and Lomo and caught up with them. I've missed them terribly and chatting online is not enough. Helena, Risa, Beni, and I helped make sure everything went smoothly with dinner and dessert afterwards. Risa did her best to only interact with Beni or Helena, and she avoided eye contact with me the entire time. She is exceptionally good at the cold shoulder.

At the end of the evening, when we dropped their gifts off in their apartment, Miko was in happy spirits, and I had no worries about her.

Now, she looks like she's going to puke.

"Miko-chan, are you okay? Do you want me to get you a glass of water or something?"

"No, I... maybe I just need to put my head between my knees."

I let Miko bend over but push the wedding kimono out of the way so she doesn't get any of her makeup on the white silk. It's a good thing she's not wearing the heavy black wig yet. That would have fallen on the floor.

She is already dressed in the *shiromuku* she borrowed for today, a silk satin, white kimono with the most gorgeous cranes and bamboo stalks woven into the fabric. The whole garment is exceptionally heavy, though, so I hope she doesn't pass out once we're outside. The temperature has already hit 35°C under the domes today. Cool breezes will be blowing up the sidewalk grates as Nishikyō recycles air past the man-made caves over a kilometer deep into the ground. Hopefully in the late afternoon, the temp will get back down into the low thirties again.

But Miko is already sweating in the cool comfort of Mariko's apartment. Mrs. Tanaka, Miko's mother, is fussing over the lighter silk kimono Miko will change into directly after the ceremony, and Mariko is doling out cold barley tea to Risa and Beni who are here to help. Helena is on her way. She had to go back to Ku 5 to pick up a gift from her parents who are also not attending the wedding today.

Crouching down next to Miko, I squeeze her knee. "What's the matter?"

"I just don't want anything to go wrong."

"Nothing's going to go wrong. You're having a nice little ceremony with your family and closest friends and then off to the banquet hall to smile and be pretty. It's going to be fine." I rub her back, up and down, up and down. "You're not worried about marrying Yoichi, are you?"

"No! No. Gods, I love him. I really do. I can't believe I needed an omiai to find him, but I'm so thankful I did."

"Good. Then don't worry. It will be easy, I promise. We'll walk to the temple. Everyone on the streets this morning will step aside and gape at how gorgeous you are —"

"Sanaa-chan," she says, grabbing my hand, "do you remember the time we were on our way to class and saw the wedding party walking to the temple... when we were, what? Ten?"

"I do," I say, squeezing her hand and smiling at her. "I remember you saying how much you loved the white kimono and the hood and how dainty the bride's steps were."

"That's going to be me in a little bit." Miko's eyes are focused far off, her voice hushed in awe. She's finally coming around.

"The day will be over before you know it. We'll get to the temple and meet up with everyone. You'll be purified, drink the sake, bless the rings, kiss, and done. Photos, then party. Nothing to worry about, right?"

"Yes. Yes, it'll be easy. You're right, Sanaa-chan. Nothing will go wrong."

"Nothing. I swear it."

I smile at her, smile at my gorgeous friend I've grown up with since I was small. She's getting married today, and I'm so happy for her.

Mariko and Mrs. Tanaka come over to fix Miko's makeup. She's paler than usual, but, thankfully, it suits her. As they're putting the black wig on her, a man who Miko hired to take photos interrupts to get a few shots.

Stepping out of the way, I smooth out the *furisode* I rented for today. It's a traditional kimono with long sleeves that unmarried women wear for this kind of ceremony. The heavy silk material is bright blue with a falling water motif that starts on the upper left shoulder and cascades down to the hem. Stitches in silver and gold thread — I was enamored with it the moment I saw it. Helena and the rest of the unmarried women will be wearing furisode today as well.

Each of the married women in the wedding party are wearing *tomesode,* black kimono with shorter sleeves, and each has a different embroidered design along the bottom hem. Mrs. Tanaka's has peacock feathers in silver, copper, and gold thread, and Mariko's has grass and flowers. They all have matching gold and silver obi with fans tucked into each on the left side.

The door chimes and Lucy enters the apartment in a dark green sleeveless dress with her red hair twisted up. Her bodyguards wait outside, and one of Sakai's men waits next to them. He'll carry all of our secondary kimonos and yukata that we'll change into once we're at the party. I say hi to Lucy as I struggle to hand off all the garment bags to the man who is waiting, and as he's walking off with them, Helena comes bounding up the stairs.

"I'm here! Damn parents have no sense of urgency, I swear."

"Good timing because we were just getting ready to walk out." I lean in and hug her.

We wait at the door, the sea of people inside part, and Miko stands before us in her glorious white kimono, wearing the traditional black wig, and the large, white circular hood. She is smiling and happy, not a hint of the green that was there fifteen minutes ago.

Helena and I catch our breath and sigh. I wonder if Helena still sees the sweet little seven-year-old Miko I see when I close my eyes. The one who ran after the boys once school was out. The one who ate chocolate candies two at a time every Christmas. The one who held our hands and dragged us to the movies on the weekend. This Miko, the one about to get married, is another one I'll remember forever.

People stop in the street and smile, or nod and say "Omedetō" and "Congratulations" as we walk past. I don't know if Miko has been at home practicing her little steps in those sandals for weeks but it looks like she was born to do it. She's holding up her kimono with her right hand so the hem doesn't drag on the ground, and her mother is holding her other hand. They smile at each other, and Mrs. Tanaka is so proud.

I try not to roll my eyes. As sweet as this is, I can't help but remember the years of her nagging poor Miko to find a nice boy. Well, Mrs. Tanaka got her wish, because Yoichi is as nice as they come.

We round the corner with the temple in front of us by two blocks, and all the men in their black kimono and gray-striped hakama pants are waiting with the rest of the wedding party. The closer we get to Yoichi, the wider his smile becomes. A man stands next to them with the red umbrella I always associate with weddings. Though we have no need to shield the bride and groom from rain, the red umbrella is still significant to the ceremony. When standing in the streets anywhere in Nishikyō, if you see the red umbrella coming and a double line of people following, a bride will certainly be underneath it.

The priest stands at the front of the line and two temple maidens follow him in their temple garb, a white kimono and red, wide hakama pants. Yoichi stands next to Miko, her mother on the other side still holding her hand, and the man with the umbrella stands behind them. Sakai stands with Mariko, and Mr. Tanaka, Miko's dad, stands on the other side. Jiro slides in next to me and holds my hand. I'm so nervous for Miko I could vomit, but his strong hand steadies me.

We're all led into the courtyard to the thrumming of traditional drums and stringed instruments. Just a few days ago, we stood here after mourning Koichi. Now, a table has been set up covered in white cloth and cups sit upon it with a pot of rice wine next to them. Miko and Yoichi stand behind the table, and we all stand in front.

The ceremony is quiet once the music ceases. The priest blesses Miko and Yoichi while waving a big, fluffy white thing over them. It takes a lot of self-control not to laugh. One of the temple maidens lays out three cups of different sizes: small, medium, and large. I'm familiar with this ritual called *san-san-kudo*, three-three-nine times. The tradition is the bride and groom each take three sips from each of the three cups, going from smaller to larger cup, until each has consumed nine sips of rice wine. Nine is a lucky number for couples because it cannot be divided equally in two, and the number three is also lucky because it's prime. So three, three times, is three times as lucky.

Miko is handed the smallest cup and takes three small sips. She gives it to Yoichi and he takes three sips. They repeat this with each cup, and then Sakai, Mariko, and Mr. and Mrs. Tanaka each step forward and share in the last of the largest cups. Their families are now linked.

I squeeze Jiro's hand and smile up at him. He gazes down at me, sadness watering his eye with tears. Is he thinking of his father? Or that this could never be us? My smile dies. Before I get choked up, I turn my eyes to my feet, and Jiro squeezes my hand even harder. I won't make it through this day without crying.

The priest motions to Jiro, and he lets go of my hand to step forward with the two rings, Miko's ring that she's been wearing since they were engaged and another plain one for Yoichi that was handed down through the family, too. It's nice that the Nishikyō government never made people give up their wedding bands to be melted down for the precious metal we need nowadays. Some things are still sacred.

After a blessing is said over the rings, Yoichi places Miko's on her left ring finger, and she does the same for him. They step back from the table and bow, and we all bow back.

Then they kiss.

Ah. It's done. Relief washes over Miko's face. See? I told her it would go well.

Now, photos, and then it's time to party.

Chapter Nineteen

I've never had so many photos taken of me in my life. I'm tempted to swear off of them for good like my mother did, but, damn, I'm going to be a highly visible public figure in a matter of years, and I will be unable to avoid the cameras. I should try and get used to them.

After the photo session, we walk behind the bride and groom to a banquet hall four blocks from the Sakai building but in the opposite direction of the Itō dōjō. This is another area I have never been to. Guests arrive in a long stream of chatter and happy faces, but we're only expecting about eighty people. Just like Miko wanted, not too big.

In a plush and well-appointed back room, Helena and I help Miko get out of the heavy white kimono. She was picture perfect the whole ceremony but her robes underneath are soaked. It's sweltering outside. I did my best to ignore the heat, but we all breathed a huge sigh of relief when we got indoors.

"I think I'd like that water now," Miko says to me, sitting in front of a fan set to high.

"My gods, Miko, I think you lost at least five kilos in sweat alone wearing that thing."

"It's a crash diet I don't recommend."

I find a pitcher of water and glasses on an end table next to the couch and pour her a tall glass she gulps down.

"Better?"

"Yes," she says, her hand reaching out and grabbing mine. "Thank you. You were right. It did go well."

I lean over and kiss her on the cheek. "I swore everything would be fine, and I always keep my word."

Beni helps me get dressed as quickly as possible in my new white yukata with the large purple flowers and dark blue obi. She pulls the collar up as high as it will go, measuring out the back by four fingers-widths, but still adjusting the height so no one can see my tattoos. Thanks, Beni.

Everyone files out of the room, leaving Miko and her mother

alone so they can spend some time together before more photos are taken. Beni and I step out the door last, and Jiro is waiting for me in the hallway with a smile.

"You look gorgeous," he says, leaning in and kissing me on the cheek. "This is the new one, right? I haven't seen it in the closet."

"Yes, it is." I smooth out the front, minutely adjusting the obi so it forms a perfect line across my mid-section. I love that we share a space for our clothes. In time, this one will smell like our whole wardrobe does now: sweet and clean. Like Jiro.

"Well, well. I'm finally getting to meet Sanaa Griffin."

From behind Jiro, a woman steps towards us with Risa at her elbow. I've only seen her in the photos in Risa's apartment, but this is undoubtedly her mother. The two look so alike it would be hard to think them not related. They both share the same small nose, the heart-shaped mouth, and thin eyebrows. If Nobu Yamamoto had less gray hair, they could be sisters.

"Sanaa Itami, actually. And you're Nobu Yamamoto."

I'd wait for her to bow, but I know she won't.

"I am." She looks from me to Jiro and back. "So you must be the one that has usurped my family."

Nobu is going straight in for the kill. No beating around the bush, no small talk.

"I haven't usurped anyone, actually," I say, clasping my hands in front of me and plastering on a smile so fake and sweet it actually makes my teeth ache from the effort. "Mark Sakai has always run this family."

We stand and quietly assess each other. Who will attack next? Risa is propped up by her mother. Only moments ago, she was helping Miko get into her kimono, and now I barely recognize her. Her smile is long gone, and she's frosty and mean.

"Before you came along, I believe Risa had a claim on Jiro."

"Nobu..." Jiro says in a warning voice.

Risa felt like she owned Jiro just because she wanted him? I never realized what a spoiled brat she was.

"Ah, I know, Jiro-kun. You like this one." Nobu purses her mouth in a sour expression. "Risa has expressed her regret over it."

"Risa never had a chance." Jiro is cold and still, his passive expression leaving no other emotion than hatred.

"But Jiro..." Risa shocks me by stepping forward and trying to actually touch Jiro's face, like a lover leaning in for a kiss. He jerks back, her fingers grazing empty air while I stand with my mouth gaping open.

"Don't touch me," Jiro says, taking one step closer to me.

"You used to let me touch you, Jiro."

Beni gasps next to me and grabs my arm. Good thing too because I have the undeniable urge to kill Risa right now. And if looks could kill they'd both be dead under Jiro's stare.

"Risa, Nobu," I say, trying to keep my voice like steel and not let it waver, "you are not to get within two meters of me ever again." Usagi is making his way towards us now. "Usagi, please see the Yamamotos to their table."

"You will not boss me around, Itami." Nobu looks over her shoulder at me. "I've been a part of this family longer than you."

I turn my back on her before I say something completely stupid, but not before seeing Risa raise her eyebrows at Jiro.

"Is she serious?" I ask Jiro. "About having a claim on you?"

"Only in their delusional world. Neither Mark nor my parents would ever think of betrothing me especially not to Risa. This is not the middle ages. Besides, you know they hoped you and I would be together." He puts his arm around me. "The only thing they tried to do was set me up a few times."

I smile at him. "I remember. Wusses. All of them."

He laughs and kisses me on my temple.

"I'm glad your reflexes are fast. If she had touched you, I would have had to break her arm or ask for Kazenoho and cut her down." I haven't drawn my sword in a while.

"Ah, no blood shed today, thankfully. Though I appreciate the sentiment."

"Let's go, Beni." I grab her hand and pull her along even though she's pale, her eyes trained on Risa through the door and across the dining room. I think that's a side of Risa no one has ever seen.

In the dining hall, I sit at a large table with Jiro, Mariko, Sakai,

Lucy, Helena, Usagi, and Beni. I can't let Risa's actions ruin the day, so I take a deep breath and put her out of my mind. The hall is noisy with the clamor of voices and music, everyone talking to their closest neighbor.

Jiro leans over to my ear. "How was Miko today?"

"You mean before we left? Positively green," I say with a chuckle. "But she was worried something would go wrong during the ceremony. What about Yoichi?"

"I made him drink so he would stop talking. When Yoichi is nervous, he can talk up a storm. Got that from our father." He smiles sadly, and I reach over and hold his hand. "I miss him, Sanaa." Jiro closes his eyes and rests his forehead against mine. I silently say my mantra for today — don't cry, don't cry, don't cry — before he pulls away and squeezes my hand with a deep breath. "So I'm afraid he might have been a little drunk during the ceremony, but no matter. It's not like he messed up or anything."

Across the table, Lucy and Sakai are chatting and laughing, and Sakai is pouring sake for Lucy.

"I suppose those two will be married in about a month, too, right?"

Jiro strokes his thumb along my hand. "Mark wants me to go with him and Lucy to Ku 1 late next week to be the witness on their marriage license." He smiles, his shoulders squaring.

"That's great. When's the party?"

"My mother is working on it for mid-July. Today is the twelfth of June, and they want the party to be a month after the license is signed. Lucy needs time to pack and move to Ku 6 even though she's coming with us to Yūsei."

"Well, then, everyone seems to be on their way to getting married before we leave." I lean forward and grab two cups for us with my free hand and pour the sake. I'm happy for my friends and family, I really am, but it's hard not to be selfish.

"Thanks," Jiro says as he lifts his cup. "To the happy couple."

A smile flits across my face before we both say, "Kanpai," click our cups and drink.

Change the subject.

"After today, I'm going to need a sake detox. Nothing but good food, lots of water, and exercise for two weeks at least."

He nods and smiles. "Sounds like an excellent idea. I'll have

Oyama take sake off the shopping list for a while."

The waitstaff door opposite us opens and Oyama comes into the dining room and heads straight for us. His job never ends. As long as I'm alive and eating, he is always watching what goes in my mouth.

That sounded really dirty in my head. I place my hand over my lips to stop a tired and light-headed giggle from erupting.

Oyama carries with him a plate of appetizers he slides onto the table in front of me. Thank the gods, I'm starving.

"Sanaa-san, I have supervised your dinner for the evening. Please do not accept a plate from anyone else but me."

"Okay, Oyama. I'll wait for you. Thank you."

He reaches forward and quickly tips back the three sake bottles on the table which are all marked with a red stamp on the bottom. He nods his head and seats himself at the table next to us.

I raise my eyebrows at Jiro, and he grabs the bottle and tips it again. The red *hanko* signature stamp is the kanji for yama, mountain.

"Did you never notice the bottles we all get at home and at the izakaya are stamped with this? He carries the stamp with him everywhere. He either tastes the sake first and stamps it, or he picks out bottles from the distributor. He has a whole system."

Shaking my head, I watch Oyama drinking sake at the table next to us. He had years to work on this system before I even arrived. And this reminds me...

"Excuse me, Jiro. Be right back."

Lucy has left the table, and Sakai is sitting alone, so I sit myself in Lucy's chair with my cup in my hand.

"Hello, Sanaa-chan, more sake?" he asks with a smile on his face.

"Yes, please." He fills up my cup, and I take a sip. "Mark, Jiro told me that, a long time ago, Oyama, before he became a full-time dokumiyaku, had a girlfriend who died."

Sakai nods his head. "He did, indeed. A sweet, little girl. Long hair, bright smile. Very confident and outgoing."

"Jiro also said Oyama slipped into a deep depression after she died, and that one day you went to him, and afterward, Oyama just up and turned it around."

Sakai face melts into passivity, and my smile broadens. He should know by now that will never work with me again.

"What do you want to know?"

"What did you tell Oyama that day?"

He sighs, looking away from me. "I told him there was this pretty, smart, and lovable girl who needed his help. That she was strong and capable of ruling a whole world but people would always try to do her harm. That he could use his skills to help watch after her, and, if he took on the challenge, he would never regret it. You're never going to make him regret it, are you?"

Looking him in the eye, I shake my head. Sakai is incapable of lying to me now. This is the whole truth. He really told this to Oyama, and not just a few months ago, more like several years ago. Sakai has been watching out for me for so long, I wonder how many years of my life were not taken care of. I'm guessing none of them. He has been behind the curtain for a very long time.

"Thank you, Mark. I'm glad to know you find me lovable."

"Don't rub it in, Sanaa-chan."

Standing up, I grab my cup from the table and put my other hand on his shoulder, squeezing quickly before letting go. He likes to think he's this hard, demanding, all scare-tactics kind of guy, but Sakai is a softie and has gotten even more so since he proposed to Lucy. Six months ago, he would have avoided that question about Oyama like the plague because his answer reveals too much about how he feels about me. Now he doesn't care if I know. Another reason I love him so much.

Jiro stands and fills my cup when I return to him.

"Quick, drink. And then let me introduce you around before the bride and groom make their entrance."

Jiro's closest cousins, actual first cousins, Mayumi and Makoto, are the first people I meet. Mariko has a brother, Matsuo, who is two years older than she is, and he was married around the same age as Mariko and Koichi were. Makoto is the same age as Yoichi, Mayumi the same age as Jiro. They don't live in Ku 6 which is why I never met them before.

"Makoto lives in Ku 9, actually," Jiro says, "and that's how he met his fiancée, Jenniko." Jiro gestures to the young woman standing next to Makoto. She's Caucasian, tall with curly brown hair, and a super sweet smile.

"Jennifer, actually, but, yeah, everyone calls me Jenniko. Nice to meet you."

"I used to live in Ku 9! About five blocks from the Colonization Committee building." Every now and then, I miss my old home and the freedom I had.

"Ah, we live on the other side of the ward. Makoto and I both specialize in the bot machinery."

"What fun! I love the bots. I was in engineering before I... well, before now, that is." I smile and bow a little. There I go, covering up my insecurities with a bow. Jiro thought I wasn't very Japanese in the beginning? He has no idea how deep it runs.

I'm then introduced to Mayumi, her husband Henry who's a doctor in Ku 2, and several other cousins around the table. It's a lot of family. A lot more than I have.

We make more of the rounds and everyone is either married or engaged, or in the same generation with Sakai and Mariko. Same goes for Miko's family across the room. I think Jiro and me, Helena, Usagi, Beni, Risa, and Oyama may be the only single people in the room.

"I'm not going to introduce you to Risa's father for obvious reasons," Jiro says, and I nod at him.

"Everyone you've introduced me to is either married or engaged. Some already have kids."

Never before this moment have I ever felt the crushing desire to marry and have children, to have a real wedding, to expand my tiny family and be joined with another. Ugh, I'm so selfish. Why can't I just be happy with what I have?

Jiro looks at me and despite the festive atmosphere, the people around us talking and laughing, I'm not smiling. I just can't smile when I'm trying to keep the thoughts away, the thoughts about my own future and what's in store for me on Yūsei.

He pulls me in, and I close my eyes and wrap my arms around him, resting my head on his chest. We don't say anything, but this is exactly what I need. I need to know Jiro's fine with all the terms and conditions that come with me. A bright flash illuminates everything around us, and I know our hug has been captured by the photographer. I hope I don't look ridiculous.

"Come on, Sanaa. Miko and Yoichi are at the door."

Sure enough, they come into the dining hall propped up by the thundering of our applause. Mr. and Mrs. Itō. Miko Itō. She told me she was thinking of keeping Tanaka because of the izakaya, but ultimately, she likes the idea of changing her own name and leaving the business name as-is. Maybe I should legally change my name to Sanaa Itami. Maybe a change would make me feel more in control.

Gods, some days I think my brain is broken. I can't stop thinking about this mess I'm in. If I choose to stay with Jiro, I'm robbing him of his ability to marry, too, and that's important for the leader of a big family. Beni tried to convince me everything would be fine. But I'm watching Miko and Yoichi walk to each table and talk to their guests as the waitstaff serves dinner, and I'm not sure.

I'm really not sure.

My leg bounces under the table, and my knee knocks up against Jiro's. His hand comes down on my leg, and I try to tuck my hair behind my ears like I used to do when I was nervous and can't. I have very little hair left on my head.

I search the room from my chair for support or distraction. Lucy and Sakai are laughing and drinking together, and they both seem so happy. Helena is at the next table over being introduced to Usagi's parents. Oyama is standing next to them, smiling and nodding his head. My knee bounces even more.

Jiro turns to me with sadness in his eyes again, like he did during the ceremony, and my stomach sinks. He's regretting this, isn't he? Regretting us because we can't have what everyone else has. Looking around at the table full of people I love, they all have the freedom to choose and be with whomever they want. I want to be with Jiro. I am with Jiro but suddenly it feels so temporary, like our relationship can't last.

I can't sit here anymore.

Chapter Twenty

I push away from the table, set my napkin on my chair, and mumble, "I'll be right back," to no one in general.

Without knowing where to go, I weave through the tables in the hall, not talking to or smiling at anyone. I just see the exit to the dining room and head straight for the door.

Out in the lobby, I weigh my options. I can't go outside because I need a bodyguard, and I'm not that stupid to try to walk out of here alone. Instead, I walk around to the side hallway. A coat check room stands dark and empty, and the bathrooms are on the other side of the building. The hall is quiet but not calming me.

"Why can't I just be calm?" My feet start to move. There is no standing still when I'm this conflicted.

I'm angry with my mother. She got this situation all wrong. I don't know how many times I watched that video, but I keep thinking about the part where she tells me I can end the imperial line by not having children. No. That's not acceptable. I want to have children, *and* I want to end the line, and I can do that by marrying. Why did she not think to tell me that? Why? Because she never thought of marrying. She never wanted to marry my father and didn't think I would want to marry either.

Obviously I could go through life and never marry, still have kids, and be happy, but what about Jiro? Is this fair to him?

Beni rounds the corner and breaks my stride, halting me with strong hands on my shoulders. She must have sensed something was up when I bolted from the table.

"What's wrong, Sanaa-san? You've been unhappy for the last hour."

"This is completely unfair to Jiro," I say, throwing my arms up and slamming them back into my sides. "He needs someone to take the name, take care of the family."

"I told you. Jiro doesn't care. He wants a good match."

"Beni, I can already tell he hates being a consort."

I know we love each other, but I'm not sure love is enough. We both have obligations. My feet are aching in these shoes, but I pull away from Beni and start pacing again, measuring my breathing, keeping my raging, smoking dragon locked away.

"Sanaa-san, you have to trust me on this. I've known Jiro my whole life. He may seem like this enigmatic, stoic, controlling guy, but really, he's a romantic." Beni laughs, and I stop. "Hard on the outside and soft on the inside. I'm sure you've seen this and not even realized it, but he's only this way with you. I never even saw him come close to this with any other girl in the past."

"I don't understand." I assumed the way he treats me is the way he treated all of his ex-girlfriends.

"He is so Mariko's child," Beni continues when she has my attention. "Everyone thinks he's just like Koichi when, really, he's a romantic just like his mother. You should see the way he talks about you to other people. You'd never pace again." She nods her head, her word on this final.

"Really?" Huh. I never think of Jiro talking about me to anyone. I feel like we spend all of our time together, but then again, we don't. We're apart most afternoons and most evenings too, and I have no idea what he does. "What does he say about me?"

My eyes must light up like paper lanterns because Beni laughs.

"I'm not telling." Her arms fold across her chest, and she shakes her head with a wicked smile.

"Beni, you're fired." I smack her away with both my hands on her chest, and she laughs again. I'm kidding, of course.

Back and forth. Back and forth. My feet pick up the rhythm again, but this time I'm faster. I want to be running and jumping and fighting this aggression out, not stuck in a yukata at a wedding. I hop and take off one shoe, throwing the hard flip-flop at the wall. Smack! That felt good. The other one is next. I kick it towards the empty coat room.

"I hate this situation. So much is expected of me. Watching Miko get married and have the life she's always dreamed of makes me want it too. Stupid bloodline. What am I going to do with my life?"

"Sanaa, stop driving yourself crazy with all of this and come back to the table." Jiro has put himself directly into my path, and I slam straight into him and push him away.

"Leave me alone. Can't you see I'm dumping all of my frustrations on Beni?"

"That's not fair to Beni." He shakes his head with a mock frown, trying to make me laugh. "You're going to spiral out of control if you keep this up." He steps closer to me, and Beni backs up next to Usagi. Jiro and Usagi must have come out looking for me together.

I stop my pacing, my anger bubbling over the lid I've put on it, anger at my circumstances, anger at Jiro, anger at the world! A blush heats up my neck, and I turn my fiery temper on Jiro.

"You don't want to be a consort. You can barely say the term out loud!" I punctuate with a foot stomp, my hands balled at my sides. I wonder if Maeda called him a consort to his face. Jiro specifically used the term "linked" like he couldn't label himself that. "You don't come right on out and tell people we're together because..."

It hits me.

"You're ashamed of me, ashamed my station is so much higher than yours." Groaning, I deflate into a lump. "I'd give it up if I could. I don't want this obligation."

He shakes his head at me and takes a step closer now that I'm not pacing anymore.

"I know that. Look, I'm not ashamed of you. Not in the least bit. I'm proud I've snatched up a pretty and influential girl. I want to show you off and tell everyone we're to be married."

"But we can't!"

Jiro waves his hand and shakes his head. "Fuck that. Semantics."

"But you've been so sad..."

"Because I want to give you everything, everything you deserve because all this shit has been dumped on you. You denied it in the beginning, but you want to be married. You look at Miko and want that for yourself, and it kills me I can't give you what you want."

"But..." My blush is dying down along with my anger, and Jiro and I stand quietly while Beni and Usagi watch us.

"Your temper is so damned sexy," Jiro whispers, stepping even closer so no one else can hear him, "and I talk you out of it too easily for my tastes. Should I go get something you can destroy? Another chair?"

I cover up the sloppy giggle that bursts from my mouth with my hand and turn from all the watching eyes.

"I think that's why we fell in love in the dōjō. You know what I adore about you?"

"No, what?" I shake my head. I love when he tells me what he thinks of me.

"You often forget about all this imperial stuff. You think you're just a plain and ordinary girl who wants the same things other girls want. You've never once let this go to your head. But you keep pushing reality away, and it keeps coming back. The continued injustice of it all drives you nuts."

I'm just an ordinary girl who has this extraordinary burden, and I want so much for it to go away most days.

"Jiro, it's so unfair, and I don't want to burden you too."

"You could never be a burden. I don't tell people we're together right away because you're a private person, that's all." He steps so close to me I can feel his heart racing in his chest, takes my face in his strong hands, and looks me straight in the eye. "This is something you want too? To be with me and have other people know?"

I nod my head eagerly in his grip. Yes, please. I'm just as proud I've caught him, and I want to take out a marker and write, "PROPERTY OF SANAA," all over him.

"Good. We'll show everyone you can have it all: the husband, the family, and the throne. Throw the rules in their faces."

Rules? I hate rules. Rules are for people who toe the line. Certainly not for me.

"No one tells me what I can or cannot do," I respond with a smile, and he leans forward and kisses me. It's not one of those small kisses we sometimes exchange in public. This is one of our deep, slow kisses, the kind of kiss that reaches down to my toes and pulls my soul up into his. I'm tingling with relief and excitement and trying to ignore Beni and Usagi who are watching us. Jiro and I are in love. I love him, and he loves me. He's not ashamed of me, he's proud.

I want to make this kiss last a lifetime, enjoy our moment of romance, but he pulls away, groaning lightly.

"That's my girl," he says, his forehead pressed against mine. "Don't worry about the family. Sakai clan will go on forever whether I marry legally or not. I have no regrets, so stop all of this nonsense."

I take a deep breath and blow it out. Blow out my anxiety and anger. "Okay."

His smile returns, devilish and wild. Uh oh, what is he thinking? "I'm going to surprise you soon. Do you think you can be patient and wait?"

I want to hit him. Jiro's such a tease! Why tell me he's going to surprise me? Because he knows it will drive me crazy with anticipation.

"A surprise? How long?"

"Hmmm," he says, his eyes turned to the ceiling. "About a month."

"A month? I can do a month." A month? A month is an eternity! How will I ever wait that long?

Someone clears his throat, and when Jiro and I part, Sakai is standing next to Usagi, his arms crossed, and his face passive. How much did he hear? Whatever it is, he's not giving anything away.

"Jiro, Sanaa, you're missed at the table. We have food to eat, sake to drink, and cake to take home."

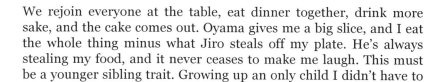

We rejoin everyone at the table, eat dinner together, drink more sake, and the cake comes out. Oyama gives me a big slice, and I eat the whole thing minus what Jiro steals off my plate. He's always stealing my food, and it never ceases to make me laugh. This must be a younger sibling trait. Growing up an only child I didn't have to share my food. I wonder what it's like to have lots of siblings, more than two kids. I'd love to have three or four kids.

After another hour of talking and laughing, the festivities are winding down. Miko wanted a dinner and dessert. No dancing. She has definite opinions on what's fun at a wedding.

"I'm going to get us cake for at home," Jiro says, rising from the table. "We can spend the evening just the two of us, okay?"

I nod and smile at him. That's definitely what I want tonight.

"Jiro, grab an extra slice for Kentaro. I thought I'd drop it off to him since he wasn't invited."

"You're a lot nicer to him now than you were last week. What's changed?"

"He didn't try to kill me. That's enough."

Back on our floor in Sakai building, I send everyone on without me and climb one more flight to Kentaro's apartment. As I'm walking down the hall, I notice his door is open and a young man stands and talks quietly with Kentaro inside. I walk a little slower because I may be interrupting something when the young man leans forward and kisses Kentaro.

I freeze, my eyes widening. I was right! When I said for Kentaro to find a girlfriend or a boyfriend, I was acting on instinct. Jiro said he likes blonde girls, but I got the feeling Kentaro likes boys. Maybe he likes both. I don't really care, but something about this situation makes me smile and want to laugh.

The young man turns and walks away from Kentaro. He's handsome, tall, pale, curly brown hair, and blue eyes. I smile at him and nod as he walks past, watching him descend the stairs.

When I turn around, Kentaro is frozen in fear at the door, but I smile and walk to him.

"I brought you cake from the wedding. I thought you might like some." He stares at me hard for a minute before reaching out to take the box I'm offering him. "So, I'm curious, Ken-chan. Why did you come watch me and Jiro fight the other day?"

He looks from the end of the hall to me and back. "I've never seen Jiro so devoted to anything in my life. I had to know why." He shrugs his shoulders and stares at the cakebox before leaning inside and gently setting the box on a table inside the door.

"Um, about that…" Kentaro jerks his thumb at the stairs.

"You don't have to explain yourself to me. I said to get yourself a girlfriend *or* a boyfriend, and I meant it."

"I thought you were just kidding."

"Well, I *was* joking around, but I don't care who you date. Whatever makes you happy."

"Really? I thought…"

"I wouldn't approve? Please. I was raised by my lesbian aunts." He raises his eyebrows. "Yes! You didn't know this? My parents died a long time ago, and my aunts raised me. They're very happy. Been married over twenty years now. So if you want to date girls and guys, I don't care."

"Huh."

"Let me guess, your father wouldn't approve?"

"Definitely not. He wants me to get married and have children.

It's why I never invited Kevin over when anyone was around. You were all at the wedding so..."

"Yeah, this all sounds familiar. I'm not going to tell you how to deal with your father on this issue, but as long as you live here with me, you can date whomever you want, whenever you want. I know things are old-fashioned amongst the clans, but I have never once cared who others loved as long as they are loved in return. Are you and Kevin... exclusive?"

He nods. "Mostly. We have an on-again, off-again thing. Since I broke things off... with Jiro's ex." He sighs, rubbing his hand through his short spiky hair before shoving his hands in his pockets.

"I think you and Jiro should patch things up."

"Jiro's still really angry —"

"Honestly," I say, placing my hand on his chest. "I don't think he is. I'll take care of it. Next time we go out, you should invite Kevin along." I punch Kentaro lightly on the shoulder. "He's handsome. Nice, blue eyes."

He lets out a laugh and wags his finger at me. "Back off, Sanaa-san. He's mine."

I throw my hands up. "I'm already spoken for. Good night!"

I can't wait to get downstairs and tell Jiro.

Chapter Twenty-One

"Reach a little more to your right, Sanaa. Just two more centimeters, and you'll have a handhold."

Tonight, Jiro is my eyes below. Yesterday, Usagi helped while Sakai stood and watched. Two days previous, I actually let Kentaro hold my line and guide me. I must trust him now. Even Mariko has been out here to witness me climb though she couldn't take more than a few minutes before she claimed I was going to give her a heart attack.

Reaching out with my right hand, my fingertips graze the brick sticking out from the building. That must mean there's another brick below by about a meter. Never mind the fact I'm four stories above the ground, and my only other handhold is the window to my left.

I'm not afraid of heights. Don't look down. If I can climb over one more section, I can make it to the fire escape and then I'm half way to my first sake in over two weeks.

True to our word, after the wedding, Jiro and I went on a sake detox diet. We have been eating three healthy meals per day and not drinking. I've been training at the dōjō with Kentaro every day and Jiro joins us twice per week. I travel with Usagi to Ku 1 every afternoon I'm free from my Sakai or Lucy obligations to watch Maeda and all the minor players left. Most evenings, I spend alone and go to bed early unless Jiro is home which isn't often. He has been working hard, gaining ground for me with every possible connection he has in the Ku 6 community.

But starting this past week, Jiro decided I should learn to climb, and I was all for it. I want to obtain as many new skills as I can before we leave, and I've wanted to learn to climb after the fight at the theater. Jiro traveled to Ku 5 and bought rock climbing gear so I wouldn't fall to my death while practicing. Sweet of him, really. I wasn't aware rock climbing gear existed anymore, but Jiro is friends with someone from school who works in and out of the caves below Nishikyō. This is standard equipment for him.

Jiro doesn't need this sort of thing anymore. He's been climbing since he could walk. I found out recently he broke his arm when he was six years old climbing over dumpsters in his spare time. I'm surprised Mariko has not gone completely gray yet.

I only climb at night. If I try to do this during the day, too many people will see me, so I'm getting used to feeling my way in the dark. I only wear the harness. We belay a line between the roof of the Sakai building, me, and the ground, and I refuse to wear a helmet because the extra weight impairs my sense of balance.

For clothing, I wear a tight, long-sleeved, black shirt though it's hot as hell out here and a pair of tight-fitting black pants I had Beni buy for me. Jiro calls them my "sex pants" because they "make my butt look good." Or so he says. I roll my eyes every time he sees me get into them. And he thinks my libido is strong?

I'm trying to dress the part of being inconspicuous. I need to learn to fight and climb in these clothes because they are my shinobi wear. If I'm ever able to go out and spy, I'll slink through the night in this.

"Stop buggering around! There's sake to be consumed."

I heave a deep sigh and carefully throw my body weight to the right, stepping onto the brick.

Kentaro is on the roof hurling British insults at me again. He has opened up since coming out to me and jokes and pokes fun at me, Jiro, Usagi, everyone. He must have felt all bottled up those first two weeks. Turns out Kevin, his now on-again boyfriend, is English and lives in the British quarters in the "Little Europe" section of Ku 4, not far from my Aunt Sharon.

"Piss off, Kentaro!"

I'm totally on board with the Briticisms.

Digging my fingertips into a raised edging above me by ten centimeters, I swing myself, with no footholds, to the right another meter and get my toes onto the fire escape, then climb over the railing to the platform. I wave to the people sitting inside watching a show on their tablets. They are family friends and are used to me outside their window now.

"Gods. I knew you would be a good climber, but I didn't think you'd be better than me!" Jiro shouts up from below.

I lean over the railing and smile down at Jiro. "Thanks, love."

"Ugh, you guys make me sick."

"Shove it, Ken-chan, or we're leaving you at home." Jiro can only take so much of Kentaro before he wants to kill him. Kentaro's a lot of fun but he's not a romantic like Jiro.

"Ow! Ow ow ow." My hand seizes up, radiating pain straight up my arm.

"What's wrong?" Kentaro peers down at me from two stories above. He sounds concerned for me, and I'm glad he always knows when to stop joking around.

"My body says it's quitting time." While shaking out my hand and unhooking myself from the line, I climb down to Jiro. He takes my hand in both of his and rubs out the cramps in my palm and fingers, and it's so intense I actually want to cry. I've been pushing my body to the limits lately.

"You need to deaden this pain with some sake for sure."

"Holy hell, yes," I flex my fingers, releasing them from contorted frozen manacles. A tear rolls down my cheek, and I swipe the drop away angrily. I hate when my body doesn't obey my wishes. "Gods dammit, that hurts."

"Good thing we have tomorrow night off from climbing. Now," he says, reaching around me and grabbing my butt, "you should probably go inside and change out of the sex pants before we go to Izakaya Tanaka. I can't have other men looking at you in those."

"Other men don't look at me," I say with a huff.

"Oh, yes they do. All. The. Time."

"You're not serious."

"Completely serious. Usagi stopped some guy from coming over and hitting on you at dinner the other day before I arrived."

"Really? I don't believe you." Never in my life have men flocked to me like Jiro seems to think they now do. He's delusional.

"Ever since you cut your hair, I swear you've become a thousand times sexier, and I'm constantly narrowing my eyes at other guys who have their sights set on you."

"Do *you* think I'm a thousand times sexier?" I wrap my arms around his neck, even though I'm very less than sexy all sweaty and gross from climbing, but Jiro doesn't care.

He leans over and kisses my neck. "I do."

"Ugh, you guys really need to stop that!" Kentaro says from above.

Jiro smiles at me, and I know that's our cue to start making out. I jump up and wrap my legs around him, and we kiss and kiss and kiss until the rope I was using hits me on my back, thrown from above by Kentaro. We win this round.

We quickly change and meet up at Izakaya Tanaka. Miko's mother has effectively retired from work. Once the wedding was over, Miko told her she didn't need to come any more unless she wanted to socialize, and Mrs. Tanaka smiled, nodded, and hasn't been seen here since. Miko says she stays home each night and does needlepoint or has her friends over for mahjong. Mrs. Tanaka is beyond happy. Mr. Tanaka will probably never leave the izakaya, and that's fine with both Miko and Yoichi. They all get along famously.

Kentaro and I sit in a booth, eating pickles and rice, and drinking sake. Ah, I missed sake. Jiro is at the bar talking to Sono, Yoichi, and Usagi. Oyama is in the kitchen as always. The cooks love him back there. They are forever laughing about something. Now that Kentaro has the freedom to date who he wants under my roof, he has been inviting Kevin over more often. When we meet up in public, Kentaro is not as forward about his affection as he is in private when it's just us.

"I'm not worried about my father spying on me. You know I go back to our building and talk to him once per week, though I have no idea why. I keep an eye out for our family spies, but I never see them. I'm more worried about friends of the family seeing me and reporting back to him. You never know when you'll run into someone on the street or in a restaurant or wherever."

"It's too bad he can't accept it. I'm sorry, Ken-chan."

"Don't pity me, Sanaa-san."

I blink and pull back into my seat. "I'm not pitying you. Don't get all huffy with me. I'm just showing a little sympathy for your situation. My Aunt Kimie was disowned for the same reason, and it still makes me angry."

"Sorry," he mutters into his drink.

"See? Don't pity me either." I chuck a pickle straight at his head, and the slice lands in his hair, making us both laugh. Kentaro can go from happy and joking to sad, abusive, and lonely in no-time flat. But I never harp on him for his swinging personality. I have one of my own to deal with.

"Is Kevin coming?" I sit up a little in the booth and turn towards the door.

"Not tonight. He has to be up early tomorrow." Kevin is a doctor, a pediatrician who loves kids.

"Sanaa-san," Kentaro starts, but stops, playing with the cup in his hand, "how long have you and Jiro been together?"

"Ummm..." I think back. How long has it been? "A few months now. We met for the first time on New Year's Eve. Well, as adults, that is."

"You met earlier than that?"

"Sort of. Our families were good friends when I was a baby and supposedly we played together. Our parents were hoping we'd get together but we moved away when my parents died."

"Huh. Funny how that happens." He stops for a moment, and I put my chin on my hand and study him. Why do I get the feeling he's digging for specific information? He only gets serious now when we talk business. I put on my passive face and push my emotions aside and wait. I'm getting better at this, as long as I'm not involved in a stressful situation.

"You know Jiro and I grew up together."

"Yes. Jiro said his family and yours were pretty close but not as much in the last ten years. I've heard the term 'best friends' used."

Kentaro fills up both our cups, and we drink. "Jiro and I, we've always been, sort of, competitors, but yeah, we were great friends. We were constantly trying to best each other, climb the highest, fight the hardest, get the prettiest girl..."

I blink and remain otherwise emotionless.

"My father tells me you two are traveling around to all the families together — that Jiro's introducing you as his fiancée."

Fiancée, a term I never expected to be applied to myself. Then two days after Miko's wedding, we went to visit Masa Suzuki, the man who made my shinobijō, and Jiro introduced me as his fiancée. I've never had such a thrill from openly rejecting someone else's rules and laws. Jiro's been telling everyone, and I haven't stopped him. People ask us when the wedding will be, and we just say "later" then concentrate on talking about the colonization and what people can expect from me.

I can't hold back a small smile, but I try to cover it with a sip of sake. "We've been to all the minor families in the last couple of weeks connected with Sakai clan — the Suzukis, Saitos, Moris, Takahashis — and then the rest of Mariko's family, the Kurokis. It's been good meeting people, hearing what they want out of Yūsei." Hearing Jiro call me his fiancée over and over, that's been nice too.

"My father, he's not very happy about this."

When I look up from the plate of pickles, I expect Kentaro to be frowning, but he's smiling widely at me.

"You have pissed him off to no end, Sanaa-san."

Kentaro's still smiling, but a chill races up my spine. I never considered this would anger Minamoto. Jiro and I aren't planning on being legally married, but we're also not telling anyone that. My thoughts on the matter? Let them think whatever they want. It's none of their business what I do with my personal life. What matters is doing my job and listening and acting.

Maybe Minamoto suspects I'll care less about his interests if I'm aiming to get married and end the whole imperial line. Or maybe he's angry that I'm siding with Sakai clan?

Shit. I think Jiro and I have made a big mistake. We should have gone to Minamoto first before doing our tour of the minor families. What the hell was I thinking? He's my ally now.

My stomach is on its side, twisting into a little knot, and my throat is so dry no amount of sake is going to wet it. Jiro walks over to the table, and it takes a lot of effort to pull myself up and appear normal.

"Sanaa, finish up your sake. It's time to head home," Jiro says, a small smile crawling across his face. I bet he's thinking of sex. He winks at me, and I know he is. It's been days since we were last awake together in the apartment. "You have the dōjō in the morning, lunch with my mother, coffee with Lucy in the afternoon, and then dinner with Helena and Miko, remember? A long day."

"Yes, another long day." They're never not long anymore. And at some point, I need to talk to Sakai and Jiro about this mess with Minamoto.

Chapter Twenty-Two

After the dōjō and a shower, I spend lunch with Mariko in her apartment. When she answers the door, she's genial, almost cheerful, and it's such a marked contrast to all of our previous lunches that I can't help but feel hopeful. Maybe Mariko and I will be friends after all. There are times when I'd give anything to go back to the days before Koichi died. Everything was so much better then including my relationship with her. But we can't go back. I need to stop hoping and wishing things were better.

Instead of eating at the table, she sits me down on the couch with a bowl of food and gets out her tablet so we can browse through pictures of my parents. She has so many of them. I thought my mother hated having her picture taken, but it appears she only liked having photos taken while she was drinking.

Mariko's tablet has plenty of photos to soak in: Arms-length self-portraits that never seem to go out of style; one of her sitting on my father's lap at a party; my mother and Mariko and Charlotte, the aunt I never knew I had; Mariko and Koichi; one of my mother and Sakai that makes my heart stop. I never see photos of Sakai young, and he looks so much like Jiro, and my mother and I are so alike this photo could be us twenty years ago. They're sitting in a booth at a restaurant, and Sakai is sneering at the camera, his hair chin-length and dark. My mother has her face turned to him, her chin propped on her hand, her other hand on a sake cup on the table, and everything about her expression screams, "I love this man."

Mariko sits next to me as I wipe away two tears that have rolled down my cheeks. "Gods, look at how young we all were." She shakes her head and swipes the photo away, on to the next one, but I stop her.

"Wait. Mark. He's so..." What do I want to say? I'm conflicted because I find the Sakai of twenty years ago attractive. Hell, I find the Sakai of now attractive too, but that's another story entirely.

Mariko glances from me to the tablet and back again. "Those Itō genes are pretty strong, right? Mark's father was handsome too. I swear the whole family has animal magnetism oozing from every pore." She laughs and waggles her eyebrows at me. "I'm glad I had sons with Koichi. I have had a lot of handsome men in my life."

Jiro and Yoichi, too. I wonder what a girl born into this family would have been like.

"Your mother was infatuated with Mark for some time before she came around to Max." Mariko eyes me carefully, and I quickly swipe past the photo to another to get us away from the obvious display of affection there.

The next photo doesn't make me feel any better though. My Aunt Sharon stands with her arms around both my father and mother.

"Mariko, what do you think of my Aunt Sharon?"

She finishes off a bite of rice and mock fish before answering me. "I think your aunt had a lot of problems to work out. She's not a bad person, just... troubled."

"I've been thinking of her lately. Wondering if it's worth the effort to get back in touch before we all leave for Yūsei."

Mariko purses her lips. "I haven't spoken to her in years. Maybe she's better, maybe not. Do you really want to know?"

I shrug my shoulders. How could I live out the rest of my life without knowing?

"Jiro seems to think it's worth it."

"Watch out for Jiro," Mariko says, and I raise my eyebrows at her. "He's an optimist at heart and even with all that we've asked of him to do for the family — the sword fighting, the role of protector — he still thinks the best of people deep down inside. He's so good at reading someone on first glance and gauging their personality, though. Much like Mark and Koichi."

Picking up my lunch, I hand the tablet back to her and eat the last bit of food in my bowl while she stares into space for a moment. I think she's remembering Koichi, but a smile quickly comes to her face.

"I just remembered something. When Kimie and Lomo adopted you and moved to Ku 5, they effectively shut everyone here out of their lives. And I couldn't blame them with everything that happened, but I missed you all a lot. My brother, Matsuo, was living in Ku 5 at the time you were, hmmm, six and Jiro was eight. Yoichi was ten. Koichi and I joined Matsuo at the temple on New Year's Day before dinner at his place and we all ran into each other!" She laughs and jumps up from the couch.

Wait, I remember this. My aunts talking to strange people and... "Oh my gods, Jiro pulled my obi bow out and made me cry. It was Jiro, wasn't it?"

She nods her head and smiles. "Koichi was so angry. I remember him grabbing Jiro and asking him, 'Why did you do that?' and Jiro just said, 'I don't know. I wanted to talk to her.' Little boys. I swear they drove me nuts for ages."

Aunt Lomo had removed me from the crowd at the temple, dried my tears, retied my obi, and then we sat and waited for Aunt Kimie to return. We had dinner together, and I forgot all about the incident.

I barely remember that little boy Jiro. We smiled at each other politely, like we were taught by our parents, and he just lunged and pulled out my bow when I turned to look at something behind me. When I burst into tears, he immediately bolted with Koichi running after him. We never did talk.

"Koichi..." Mariko says softly, her watery eyes directed at a photo of him on her tablet. "I can't help but think he'd still be here if..."

Her voice trails off, and I'm not sure what to do. She went from laughing and happy to crying so quickly.

But I should do something.

I've been meaning to talk to her about the family, about how I want to take care of everyone like she does, despite all of my obligations. Now is a good time to show her how committed I am, how I love this family more than anything in the world.

I reach my hand over to hold hers, but she flings my affection off violently, her head snapping away from me, and my heart beats wildly.

"I'm sorry. I didn't mean to intrude..." Apologies start to tumble from my mouth, my hands shaking with fear I've completely screwed this up. I'm about to throw myself in a bow at her feet when the door chimes and opens with Usagi standing in the doorway.

"Sanaa-san, you're going to be late to meet Lucy if we don't leave right now." I jump from the couch and sprint for the door, eager to leave this situation far behind me.

Usagi escorts me from the Sakai building, and I spend the entire time walking and thinking about what just happened. I've offended Mariko somehow. There's no doubt in my mind now. I fear I'm being way too informal with her, too personal. I've overstepped, and I shouldn't have. I need to take a big leap back and stop being so aggressive. Just because she's Jiro's mother does not give me the right to touch her or be too familiar. Ugh, I hate this stuff. I should confront her, but if Jiro and I are going to last, I can't damage this relationship. I'll have to think of something else.

We walk in silence, and two blocks parallel to the Itō dōjō, we come upon a little French cafe with twinkle lights in the window and an erasable sign out front with handwritten daily specials in both French and Japanese. *Café les pivoines.* I recognize this name. It was on the cake Oyama brought for me the night I had Miko and Helena over.

As we approach the door, it flies open and clangs with metal bells that I reach out and silence with my hand. A young Japanese man in his mid-twenties bumps into me and jostles his iced coffee.

"Excuse me! I'm sorry. I wasn't watching where I was going." He laughs and grabs me by my shoulder, looking me in the eyes for a moment and taking in every detail of my face and body in an instant. But before Usagi can even turn and dislodge the man from me, he leaves, waving over his shoulder at us. "Sorry!"

"Hmmm, let me get the door, Sanaa-san." Usagi holds it open for me, and we enter together, brushing off our encounter with the hurried young man.

The cafe is pleasantly busy. Ten tables line the window in the front, five of them occupied, and a line of cushioned booths sits along the back of the cafe. Sakai waits at the front counter, and he's talking to the owner. I thought I was having coffee with just Lucy today.

I smile as I inhale the sweet scent of coffee, airborne sugar, and baked goods. I really do love desserts. Chocolate is my serious downfall.

"Hi Mark, I didn't know you'd be joining us." I try to smooth my hair down and straighten my shirt. I'm out of place amongst the stylish clientele in the cafe. Dressed all in black, carrying a sword and my every day messenger bag, no makeup, and my hair a mess, I don't fit in here even if I could eat chocolate cake every day for the rest of my life happily.

Sakai smiles but doesn't say anything and gestures to the tall man behind the counter.

"Remy, this is Sanaa, Jiro's *fiancée*. Sanaa, Remy."

Sakai is pissed, and I can already tell I'm in a lot of trouble. He stressed fiancée a minute amount, but the emphasis was like a slap in the face. We're usually so familiar that he hugs or puts his arm around me in some fashion when we see each other, but he's not making a move to greet me other than to introduce me. I'm getting the cold shoulder, and after seeing the photo of him and my mother, I want to cry. I falter for a moment but put on a smile for Remy whose curly hair stands up and gives him a few extra centimeters. He smiles and his green eyes shine.

"A pleasure, *mademoiselle*." He nods at me, and I bow back.

"Remy's been running this place for about eight years now, right?" Sakai turns from me slightly to speak with Remy, and my heart aches.

"I have. I'm lucky to have such a great landlord." Remy and Sakai smile at each other. Sakai must own this building, too.

"Remy, let's get Sanaa an espresso since it's nice and cool in here. No problems with the air coolers?"

"None. Even the kitchen has been good." Remy turns to me. "Anything to eat, Sanaa?"

I examine every last pastry in the case carefully. It's hard to decide. "I'll have a chocolate croissant, too."

"*Très bien.*" He reaches into the case and plates a chocolate croissant for me. Another woman working behind him pours espresso into a dainty white porcelain cup. Sakai doesn't ask for anything, but Remy puts a glass in front of him, drops two ice cubes in, and about three fingers of Scotch that he pours from a bottle he has stashed under the counter.

We meet Lucy in a booth at the back, and Usagi sits at a table next to us with tea and his tablet. I slide into the seat and prop Kazenoho up next to my leg under the table. No one even looked at it. Everyone minds their own business here.

"Sanaa..." Lucy leans forward, and we kiss on the cheek, her preferred method of greeting, though I'm always trying to hug her.

Silence brews while I sip my espresso, Lucy her coffee, and Sakai his Scotch. We're engaged in a waiting game. Who's going to break the uncomfortable silence first? And damn, why isn't Jiro here to back me up? I'm all by myself, and it was his idea in the first place.

"So..." Sakai says, and I breathe a sigh of relief. Him first. "Fiancée, huh?"

An embarrassed blush bursts onto my cheeks, and I study my cup instead of looking at the both of them.

"You have a lot of damage control to do now." Sakai is not admonishing me, Lucy is. "We've been propping you up as the colonization leader, though you're twenty years old and have no clue what you're doing, all because of your bloodline. And this only works if you don't marry."

"I know." I'm a four-year-old child being sent to time-out by my mother.

"Please tell me you're not going to do anything legally."

"We weren't planning on it, I don't think."

"You don't think?" she asks, her voice rising slightly. I've spent many afternoons with Lucy since she came into our lives, talking about my family lineage, the history of Nishikyō, the different governments that have worked on Earth, and I've even confided in her about my hopes and fears, about the future. But never once has she shown so much as a drop of anger like she is now. Sakai sits and watches me passively, giving nothing away while he sips at his Scotch.

"Look," I say, and my temper rises immediately. Whenever I start a conversation with "look," I'm already half-way to losing my cool on someone. "I want to get married. I want to have a husband and kids, and no, I don't want a consort. It's not good enough. A consort means there's room for other consorts, and it's stupid, but I just want Jiro. That's it."

Why is this so hard for Sakai to understand? Unexpectedly, his passivity breaks and sadness clouds his eyes. I want different things than my mother did, and he's still measuring me against her. My mother would have taken the consorts and screwed the marriage. After everything I've learned, she was probably with both Sakai and my father at the same time, breaking both of their hearts.

"It's not stupid," Sakai says, quietly.

"Really?" I was expecting a fight. A big blowup where I get up and denounce everything, quit it all, and have to come back later and apologize.

"It's unexpected. We spoke to Jiro today before this and he's... determined as well."

My blush fades, and knowing Jiro hasn't backed down either, I'm more confident about all of this.

"Lucy and I are unhappy you didn't talk to us about this before broadcasting your relationship to the minor clans. And now you have a Minamoto problem and possibly a Maeda problem. I know you were thinking about going to visit Kimie and Lomo soon, but you should postpone and concentrate on this. It's July now, and you have less than six months to get everyone in line before we leave."

Shit. I miss my aunts so much. It'll kill me to have to postpone a trip to call on them. Again.

"Way to put the pressure on, Mark. And last time I checked Maeda has ignored every one of our messages."

"You'll have to think of some other avenue to talk to him."

"Fine." I'll have to come up with something, I guess. More time in Ku 1 with Usagi when he's available to take me.

"Well, well, listen to Sanaa, our future empress, getting scolded. I never thought I'd see the day."

Risa unexpectedly stands at our table, her shoulder-length hair falling in perfect waves around her pretty but detestable face. She always looks gorgeous, like she just stepped out of a salon, and I always look like a pre-pubescent girl. Whenever she's nearby, my tomboy nature is amplified tenfold.

"Hmmm, maybe Sanaa's not as perfect as she pretends to be." Risa taps her rounded fingernail against her lips and blinks her eyelashes at me.

"What the hell do you want? I told you to stay away from me." I nod at Usagi, and he comes to Risa's side, grabbing her arm, but she snatches it back. Sakai and Lucy exchange glances, and Sakai moves so he can get up.

"You won't boss me around. I'm surprised anyone wants to be friends with someone as annoyingly superior as you." She sneers at Lucy, and I almost laugh. The girl has guts, I'll give her that. "For example, poor Helena..." She clucks her tongue against her teeth. "She definitely doesn't deserve the treatment she gets by being your friend." She picks up her bag from the table next to her, throws her hair over her shoulder, and leaves.

What?

"Helena? What's she talking about?"

Everyone freezes, the same light flickering on in each of our heads at the same moment. I'm supposed to have dinner with Helena and Miko tonight, supposed to meet up with her for drinks at her place beforehand in thirty minutes. The cafe is steamy and warm, but goosebumps pop up all over me.

I grab Kazenoho and throw the sword over my shoulder with my bag, running for the door with Usagi, Sakai, and Lucy right behind me. Helena's apartment is five blocks from here, and if we run, we can make it there in only a few minutes. She usually works till eight or nine every night but decided to shorten her shift today so we could hang out together. She should be home by now.

I weave in and out of people on the sidewalks, sweat streaming down my face, and my legs pumping as hard as they can, trying not to think about what I'll find when I ring Helena's doorbell.

When we reach her building, I bypass the elevator and climb the stairs two at a time with Usagi right next to me. Scanning my hand at the door, we wait... and wait. Why is she not answering?

Usagi leans towards the door and listens as Sakai and Lucy run up behind us. Light but irregular steps sound through the doorway before it opens.

Something is very wrong with Helena. She stares at us, blank, her eyes are vacant, and her pupils are almost nonexistent in her deep blue irises. Her body convulses, and I lurch forward and wrap my arms around her before she falls and hits her head.

Chapter Twenty-Three

"Usagi, call an ambulance!"

Usagi quickly reaches over to the door's panel and hits the medical emergency button.

A voice comes through the speaker, "Medical teams have been dispatched to your location. Estimated arrival time is three minutes. If this system has been used in error, please cancel within the next thirty seconds."

I've never had to use the medical emergency button, and I'm panicking now hearing the voice come out of the panel. Lucy helps me lay Helena on the floor, and Usagi crouches down over her. He puts his hands on either side of her face and leans close to her.

"Helena, can you hear me?"

She blinks her eyes a few times but remains mute. Her body convulses again, and I have to stop myself from bursting into tears. I'm not good with this kind of stress.

Sakai steps past us all and scans the room. He takes in every single thing he passes as he quickly walks her apartment: Helena's kitchen table loaded with neatly stacked dishware, her collection of shoes at the door, her bag lying on the floor next to the couch, and finally the takeaway cup of coffee spilled all over the couch and coffee table. He picks up the cup, smells it, and tastes a remnant of liquid still clinging to the lip.

Usagi looks from Sakai to me, and I'm sure we're thinking the same thing.

Leaning over Helena, I search her vacant eyes. "Did you come straight home from work, Helena?"

Her head shakes right before her eyes close, and she loses consciousness. She's still breathing, and her body continues to convulse. Footsteps pound down the hallway as three medics come flying into her apartment. Usagi and I step back.

"What happened?" the lead medic, her badge reading "Harper," asks us.

"She was expecting us over for dinner, but she opened the door and something was very wrong with her. Her pupils were tiny, and her footsteps were uneven, like she was drunk." I'm surprised I can even speak and report this. I feel detached from my own body.

"Check her for head trauma," one medic says to the other.

"No. She's been poisoned." Sakai hands the cup over to Harper, and she zips it into a bag while the other medics attend to Helena.

"Are you sure?" Harper asks, her eyebrows drawing together, skeptical of Sakai, but then turns and spots Lucy in the room with us.

Lucy nods her head. "If he thinks it's poison, it most likely is. So get moving."

Two more medics arrive with a stretcher, and they quickly lift Helena onto it.

Harper directs them out the door. "You will all need to follow us to Ku 2. Can you hail a taxi?"

Lucy and Sakai nod, but I push shocked and pale Usagi out the door behind them. "Usagi will go with you!"

The medics carrying Helena in the stretcher are so fast on the stairs I worry they'll dump her out, but they get down and out of the lobby in no time flat.

Usagi jumps into the ambulance behind the stretcher.

"Call Oyama," he says as the doors close on him. The sirens start, and the driver takes off down the street heading straight for one of the tunnels that leads directly to Ku 2.

We hail a taxi that pulls up right after the ambulance departs, and Sakai gets in the front with the driver who speeds away from the curb towards Sakai building.

"We'll run by home, and I'll jump out to get everybody we need. Sanaa, you and Lucy go on to Ku 2, and I'll follow." The car stops, Sakai jumps out, and runs into our building and up the stairs.

"Don't worry, Sanaa." Lucy takes my hand as we speed away. "Hopefully, we got to her fast."

Fucking Risa. She came in, rubbed my face in her power over my family and friends, and left, giving me the smallest clue Helena was in trouble. And she blamed everything on me. Helena is in this situation because of me.

"No, no no no no..." All of the blood leaves my head, and I bend over in the backseat of the taxi, putting my head between my knees. "My fault. They went after her because of me!"

"Don't jump to conclusions."

"Lucy!" I raise my head up and clutch her hand to my chest. "Don't patronize me!"

Our car speeds towards Ku 2, the Medical Services Ward, at the center of the city. The dark tunnel providing easy access to the emergency wards blinks with lights every hundred meters hypnotizing me into a panicked trance. Traffic is light, and the tunnel bends to the right as we approach our destination. Ku 2 is round in shape and divided up into pie pieces for each ward it's closest to. Around the outside crust of the pie, a series of emergency rooms accommodate urgent care, then the specialities, surgery wards, and hospital rooms are closer to the center.

Lucy and I enter into the hospital via Emergency Room 6C. My tablet pings with a message from Jiro. They are on their way, so I message him back with our location and sit next to Usagi after wiping away my tears with a tissue from the admitting desk. Lucy is helped immediately, of course. Everyone in this city knows who she is.

The waiting room is quiet. Only two other people are in here with Usagi and one of them, a graying man in his early thirties, is looking at Usagi and his sword and wondering whether or not to call the police. I stare him down, and he goes back to reading his tablet. Medical advances have eliminated the majority of diseases from the human race — no more chronic illnesses, auto-immune disorders, or sexually transmitted diseases — but people still get into accidents. People still get sick and die from things like poorly handled or stored food, and everyone's body deteriorates in middle age from the ambient radiation that seeps through the domes. This man glancing back up at Usagi and me doesn't appear to be injured. He must be waiting for someone.

Ku 2 is not like the old hospitals I've seen in movies, and luckily, I'm hardly ever here. The waiting room and admitting desks are orderly and tranquil. Sitting down next to Usagi, I hold his hand which is something I've never done before. I've hugged him and played around with him in the dōjō, but I've never had to offer him comfort. He smiles weakly at me, and guilt drains into my chest.

After five minutes of sitting, anxiety overcomes me, and I get up from the seat and start to pace. I'm pretty sure Helena said she didn't come straight home from work today. She's been working at this one onsen for two or three weeks now and already has a regular routine, a regular place she goes to for snacks or coffee or food.

Someone could have easily watched her for a few days and then made their move.

But why? My only answer is because she's connected to me. She's connected to Sakai Clan through both me and Usagi. She's not protected. She's easy to get to. If they want to hurt Usagi, me, Miko, or anyone in Sakai Clan, then they would go for her. She is the sweetest thing ever, and hurting Helena is the easiest way to hurt us all. Even Sakai loves her.

The door opens, and Jiro, Sakai, Mariko, and Beni enter in a stream of concerned and angry faces. Oyama is right behind them, but he heads directly to the front desk, his hand is scanned, and he's sent back into the hospital. Mariko and Beni sit with Usagi. Jiro walks over but stops about half a meter from me because he can tell I'm angry. I'm pissed!

"Someone is messing with my family, Jiro. *And I do not like it.*"

My head is going to explode. My temper is way off the charts, and my face is so hot I'm starting to sweat.

"Uh oh," Jiro says, holding my face and looking me in the eyes. His fingers are icy against my heated cheeks. "Concentrate. You look close to having an aneurysm. What do you want to do? Because I know what I want to do but it involves swords and violence." He is so intense. Everyone loves Helena.

"We need Mark."

Sakai is talking to the admitting personnel at the front desk, so Jiro walks over to him, and after a few words, they both return to me.

"What do you need?" Sakai asks.

"I need you to work your magic and release the holds on the surveillance video so I can make calls to the GDB for real-time feeds. No more twenty-four-hour delay. I need answers, and I need them now. Not tomorrow."

Sakai folds his arms, not answering.

"Don't deny you have access to real-time feeds, Mark. Remember how you followed Minamoto and Matsuda to Izakaya Tanaka, and you spied on Jiro and me? You had those videos real-time. You showed me the images the next morning."

Sakai sighs. "I was always hoping you'd overlook that."

"No, I knew. I've known forever. I've just never needed the video that badly."

"Fine. I'll give you my access, but you have to be smart about using it. Understood?"

I nod.

"You'll have to log in at Ku 1 the first time. It's a security protocol for new tablets assigned to my level of access. After that, you can request files remotely if you like. Bring me your tablet."

I walk over to my bag sitting next to Usagi with Jiro right behind me.

He leans over and whispers in my ear. "Mark spied on us?"

"Yes, our first kiss and other making out we did that night."

Jiro and I look at each other, and we both blush and laugh. Oh gods, I needed that laugh. It broke my murderous temper. Now I can think logically.

While Sakai taps his credentials into my tablet, the doors open again, and Miko and Yoichi enter with Helena's parents right behind them. I haven't seen Helena's parents in ages. They've always been workaholics, and they love Helena, but she learned to do things on her own from a young age. I'm glad they've come, but I don't want to explain to them why.

Sakai hears my sigh when I see them. "It's okay. I'll go talk to Helena's parents. I've talked to them a few times over the past couple of months. They know everything."

"Really?"

"Yes, Sanaa-chan," he says, resting his hand on my shoulder. "Helena's one of your best friends. She wanted to come with you on the first wave to Yūsei. She wanted to live in Ku 6. I even tried to set her up with a permanent job at one of the onsens, but she's so independent, she was only willing to take so much help."

This news makes me smile even though our current situation is devastatingly sad. If only she had taken the offer...

"Your friends' welfare is just as important as your own. So don't worry. I'll take care of this."

Sakai walks off to talk to Helena's parents, and they're relieved to see him.

Mark Sakai, you never cease to amaze me.

Chapter Twenty-Four

Having access to real-time video is a life-changing experience already. Being able to sit in 3B, call up any camera in the city, and witness what's going on there right now is powerful. I'm like a god surveying my people. Much better than looking at feeds from days or weeks ago.

I've been here a lot lately, with Jiro as well but mostly with Usagi. I've spent many afternoons sifting through video feeds, watching Minamoto, Maeda, anyone still affiliated with Taira, and then, most recently, all the minor clans that we've visited and secured their allegiance. But never before have I come here to spy on my own family or friends. A long time ago, I followed Sakai once via the video surveillance, felt guilty about it, and didn't do it again.

Now that my tablet is logged into the system under Sakai's access, I can call up the feeds for the area around where Helena has been working the past few weeks and see what happened only a few hours ago. I find three cameras across and down the street from the onsen and point the time code at 1:55pm. Helena is always prompt, never late for anything. If her schedule is 9:00 to 5:00 then she shows up at 8:55 and leaves at 5:05. Much like me, she wants to be on time for things. Today she was working 8:00 to 2:00 so we could spend the afternoon together.

Jiro and I sit and observe her every movement, our eyes trained on the screen. Like clockwork, Helena emerges from the building at 2:06. She stops on the sidewalk and quickly chats with another woman who is leaving at the same time. They're laughing, and Helena's hands gesture wildly like they always do. She doubles over in laughter about something, and they walk away from each other with a wave.

Helena crosses the street and walks half a block to a cafe on the next corner. Pausing the video, I groan and put my head down on the desk.

"I can't watch. I cannot watch this. This is worse than following Matsuda all those months ago."

"I need your eyes, Sanaa." Jiro's warm hand settles between my shoulder blades and glides across my left shoulder, pulling me closer to him. I lift my head but rest it on his shoulder. I want to climb in his lap and never leave. "Let's figure out what happened here so we can help Helena."

Jiro squeezes me and leans forward to play the video again. We continue with our arms around each other.

My heart sinks, deep down to my stomach, as Helena walks up to the coffee bar, smiles and chats with the woman taking her order. While Helena takes her tablet out to pay, she doesn't notice the woman turn to the man who is making coffee and nod.

It's a knowing nod. Everything about her body language is wrong. She is intent on Helena, alert, not casual. The man pouring her coffee turns and waves his hand over the open cup before securing a lid on top. I'm sure he just dropped something in Helena's drink.

"That's it," Jiro says. "This man here making the coffee had this poison ready for Helena before she even walked in the door."

I pause the video on Helena's smiling face as she turns to walk out of the cafe with the cup of coffee in her hand. I want to puke.

"Who are these people? Have you seen them before?"

"I'm not sure." Jiro's expression is dark, narrowing his eyes and concentrating on every detail in the frame. "No, I've never seen them before. Let's try to get a good shot of their faces and run them through the face recognition software." He scrubs the video back and forth, zooming in and out. This man and woman must be professionals because they were aware of the cameras and never turned their face directly to them.

"Here, you try. This is frustrating." He sighs and hands the tablet to me, and I take it with a smile. I'm still better at working with the computers in 3B than Jiro.

After a few minutes, I manage to capture a couple of acceptable shots of both the man and woman, but the face recognition software comes up with nothing.

"Zero matches." Jiro sets the tablet down on the table and turns to me. "But it's safe to say that we have new adversaries." He reaches over and grabs my icy cold hand, trying to warm my fingers between both of his.

My life is in danger again. The lives of everyone I love are in danger again. I feel like we just got off this train and now we're back on again.

We head straight home from Ku 1 having messaged with Lucy and Sakai about what we found. They're still at the hospital but sent everyone but Usagi and Oyama home. Tomorrow, we'll all go back and hear what the doctors have to say.

I don't have the energy to cry. I cried earlier but now all I want to do is pace. I'm so angry at the world and worried about Helena. I kick off my shoes at the door, drop my bag on the couch, and pick up the path, back and forth from the coffee table to the kitchen table.

"Give me Kazenoho," Jiro says, his hand out. I didn't even bother to take it off when I walked in. I don't break my stride but pull the sword off my back and hand it to him, and he sets both swords on the couch. Stretching my arms and shoulders, I groan. I'm so tense, so stressed out.

"What if they can't fix Helena? What happens if I lose my best friend in the midst of all of this?"

My fault, my fault. Risa said my friends didn't deserve to be treated the way they are because of me. What about Miko? What about my aunts?

"I know what you're thinking. It's not your fault this happened."

I burst into a laugh, my feet still burning a path in the floor. "Seriously, how do you do that? Am I really that predictable?"

"Only to me," he says, stripping off his shirt. It was hot out today, at least 35°C under the domes, and the temp is about 30°C in our apartment. "Though you surprise me often. I love surprises."

"I like happy surprises. Today was full of bad ones. You should have heard the grilling I got from Lucy before finding Helena. Poor Helena."

How sick is she?

"I know you're worried about Helena. We all are. But Mark and Lucy are taking good care of her. They'll find the best doctors for her. Try to put this out of your mind so you can sleep tonight."

"I can't. I can't deal with this kind of stress. Risa is after us somehow. I'm not sure how she managed to hire assassins, but she did."

I do a double-take as I pass by Jiro, and he's in nothing but underwear now. I'm sweating again for the billionth time today.

"She's working with someone. That girl is too stupid to do anything on her own."

"She is kind of clueless, come to think of it." My feet slow. "Ugh, Jiro. I don't know what to do."

"I know what to do," Jiro says, and when I turn to him, his gaze is locked on me, a hint of a smile forming at the edge of his lips. "It's hot in here. Let's get in the shower."

I stop, all the blood leaving my head and pooling between my legs. In the shower, both of us? Now? He takes my hand and leads me to the bathroom, pressing the Do Not Disturb button on the door access panel as we pass by.

But focus on Helena, Sanaa!

My lips are dry, and I lick my bottom one and bite down, causing him to raise his eyebrows at me. Too late. All focus is on Jiro which is exactly what he wants. Focus on his chest and his tattoos swirling over the top of his shoulders. Follow the line of abdominal muscles straight down his stomach to the top of his underwear.

Our bathroom is small, and we never spend any real time in it together. Most mornings, I wake up, and Jiro is already showered, dressed, and gone. Some nights if he's home before bed, we brush our teeth side by side in front of the sink and chat about our days. I've missed him lately. With our jam-packed schedules, I only see him for short spurts each day.

He reaches into the shower and turns on the tap, the soft patter of water drowning out thoughts of assassins and my best friend lying on a hospital bed.

"Let me take away your stress, love. You know I can." Confident Jiro. I stand numb, unable to comprehend where this is going while he puts the bathmat on the floor outside the shower and hangs two fresh towels on the hooks. He pulls off my black shirt and camisole, sinks to his knees, and places a kiss on my belly. "I've missed you."

The tears I thought I could keep away fall easily now. He's missed me, too. Jiro's hands on the small of my back press me towards his kisses as they make their way up to my chest. He takes my right nipple into his mouth, and I sway with dizziness again. I never ate dinner, never ate the croissant I left on the table at Café les pivoines. I've been running on pure adrenaline all day long, and now lust is going to take over where the adrenaline left off.

Running my fingers into his hair and clutching him tight against my chest for a moment, I bring his face up to mine. Jiro's dark eyes are soft, the fold running straight across instead of turned up in anger or intensity.

"Jiro, you said you'd..." My voice catches as a new wave of tears breaks free. "You'd take care of me, and I feel weak and stupid for even saying that."

"I have been. I'm taking care of you right now. Sex doesn't solve everything, but you need a distraction." His lips come over mine, and he presses my body against his. I let my mind wander while I open up to his tongue. He's doing everything he can to make sure I'm safe and working hard at the job I've forced upon him, but he leaves me in a building full of people who don't talk to me, don't know me, and don't answer their door when I stop by to chat. I'm surrounded by people who want to protect me but want nothing to do with me.

What can I do about this? I've tried to invite myself along to all these meetings, but Jiro insists my presence will only cause people to clam up and feel uncomfortable.

And now Helena is in a mess of trouble.

I pull my face from his, my body withdrawing, only to try and unbutton my pants with shaking hands.

I. Don't. Care.

I just don't care about what's right or appropriate at this moment. Everything is screwed up now: my life, my friends' lives, my future. Why would I deny myself any time with Jiro when he can make me forget all of that?

Forget this day. Forget the stress.

Yes.

He drops his underwear once I'm naked, sliding open the shower door and pulling me in with him. The water is just hot enough to run the sweat off my skin, and I watch a rivulet snake down across my breasts to my stomach and land between our feet. Jiro wraps his arms around me from behind, reaching out for the soap on the ledge. He works up a lather between his two hands and slides his palms over my breasts, down across my stomach, and between my legs.

"Oh, yes." I moan, and my head lolls back onto his shoulder as my body seizes up so easily into orgasm, it surprises even me.

"You're coming so quickly." His fingers speed up and bring back another wave of orgasm stronger than the last that wipes my brain into an empty state and leaves me panting for air. "I thought you were going to push me away, but I'm glad you didn't."

My breath heaves in my trembling chest, and I turn my face into the stream of water to center myself. Jiro pushes me to the wall, the water from the shower now beating down upon him. I'd wash him, but I don't even think I could handle the soap. He lifts my legs up, wrapping them around his waist, and drives straight into me. I kiss him hungrily, biting down on his lip, the water running between us. I let my mind float away with each time he slides into me, allowing my body to come with him again, as he shakes and lets go, moaning against my mouth.

Oh my gods, I am, at once, the unluckiest and luckiest girl in the world. I can think of a hundred men who would run screaming from me, but this powerful, sexy, tender man is more than happy to tackle everything I come with.

I run my nose along the wet skin of his neck, kissing up over his chin to his cheek. "Mmmm. Why haven't we done this before?"

"I can't believe it's taken me this long to have sex with you in the shower. I'm sorry I've been so busy." Jiro pulls out of me, cupping my ass gently so I can put my feet back down on the floor of the shower. But I can't even stand anymore. I sink down to the floor, sit with my tattoos to the water, and rest my head against Jiro's leg while he soaps up and rinses off.

"I love you, Jiro," I say, closing my eyes and concentrating on the hiss of the shower. "I love you, and I've missed you. I'll never push you away. There are days when I'm sure you're the only person who loves me for who I really am." I'm not an empress, a sword fighter, a smart engineer, a negotiator, or Junko Itami's daughter, though I pretend to be. I'm a girl who's lost in a maze of lies, secrets, and deception.

His hand smoothes down my hair, and fingers glide behind my ear. "I love you, too."

Chapter Twenty-Five

In Helena's hospital room, introductions are made, doctors are in and out, and she sleeps peacefully through everything. I sit in a chair next to the bed, just wanting to be with her for a little bit until someone can come and talk to me about her condition. She's missing her usual rosy glow, her face so pale with her blonde curly hair spread out around her head. Her hand in mine is soft and warm but limp and lifeless, not the same hands I'm used to seeing gesture while she chatters away.

When we were girls, Helena would braid my hair for hours on end during sleepovers. Until recently, my hair was always long, and she loved to sit and talk until my whole head was covered with braids. I would brush them out the next morning, and my hair would be kinked for a few hours before reverting back to stick straight.

I was sure it was the right decision when she decided to go into massage therapy instead of medicine. She's so precise with her hands. Her mother loves to knit and Helena always pulled out any knots in the yarn. Her handwriting is lovely and neat, and that says a lot about her since so many people can barely block print nowadays. Only my Japanese handwriting is good. Every time I write something in English, it takes several tries to make my scrawl passable.

Helena, I don't know what to do! You always gave me great advice. You talked me off the ledge when I first found out about my heritage. You told me to go after Jiro. I wish I could talk to you about this too.

The door opens, and Usagi and Kentaro enter. Usagi's face is just as pale and lifeless as Helena.

"Akio, I told you to get more sleep," Mrs. Tambor, Helena's mother, says.

"I couldn't, Jess. I just couldn't."

Hearing Usagi and Helena's mother so familiar with each other drives a knife into my heart. I'd bet my sword Usagi was days away from proposing to her, and the pain of his loss is so palpable, everyone in the room can feel it.

Usagi comes over to me, I stand, and transfer Helena's hand from mine to his. Then once he's sitting, I squeeze his shoulder and make for the door.

"Sanaa-san, can we talk?" Kentaro's hand lands on my arm, and I nod to him. He and Jiro follow me out into the hall.

Once I'm out in the hall with strangers passing by, I no longer want to let my sadness loose. Kentaro faces us while Jiro and I stand with our backs against the wall, outside of Helena's door. Jiro reaches over, laces my hand in his, squeezes it, and my chest aches. I would've given anything for Helena to squeeze my hand, for her to sit up and talk to me.

"When do you think the doctors will be back?" Kentaro asks

"I have no idea," Jiro says, looking down the hall. "Lucy did say last night specialists are involved in her care. I'm not sure if they've all been in to see Helena yet."

"I wonder what they have to say." I sigh and tug on Jiro's hand. "I know nothing about medicine or biology. I'm hopelessly lost when it comes to anatomy."

Jiro smiles at me, a little half-wry smile with a raised eyebrow. Jiro, I can read your mind. Get it out of the gutter. Kentaro laughs at us both, and his chuckle is heartwarming and sweet. He's become a friend instead of an enemy in the past few weeks.

"Usagi came to me last night, to tell me what happened with Helena." Kentaro frowns and folds his arms across his chest. "This Risa is Risa Yamamoto, right? She lived in the same apartment with Beni for a long time?"

"Yes, she's a cousin on the Sakai side of the family," Jiro says, rubbing his face with his free hand. "Risa's mother, Nobu, is Mark's cousin. Beni recently moved in with my mother, and I think Risa has the apartment to herself now."

Kentaro nods, his gaze directed way off down the hall, thinking. "I don't know what I'm doing with my life. Our families used to be so close, and now my father is pushing away anyone who doesn't agree with him, including me." He turns to me, his mouth turned down and eyebrows stretched straight across his forehead. "I need someone I can trust, Sanaa-san, and I trust you."

I reach over with my free hand and take his. "I trust you, too, Kentaro. I actually like you a whole lot more than I thought I would." I smile warmly at him, and he stares down at our locked hands. Jiro squeezes my other one, pulling me closer to him. I can feel Jiro's heartbeat quicken through our linked palms.

"Helena is a good, sweet, kind person, and Usagi loves her a lot. I want to help out if I can." Kentaro nods and lets go of my hand, then squares up his shoulders, steeling himself like he does in the dōjō before I'm about to attack him. "I went home two days ago to talk to my father. Emiko Matsuda was discussing business with him and a few other people. I heard Risa's name come up in conversation. If you're looking for leads, you should start with my father."

The prognosis is not good.

"The poison did a lot of damage to Helena's nervous system," the hospital's poison specialist says, standing next to his team of doctors. "If we were to take her out of the coma right now, she would most likely be unable to talk or walk or function in any normal capacity. But, if she hadn't been rushed to the hospital when she was, the poison would've completely shorted out her brain, and she wouldn't have made it."

A heavy silence falls over the room, and we all stare into space. Sakai and Lucy, Mariko, Beni, Jiro, Kentaro, Oyama, Usagi, Helena's mother and father, and I all stop breathing and moving. How can they even fix this? I doubt they can.

I guess getting poisoned is a common occurrence. I wonder if this doctor was involved with taking care of our old Chief of Colonization, Kenji Yamada. It was only earlier this year that Yamada hung on to his life by a thread and then died the day Jiro and I had our first date.

"This is Dr. Paige Volkova." He nods to the young woman next to him and she smiles at us. Though her eyebrows and eyes are dark, her wavy blonde hair is clasped in a ponytail over her right shoulder. "She works with a team of people on new medical therapies."

"Yes, we go beyond drugs and use technologies instead to help heal the human body. Before the wars and the Decline, we had made a lot of medical breakthroughs using nanotechnology, but those technologies were turned around and used as weapons. We have since reclaimed them and are putting them to better use healing. We think Helena would make a good candidate for this therapy."

My legs itch with the need to pace. I love technology. I believe in technology, and I want technology to heal people. But Helena? Do I trust it to heal my best friend?

The door opens and Miko and Yoichi enter. The room is completely full now, but Dr. Volkova continues, her voice stronger and a hint of a Russian accent floating along the harder consonants.

"We've used this therapy hundreds of times to rebuild nerves, but Helena's damage is extensive. We believe the nanos will work and work well, but it will take a long time. The slower the nanos go, the easier the body has of adapting."

"Hibernation," I blurt out and then cover my mouth in a moment of shame for interrupting. Dr. Volkova nods at me to continue. "Put her in hibernation now for the trip. Can they work while she sleeps?"

Dr. Volkova smiles and gestures at me. "They can, and yes, that was the very next thing I was going say. Hibernation is not different from a medically induced coma. The only thing that's different are the drugs used to slow down the body's functions and aging. The nanos can still work under these conditions, and we would have six to eight years for them to work in which is more than enough. The majority of Helena's healing process would be on the other side of the trip. She would have to relearn to walk and most likely need a lot of physical therapy. Hopefully she will still be able to talk, but we won't know much until she wakes up."

Helena's mother and Usagi nod. A ray of hope shines here! I didn't expect this at all. But poor Helena. Her last memory of Nishikyō will be Usagi and I hovering over her in her apartment right before she passed out. I honestly hope she doesn't remember that at all.

"You have a few days to think about this while we prepare the nanos. If you decide not to do this therapy, we'll completely understand. Otherwise, we can put her in hibernation tonight, move her to spacedock immediately, and begin the treatment there."

She smiles at each of us. Dr. Volkova seems to be confident about this, but I'm even sadder knowing Helena will be gone from Nishikyō before I fall asleep tonight.

"On a personal note, if this is what you decide to do, I will go with you on the first wave and attend to Helena's needs myself. It would be my honor." She bows and everyone in the room bows back.

"I'm going to check some of Helena's vital signs, and then I'll be sending someone in later to take her measurements for the hibernation suit." She pulls out her tablet, gets the information she needs, and whispers with both Lucy and Sakai before leaving. The poison specialist is right behind her out the door.

Sakai and Mrs. Tambor look at each other, and Mrs. Tambor nods. "Akio? What do you think?"

"I want what's best for Helena. She wanted to go to Yūsei. I think we should give her every opportunity to make it there."

Miko edges through us all, and I move out of the way so she can hold Helena's hand. "I agree. She talked about Yūsei all the time. I know that if she could talk to us now, that's what she would want."

All is quiet except for the sound of Helena's life support machines, clicking quietly and beeping at regular intervals.

"It's a good plan, Mark," I say, finding my voice again. I was lost in daydreams of Helena walking again under a blue sky. "We should give the therapy a try." I can't help but be selfish in this. I want Helena back just as much as everyone else.

Sakai turns to Mr. and Mrs. Tambor. "Are you sure?"

"I'm confident about leaving Helena in all of your capable hands," Mrs. Tambor says, holding her husband's hand. "I wish we could go with you on the first wave but our jobs are counting on us too, and we can't leave until third wave. Hopefully we'll only be separated by less than five years."

Families will be split-up by colonization. I wish we could all pick up and go together.

"It's a good decision," Lucy says, her authoritative stare sweeping the room and everyone gathered around Helena's bed. "It's definitely the best thing for Helena... and the family."

Each person in the room takes a private moment to say goodbye to Helena before filing out of the hospital. It's only lunchtime, but I'm completely beat and sore all over. Between the constant exercise at the dōjō, the running yesterday, and Jiro's stress-releasing sex last night, I'm holding on by a thread.

Standing outside in the heat of early July, I lose the ability to remain upright and step to Jiro, letting him wrap his arms around me.

"What should we do? Back to Ku 1 and the theater? We could follow Minamoto, Emiko, Risa, her parents..." I sigh, defeated. "It's a lot of people, and we still need to figure Maeda out."

"Let's not worry about Maeda yet, Sanaa. He's maintaining the status quo, on nobody's side but his own. But I fear Minamoto is wavering especially after hearing Kentaro's confession today." He pulls back from me and takes in my wild hair, the dark circles under my eyes, and my frown. "I have an idea. Let's take the day off. There's a Bogart double feature in Ku 3 today. We should go and be irresponsible for once. Eat popcorn, sit in the dark, make out when the lights go low..." His mischievous smile is back. "And then I'll take you out for dinner."

"What about Oyama?"

"Don't worry. I'll ask him to meet us. I know a place."

"Of course you do. Okay, but back to work tomorrow?"

Jiro bobs his head back and forth. "Tomorrow is Tanabata. Work and play."

I like this idea though I feel like we should be tracking down Helena's attackers immediately. But I'm so tired I'm sure I'd fall asleep in the Ku 1 theater. I might as well fall asleep watching an old film with my head on Jiro's shoulder. So without getting permission from anyone, we take the afternoon off.

Chapter Twenty-Six

Today is Tanabata which usually takes place on the seventh day of the seventh month every year. Tanabata is a sweet, little holiday, a lovers' holiday. Citizens dress in yukata and walk the streets festooned in brightly colored paper stars with streamers hanging from them. Street vendors sell snacks, and men and women of all ages write wishes on pieces of paper and attach them to wishing trees. We have no actual trees in Nishikyō, so most homes attach their wishes to wire stars or wire trees they hang in their homes or outside their businesses.

The story behind Tanabata is a sad tale, a fable thousands of years old about two lovers in the heavens, Orihime and Hikoboshi. The two fall in love and marry quickly, but they become so consumed with each other that they neglect their work and send the heavens into chaos. Orihime's father, the King of the Sky, prohibits the lovers from seeing one another by separating Orihime and Hikoboshi, one on each side of the Milky Way. Orihime falls into despair, though, so her father relents and lets the two of them meet once per year on the seventh day of the seventh month.

I have never done anything for Tanabata before. The holiday is not celebrated widely in neither Ku 5 nor Ku 9, and, as my overworked-other-self, I usually had to be in the office. I have no idea what Jiro has planned for the day, but he seems pretty excited this morning. He wakes up happy, makes us both coffee, tea, and toast, and smiles at me before I sit down next to him and put my head on his shoulder. We slept in, and it's already 10:30.

"Do we have plans for the whole day? Or are we going to the dōjō for practice too?"

"No, we have plans all day and this evening, too."

"Shall we get dressed up? Wasn't that one of the points of doing something fun today?" I take a big bite of toast and a gulp of coffee, and then the door chimes.

"It *is* one of the points of doing something fun today, and Beni is here to help you get dressed. So get in the shower, and when you're ready, we'll leave."

When we hit the street outside, Usagi and Oyama are already

waiting for us. I head straight for Usagi and give him a big hug which he accepts gracefully.

"I stayed with Helena last night until she was loaded onto a shuttle out at the airport."

"I'm going to miss her, Usagi."

"Me, too. Let's try to enjoy the day, though. She'd have wanted that." Usagi smiles sadly at me. Tanabata was one of Helena's favorite holidays.

Jiro links arms with me and pulls me along behind some of Sakai's men out in front of us. I'm happy to be wearing my red yukata today with a black obi. It's not often I decide to go with red, but when I do, I feel alive and energetic. Red is a powerful color. I like having it in my hair.

Jiro is wearing his dark blue yukata, the one he wore to the okiya on the night we first openly flirted with each other. I do love men in kimono and yukata, but I've gotten used to him wearing all black too when we play around at night in the city.

"I've had plans to visit Minamoto today for weeks now, but we're going to have to talk business with him after what's happened."

I nod my head in assent. I need to be passive and not get emotional.

"We're going to his family's *chashitsu* in Minamoto territory. It's a favorite place of mine. Kentaro, Usagi, and I used to play there a lot when we were kids."

"Chashitsu? You want to take me to a tea house?"

"Ah, but Sanaa, it's not just tea. It's *kaiseki* and the tea house. The tea house grounds. They have a real koi pond."

"With real fish?" I remember all of the beautiful fish swimming in the aquarium in Ku 8, and I'm so fond of my haori coat with the big koi fish along the back.

"Real. Fish. You will love the fish in the pond. They are hand-fed each day so they're quite friendly."

We turn the corner onto a main street, and everyone is out. From each street lamp hangs a bright, big, round star in a million different colors with streamers hanging off the bottoms, tickling the heads of people who walk under them. Usagi and Oyama press in a little closer to us as do the other men in front. The street is loud and busy. People are lining up for lunch from the street vendors. The smell of all the food is making me hungry. Toast this morning was probably not enough.

I turn to Oyama behind me, and he smiles. "I can tell you're hungry, Sanaa-san. Kaiseki is simple but elegant and won't take long to prepare. I was at the tea house earlier. They have strict instructions not to start until I arrive, though."

A particularly beautiful and large multi-colored star hovers over the center of the street ahead of us with a little girl on her father's shoulders reaching up to swirl her hands in amongst the streamers. Her laughter is so sweet.

"Sanaa, Mark and I had a long talk two days ago, the day he cornered me and asked me why I was going around introducing you as my fiancée to everyone. The last thing I want is to lose you, and if we had gone on the way they all wanted us to, there's no way we'd be happy. Neither of us. Mark wanted me to keep my distance in the beginning, but I've made it clear that we want to be together, have a family together?"

My heart races in my chest, I'm excited to hear him talk so decisively about our future. "It's not a question. I want that more than anything."

"Good." He smiles, and I squeeze his arm tight. "And Kentaro?" he asks, his voice trailing away and losing the sudden smile his lips just had.

"What? What does Kentaro have to do with any of this?"

He stops and faces me, everyone on the street swirling around us. We're a rock in the middle of a river, an island amongst the rapids.

"He'll never come between us, will he?"

My heart jumps up to my throat. Is he afraid I'll leave him for Kentaro? Like he lost his old girlfriend?

"Jiro..." My voice cracks, and my lips shake before I press them together. "Never. I swear. I don't have those kinds of feelings for him. He's a good guy, but, no. Only you." He's almost convinced, looking into my eyes and seeing my sincerity. I know I have to say it out loud. "I would never betray you like she did. I love you. You're the right one for me."

He tried to joke with me in the past about his ex-girlfriends, like it was no big deal that the one woman he proposed to chose Kentaro over him. But I know that must have hurt a whole lot more than he's ever let on.

Jiro closes his eyes and blows out a breath, held for so long, I thought he'd keel over and die.

"I had no idea you were worried. Why? I sit and wait for you to come home most nights, anxious and excited to see you..."

He shakes his head. "I'm sorry. I know how much time you spend with him at the dōjō, and I saw how relieved he was when you held his hand at the hospital. You have such an effect on everyone."

"That's my job. You know that. I can't be cold and distant with everyone."

"You're right, of course. I won't mention it again. I promise," he says, nodding his head, relieved, and pulling me along beside him. We walk for a few silent minutes as Jiro's steps become more confident and less hesitant. I'm stunned with how worried he was. If only I could see him every day, show him how much I love him with all the simple things normal couples do. This is what comes of spending so much time apart. "I've made plans for our future. Mark and my mother will watch after Sakai clan for the foreseeable future. I will concentrate on you, your imperial duties, and on us. You concentrate on the clans, the business, your training, the government, and all the other stuff that's going to come your way. Divide and conquer."

"And you. I like concentrating on you. I love it." The easiness is returning, so I smile at him and squeeze his arm again. This sounds completely doable.

"I'll be fine. You have enough on your plate, I think." But when he sees my eager expression, he smiles back. "Okay, relationships are two-way streets, and I like when you concentrate on me, ever since the day you first started asking me questions in the dōjō."

We both dodge right as two little boys race up the street and nearly knock into us. One of them collides straight into Oyama who picks the boy up off the ground and sends him on his way.

"I actually love doing this stuff," Jiro continues, laughing at the little boy. "When I talked to Maeda at Yoichi's bachelor night? It felt like I was doing what I was meant to do. I'm just as good as Mark at handling people. Maybe even more so because I've learned so much by watching my mother."

"I've been thinking about what happened to Helena, and I think we should continue to pull in ranks until we leave for Yūsei. I don't want anything to happen to anyone else, and I don't want to be a burden to you all. The situation would be easier if I continue to stay at the Sakai building and everyone was brought to me." I was hoping, with time, we would be safer, and I would have more freedom, but Helena's poisoning has changed everything.

"We definitely need to reassess our situation. I won't lie to you about this stuff, ever, and I don't want to put a happy face on things just to make you feel better."

"Good."

"But, until we can figure out what's happened, you need to stay safe. This is not about being a burden. This is about your safety. Okay?"

"Okay," I say, reluctantly. He's right, I know it. I've already spent so much time at home, though. Should I talk to him now about his mother? About how I never see her, and when I do, our visits have always ended badly?

No. Even with the heavy topic, he's cheerful, and I don't want to ruin the mood.

"What if we have a major difference of opinion on something big?" I ask, getting back to the original subject.

"We'll have to try to work it out, I guess. Isn't that what you'd do with Mark?"

"Yes, but I'm not sleeping with Mark. I can have an argument with him and then go back to my apartment and think it through."

"Okay, well, if we argue about something, and you need to think the situation through, you can have the bedroom, and I'll take the bathroom."

I imagine us both mad at each other, me sitting on the bed with my arms crossed, and Jiro standing in the bathroom. It's completely ridiculous.

"Seriously, someday I'd love to have a house with more than one or two rooms in it."

"I'll have one built with a wide deck, wooden doors and tatami mats. It'll be perched on a lake filled with fish, and we can spend our days reading in the sun in the garden."

I can picture this house in my head. Peaceful and quiet but happy and joyful with the sounds of our children running around. Sleeping on futons on the floor. Warm summers with breezes blowing through open windows, and cold winters snuggled up under large, fluffy blankets. I'm going to love Yūsei. I know I can get over my fears of the outdoors if that's what awaits me.

We smile at each other, and his eyes reflect the same future I'm imagining. Suddenly, I want very much to get on that ship and go.

"Okay, on both accounts. We'll be fine. There's no one I trust more than you, anyway."

We turn onto a small side street away from the hustle of the main strip and in front of us is an actual tea house.

"And now I see why you wanted me to come here today. Inspiration for our future home?"

He nods and smiles. This low, squat building seems out of place here, stuck between two larger buildings. The tea house has the appearance of a thatched roof with wooden columns and a wooden deck stretched across the front and side of the house. I'm sure it's all composite materials but I'm constantly surprised by the ways composite is put to use in Ku 6.

In Old Japan, especially in the rural areas, homes were built mainly of wood with paper windows and doors. This style was a nod to nature in more ways than one. The Japanese love to be close to the gods in nature which is reminiscent of our Shinto religious roots, so traditional houses were made of natural materials. But nature was cruel to Japan. Between the earthquakes, tsunamis, floods, and typhoons, wood was easily replaced and recycled if it was damaged, but it was a catastrophic loss if the building fell down or burst into flames.

I think wood is beautiful which is why I've always loved the first drawing Jiro sent to me and the wooden swords at the dōjō. I wish composite could accurately capture its brilliance. The artificial lumber does a good job, but it's not the same.

What this tea house lacks in natural materials, it makes up for in design. Every detail is accounted for, from the rice paper shōji windows to the stepping stones leading up to the deck, including the hand-painted sign out front that reads, "Shōfū-an," Maple Hut. We step up to the wooden deck and walk slowly towards the back of the building, the boards lightly creaking and bending beneath our feet.

"Here's what you need to know about today, Sanaa. Yoshinori Minamoto, Kentaro's father, is a hard man. He has obviously been close to Emiko and Tadao Matsuda but never outright supported them even though they are in the same family."

When Kentaro told us Emiko met with Minamoto the other day, I was dismayed. I had hoped their association was done now that Tadao is dead. I keep going over the conversation Emiko, Tadao, and Minamoto had the night Jiro and I spied on them at Izakaya Tanaka, and it was never clear whether Minamoto had a hand in my parents' deaths so I let it go. I'm pretty sure the explosion was all Tadao's doing. He seemed consumed by hatred, the bastard.

"I grew up around the Minamoto family," Jiro continues, "and have watched them my whole life. It may seem like we have his support, but it could be the complete opposite."

"Not surprising." I want to trust Minamoto, but I don't. My instincts tell me he's lying, but I have no concrete evidence.

"But today is when you can shine, Sanaa, because Kentaro's mother is here, and she loves charming girls."

I raise my eyebrows at him.

Jiro laughs. "You can only imagine how disappointed she's been that Ken-chan hasn't brought anyone home to meet the family in a long time."

Kentaro has his work cut out for him.

"I know his mother better than his father. She has even met one of my past girlfriends..." Jiro clamps his mouth shut.

We let the silence sit between us. Twice in one conversation is too much for me.

"Anyway," Jiro says, clearing his throat, "the good news is that if she likes you, then you definitely have an ally in this house because no one does anything without her approval."

"Much like Mariko."

"Exactly. Just like my mother. And Tamiko Minamoto is just as shrewd, responsible, and loyal. So let's go woo her." He raises his eyebrows at me this time. "She likes *me*, too." His smile has a devious hint. Something tells me Tamiko Minamoto might have a little crush on my Jiro. I'll have to use this to my advantage somehow.

A shōji door opens as I'm about to peek around to the back of the house, but a woman who looks much like Kentaro stands and smiles at us both so I turn my whole attention on her.

"Good day, Tamiko-san," Jiro says while bowing from the waist. "How are you?"

"I'm good, Jiro-kun. It's been too long since I last saw you!" She smiles at him, and yes, a little twinkle lights up her eyes. She definitely thinks Jiro is cute, and I quite agree.

"I'm sorry I haven't been by to visit you before now, but I've come to introduce you to Sanaa Itami."

Tamiko bows low. "It's a pleasure to finally meet you, Itami-sama."

I smile at her and bow slightly back. "It's good to meet you, Minamoto-san."

"Please call me Tamiko." She smiles and nods at me, but it's not the same warmth she has for Jiro. "Jiro-kun, is it true what I hear that you two are engaged?"

Wow, what a way to be direct, Tamiko. I'm glad I have politely clasped my hands in front of me, but she is smiling at the two of us and doesn't seem the least embarrassed by her own forwardness. I like her already.

"It is," he says and smiles at me.

"Congratulations."

Tamiko and Jiro still smile at each other as Tamiko gestures us both in, and sitting seiza inside past the shōji screen door is Yoshinori Minamoto. He just heard everything we said, and now he knows straight from us that I'm itching to marry into Sakai clan. We're off on the right foot.

A low table dominates the center of the room, and Minamoto takes up one whole side. He bows low to us and doesn't crack a smile, but I'm definitely going to come in here today and be the intimidating one. Intimidatingly kind and sweet, that is.

"Minamoto-san, it is so good to see you. I haven't seen you since we last had tea at the okiya. An oversight on my part. You'll have to accept my apologies."

"Please, Itami-sama, we are all busy people."

"But your son now stays in my house, and I should take the time to come and visit you more often." I nod my head once to indicate my word on this is final. That it's my fault, not his. Really, who cares? These pleasantries are all about making excuses for things that don't matter.

Jiro and I sit down on the other side of the table from Minamoto. Oyama's soft voice trickles in from the kitchen and the ladies back there titter away at whatever comments he's making. I purse my lips to stop a smile. Oyama is the king of charm.

"And I hope my son is helpful to you, Itami-sama?" Tamiko softens when she speaks of Kentaro. Mama's boy, for sure.

"Kentaro-san is more than helpful. He's a delight. I'm very glad he joined my staff. I know you must miss him."

Minamoto's eyebrows draw together in confusion, but Tamiko suddenly thinks I deserve as much warmth as Jiro.

"I have him coming to the Itō dōjō with us a few times per week and teaching me new skills. He's a good listener, and his opinion is always different from the opinions I get from other people. His viewpoint is exceptional and unique. I'm quite grateful for him."

I wish I could read Minamoto's thoughts right now because he is oddly still. Maybe I just said words out loud he never expected to hear about his son. Now I feel even better about bringing Kentaro on board. I, no doubt, saved him from a lifetime of derision and boredom at the hands of his father. I hope Kentaro gets more appreciation from him now. His mother is reserved, but her eyes are smiling brightly.

"Sanaa doesn't realize what a pain Kentaro was while we were growing up," Jiro laughs and causes everyone to smile. "I can't tell you how many times he pushed me into the pond out back."

"I have paid a fortune over the years to have that koi pond restocked many times." Minamoto huffs, but he's amused.

"My mother was so sick of me coming home soaking wet," Jiro shakes his head. I wonder about what it would have been like to grow up here. I missed out on a lot. "I ruined at least a dozen pairs of Nishikyō grays and yukata by coming over here."

"I'm sure your mother was very forgiving, Jiro-kun," Tamiko says, swiping out with her hand at a piece of dust on her yukata. "How is Mariko? Is she doing well?"

"She is doing well, thank you for asking. She's still in mourning but keeping busy with the family."

Another woman about the same age as Tamiko opens the door to the kitchen, and she comes out with a tray of food. Thank the gods, I'm starving. She smiles as she places the tray in front of me, and my face lights up. What a gorgeous meal. Everything is presented in black and red lacquerware, perfectly arranged, and smells so good my mouth is watering.

"Itami-sama, this is my sister, Shizuka. She runs this tea house which has been in my family for over a hundred years." Tamiko raises up her shoulders. She's proud of the place and rightfully so. I am definitely impressed.

Shizuka bows to me from seiza. "Thank you for visiting us today."

"It's my pleasure," I say, inclining my head back. I look at Jiro, and he has the same prideful expression on his face that Tamiko has but it's directed at me.

Passive face, deep blue sky, dunes. I almost blushed.

Shizuka gestures to every dish and explains what each is. A large bowl of rice is on the left, a bowl of miso soup sits in the center front, and three larger side dishes line the edge of the black and red tray. Each lid is taken off and reveals food artistically arranged: a simmered soy salmon paired with sesame carrots, broiled mock whitefish with lemon slices, grilled eggplant, and a small bowl of mushroom stew smells delicious, peaty and rich.

"This is really beautiful! I've never had kaiseki."

I'm so hungry it's taking all of my willpower to not dive in right now. Each person gets their tray of food, but I wait for Minamoto to start eating first. Once he does, I sip on the soup.

"I'm pleased your first kaiseki is at my sister's teahouse. You didn't grow up in Ku 6, ne?"

"No. I grew up in Ku 5 and never had much chance to make it to Ku 6 for such lovely things."

Tamiko doesn't say anything more. My smile is tight, but I can be charmed by the food. Conversation for the rest of the meal hovers around what everyone is eating. Jiro asks after Minamoto family members he knows, and Tamiko obviously enjoys sharing stories with him. Minamoto and I stay silent and eat, nodding our heads when comments are directed at us.

I finish everything on my tray and even sip on the tea. Despite my best efforts to hate tea, it's growing on me. I'm sure Sakai will be pleased.

"Minamoto-san, thank you for such a wonderful meal. I enjoyed it immensely."

"You're welcome, Itami-sama."

"I have one piece of business before the tea ceremony..." I'm being as passive and businesslike as I can be. Minamoto's ears prick up. "As you have heard, Jiro and I are engaged to be married. I'm here to tell you that though I'm aligning myself permanently with Sakai clan, we will not be making our marriage legal for quite some time. I am merely stating that our relationship will be monogamous, and no other consorts will be taken. Any allegiances made with me will be in good faith, with loyalty and honor, not bought with anything else. Much like my alliance with you."

Minamoto's stare turns hard and cold, yet he smiles and waves his hand in a friendly manner. "I completely understand. Thank you for your candid words." He bows down but goosebumps rise on my forearms. He's not convinced, but he's not prepared to denounce me today.

"Shall we walk around outside while the room is being prepared for the tea ceremony?" Jiro asks.

He helps me up — we've been sitting seiza now for a while — and I let the blood flow back into my legs before we start to walk. He opens the shōji door to the backyard, and once again, I'm stunned by this place.

It's not grass out back, nor bamboo, nor trees, but it might as well be. I step down off the wide porch and instead of putting my flip-flops back on, I put my feet in the "grass." The blades are soft and green but definitely not alive. Still, when I squat down and run my hands over the lush lawn, the ground feels spring-loaded. My feet sink into it like it's real earth, real turf.

"This is a newer version of fake grass. When Kentaro and I were kids and played back here, it was not as nice nor, um, soft." He rubs a spot on his elbow, probably from where he fell or was wrestled into the ground.

"Aw, Jiro. Was Kentaro rough on you as kids?"

He shakes his head. "He never knew when to give up a fight."

I glance back at Minamoto and Tamiko, and they are standing and watching us from the porch.

"Walk with me," I say, holding out my hand to Jiro with a smile, and he takes it without a second thought.

We amble through a long arbor of bamboo taller than our heads, and I keep closing my eyes and breathing deeply hoping for that same clean air I inhaled in Ku 10, but it's not here. I'm sure this is good enough for a lot of people who just want to see something green or feel connected to the Earth we all long for. The tea house grounds are fun and novel for me but not real.

"Did you see what I saw back there?" I whisper to Jiro, and he nods. I wasn't imagining the look on Minamoto's face. We have a lot of work to do with him.

When the bamboo parts, the koi pond is in front of us. It's not very big, maybe five meters across, and the water is murky, the color of soy sauce. Dark gray stepping stones dot the water from one edge of the pond to the other, the circumference rimmed with more grass. Jiro looks back and Minamoto and Tamiko are arm-in-arm, following us at a polite distance.

"So, you want to meet the fish?" Jiro knows how much I love animals. I still talk about the trip I made with Sakai to Ku 8 all the time. He gives me a little shove towards the stepping stones, and I walk towards them but hesitate.

"How deep is it?"

He looks me up and down and measures me against his last memory of ever falling in the pond. "Up to your thighs, but I don't think you'll fall in. Just go out two steps, and they'll come to you. You're wearing bright red. I'm sure they can see you."

I leap to the first stone and bring both my bare feet onto the second one. In the dark water, flashes of white, orange, red, and gray start to appear around my feet. Soon the fish are so eager to see me they're swimming over and over each other, their mouths opening and closing at the surface.

I crouch down and lean close to them, and they get so excited water starts flying everywhere, causing me to screech and Jiro to laugh from the bank. The fish look so soft and smooth... and hungry. Jiro wasn't kidding about them being hand-fed every day. I reach down and stroke the top of a white fish with huge red spots on it, then snatch my finger back quickly.

"Ow!"

"Sanaa!" Jiro is on the verge of making a run for me when I smile and pop up.

"Just kidding!"

Minamoto behind us bursts into a low laugh. Jiro's expression turns from fearful to playful, and I make a mad dash across the stones to the other side with him hot on my trail. I let him chase me around the pond, laughing and dodging his lunges, and then run back through the bamboo before coming to a halt and acting more ladylike. He swoops in behind me and picks me up, swinging me around twice before letting me down, and I can't help but throw my arms around him and hug him tight. He is my love and my best friend all at once.

Thank you, Jiro. I haven't laughed and played like that in a long time.

Chapter Twenty-Seven

We have the tea ceremony with Minamoto and Tamiko, and after our little walk by the pond, they are both more relaxed. I think we showed them we can conduct business and be kids in love, and that is endearing to everyone. I've noticed how much softer around the edges Sakai gets when Jiro and I are sweet to each other. Thankfully, this is very easy to do.

Minamoto opens up a little more and talks about business in his main restaurant. Jiro's been there before, of course. Minamoto, Taira, and Maeda don't mix amongst themselves, but Sakai clan mixes with everyone. They are the ambassadors between them all. I love how neutral Sakai's family is, but I'm sure this is why they're perceived as a weaker family.

When the tea ceremony is finished, we gather up Usagi and Oyama and make our way back to the main street. We had a long lunch and tea with Minamoto, and it's around 4:30 now. Jiro's not done with the surprises, though. He takes me to a small sake bar where the four of us sit and drink and eat together for a few hours. Usagi pops into the business next door and grabs paper for each of us and a brush pen. We write our Tanabata wishes and tie them to the wire tree outside when we leave.

I wish for peace and health for myself and my family. I just want a few quiet months before we leave and more to come when we get to Yūsei. I hope that's not too much to ask.

After we're done at the sake bar, we walk back to the Sakai building the long way and drop off Oyama. Jiro pulls my hand and takes me to the transitway with Usagi in tow. We take the train up and around the city, and I close my eyes and rest my head on his shoulder, not paying attention when the train glides into the station.

"This is our second to last stop." Jiro pulls me off the train at Ku 10, the farming ward, and I immediately freeze up. Usagi is right behind me, though, so I can't turn and sprint for the doors before they close and the train pulls away. Only a few people disembarked at this station, and they have already scanned themselves and gone inside.

"Jiro, I haven't been outside in a long time now. You *are*

planning on taking me outside, right?"

"I am. Do you know what time it is?"

"Uh, sometime after 8:00?" I haven't checked the time since before we left the sake bar, but the lights were dimming in the domes, and I can only assume that it's night now.

It's night.

I remember all of those nights I spent at the house with my cheek pressed against the window, gazing at the stars and the moon, watching for the shuttles zipping back and forth from the elevator to the space station.

I want to run all the way up to the top of the hydroponics tower now. I'm not even remotely afraid of the outside when the stars are out.

Now it's my turn to pull Jiro, and I take his hand and drag him along with a huge smile on my face. "Come on, Usagi! Don't dawdle!"

Usagi chuckles, and I think that might be one of the few times he has ever laughed in my presence.

We enter the hydroponics tower and let our eyes adjust to the light. I love the fresh air that only comes from green plants and bubbling water, fresh air that was painfully absent on the teahouse grounds today. The air is clean and new, and so light and cool on my lungs. Instead of walking down the spiral like Jiro and I did our first time here, we walk up, around and around, until we get to the spot where the elevator lets off on the top level.

The long corridor to the outside stretches before us, and I shudder with a small twinge of anxiety when I think about the last time I was here. I grip Jiro's hand even tighter and pull him closer to me.

"Will you be all right, Sanaa?" He turns his smile on me. "I know how much you love the stars. Maybe we'll see Orihime and Hikoboshi tonight."

"Jiro, you're such a romantic," I say, pinching him on the arm.

He turns and backs into the door, opening the latch with his elbow. "It's true. I am. But nothing is more romantic than the stars."

The night is hot and clear, and the sky is bright with millions of pinpoints of light above us. The moon is absent, but its light would have obscured the cloud of the Milky Way stretching from one end of the horizon to the other. I only look up; the sky is amazing in its brilliance.

If this were day, my eyes would be on my feet, and I would hope I wouldn't pass out, but I can't tear my eyes from the stars. Jiro gently leads me out farther and farther past the door and the tarp that shelters the entryway. When we get far enough out, he pulls me to him, and I turn my gaze as high as it can go, past his face which is soaking in the stars as well.

We stand quietly for a while, just watching, and when my neck begins to ache, I close my eyes and bring my face down to his chest.

I take a moment to breathe in Jiro and place this memory safely in my head. I'm lucky tonight. When I open my eyes, Beni stands with Usagi off to the side and both are smiling at us.

"Beni, what are...?"

I stop when my eyes hit the ground. A blanket is laid over the tan gravel with a pot of rice wine and three cups. My heart starts hammering in my chest, and I look up at Jiro who is smiling down at me.

"Yoichi's wedding was an eye opening experience for me in many ways. Watching you pace that floor and worry about me and my family, agonizing over doing the right thing? You're a very selfless person."

Thinking back on that day now, I'm so embarrassed by the way I acted. "No. I'm completely selfish. I panicked because I wanted to keep you, and I was sure there was no way we could be together."

"I love that, too. Before you, every girl I met freaked out and broke up with me. Getting married was the furthest from their mind because they were afraid of this life. There are a lot of reasons for us to not be together — laws and family obligations. What do you want?"

I close my eyes and lean my forehead against his chest. "I want us to make our own decisions, for us, not for anyone else. I told Mark and Lucy I would have no consorts, only you. I didn't ask their permission."

His hands come up and hold my face, and he shakes his head and laughs lightly. "You're so full of fire, it kills me. I'm only sorry about one thing. I called you my fiancée, and I didn't make it official. I've had this planned for weeks now. I've gone to your aunts and asked their permission. I've informed everyone in the family. Sanaa, will you marry me? Right now?"

Beni comes forward out of the shadows and opens her hand and in her palm are two rings. One for me is platinum with a series of three square diamonds. The other is a plain matching band.

Jiro takes them both from Beni's hand. "These are from my other side of the family. My mother's mother and father. I visited my grandmother and got them both."

I'm speechless. I just keep looking at the rings and then Jiro and then the rings and him. The look of shock on my face turns to a wry smile. "Aunt Kimie and Lomo must have died when you came to them."

"Lomo cried and Kimie rolled her eyes." I burst into a tear-filled laugh picturing the two of them with Jiro. I bet it was quite a scene. "So, is that a yes?"

"Oh! Yes, Jiro! My gods, I've been saying yes in my head for the past minute and not saying it aloud."

He laughs and kisses me, kisses me under the stars with the rings clasped in his hand between us.

"Come and sit down."

Jiro leads me over to the blanket, and we sit seiza opposite each other with the cups between us.

"San-san-kudo. You weren't kidding about getting married right now."

"There's no priest here to purify us or bless the rings, but we can drink from the nuptial cups. Beni and Usagi will be our witnesses. From here we have a party to go to." He hands the rings back to Beni who sits next to me, and Usagi sits next to Jiro.

"A party to celebrate? You've been busy. I love this. It is over-the-top romantic, even for you."

"Yes, I know. Let's be thankful Kentaro is not here."

I can't think of a better wedding ceremony than this, a grand gesture and us sitting and poking fun at it because that's what we do.

Beni pours the rice wine in the smallest cup, and Jiro and I pass the cup back and forth and drink three sips apiece. Then the next cup and the next. I want Usagi and Beni to be a part of this too — they are now as much my family as anyone else — so after Jiro and I have sipped from the last cup I pass it to Usagi and he passes the cup to Beni.

Beni gives us back the rings. Jiro puts mine on my finger, and I gaze down at it for a second. The diamonds are bright and sparkly, and the ring fits a little loosely, but I love it. I'll have to thank Jiro's grandmother next time I see her. She never came to Miko and Yoichi's wedding because she's housebound. I take Jiro's ring and put it on his finger. I wiggle it around, and it seems to fit nicely.

Leaning across the blanket, I put my hands on his knees, and he holds my face and we kiss. Jiro and I make this last, deeper and deeper, our lips alternately light and strong. My heart is beating so fast, and my head is so light and happy, and then he literally takes my breath away when he gasps from the strength this love between us. I press my cheek into his hand and feel the ring around his finger, and when we break apart I look up at the sky and the stars. Perfect.

"I love you, Sanaa."

"I love you, too, Jiro."

"Congratulations!" Both Beni and Usagi say bowing.

Jiro and I bow back. "Arigatō gozaimasu."

I laugh and look down at my hand. "For some reason, I thought I would only ever get weapons from you and never a ring."

He shrugs his shoulders and smiles. "I like to surprise you."

I like it, too. I'll never bug him to tell me things when he wants to be secretive ever again. It would ruin the fun.

"We have to go. Thirty minutes outside tops. Even tonight when the radiation is low." Jiro is the voice of reason, though I don't want to leave. I want to lie down on this blanket with him beside me and watch the stars all night long.

We stand up and Beni packs everything away into a bag. I slip my arm into Jiro's, and we walk back to the door.

"Sanaa, this is for us, this ceremony, these rings. As long as the law stands in our way, we can never be married legally. I promised Mark."

Don't feel sad, Sanaa. "It's a good compromise."

"I'd like to call you my wife when we're with family and friends, fiancée when it's business. Is that okay?"

"Deal, husband. Maybe we can change the law someday when things are settled. Who knows what'll happen when we get to Yūsei?"

Jiro holds open the door for me. "Yūsei could be anything or everything. But we'll worry about that when we get there."

From the top of Ku 10 to a party at Izakaya Tanaka.

It's probably for the best I won't have a real wedding with a ceremony and reception since my only family members are Aunt Kimie and Lomo. I don't have the kind of extended family Miko or Jiro has, and a real wedding would call attention to my unbalanced life. My eyes search the room for Helena before I remember she's not here. My circle is even smaller than before.

"I'm sorry... about the timing." Jiro is sad, too. It's not his fault, of course. It's mine, much like every last damned thing that has gone wrong this year.

I hug my aunts first before I sit with anyone else.

"Lomo and I are so pleased, Sanaa-chan. We worried the strain of leadership and the colonization would pull you and Jiro apart. But with him coming and visiting us at least once per week..."

"Wait, what? Jiro's been visiting you?"

"Yes! He comes while you're with Mark or Lucy."

"Really? He never told me this."

"I know." Aunt Kimie pats my face with a smile. "But he loves you so much and wanted to know us better. We understand how busy you are and what a pain it is security-wise for you to come visit us. It's been nice to hear about what you've been up to through him."

I lean forward so I can see Jiro at the table in the back, laughing and pouring sake for Usagi, Yoichi, and Kentaro. His left hand is on the table, and I catch sight of the ring, the one I placed on his hand an hour ago. Mine.

Maybe I don't have the biggest family or largest group of friends ever, but at least they're all people that I want in my life and want me in theirs.

When Aunt Kimie moves to the back of the room, my eyes fall first on Sakai and Lucy, who both smile warmly, and then on Mariko. Does she want me in her life? She's the only one I'm uncertain of. Her expression is neutral for a moment before she realizes I'm watching her, then her mouth forms a smile, and I let out a huge sigh of relief. This is so hard. She probably wishes Koichi were here, which softens my heart. I should cut her more slack. She doesn't have to be overjoyed at anything, not when her husband is gone.

I'm distracted by my thoughts when I turn to greet Sono at the bar and crash straight into a waitress nearly knocking her over and all of her drinks as well.

"Oh no! I'm so sorry." I say as I catch her arm. "I didn't see you coming."

"It's okay, really. Nothing's broken." She pulls her arm from my grasp and bows to me as she sets the tray on the bar.

"Are you new here? I've not met you before." She's in her mid-twenties, long hair braided and then twisted up.

"Yes, Miko hired me a few days ago. Excuse me." She wipes her hands on her apron, turns, and leaves for the kitchen. Sorry. I keep crashing into people this week. Must be the lack of proper sleep.

After chatting with Sono, I do the rounds, talking to and kissing everyone at the table, imitating what Miko and Yoichi did at their wedding before I sit down with a tired sigh. I'm happy, but it's been a long day.

Kentaro leans over and gives me a kiss on the cheek. "Congratulations, Sanaa-san."

I glance over at Jiro, and he's smiling. Good because I was afraid that was the end of Kentaro's life for planting his lips anywhere on my person. I guess my reassurance today worked. They both are more relaxed.

"I hear you went to Shōfū-an for kaiseki. What did you think of the place?"

"It's beautiful. You're lucky you got to grow up there."

"I love the time I spent at the tea house with friends. Not so much my family." He leans even closer, right up to my ear. "We should talk tomorrow."

When it's time to go, Miko pushes presents into my hands and hugs me. "I miss Helena so much. She would have wanted to be here for this."

I press my cheek into hers. "I miss her, and I miss you, Miko. You live across the hall, and I never see you."

"I know. I'm sorry I've been so busy. Just trying my hardest to get things taken care of around here. Only a few more months before this is all gone, and the izakaya is my responsibility now. I guess now that Helena is gone, Usagi will bring you by more often?"

Looking past her to Usagi in the back of the restaurant, he's sitting silently, alone at a table, staring into his cup. Slowly, he rubs his bald head and sighs. Helena's absence is painful for me. It must be hundreds of times worse for him. My wedding day is bittersweet for most of us.

Chapter Twenty-Eight

We sleep in the next morning, and I invite Kentaro down to our apartment instead of meeting him at the dōjō. In all the time he's been staying with us, we've always met on neutral ground, in the hallways, lobby, izakaya, street, or dōjō. I don't know how we ended up this way, but we've never trespassed on each other's private space before. When I open the door and invite him in, he's careful to take off his shoes in the genkan before presenting me with a bag of food.

"From Oyama. I just ran into him in the hall."

"Breakfast for us all!" I cheer. I'm starving as usual. "I hope you like omelets with rice and mock ham."

"Love it," he replies, standing in front of the couch and looking at the framed drawing.

"Coffee or tea?"

"Tea. Whatever Jiro drinks, thanks." My coffee drinking is legendary.

I leave the bag on the coffee table and go to the kitchen for plates and silverware but keep my ears open.

"You still sketch, Jiro?"

"Yeah," he replies. My stomach sinks. I love that he still draws but he hasn't shown me anything in a long time, and I wonder if he's keeping his sketches from me because I haven't been supportive enough. I hate our busy schedules, and I'm sure they will only get worse. "I try to fit it in during my free time, though there's not much of that."

"I sometimes think I have too much free time."

I join them at the coffee table and unload the food, setting the steaming mugs in front of each of us. Our kitchen table is small, and it's nicer to sit around in the living room and eat.

"Ken-chan, when I asked you to join us, I used the title of 'advisor' in front of your father but had no idea how we would work together, relations being what they were in the beginning." I hand him a plate of food, a large omelet stuffed with rice and gesture for him to sit on the couch. "I hope you'll agree things are better now."

"Sanaa-san, you sit on the couch."

"No thanks. You and Jiro sit there. I'm going to sit at the table." Handing a plate off to Jiro, I grab a floor cushion and sit. "You said we should talk today. What's going on?"

"My mother called me home yesterday afternoon, after you had gone." He shovels food in his mouth and swallows quickly. "She loves you. Love may even be too weak of a word. She said you were charming and sweet and obviously you and Jiro were made for each other, et cetera." He rolls his eyes, and Jiro laughs. "And then said, 'Your father is not happy.' And you know what? I don't give a fuck what my father is happy or sad about. He doesn't talk to me, meets with Emiko all the time, and doesn't tell me what they're doing."

Shit. I chew my mouthful of omelet extra long before trying to swallow because a lump has formed in my throat that food has to get past.

"I hate Emiko. Always have. She's the most duplicitous woman I have ever met. She would smile and simper at me when I was a kid and turn around and tell other people I was annoying. And then she married Tadao. Ugh. They were gross."

Jiro is not eating, just sitting and listening. He's so good at waiting. I want to interrupt Kentaro and ask him questions about everything, but instead I eat. If I keep my mouth busy with food, I won't talk.

"Anyway, I've made a decision for the good of my family. I'm going to help you. I'm upset about Helena, and I have a feeling my family is involved somehow. It's just a feeling, but it can't be a coincidence that you and Jiro got engaged, my father started showing his disapproval, and then Helena was poisoned. I can't prove it, though."

Wow, Kentaro really does trust me. I thought maybe our shared moment in the hospital was a fluke, but he's come around, and so have I.

"We know Risa was involved, and I think she must be meeting with the people who poisoned Helena. We obtained video of the cafe where Helena got her coffee that day, and the whole attack was all perpetrated by a man and woman, a team."

"A team? Really? Did you see what they looked like?"

"No," Jiro says, returning to his food. "They kept their faces turned from the cameras, and what little of them we identified wasn't enough for the face recognition software."

Kentaro drums his fingers on his knee, a nervous tick I've seen his father do on occasion. "Hmmm, I have an idea, but I'll need a little more evidence before coming to any solid conclusions." He picks up his food and inhales the last of his omelet. What is it about boys that makes them eat so fast? I'm only a quarter through my breakfast and still sipping at my coffee.

"How about I follow Risa?" Kentaro laughs and rubs his hands together gleefully. "It's been ages since I last spied on anyone."

"You'd do that?" Jiro is surprised but pleased. "You don't have to. We have access to surveillance videos and can set up jobs to watch her."

"I would imagine you're already watching plenty of people." Kentaro raises his eyebrows. He reads situations well. Though I've never told him about my time with the GDB and video feeds, he accurately guesses I have a lot of access. "I'll follow her and report in regularly. If something major happens, I'll take note of nearby surveillance, and we'll watch it together. Deal?"

Jiro nods at me happily. He has his friend back, and I have a much better ally in Kentaro than I do in his father.

"Deal."

We all reach forward and click our mugs together.

Chapter Twenty-Nine

Two sweltering weeks go by, and Jiro and I spend them in our apartment. I wanted alone time with him, and I got it, and I'm certainly not complaining. We're newlyweds, and I'm so happy I could die. Warm apartments call for little in the way of clothing, and we spend a lot of time doing role play — him in charge, me in charge — and our time together is hot in the same way the summer is. The dōjō is in the high thirties every day so we can't go there for exercise. It doesn't matter, though, because Jiro keeps me fit at home. Mmmm.

But, unfortunately, that's all I get of him. After the two weeks are over, Jiro ramps up the business. He's obviously happy doing this kind of work, scheduling meetings, talking, negotiating, making plans for me and Yūsei with Sakai and Lucy. I can't believe someone as young as him can handle all of these men and women, heads of houses, government officials, and be so organized. I was always good at organization and logical thinking, but Jiro takes everything to a new level with to-do lists and plans and negotiations that hinge on other plans and negotiations.

Being good at it means he spends a lot of time at work, though. This is such a Japanese thing to do, to work ourselves to death, and I used to be just as bad. I miss long days on the job and *nomikais,* all night drinkathons, with my coworkers. Some mornings, Jiro is around for a quick breakfast together, during which he is shoving food in his mouth at a rapid pace, chugging down green tea, and kissing me on the forehead as he sprints out the door, while I slowly sip my coffee. I only attend half the meetings. When I do, I have opinions on almost everything and everyone listens, but the real heavy lifting is done after I leave. So I go to meet with these talking heads, and then Usagi escorts me home. When I don't have meetings, I spend the mornings running quick errands because it's too hot to do anything else. I rarely have lunch with Jiro, and most nights I fall asleep before he's home. I miss him so much my chest aches when I think of him.

I get out of our space as often as possible, going to Mariko's or Sakai's, scanning my hand at the door, but usually finding no one at home. I swear most of the palm scanners can see me coming and are whispering to each other about how many times I've been rejected. Miko has closed Izakaya Tanaka for summer holiday which means I can't even get Usagi to take me out for drinks. I'm always wandering the halls trying to find someone in the building and never succeeding. Never. I try every day without fail. I really should give up because this dismissal of my love and company is doing awful things for my confidence. If Mariko, Beni, Usagi, Miko, Yoichi, Sakai, and Lucy wanted to spend time with me, they would come to me, right? I do often find Oyama at home, but he's always cooking or baking. I interrupted him once, and he burned a cake he was working on. Now if I smell food coming from his apartment, I don't bother to ring. I've even tried to catch Kentaro at home, but I know he's been tailing Risa or out with Kevin.

So the days when I'm not able to find anyone to spend time with, I comb through video surveillance. I still like to have tasks to do. I have jobs set up on Emiko Matsuda and Yoshinori Minamoto, and I watch them every day, but they don't do much outside of eating together on a regular basis. I let the jobs on Risa's parents, Nobu and Yukio Yamamoto, pile up, and Jiro watches them for me since he knows more about that side of the family than I do. According to Jiro's messages to me, they are the most boring people alive. They go to the theaters, out to dinner, to the casino, and have once spent a weekend at a *ryokan* in Little Kyoto but that's it.

Maeda is still a problem. I messaged him again, inviting him to an okiya for dinner with the geisha, and he declined. Just outright declined and gave no reason why. His avoidance is starting to get under my skin, and I need to figure out what to do before he thinks he can walk all over me. Ugh, he already has walked all over me, and I've felt powerless to stop it because I need to be proper about approaching him, according to Sakai. I hate being proper.

With no dōjō, no Jiro, and no companionship, I'm forced to wander the halls of the building for hours at a time. I run up and down the stairs until my heart is pounding, and I'm sweating buckets, getting the same kind of exercise I would have sword fighting, but it's not as fun. Akira, the main guard on my floor and the one above me, is a nice guy, older and married. He counts my runs up and down, and we converse lightly about things like the weather ("Hot one today!"), his kids, and his favorite subject, origami. Some days, he's the only person I talk to.

This morning, I chat with Chad online. We talk about work and his girlfriend, and I try to tell him what I can of Jiro without giving anything away about my circumstances. It's hard, though. My whole life is wrapped up in this now, and I have very little else to talk about since I don't go out, don't see shows, don't attend summer festivals, don't do, well, anything public anymore. The last time I was out and about was Tanabata and that seems like ages ago.

I'm leaving the apartment just before lunch to do my usual rounds of everyone's door scanners before running laps up and down the stairs when Miko and Yoichi's door opens. I nearly burst with happiness. Someone is home!

"Miko! Yoichi! It's great to see you." I smile and bounce on my tip toes. I hope I don't look too eager.

"Sanaa-chan," Miko leans in, and we kiss on the cheek before she looks me up and down. I'm in my casual workout clothes. Nothing too ratty. I still care about my appearance even if no one ever sees me.

"What are you up to?" Miko asks.

"I was just about to see if anyone was home. Maybe get some lunch?" I would give up my exercise plans to have lunch and human contact any day of the week.

"We actually have a lunch date planned," Yoichi says, taking Miko's arm. They smile at each other, and my heart flops down into my stomach. My poor heart. It keeps getting broken or squashed by circumstances.

Fake it, Sanaa.

"How lovely! Where are you going?"

"The new sushi place that's opened a few blocks away. The food is great, really fresh, and super tasty. I'd like to poach the chef if I can."

"Well, I'm sure you'll enjoy it." I nod at them both. "A lunch date sounds just... lovely." I already said lovely. I'm repeating myself.

"One of the perks of having a husband now." Miko flashes a smile at me over her shoulder as Yoichi leads her away.

Yes, I'm sure it is. Funny that I haven't seen mine in days. Or been out on a date since Tanabata.

I pace the halls today and consider what's happened to my life. Is Jiro away at these meetings because he likes his work or because he doesn't want to be with me? No, don't think like this, Sanaa. If he didn't want to be with me, he never would have married me. He still comes home when I've been asleep for hours, wraps himself around me, and kisses me. There's no way he'd do that otherwise. He's always been sincere, never fake. I can trust him.

But with no one ever around, and they all know I'm here, they haven't just left me alone. They've abandoned me.

Chapter Thirty

Izakaya Tanaka doesn't open again until the first of September. It's a good thing the colonization is starting this year because the summers are getting brutal in this part of the world. I can only imagine what the weather is like on the equator where the space elevator is. Hot as hell.

Sakai and Lucy got married not long after Jiro and I did our ceremony on the top of Ku 10. They were supposed to have a party at a tempura restaurant in Ku 6, but a fire in the kitchen on one of the hottest days of the year sent the building up in flames. Over thirty people died in the fire, and we smelled smoke for a week. Instead of trying to find a new place in the dead of summer vacation, they postponed until Izakaya Tanaka reopened.

"Why bother renting out a stranger's restaurant when we have one of our own?" Sakai says, and I laugh. I guess the izakaya belongs to him now too, though it will be liquidated with all of the family assets when we leave in November.

We've celebrated Sakai and Lucy, and now the real fun begins — a night of endless drinking ahead of us. It's such a happy occasion for me. Anytime we can all get together, I try and soak in as much of everyone as possible. To top off this fabulous evening, I don't drink when I'm at home alone, so my tolerance is low again.

Sitting with Sakai at the bar, he sips on his Scotch that Miko keeps for him, and Sono dispenses with a heavy hand. I have sake.

"Can I try your Scotch?"

"Of course," he says handing me the glass. I've never had Scotch before. The sip fills my nose with alcohol, vanilla, and a hint of orange. My first instinct is to inhale when the Scotch hits my tongue, and my breath makes the flavors even more intense. With the little bit of water from the ice, it's smooth, and, well, I like it, too.

"Mmmm. I could get used to that."

"You surprise me. But you do love sake, and I've never seen you drink a sweet alcoholic beverage before. I'm not even sure you liked the wine your aunts had." I shake my head. The wine was fine, but I like the strong stuff.

"Mark, why are you the only one in your family with a Western name?"

"Ah," he says, turning his glass around a few times. "I get this question a lot, and no I'm not the only one with a Western name. I have cousins named Jon, Sara, and Gina. My mother studied theology. If she had had more children, we would have all had Western, Christian names."

"Mark is from the Bible, right?"

"Yes, have you read it?"

"No. I have no interest in religion, to be honest. I just follow the customs from my family."

I'm a science girl, and Sakai knows this.

"The Gospel according to Mark is the part of the Bible that tells the story of Jesus's life before he died. My mother loved it. I wanted to change my name when I was growing up to something more Japanese, but being Mark has served me well. As the leader of Sakai clan, I deal with more than just the Japanese every day and having a Western name that's easy to remember comes in handy. It was a good choice."

"Is that why you chose the name Sanaa for your child?"

He smiles at me. "I'm so glad you carry the name and like it. Yes, Sanaa is a name that is easily remembered and also written in katakana. If I had married Charlotte maybe my daughter would have been Sanaa Sakai. I don't know. Regardless, Sanaa Itami is also a good name."

I had always wanted to learn more about our names. I'm glad I asked even though this topic makes Sakai melancholy.

"I never want to be Sanaa Griffin again. I've avoided going to visit Aunt Sharon, because I feel like a reunion is a lost cause."

He puts his hand on my shoulder. "It may be, but I'm going to change my opinion on this and say you should go see her before you leave. You should know and understand it's not your fault they left you."

It *is* my fault, like so much of what's happened lately is. Sakai's hand is strong and warm, and I lean into him so I can force him to hug me. I need him in my life as much as I need Jiro.

"Will you do me a favor?" I ask, resting my head on his shoulder.

"Anything."

"Change my name legally, please. It would mean a lot to me if you took care of this for me."

"Sure."

"Thanks." I give him a kiss on the cheek and sit back up again.

Excusing myself from Sakai so he can sit with Mariko and Lucy, I join Jiro and Kentaro in a booth. They're talking about Risa and cursing the heat from keeping Helena's attackers indoors and undercover.

"I feel useless. I swear I've followed that stupid girl all over Ku 6, and she's done absolutely nothing except go to the damned salon." Kentaro throws back a shot of sake and slams the cup down on the table. "Do you have any idea how many massages she gets? Pampered, spoiled little rich girl."

Jiro and I burst into a laugh that causes everyone's head to spin around from the bar. Usagi sits down with us, and we all fill up our cups. Usagi has been so quiet lately, more than usual, and his somber face lacks any uplifting emotions. I dip my head a little to meet his eyes with a smile, and he smiles quickly back at me before turning his attention on Kentaro.

"I don't know what else to do for now. I guess we'll just have to wait. The weather is cooling off so I think they'll all be at it again soon, whoever they are." Kentaro turns his cup around a few times before sipping this time.

"I hate waiting," I say, sitting back and closing my eyes for a moment. I'm already drunk.

"Well, we could figure out what the hell we're going to do with Maeda," Jiro says, and I sigh, deflating into a lump. "No really. It's getting ridiculous. He's just going to keep pushing you off until we all board the ships and leave."

"What can we do? I can't force him to meet with me."

"Of course you can," Kentaro says, leaning back and propping his foot up next to him on the booth bench. "Who says you have to be proper about this? Maeda's not. He's the most improper of all the clan heads. He doesn't bank on loyalty or honor because he bases everything on money."

I blink my eyes at Kentaro. "Are you actually advising me on something, Ken-chan?"

"Isn't that what you asked me to do?" He smiles and pokes

himself in the chest. "I've got intuition, and my gut says he's waiting for you to make a decisive move."

"Like what?" Jiro sits forward, hanging on Kentaro's every word.

"Ambush him. Don't give him any reason to say no to seeing you."

"Hmmm, I like this idea a lot." Jiro sits back in his seat, crossing his arms over his chest and letting his eyes take me in from head to toe. I swear he's undressing me with his mind when he does that.

"Here you go." A plate of onigiri rice balls hits the table, and I look up at the waitress confused. "From Miko," she says, shrugging her shoulders as if she has no idea why.

I crane my head to peer past Jiro and silent Usagi, and Miko's nowhere to be seen.

"Thanks, but have you seen the big guy? Oyama?"

She shakes her head and walks away.

"I can always eat." Kentaro's hand snaps out, but I smack it away.

Where's Oyama? He's always within eyesight when I get food, even snacks, and his absence now is suspicious. And where's Miko? Since I'm so small, I get up on my knees in the booth and scan the izakaya, but the dining area is virtually empty, only a couple sitting in the front booth, a private party in the room at the back, and all of our family at the bar.

"What's wrong, Sanaa-san?" Usagi turns around as well, and when my eyes land on the waitress again, she's dropped her apron by the door and all I see is her bag as she ducks out under the noren curtains and exits the izakaya.

"Find your brother. Now." I pick up the plate, and Jiro jumps out of the booth next to me, running for the bar.

"Nobody eat anything!" Jiro grabs another plate of onigiri from the bar and pulls it away. Sakai, Mariko, and Yoichi back away quickly, and Beni drops the onigiri she had in her hand. My instincts are screaming at me something is really horribly wrong so I leave the plate with Jiro and head straight for Miko's office in the back.

Opening the door, I find Miko, passed out at her desk with a pool of vomit next to her on the floor.

Chapter Thirty-One

"Mark! Yoichi!"

Jumping over the mess on the floor, I dive straight for Miko. She's breathing, and when I shake her, she moans. Oh, thank the gods! Her restaurant terminal, where she handles all the izakaya's transactions and correspondence, is open and on, so I navigate to the home screen and tap the emergency button. Ugh, second time in one year.

"What is the nature of your emergency?" A voice comes out of the speakers.

"Medical. Poisoning."

"I'm dispatching an ambulance to your location now. Estimated time of arrival is two minutes."

"Miko!" Yoichi bolts into the office, straight over the mess, and I press myself against the wall, out of the way. This little office is too small for three people. "Is she breathing? Did you call an ambulance?"

"Yes. I think she's just sick. Let's get her out of here and out the door. The medics will arrive any minute."

Miko lifts her head a little and groans, squinting her eyes at Yoichi. "Pickles," she whispers before laying her head down again. A plate of pale yellow pickles sits next to her, several gone and one half-eaten. These are definitely not Miko's usual pickles. Hers are always bright green with pepper flakes. The pickles were probably in the onigiri, too.

Yoichi props Miko up, I duck under her arm on the other side, and we carry her out to the main restaurant as an ambulance pulls up outside. Beni takes my place as Sakai and Jiro exit the kitchen.

"Oyama was in the back store room, completely unconscious, and one of the new chefs is gone," Jiro reports, scanning the rest of the restaurant for suspicious activity. "They must have used chloroform on him and a lot too. Oyama's hard to knock out."

"I'm going to get in a taxi and follow the ambulance to Ku 2," Mariko says, grabbing her bag.

"I'll go, too." Lucy is right behind her.

"Oyama, is he going to be all right?" My heart flutters with anxiety and panic; I can barely catch my breath.

"He'll be fine. He's half-conscious now." Jiro wraps his arms around my neck and squeezes. "Good job, Sanaa. If you had just eaten those onigiri, we'd all be sick or dead right now."

Once he lets go, I pull out a chair from the table next to me and quickly sit down, putting my head between my knees. "I think I *am* going to be sick. Someone needs to clean up the mess in Miko's office."

"Don't worry. I'll take care of everything, and we'll close the place up early." Sono's hand lands on my back before I watch his shoes walk away towards the office.

"Up, Sanaa-chan. We need to act fast." Sakai grabs me under my arm and hauls me up even though I waver and my head spins. Too much stress. Too much sake.

"Okay, okay." I take a cleansing, centering breath and let it out slowly through my mouth. "That waitress has been working here since Tanabata, probably not as much in the intervening months with the weather being so hot and the place being closed."

"I thought she looked familiar, but I can't place her," Kentaro says, rubbing his chin. "I originally thought she was someone I went to school with."

"So whoever's in the business of hurting us is at it again," Sakai says, scanning the restaurant again for strangers. "They knew to infiltrate Izakaya Tanaka and have probably been planning this for months waiting for us to show up. Okay, this is what we do." He rubs his hands together, taking charge of the situation. "Usagi, you watch Risa. Kentaro, I'm going to give you the same access to video that Sanaa has. Can I trust you?"

"Yes!" His face lights up in genuine happiness. "I promise nothing we do will ever make it back to my father."

"I believe him," I say, squeezing Kentaro's arm.

"Tomorrow I'll take you to Ku 1 in the morning to get your tablet setup. You'll access the video feeds for this area and track the waitress. Sanaa and Jiro, after you're done attending to Miko and Oyama, you'll track the chef who also went missing. We'll all meet tomorrow at lunch in my apartment."

We all have our missions, and if I just concentrate on the work,

I won't be able to feel scared out of my mind.

———————————◆———————————

"I'm fine. Really. You can go home now." Miko pats my head which is resting on the edge of her bed in her apartment. She was discharged after spending only two hours at the hospital. The doctors purged her stomach and hooked her up to an IV for meds and fluids, and she improved immediately. Maybe the poison wasn't strong because these assassins wanted to weaken us before moving in for the kill.

I'm beginning to think we dodged a bigger bullet, and someone is going to be very angry about it.

"Okay." I look over at the clock. "Gods, it's 3:13am. Sorry I'm still here." But we both hear Jiro and Yoichi talking out on the couch, so it's not like I've kept them up. I squeeze Miko's foot under the covers, and she pulls them up and lies down as I head for the door.

"This is getting way too dangerous, Jiro." I stop with my hand on the doorjamb, not wanting to intrude in this conversation. Yoichi's voice is tense with anger. "I don't know what you and Mark got us into when you hooked up with Sanaa, but I can't let them hurt my wife and family. I told our father ages ago I wanted no part of this clan nonsense. Now we're right in the middle of a big mess because of her."

My heart stops and tears jump to my eyes. When I glance back at Miko, she's already asleep. No, don't cry, Sanaa. Crying makes me appear weak.

"Be careful, Yoichi. I don't like what you're implying."

"You married her against our wishes. What about our mother? And the rest of our family? Our cousins? Do they deserve the kind of danger that she puts us all in?"

This is almost exactly what Risa said and hearing the same words come out of Yoichi's mouth is even worse. I love Yoichi as much as one can love their brother-in-law and best friend's husband. What he's saying betrays my love for him and hurts so badly, his words sit in my chest like a cancerous lump. No. *I'm* a cancer that has laid dormant in this family and is unexpectedly consuming them all one by one.

The night Jiro and I married, on Tanabata, I thought everyone in this family wanted me in their lives. Now I see the real truth. I remember the way Yoichi pulled Miko towards him when I almost interrupted their lunch plans. Cautious and protective. Mariko is not the only person who regrets me being here. It's better I'm constantly in my apartment. I can only imagine what kind of damage I would do if I spent more time with them all. How will I ever make it up to them?

I force my feet to walk from the bedroom, past both silent brothers, straight to the door. "Jiro, I'm tired. Can we go home now?" I keep my eyes low and don't look at either of them as I open the door and pick up my shoes.

"Yes, of course. Let's go home and get some sleep." Jiro's hand pushes me lightly on the small of my back, and I make the three steps over to our apartment without saying good night to Yoichi.

Jiro and I remain silent while we brush our teeth, grab glasses of water, and get ready for bed, and the whole time I can't make eye contact with him. I'm so ashamed of what my presence has done to this family, to my friends.

Jiro turns out all the lights in our apartment before turning on our bedside lamp and closing the door behind him.

"He didn't mean it. He's just upset and tomorrow he'll regret saying anything."

"I don't want to talk about it." I strip down to my underwear and finally look at him. Mistake. Seeing his concern for me makes the tears come fast and furious, plopping down on our hard floor so loud I can hear them splash.

Jiro takes two swift steps and pulls my face into his hands, looking me right in the eyes. "Not your fault."

"How many times have you said that since we've met? How many more times will my very presence bring danger to your family and friends? Yoichi is right. It was all a big mistake to get hooked up with me, a mistake to marry me and be linked with me forever."

"No." He shakes his head and presses my face even more. "No. I will never feel that way. And Yoichi gets no say in the matter."

"I do nothing but bring death to your family, to your poor father." I sink down in agony, but he pulls me back up.

"This is ridiculous. Don't you remember the innocent girl you were before all of this? I do." He smiles into my teary face. "It's not as if you planned to hurt people."

"I'm as good as the harbinger of death."

"Someone as cute and wonderful as you could not be the harbinger of death. Anyway, isn't that usually a guy in a black robe with a huge sickle-like weapon?"

My sobs turn into a big guffaw of laughter, and Jiro hugs me. "No, that's the Grim Reaper. Get your facts straight."

Seriously, I have no idea how he always manages to make me laugh and cry at the same time. It's a gift.

All of my protests die in his arms. Who's to say that if I left them now they would be safe? The damage is done. It's beyond done.

Jiro's head relaxes, and he breathes into my neck, his arms in a vise grip around my shoulders.

"Jiro, the only way I can live with myself now and know I've done my best to protect you all is to do everything I can to stop them from hurting us again."

He squeezes me and picks me up off the ground. "That's my girl."

Chapter Thirty-Two

My mind and body wake of their own accord at 9am. Five hours of sleep is not enough to accomplish the kinds of things I have to do today, but it'll have to do. Jiro is still asleep, and for once, not attached to me like a barnacle so I get up to take a shower. The temperature is exceptionally warm in our apartment so I make the shower cold and laugh through half of it, dancing back and forth over the drain and washing my hair and face as fast as I can. The water's not frigid like in winter, but it's cool enough to be bracing.

I stand in front of the mirror for several minutes. My face is getting angular again, like it was at the house in the desert. Stress knots up my stomach and makes it impossible to eat most days, and I find when I'm alone, I don't eat as much as I do when I'm with other people. Somedays I will forget to eat at all. Dark circles hang under my eyes, and my eyelids are swollen from crying last night. My hair is growing out and getting shaggy, the red faded to burnt orange. I want my long hair back. I miss it. I really do.

That's it. I've decided I'm not going to get my hair cut again, but I will re-dye the patch red until we leave. I'll have to do something with this style in the meantime so I put hair goop in while my hair is still wet and make it messy, on purpose. Ugh. I do not look feminine or attractive at all. Forgetting the messy look, I finger-comb it back to a style less insane and blow dry my bangs flat, clipping them with a hair pin. That's better. Now I look like a girl.

Jiro's up and making the coffee and tea I was just about to get to, so I dress in Nishikyō grays and join him in the kitchen when the door chimes.

It's Oyama, bent at the waist, his hands by his side.

"I've come to offer my resignation. My inattention to my surroundings led to Miko's poisoning. I have completely let you down —"

"Oyama, stop and come in, please." He stands immobile, and I sigh. "Please. I don't want to have this conversation in the hall. You are not quitting. I will not allow it. Your absence yesterday was the trigger in my brain that something was wrong. You taught me well. There's a reason why you're in my life, and you can't quit. I will certainly die if you do."

"Sanaa-san —"

"I hope you brought breakfast. Jiro and I got less than five hours sleep, and if I turn on the stove, I'm going to burn the place down."

"I... I did. A peace offering?" He kicks off his shoes and shuts the door behind him.

"Trust me. You're not the one I'm angry with right now." My sadness at Yoichi for betraying my love and devotion to this family has turned to dark, smoldering anger this morning.

Oyama glances past me to Jiro, and Jiro shakes his head. "Not me, thankfully."

"Anyway," he says, lifting the bag next to him. "Here. I made a lot. I heard someone in the shower a while ago and got these on the griddle right away."

Griddle! I open the box on the kitchen table and inside lies giant stacks of chocolate chip pancakes. I nearly cry from joy. Coffee and chocolate chip pancakes are just what I need.

The door chimes again, and this time Kentaro is waiting when I open the door. Now, I'm giddy with joy. I wish I had this much traffic in our apartment every day.

"Hey, we need to talk," he says with no other preamble and comes straight in. Miko and Yoichi's door opens behind Kentaro, and my eyes meet Yoichi's.

"Sanaa, I'm so sorry —" He starts, but I shoot my hand up, halting any easy apologies.

"Don't talk to me for at least twenty-four hours." I shut the door on him as he's about to say something else and stalk back to the table. "Pancakes. Please." I bite off each word, clip them short so they're barely P's. Kentaro's eyes skip from me to the door to Jiro. Jiro shakes his head and makes a cutting gesture across his throat while mouthing, "Don't ask."

I plate my pancakes and sit down at the table with some coffee. Wasting no time, I eat one after another until I feel the rush of sugar and caffeine start to take ahold of me. When I look up, all of the boys are frozen watching me. They've barely eaten, and I've finished half a stack. The tables are turned today.

"Can we talk?" Kentaro asks, sitting across from me.

"Of course. Did you get any sleep last night?"

"None. I just came from tailing the waitress and Risa all night with Usagi. When you left to go to the hospital, Sakai took out his tablet, and we sat down to see if we could figure out what's going on. We tracked the waitress and Risa to an alley in my family's territory behind an udon restaurant, one I'm quite familiar with as it belongs to distant cousins of mine. Here. Give me your tablet, and I'll show you what we found. Sakai-san showed me how to do all of this."

He takes my tablet, taps parameters into the GDB surveillance feeds, and we sit and wait. "Yes! This is it. No audio, as you know."

The camera is pointed on a back alley behind a restaurant, boxes and trash bags stacked next to a door for incoming produce. From one direction comes Risa and looking at the time code, it wasn't long after we called the ambulance all the way in Ku 7.

"She waits here for fifteen minutes before the waitress finally shows up. She left the izakaya and took a circuitous route through the neighborhood before getting on the transitway."

Kentaro scrubs the video forward, and the waitress appears. The two talk for a moment, both becoming more animated as the conversation heats up. Risa is pissed. She's balling her hands into fists and running her fingers through her hair. I blink, and they're fighting with each other.

"Whoa!" Jiro says and laughs. "She's a horrible fighter." He shakes his head and smiles. He's right. Risa's smacking at this woman, and the woman blocks her every move until she grabs Risa's hand and twists her arm behind her back. "That'll teach her." Jiro nods, satisfied.

"Then..." Kentaro points at the screen. A man joins both women. The camera angle is the same from the cafe when Helena was poisoned, and I'm sure this is the same man who spiked her coffee. I can tell from the long slant of his forehead and nose, the edge of his jaw. All things I can see from above. He breaks up the two girls and yells at the waitress before she stalks off. Risa turns to him, and they're yelling at each other too, but he backs her to the wall, pins her there with one hand, and kisses her.

"Ew!" We all say at the same time.

"Disgusting." Jiro puts down his pancakes.

"Revolting." Kentaro closes his eyes.

Oyama doesn't say anything but shakes his head.

As horrified as I am watching Risa and this guy make out, I'm thinking about how I can use this information to our advantage. "I need more pancakes if I'm going to watch any more of this."

Kentaro turns off the tablet and sighs. "It goes on like that for a little while and then they go their separate ways. The waitress went to an apartment in Ku 6, Risa goes out drinking till the wee hours, and the man... I don't know where he went. Sakai said he'd track him. I sent Usagi to bed at 5:00 and was watching both the waitress's apartment and Risa's new place — she has an apartment now in the same building as her parents — until twenty minutes ago. I'm handing off the jobs to you two so I can get some sleep. Still haven't found the temporary chef who drugged Oyama." Kentaro nods at Oyama and he nods back. "You all right?"

"I'm fine, thank you. Back on the job."

"Excellent. Thanks for the pancakes. Come and get me later but not before 3:00pm. I'm going with Sakai-san at 2:00pm to Ku 1, and I'll be back after. No lunch at his place today. He'll send a message with more news later." Kentaro waves and lets himself out.

The sugar and caffeine are not doing enough for me, and my eyes keep drooping.

"Go back to bed. I'll watch the feeds and catch up on correspondence." Jiro smiles down at me, and I rest my head against his stomach.

"I don't want to leave you with all the work, and I bet you're pretty tired, too." I'm also happy to have him home and not at meetings. I want to spend every minute I can with him, but I can't keep my eyes open.

"I can live for days on no sleep. This is nothing. Go. And don't set an alarm."

I'm too weak and tired to argue, so I go, but only after I eat another bite of pancakes.

Chapter Thirty-Three

Jiro wakes me up at 3:00pm and waves a cup of coffee under my nose.

"I tried waking you up around noon, and I actually thought you might be dead because you just wouldn't budge. But you were still breathing, so..."

I sit up in bed and blink the sleep from my eyes. Jiro sits next to me on the bed, his hand on my leg.

"Are you hungry? I have rice in the cooker, and Oyama dropped off teriyaki vegetables."

"Yes. The pancakes were good, but I need some real food in me," I say, taking the mug and yawning before sipping.

"I talked to Yoichi while you were sleeping. Supposedly, Miko yelled at him for an hour this morning. I know you heard everything he said last night, and I'm sorry. That must have hurt."

I nod my head and look down into my coffee. More than he'll ever know.

"He wasn't kidding when he said he wanted nothing to do with the family business. You remember when you found out about who you are, he was just as clueless as we were and still never got involved with anything after. I haven't been forthcoming with him regarding your past because you're so private. I figured you'd tell him when you're ready."

I love that Jiro doesn't go around blabbing to everyone about my broken family and how they won't associate with me anymore. He understands it's something I keep held tight to my chest.

I've never opened up to Yoichi. We've only been friendly to each other. I love him, but I don't confide in him. We talk of everyday things, Miko, the business, starting a family, but I don't reveal my hopes, fears, and secrets like I do to others. Arms length. And why? Because he's never shown interest in those things, and Jiro's right. I'm private and don't like confiding in people if they're not genuinely interested in me.

"I can't go through life with your brother hating me and thinking I brought destruction on your family. Especially if he's married to one of my best friends in the whole world."

"He doesn't hate you..."

"Oh gods, I just realized Miko is my only best girl friend in the whole world. Helena is gone, and I'm not sure if I'll ever see her again." Damn, I'm crying, right into my coffee, and Jiro squeezes my foot again. "Jiro, you're my best friend, too. I don't know what I'd do without you."

Leaning forward, Jiro takes my mug away and holds my left hand, playing with the ring he put there only eight weeks ago.

"I don't think I realized just how important a person you'd be in my life when I put this ring on your finger. You know how much my family means to me, but I would shun them all if they hated you."

"You would?" I'm surprised. His family means everything to him, and now I'm doubly afraid to say anything about the way his mother treats me. I still think he has no idea, and if I told him now, their relationship may be ruined for a long time. I can't be responsible for that, too.

"You're the most important part of my family. I want to spend the rest of my life with you, have kids, and be together till we're old. You're the best thing that's ever happened to me. I found love and a purpose in life all because of you." He cocks a lopsided grin and looks down at my hand again. "Sorry. I sound terribly sappy and romantic for a twenty-two-year-old boy."

"Your mother and father were married at our age. I think your mother was pregnant with Yoichi when she was twenty." He nods. We're all so young, but our responsibilities make us ancient. "I love that you're terribly sappy and romantic. And kind and loving. And strong and forceful. And commanding and sexy." Our eyes meet, and his are eager and excited. It makes me laugh. "They're all the things that make you you."

"Don't worry about Yoichi. He feels horrible. He didn't understand, and now he does. I'm sure he'll apologize." He kisses my hand and stands up from the bed. "I hear from Usagi the dōjō is back to normal temps. Let's go for a little while. The people we're watching are sleeping and eating the day away. We'll come back to them later."

The mats squeak under my feet as I run back to the center and wait for the men. Kentaro, Jiro, and I have been pummeling each other for a solid hour already, laughing, striking, and lobbing challenges at each other. It's great to be back in the dōjō again. I've missed my regular workouts and the routine of seeing Jiro and Kentaro all the time.

"Come on, Sanaa. Come and get me."

Jiro taunts me, and I laugh, laugh off the stress, the anxiety, the tension that's been building between my shoulders, a knot the size of my fist. Kentaro is laughing, too. He gets a kick out of watching us fight one another especially when we're like this.

But I have my wooden sword out in front of me, my grip is loose, my body is warmed up, and all I can think about is the last moment when I looked into Helena's eyes.

"Mmmm, Jiro. Look at you talking dirty in front of Ken-chan."

I lunge at him with a stab to his upper chest. He blocks me but I circle around and cut at his shoulder. Jiro is so fast. I don't think I've ever seen him slow down, and I've never truly beat him in one of our sparring matches. It's the best exercise around. My heart pounds. My vision is focused. Sweat is pouring off my face.

Jiro's eyes flick to my left, and I back away quickly before Kentaro can come at me.

"You guys are sick, you know that?"

Kentaro has been working on my offense and defense. When I fight with the staff, he teaches me how to disarm Jiro fighting me with the sword. Then at times like this, when I fight with the sword, he teaches me how to hold onto my sword when someone tries to disarm me with the staff. He's a fantastic fighter.

"Kentaro, you love it, and you know it."

He tries to wedge his staff in between my arms and force me to drop my sword, but instead I step forward and purposely let my right hand come off the sword and swipe down with my left. He jumps out of the way, and I do something I've never done before. I reach out with my right hand, grab the staff, and yank with all my might. Kentaro flies forward, knocks into Jiro, and they both go sprawling to the ground.

Before they can get up, I quickly sit my butt down directly on Jiro's chest and poke Kentaro in the side with my sword.

"I win. And you thought I couldn't fight. Little ol' me."

Kentaro laughs. "I'll admit you can fight. You can climb. You can drink. And, you can charm the pants off my mother."

Jiro laughs underneath me, and my whole body shakes. He could easily lift me up and remove me, but his head is laid back, and his hand traces the bones in my foot.

"She can't wait for you to come to Shōfū-an again."

"We should all go soon, but I think it's time I took your advice, Ken-chan. How do you feel about a little gambling tomorrow night?"

"Perfect. An excellent idea."

"Great. We'll spread the word. Seven o'clock tomorrow."

"I'm going to go get cleaned up in the bathroom. I'm meeting Kevin in an hour back in Ku 4."

Kentaro gets up to leave, and I watch him exit the dōjō, rubbing my sweaty face and hair until it all stands straight up. Looking down at Jiro's chest under me, I can't help but smile. I love seeing him like this. I love being active. I love being with people, especially Jiro.

"What are you smiling at?"

"I was just thinking of something I haven't done in a long time." I shift my weight and bring my legs down on either side of his body. "In fact, I think it has been a *very* long time since I pinned you down and had my way with you."

"Mmmm, a little role reversal? But what about?" He jerks his head at the cameras, and I lean over and graze my lips against his ear.

"I think I can forget about them for once." I laugh and wink at him, and his face lights up with excitement. I kiss him right here on the mats in front of everyone to see. Well, everyone who reviews the video from these cameras.

And Kentaro.

"Ahem, I came back for an extra towel," he says, quickly walking past us on the mats to the towel rack, but Jiro and I don't stop. "Oh well, um. Carry on."

He didn't kick us or tell us we're disgusting! We've won him over for good.

Chapter Thirty-Four

I told everyone to make plans for a night out at the casino, and I mean everyone. I have called in Miko and Yoichi, Sakai and Lucy, Mariko and Beni, Kentaro, Oyama, Usagi, and Jiro to come and support me. If anything, we'll all have a great time. The casino can provide endless hours of entertainment, and Miko and Helena were both jealous of the boys going before the wedding. I just wish Helena were here to enjoy the festivities.

We all dress up except this time, I leave the yukata behind and slip on a little black dress I've had stashed away in the back of the closet. There's nothing better than a little black dress that fits perfectly in all the right places. This is one I picked up while shopping with Miko two years ago, when I still had hopes of dating after Joshua and I broke up, though I never wore it. The black dress is sleeveless and short and has a cowl-like collar that gathers high up around the back of my neck but dips down low up front. The cut is a tad scandalous, especially since I don't wear a bra and everyone will be able to tell. I lack a curvy body or cleavage to show off, but my legs and arms are pretty hot. All of the hard work I put in at the dōjō has paid off. I even have a pair of black high heels I can wear and not fall out of. Being short makes it easy to walk around in such contraptions.

When I come out of the bedroom all dressed, Jiro shakes his head.

"No way, love. That right there is worse than the sex pants."

"Stop. It is not."

"It is so, and oh gods, I'm going to be pushing the men off of you all night." He narrows his eyes and crosses his arms. Possessive Jiro is not having any of this.

I roll my eyes at him. "Please. I'm a married woman now. They'll take one look at the ring and know I can't be swayed by their masculine charm."

He bobs his head back and forth. I love this gesture of his. I always know when I've hit on something he agrees with when his head makes this movement. "This is true. Another thing those rings are good for."

"Besides, you wanted to show me off." I turn slowly and glance over my shoulder with my back to him.

I don't think I've ever seen Jiro so speechless, so... I don't know. He's happy, sad, lustful, and shy all at once.

"Sanaa, I'm gonna love spending the rest of my life with you."

Maybe he's a little lovesick. I'll have to remember this look on his face so I can identify it later.

"Well, you're stuck with me now, because I'm not going anywhere." Smiling, I step up to him and open his hand, dropping my bracelet onto his palm. "Will you?"

"This is pretty. I don't think I've ever seen you wear it."

This simple silver bracelet is a series of interlocking chains with a fish charm hanging from the clasp. Fish seem to be a recurring theme in my life.

"I haven't. I always forget about it since I can't wear it to the dōjō and don't go out much. It was my mother's, of course."

Jiro secures the bracelet to my right wrist. He's wearing a white button down shirt with gray vertical stripes, casually untucked, and dark tight pants.

"You're pretty handsome yourself, Jiro Itō." Running my hand down his crisp, clean shirt, I tug the hem and then reach around him, slipping my fingers into his back pocket.

A rumbling purr emanates from deep down in his chest, and he stops breathing for a moment. He's had a chance to look down into my dress and notice I'm not wearing any underwear. "Let's go before I make you take off the dress, and we get delayed by at least an hour."

We meet everyone downstairs, and they're all ready for a night on the town. Perfect.

Noboru Maeda owns several casinos in both Ku 6 and Ku 7 but his main casino where he brings in the most business is in Ku 6. He is a man of habit. Every morning, he wakes up in his penthouse apartment, dresses, and then has breakfast in the restaurant of his building. After breakfast, he travels by car to his two casinos in Ku 7, goes over the take from the night before, tours the floor, meets new employees, talks to old ones, shakes a few hands, and leaves.

He's back in Ku 6 by lunch time and has a meal at his biggest casino, Akaboshi, with his main floor manager where they talk business. He then spends two hours in his office going over the books and meeting with the managers of the love hotels he runs. Not everything he does is above the table and legal. The love hotels would be perfectly fine if it weren't for the prostitution that takes place in and out of them.

Just like the time Jiro took the boys to Akaboshi for Yoichi's bachelor night, Maeda will be here tonight. He rarely travels to any of his other casinos in the evening unless a problem occurs at one of them. I made sure this visit was going to be a complete surprise for Maeda. Jiro didn't tell him we were coming ahead of time and none of us talked about our plans out in the open.

There are a few things I need to remember about Maeda. Though he is married and has two daughters, he is a ladies' man. He likes bright and beautiful women, and the younger the better. He appreciates the old ways of Japan, but ultimately, he is more Western at heart. He believes in capitalism and money, and the allure of a successful business venture is more enticing than honor.

So even though I pissed him off by making him bow to me the first time we met, I can salvage this relationship by smiling, being pretty and cute, and showing interest in his business. I plan on doing all of these things. I warned Jiro before we left that I was going to mercilessly flirt with Maeda, and he shook his head and said, "That poor man."

We're two blocks away from the casino, and Jiro and I are in front with everyone behind us. Akaboshi means "red star" in Japanese, and hanging over the posh and opulent entrance to Maeda's grand casino is a giant red star surrounded on both sides by white paper lanterns. The entrance is busy with people coming and going or waiting for taxis on the sidewalk outside. I can already hear the electronic noise of slot machines, and the clamor brings a smile to my face. This is going to be fun, and I'm already completely high on the excitement of being out with everyone.

The time has come to ramp up my personality and pour on the sex. Instead of walking in my usual stride, I make sure to put some sway in my step and let my backside be the major attraction. Jiro catches sight of it right away, and I can tell he wants me to stop, but he doesn't say anything. We're in public now, and I'm in charge. It's a tacit agreement we have, though I should be careful not to push him too hard. I glance back at Sakai behind me, and he is actually checking out my ass. Lucy reaches up to put her hand over his eyes.

"I think Mark's in trouble," I whisper to Jiro.

"I think we're all in trouble tonight. You even turned on Kentaro when you were walking down the stairs."

Good. Kentaro's a tough crowd. I'm sure to win this night. Just remember, Sanaa: you're in it to win it.

Jiro opens the door, we walk in, and immediately we're noticed. I bet Maeda's people saw us coming two blocks away. To think that my night out in my little black dress, all sexed up to catch a clan leader, will be immortalized on video forever so, generations from now, people can witness the last living empress in this situation is humbling. I can only imagine what my grandchildren are going to think. I better do an extremely good job tonight.

Three men scurry to a stop in front of us, and I wait while they line up and bow.

"Itami-sama, Maeda-san is pleased you would come and visit him at Akaboshi this evening," the man in the center says as he comes up from his bow. I know from my time in 3B that this man is the general manager of the casino, Ian Kondo. He's half-Japanese, much like me, but his other half is South African. He reports directly to Maeda.

"Please give our apologies to Maeda-san for not calling ahead, but we had a free night and decided it would be best spent here. I have brought all of my family and friends." I turn to smile at them all, and they smile back. "Will you please be sure they are well taken care of, Kondo-san?"

"Yes, absolutely," he says bowing again. "My staff will have their gambling cards prepared immediately." He turns and snaps his fingers and several other men join us to escort away Usagi, Kentaro, Mariko, Beni, Yoichi, and Miko. I wave to them as they head off. They'll have their hands scanned, money added to their gambling cards, and be off and having fun in no time. Meanwhile, Jiro, Sakai, Lucy, Oyama, and I will go on to meet with Maeda.

"Please follow me."

We're led across the casino floor past slot machines, card tables, roulette and craps tables. Two restaurants along the way are brimming with people, and a hallway between them leads to the main offices. We pass blackjack tables full of gamblers with others standing and watching. It looks like a lot of fun especially when someone wins big and everyone cheers.

Close to the back of the casino, we skirt around a bar, and a man in a suit tries to approach me. He has a drunken smile plastered on and a martini in his hand. Jiro sighs next to me. He puts his hand in front of me and says, "No. I don't think so," to the man. One of the casino security guards intervenes and escorts him off as Sakai laughs behind us.

"See? I told you," Jiro says, leaning into my ear.

"I swear I had no idea I was such a man magnet though I admit to the dress being pretty sexy."

"The dress is beyond sexy. You have no idea what it's doing to me."

"I'd like to find out later."

"Sanaa, that is inevitable."

"Itami-sama!"

Maeda is finally right in front of me with a grin and his arms open. He's another one of these big and boisterous men who prefers to rule by harsh glare and sheer force of size. I'm sure with a scowl on his face he's quite intimidating, and underneath his expensive dark gray suit, he is covered in yakuza tattoos. But when he smiles like he is now, he has a boyish charm about him that, yeah, is pretty attractive. I can see why women like him other than the fact that he has a lot of money and a whole lot of influence.

"I'm so glad you and your family were able to spend the evening in my establishment." We've made our way to the private lounge at the back of the casino, and he has cleared out half of the area for us. I don't recognize the people in the other half of the lounge, but a few of them nod to me and Jiro, and he smiles and nods back, a product (no doubt) of all the evenings he's spent away from me.

"Maeda-san, I'm sorry I wasn't able to come sooner." Might as well get the formal apologies out of the way as soon as possible. "I have been meaning to come since Jiro was here last, but the summer just slipped by."

I incline my body the smallest amount in a bow. Really, I would bow lower if I weren't wearing this dress. I don't mind showing Maeda more respect than he deserves since the rewards from such actions are usually paid back in full.

"Itami-sama, you should not be apologizing to me," he says surprised. "I'm the rude one for not having invited you sooner. Had

I known you'd be interested in coming, I would have arranged for this immediately after our first meeting."

"I'm glad to be here now." As I suspected, he has no idea the kind of woman I am despite his conversation with Jiro. You're in for a treat, Maeda!

"Please sit. Can I get you refreshments?" He gestures to a waiter who is standing by for orders.

Several modern, black velvet couches with arm chairs and tables between them sit empty in front of us. Jiro, with his hand on my lower back, guides me to sit on the couch with him next to me.

"Maeda-san, perhaps you've met my dokumiyaku, Oyama-san. He will be more than happy to supervise my drinks and food this evening."

Oyama bows to Maeda, and Maeda pauses a moment before responding. "Of course. I completely understand."

He's probably already aware of Helena's poisoning and the incident only a few nights ago. Maeda has ears everywhere.

Sakai and Lucy sit down in the armchairs across from Jiro and me, and Maeda takes a seat on an end armchair between us all. I place my bag on the table next to me and smile up at Oyama.

"I'd like Scotch, whatever Sakai-san usually drinks."

"Fifteen-year or better," Sakai says, "and another for me. Lucy likes a vodka martini with a twist." Lucy smiles, her eyes sliding to the side at Sakai. I wonder how often he orders for her.

Jiro raises his eyebrows at me. "Hmmm, Scotch? Oyama, I'll have bourbon. You know how I like it."

Oyama bows to us and then steps up to the bar and supervises our drinks.

I said this dress was short, and I was not kidding. Sitting down, I'm showing an unbelievable amount of leg, and Maeda seems to approve. His glance has made its way to my thighs twice already. I cross my ankles and let my knees shift to one side. I can be sexy but ladylike.

"Jiro tells me he had a fantastic time here in June. My guess is he'll want to play poker tonight as well."

"Most likely," Jiro says with a smile. "Especially if Sakai-san is going to join us. I haven't played against him in ages."

"It's true. It's been at least a year since we've played Jiro. Don't count Lucy out, though. She has an amazing poker face."

"I believe that," Maeda says with a laugh. "I've sat across the table from you in more than one governmental meeting to know you don't give anything away. Very well, very well. I'll have a private room prepared for you all."

"I'm sure I'd like to learn to play, Jiro." I take my Scotch from Oyama as he hands each of us a glass. "But I also want to see everything else here." I nod to Maeda. "I have a terrible poker face, and they all know it."

Turning to Jiro, Sakai, and Lucy, I raise my glass. "Kanpai!" We all drink. Mmmm, Scotch is delicious.

While we have our drinks, I make small talk with Maeda since I've learned it's never appropriate to jump right into business unless I'm speaking with family. I'm getting better at this having spent more time in Ku 6 and practiced with everyone from the grocer across the street to the man I've hired to restore the royal kimonos. I like to pick out a few topics ahead of time and make my way through them before getting down to my real motives for our conversation. I ask Maeda about his wife and daughters and how his casinos fared during the earthquake. But I can tell his time is limited so once these two subjects are exhausted, Jiro steps in.

"When I was here last you and I talked about your plans for Yūsei. Have you secured all of your permits?"

Jiro reclines in the couch and puts his hand on my back. I smile at Maeda when he looks down and realizes Jiro and I are wearing matching wedding bands. This news has been slow to reach him apparently.

"I have secured the majority of them. All of my permits for second wave are done but none of the first wave permits. My equipment, employees, and family are ready to go for first wave, we're just waiting on this matter."

Looking over at Lucy, she nods her head at me while sipping on her martini.

"I'm sure this must have been an oversight in the committee," I say, setting my drink down on the table next to me. "Your businesses on Yūsei are important to the fabric of our colonization. I'll look into this personally and make sure you receive those permits as soon as possible."

Maeda sits in stunned silence for a moment. Looks like I came in here and turned his night, and his view of me, upside down.

"That is certainly very generous and not what I expected of this visit."

"I know we got off on the wrong foot, Maeda-san. And you don't know me very well, but I am completely capable of having a good time."

I smile at him, and he smiles back, but his eyes crinkle around the edges. I get the feeling he is cursing the people who gave him false information about me.

"I see nothing wrong with casinos, bars, restaurants, or love hotels as long as you operate within the law, which you do." This is a little white lie, but I'm going to gloss over it. "It's quite possible you got the impression from someone I would never be interested in your businesses and that couldn't be further from the truth. In fact, we've come here tonight to have a good time, and I don't want to keep you from your duties."

Jiro stands up, and I take his hand and stand. Maeda hesitates, blinking his eyes a few times, before standing as well.

"I'm sorry it's taken me this long to come here and tell you these things in person. I should have come sooner. We will get you those permits, and your businesses will be just as profitable on Yūsei as they are here. I'm sure moving to an open-air environment will not keep people from gambling and having a good time."

I hold my right hand out to him, hoping he'll take it and we'll shake on the matter. But instead, he takes my hand, lifts it, and kisses it. Jiro steps forward, but I squeeze his arm tight with my left hand. It's okay, Jiro. He's not going to bite.

"Itami-sama, please sit and enjoy your drinks. My floor manager will be back soon to set up your private poker room and gambling cards. All your food and drinks are on the house tonight."

"Arigatō gozaimasu. We will see you again before the night is through."

He bows to us and leaves.

I sit back down with Jiro and sip on my Scotch, and we don't say anything for a minute.

"Jiro, let me try your bourbon."

Sakai lets out a large laugh as Jiro hands me his glass.

I take a sip and roll the liquid around my mouth, and it has the same feel Scotch does but the taste is smokier. "Mmmm, I like bourbon, too. This may be a hard habit to break."

"Your next drink should be a Manhattan. I think you'll enjoy it," Jiro says as I hand back his glass.

"Sanaa, I actually think you're better cut out to do this job than your mother was," Sakai says, setting his empty glass down. "Not only was she not a big drinker but she also did not approve of gambling."

"Nor did she approve of the swords or the fighting, am I right?"

"You are."

"I have a feeling this information was relayed to Maeda via Matsuda and Miura. That I am just like my mother, and that since she would never approve of these things, neither would I. I've just fixed that. To be honest, I'm not much of a gambling woman. I think maybe I just need to find the right game to play."

"Uh, I think you already found the right game to play, and you're incredibly good at it." Lucy straightens out the hem of her dark green dress. The color goes nicely with her eyes. "You knew exactly what he wanted when you walked in here tonight, and you gave it to him *and* made him think he didn't have to do anything for it."

"Yes, well, the illusion of getting my support for free is just that, an illusion. There are no free handouts." I recross my ankles and shift my legs closer to Jiro, placing my hand on his knee.

"The dress was a good choice."

"Thank you, Lucy. I know Jiro likes it."

Jiro chuckles. "Evil." He sighs. By wielding my power just now I have completely turned him on. It'll be a miracle if we make it past midnight without tearing each other's clothes off.

"We should eat some food and have more drinks before getting on with the night." I motion to Oyama from across the room, and he smiles and nods at me. Even Oyama approves. I am definitely winning it, but my night is far from over.

Chapter Thirty-Five

Jiro and I break off from Sakai and Lucy, and he takes me around to all the areas of the casino. I'm careful to watch each area I'm introduced to so I can get an idea for what's most profitable, but on a night like tonight, when it seems everyone is out gambling, it's hard to tell. As I suspected, I'm not at all interested in getting involved myself though I have plenty of money to gamble with. Then we happen upon Miko playing roulette, and I'm sucked in. Badly. I thought I might like card games that rely on skill, but no, games of chance are more my speed.

We play for an hour straight with Jiro, Yoichi, and Usagi standing behind us. Yoichi and I still haven't spoken, but I'm sure to turn and smile at him, letting him know that I'm not mad anymore.

When our time is up, we leave the roulette table reluctantly, pick up Kentaro playing craps, Beni playing slots, Mariko, Lucy, and Sakai all having drinks at the bar, and head to the restaurant for dinner. Waitstaff are already serving salads and glasses of wine. Oyama hand-delivers my food and sits at the other end of the table from me so he can watch anyone who approaches. I skip dessert but steal chocolate cake off of Jiro's plate.

"Turnabout is fair play." I wink at him when he laughs.

"I'll make you pay for it later."

"Mmmm, then I'll have more, please." And I take what's left on his plate with a smile. Miko laughs next to me, but I can't look at her without a blush forming.

After dinner, it's poker playing time, and everyone files into the private room Maeda had set aside for us, but as we're approaching the door, Yoichi lightly brushes my arm.

"Sit with me at the bar for a minute?"

Behind him, Jiro nods at me eagerly. It's not really the time for apologies, but I've had a lot to drink, and I'm feeling sappy. I let Yoichi lead me away, and Jiro whispers to Sakai then sits on the opposite end of the bar.

Perching myself on a bar stool, I'm two meters tall, and with the Scotch and wine in me, I giggle as I try to not fall off. I'm a happy drunk.

"I don't know where to start..."

"It's okay. If I were you, I don't think I'd be happy with me either. I'm sorry about Miko and all the upheaval in your family the past couple of months."

"It's not your fault," he says, and I laugh. I swear he sounds exactly like Jiro.

"Yoichi, it's sweet you and Jiro and everyone else want to make me feel better about my circumstances. It's not something I planned or wanted to happen." I reach over and take his hand. He's a lot like Jiro, and holding his hand, I can see why he was a good sword fighter before he gave it up. "I come from a broken family. My aunts are my only saving grace. I grew up without a mother or father, removed from my culture, and shunned by my father's side. I won't say I had a sad childhood or anything — I was still pretty happy — but I didn't have what you have, what Jiro has."

It hurts physically, a punch in the stomach, to say these things out loud, to admit my family is damaged beyond repair. Thankfully the amount of alcohol I've consumed tonight is deadening the pain somewhat.

"Did you mean what you said, about Jiro marrying me against your wishes?" Yoichi closes his eyes and nods. Well, at least he's honest. "I understand. Jiro does what he wants, and that's another reason why I love him so much."

"I'm sorry about what I said the other night. Really, really sorry," Yoichi says, squeezing my hand.

He seems sincere, I think. I hope.

"Thanks. I understand how you feel. Please just know if other things happen, I don't mean them to. I would never deliberately hurt any of you. I'd rather give up my life."

I pick up my drink to sip, and the man who approached me earlier is eyeing me from across the bar, only a few people away. He's serious before cocking a smile in my direction, playful and flirtatious. I wiggle my left hand with the drink at him, the diamonds on my ring finger catching the light. He shrugs his shoulders sadly and walks off to the blackjack tables. When I look down the bar past Yoichi, Jiro watches the man leave, his eyes cold and hard.

"Sanaa, despite my earlier misgivings, I'm glad you and my brother are together. I think you're good for each other. I hope I didn't ruin our relationship."

"Help me down from here, please, before I fall off." Once my feet are on the floor, I reach up and give him a kiss on the cheek. He's a centimeter or two taller than Jiro, and even in these heels, I'm miniscule. "Our relationship is fine, but I'd like it to be better. Let's spend more time together? I'm in the building all the time and would love to hang out."

"I'd like that."

We walk back to the poker room together with Jiro right behind us.

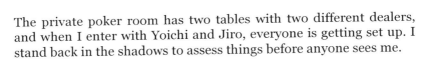

The private poker room has two tables with two different dealers, and when I enter with Yoichi and Jiro, everyone is getting set up. I stand back in the shadows to assess things before anyone sees me.

Miko and Mariko are off to the side of the tables, talking low, their heads tilted towards one another. They both laugh and smile, Miko's eyes shine happily, and Mariko reaches over to her hair and smooths out a piece that has flown away. Such a sweet, kind gesture, my chest constricts. Mariko touched me the one time when I came back from the desert months ago. Since then, I've been frozen out, never given even an ounce of this warmth. Before Miko leaves, Mariko kisses her on the cheek, and I have to look away. Look anywhere else, Sanaa.

Miko sees me, smiles, and comes straight to me. Smile, Sanaa. Put on the mask.

"Are you and Yoichi all right?" she asks, her hand stroking my shoulder before squeezing.

"We're fine. Thanks." I nod and continue smiling though I'm aware I'm not showing happiness in my eyes. They're the hardest part of my body to trick. "You and Mariko are close."

Shit. Why did I say anything? What is wrong with me? I've had too much to drink.

"Of course we are!" Miko says with a laugh while going through her purse. "She is my mother-in-law, after all."

My feet won't sit still even in these heels, and when Miko looks up, her smile is gone. Her eyebrows knit together, and I have to direct my eyes at my feet that are tapping away.

"But you're close with Mariko too, right?"

Clearing my throat, I try to make light of this situation. "Not especially... not like that." I wave my hand at where they were, and Miko's head turns to the empty space she just came from.

"But your families were so close. I thought..." Miko is prompting me to agree with her, but I can't lie about this when asked so directly. I can only shake my head.

"Sanaa-chan..."

"Anyway, are you not playing poker?"

"Sanaa-chan..." she says more forcefully.

I sigh and deflate, pulling her closer to me. "I think... I think she hates me, but I must be blowing things out of proportion."

"Have you discussed this with Jiro?" Miko asks, her voice colored in shock.

I shake my head at her. "I mentioned this months ago, when I was still in the desert, and he told me I was crazy. Jiro and Beni both believe she loves me, so I must be reading her wrong."

"I don't know. You're so good at reading people lately. Maybe she's upset you never come out with us for the family dinners?"

"What? What family dinners?" I whip my head around to see if anyone is listening, and the room swims. The alcohol in my system is running my paranoia to extremes. Usagi starts across the room towards us.

"She said you were busy." Miko grasps my upper arm, looking directly into my eyes.

"I don't know what you're talking about." I want to take this discussion to the ladies' room, but Usagi is next to Miko with a smile.

"Shall I take you to the roulette table on my way out to play craps with Kentaro?"

Miko nods, Usagi leaves to get Kentaro, and I can do nothing but stand in shock. What's going on in the family behind my back? I shake my head and steel my emotions that are threatening to churn with all the alcohol I've consumed tonight. Miko, please change the subject. Fast.

"Won't you come with me? You were having fun earlier." Miko drops her betting card in her purse and snaps the clasp shut.

"I'd love to, but duty calls. Maeda will be back soon, and I have to be charming and flattering once more."

"I didn't know you could flirt like that. Jiro's been ready to take you home all night. I'm surprised he let you leave Sakai building."

Across the room, Jiro is talking to Oyama but watching us at the same time.

"I'm teasing him on purpose."

"The sexual tension is palpable." She fans herself with her hand for a moment before winking at me.

"Go have fun, Miko."

"I wish you could have more fun," she says, smiling sadly at me. "This all seems less than fair."

"Those days are over, but I have to do something for entertainment, so I torture Jiro when I can. It's the least I can do." Because my public persona is so strict, my private persona is playful and submissive. We have a head-swirling dynamic, thrilling in every possible way. I look forward to each turn of events that lets me switch back and forth.

Miko smiles and nods her head. "We'll talk about Mariko later. I promise," she says, leaving the room with a wave of her hand. Then I kick myself as a waitress walks by and raises her eyebrows at me. I've said things to my friends tonight in public I would never say to strangers. That's what I get for drinking and having a good time.

Business, Sanaa. My life is all business now. New rule: if I'm not in my apartment, I don't open up to anyone, even Jiro.

After watching everyone play poker for thirty minutes, Maeda checks in on us. I'm sure to stand next to him and talk about the dinner, the roulette tables, and how everyone makes fun of my lack of a poker face. I even lean forward to whisper in Jiro's ear once or twice about non-sensical things so Maeda can get a better view of my legs. I'm shameless, really. I don't even blush.

"Will you be playing before the night is through, Itami-sama?" Maeda asks as we walk to the door.

"Possibly. I'm going to get another Manhattan and see if that gives me an advantage."

He lets out a large chuckle and reaches for my left hand. I fight every instinct I have that tells me to snatch it back and defend myself, but I do a good job of covering up the urge because Maeda doesn't notice. He examines my ring, his smile straightens across his face, and his shoulders square up.

"Are you married to Jiro? Because something tells me you would not be that stupid to break the law before we leave for Yūsei."

His grip on my hand tightens, and I put on my passive face and relax, doing everything I can to stop my heart from racing into a panic.

"We're engaged and both wear the rings, but no, we're not legally married. It is our way of saying I am… not for sale."

"Off the market, ne?"

I nod my head, he releases my hand, and I clasp both in front of me to keep them still. You're in charge here, Sanaa. Not him.

"Sakai clan has come up in the world," he says with a nod of his head.

I'm unsure whether to take this as a compliment or a threat. Does he think of Sakai clan as a competitor now instead of an ally? I decide to go with compliment.

"Yes, well, supposedly I'm quite the catch." I let my eyes slide to the right. Jiro is two tables over watching us. Possessiveness makes his eyes sharp, and I slightly shake my head to tell him there's nothing wrong. I can handle this.

"Indeed," Maeda says, leaning in. "Something tells me once Miura and Taira clan are awake again, you will need your family and Sakai clan to keep you from becoming someone else's catch."

Ominous but most likely true. I'm sure now Maeda is not the one I have to worry about. He seems concerned for me, but the emotion quickly fades from his face. Maybe I was imagining it.

"Your bracelet has a koi charm on it. It was your mother's, ne?"

I nod. Perhaps he knew my mother better than I thought.

"*Koi no takinobori*, Itami-sama." Maeda bows and leaves with no further comments.

I've heard this proverb before. It literally means "koi climbing waterfalls" but is translated to mean "succeed vigorously in life." It would appear Maeda is giving me his best wishes. At least, I hope so. Who can tell for sure?

I sigh and go to Oyama to order another drink. I need one now after that exchange. Once he sets me up and starts playing, I stand back with Kentaro.

"Hmmm, Maeda seems interested in you." He keeps his voice

low and steps a little closer to me.

"Yeah. I get the feeling he's not the only one I'll have to say no to in my lifetime."

Kentaro raises his eyebrows at me and smiles. Yes, I've already said no to Minamoto too concerning Kentaro. We each take a sip of our drinks and watch everyone play cards for a moment.

"Well, I like craps, and I'm crap at poker." He gestures at the poker table with his glass in his hand.

"I thought you were out playing craps with Usagi?"

"I wanted to stick around and see how you dealt with Maeda. Playing with his baser instincts is something Jiro nor Sakai-san could do..." Kentaro leans his head forward, and I catch him looking down my dress. I cock my head and blink my eyes at him.

"See anything you like?" I whisper.

"No comment. I'm off." And he turns to go before he blushes. I don't think Kentaro hates me anymore though he will always be the same idiot boy he was in the beginning.

Looking at the clock on the terminal in the room, it's after 2:00am, and everyone is still having a great time even Mariko. I want to go back out to the roulette table, but I can't leave without having either Usagi or Jiro with me... or Sakai. Gods, I am beholden to other people for my own safety for the rest of my life.

I slowly walk around the outskirts of the room. Everyone is playing poker but me, Mariko, and Sakai. Mariko and Sakai are having a conversation so I won't interrupt them. Sakai wouldn't leave without Lucy anyway. Lucy and Beni are the biggest surprise players I've seen yet. They have stacks of chips in front of them higher than Oyama's.

I'm ready to go home, and I know what I want, so I cross the room into Jiro's eye-line.

Come on, Jiro. Look at me.

He looks up and sees me watching him. I raise my eyebrows at him and run my index finger from my neck straight down my front along the deep V-neck of my dress which ends just below the bottom of my breasts. Licking my bottom lip, I shrug my shoulders a little bit. Jiro swallows and stares. I smile and pick up my empty glass, lightly gesturing my head at the door.

"I'm cashing in," he says pushing all of his chips away from him. "Sanaa looks tired."

I set my drink down while faking a yawn, grab my card and purse, and Jiro and I say goodbye to everyone in the room. He leads me through the casino at a fast pace and outside he takes one look at me in my dress with the high heels and hails a taxi. We're home in five minutes, and it was the most excruciating five minute taxi ride I have ever taken. Even with the relative privacy of a taxi, I still can't break my public persona though I want to jump into Jiro's lap and make out with him.

I kick off my shoes in the lobby, and we run up the stairs, past the security guard to our apartment. Once we're inside, I tear at Jiro's shirt and try to get it off of him as fast as I can without actually ripping the buttons off, but I don't succeed. They pop off and skitter across the floor. He's kissing me on my neck and down my front, and I throw my arms around his neck as my knees weaken.

"Sometimes I think we're at a major disadvantage because we can't have sex in the back of a taxi or in a coat check room or wherever because we have to be on the lookout for assassins and not be distracted."

I catch my breath as his hands travel up my legs and under my skirt, and he hesitates for a moment. "Sanaa! You aren't wearing any underwear at all."

"No." I reach down and unbutton his pants. "I thought you knew."

His hands keep going, and I think I may faint.

"If I knew, I doubt we would have made it out tonight."

"Mmmm, I continue to surprise you."

Chapter Thirty-Six

Jiro and I have a lot of correspondence to go through for two whole days after the casino. First, I deal with Maeda and his permits. Lucy comes down for coffee and food that Oyama whips up in our kitchen. Jiro travels up to Sakai's penthouse with Kentaro and Usagi to discuss all the people we're tailing.

Maeda is grateful for all of the permits but refuses to back me.

"Here, listen to this, Lucy. *Though I'm extremely fond of you, your late mother, and all of Sakai clan, I have been advised by the members of my board that I should not officially support any government system for Yūsei. We will continue to remain neutral and provide help as needed. Thank you for visiting Akaboshi the other night. Please feel free to come back again any time before we leave.*' What kind of nonsense is this?" I slam my tablet down on the table, and it bounces and flips over.

"And Mark thinks I'm the fiery redhead?" She laughs and rights my tablet. "Don't worry about this. It's a temporary setback. He won't be able to remain neutral for long once we're on Yūsei and all of Clan Taira is awake. He has the luxury of saying no right now because you've been so good about going around to all the minor clans and securing their support."

I cross my arms and pout. I wanted Maeda. He has so much money and power. He's lucky I don't go back to his casino and burn it to the ground.

"No, really. I know I was harsh with you about telling the minor clans you and Jiro were engaged, but they've all contacted us and are on our side. Maeda can say no because he's aware you have power too and, hopefully, won't be bulldozed by Miura when he wakes up. It's not 'game over.'"

Ping! Lucy picks up her tablet and reads her message while sipping coffee.

"Mark and the boys are on their way down. It's about to get very crowded in here." As she's removing all of our excess belongings from the table, the door opens and in they all come. I've had three bites of fried rice, and I'm in a horrible mood now, so I'm not sharing my food with anyone.

"I have extra rice," Oyama says from the kitchen and both Jiro and Kentaro ask for some while Sakai and Usagi sit on the couch. I grab a floor cushion and pull up to the coffee table.

"We have a few pieces of news. First, the temporary chef Miko hired is dead."

My throat closes up, and I break out into a sweat. Chew the food, Sanaa. Don't choke.

"He was found in a dumpster yesterday morning, and I saw the bulletin about it a few hours ago. Miko, Yoichi, and I have discussed this, and she will not hire on any new staff before we leave for Yūsei. They'll be packing up the izakaya in another month anyway, and if they need help I can loan out some of the security staff or we can go and give them a hand." Sakai refuses food from Oyama but takes a mug of tea from Jiro.

"The waitress had a fake record in the GDB, and I still have no idea who the other man is she was working with." Sakai takes a sip of tea and misses my glance at Kentaro. When we first started following these two, he said he had a feeling about something, and I thought he knew who they were. But he just sits in the armchair eating and thinking. Maybe his idea didn't pan out.

"We need to get back to tracking these people," Sakai continues. "The next steps are to tail Risa and her parents again and pick up the trail with her. I'm handing off to you and Jiro now. Lucy and I have government business to attend to. I've asked Usagi and Beni to help Miko and Yoichi get their packing materials ready for the move. Another six weeks and we're gone."

"I can help Jiro and Sanaa. I'd be more than happy to," Kentaro says.

"Thank you, Kentaro. Please be sure to check in with your family often. Don't forget they will need assistance packing up for first wave as well."

Kentaro frowns. He's much happier when he's here with us.

"So, Sanaa," Jiro says, between mouthfuls of food. "What's it going to be? Shall we divide up the work since my tablet has real-time feed access now too?"

"Sure. Let's do Rock Paper Scissors. Winner gets Risa. Loser gets her parents. One shot?"

Jiro narrows his eyes at me before nodding.

"Ichi, ni, san!"

I throw: scissors. Jiro throws: paper. He's learning, but I'm one up on him.

"Damn," he says with a sigh. "I married my mother."

Sakai laughs, nearly spitting out his tea. I grab my tablet and open up the jobs I have on Risa while chewing on my food. Let's see. Where is she now?

Wait. Two minutes ago, she scanned her transitway card at the exit to the station around the corner. I set down my chopsticks and access the video feeds from here to the station.

"Guys... Everyone! Risa just walked into the building. She's here. Right. Now."

Risa is definitely not happy.

She entered the building, and, because she claims residency here, the security staff let her up to her apartment, right down the hall from us. But Smart Beni had taken her off the occupancy list a while back, so Risa went to Mariko's apartment.

Now, she's sitting on the couch and refusing to make eye contact.

Sakai sits right in front of her on a chair with his tablet on his lap. Jiro, Usagi, and I are behind him. Lucy, Mariko, and Beni are in the kitchen. All of our eyes are boring into her head.

"We have you on video, Risa, meeting with your parents and Emiko Matsuda. We know you told Emiko about our trip to the theater, and we know you've leaked other information as well. We've even seen you with the man and woman who poisoned Helena and tried to kill all of us at Izakaya Tanaka. The evidence is quite damning."

Risa sits in silence, ignoring us all, while examining her pink, rounded nails. If she were denying it, I'd be inclined to forgive her but she's not defending herself at all. I have to admit I hate her. Hate everything about her, her stupid face, perfect makeup, perfect nails, perfect hair. My temper is simmering and bubbling, red hot like one of Oyama's curries cooking away on our tiny stove.

"So, what do you have to say for yourself?"

Risa makes eye contact with Sakai, her face full of hatred, her arms crossed over her chest. "I have nothing to say."

"Nothing?" Sakai's face is getting progressively more passive, and he's trying to rid himself of emotions because he doesn't want to blow up at her. I am not doing such a good job of this. "Are you unwilling to apologize for betraying this family?"

Risa shakes her head and narrows her eyes. She's even more bitter, angry, and downright evil than she was at the wedding or at Café les pivoines.

"You are the one betraying this family. Not me."

Sakai sits and waits. How does he do that? I want to yell at her.

"You're the one siding with the bastard child over your own family." Risa looks directly at me, hate practically pouring out of her straight onto me.

"Excuse me?" My voice rises and cracks, and Jiro puts his hand on the small of my back. "Are you talking about *me*?"

"Of course I'm talking about you. You and your whore of a mother have done more damage to this family than I ever could."

Beni and Mariko gasp at the kitchen door. What? My mother a... whore? Instead of shock, I'm seeing red. No one insults my mother.

"This is my family, too," I say, stabbing the air between us with my index finger. "Your actions have caused us all to lose people. People we love." My forehead is breaking out in a sweat. Helena. Koichi. I don't think I was meant to handle these kinds of confrontations.

Sakai is turned a bit and watching me with his passive face on. He's hoping I don't do anything irrational.

"This is not your family. You and Jiro are *not* married, and you most likely never will be. I'd be careful, Jiro. She's probably just as much of a whore as her mother was."

That's it. I lunge across the coffee table and get my hands around Risa's throat for two whole seconds before Usagi peels me off of her. Before I can be hauled away, I lash out with a kick and hit her squarely in the jaw, messing up her perfect face. She's lucky I have no shoes on.

Interestingly enough, no one else moved, and no one is looking at me like I'm the crazy one.

Jiro walks over to Risa who is coughing and rubbing at her throat and gets right in her face. "Never speak to my wife that way again. Do you think you could beat her in a fight? She could snap your neck before you blinked." He straightens up and takes a step back. "Never forget that she is your empress. She has every right to take your life, right now if she wanted to."

I have never felt vindictive in my life until now, and it's not a pretty emotion, but it's apt. That's right, Risa. Jiro's on my side, not yours. If you ever thought you had him, I hope you realize now, you never did.

My temper got the better of me this time, but it looks like I didn't offend anyone but Risa. Tears flow from her eyes, and her cheek is red and swelling. I relax and Usagi lets go of me but not without giving me a little squeeze first.

"You weren't supposed to fall for anyone but me," Risa chokes out, "especially not her."

"I find you completely disgusting. There is no one for me but Sanaa. Ever."

Sakai and Jiro nod to each other, and pride wells up in my chest, calming my temper. I have the approval of the two most important men in my life. I don't need much more than that.

Sakai turns back to Risa. "Now that Sanaa has taught you a good lesson, you will leave this building and never enter Sakai territory again. If I ever catch wind of you, you will regret it."

Risa stands up, grabs her bag, and starts for the door. "Don't think this is the end, Sanaa. I'm not the only one who wants you dead. Have my stuff boxed up and sent to me, Beni."

I hope her face turns black and blue for a very long time.

Sakai nods at Usagi, and Usagi follows Risa out. Now that Risa is gone, everyone turns to me, but I'm still angry, my arms folded across my chest.

"Sanaa, I know we haven't talked about this much in the past few months, but you need to go see your aunt. Tonight."

"Why?" My temper evaporates quickly, and my stomach clenches. "Do you think she's involved in this somehow?"

I was thinking I wouldn't visit Sharon at all. I would just pick up and leave, "let sleeping dogs lie" as the saying goes, though I've never seen a dog. What did I hope to gain from opening past wounds? Nothing. I don't need Sharon's approval.

"Sanaa-chan..." Sadness sweeps across his face, and Lucy closes her eyes. "Your mother was a private person, much like you. For Risa to know anything about her, she would have had to go to your family. There's no way Kimie or Lomo would speak ill of her. That leaves only Sharon."

I nod my head slowly, my insides trembling at the idea of facing her.

He squeezes my shoulders and nods back at me. "Time to clear the air."

Chapter Thirty-Seven

I close my eyes and meditate, standing in the darkened hallway with Jiro and Usagi behind me. I can do this. I can do this. "I can do this" is my new mantra for this evening. Placing my hand on the palm scanner at Sharon's door, I wait while the chimes ring inside, and the readout on this side states "Sanaa Itami." I catch my breath and smile at Jiro and Usagi behind me. Sakai finally changed my name.

From this side, I hear footsteps and then silence before a barely audible "shite" comes from the other side.

"Aunt Sharon, it's Sanaa. Open up, please."

A few seconds wait pass by before the door opens, and she finds the three of us standing in the hallway. I can only imagine what's going through her head right now. Two formidable, young Japanese men in black carrying swords and me, her only niece, also in black, sporting short hair with a shock of red to it. She hasn't seen me since I was twelve.

She's the same, though. Same auburn hair with a little more gray than before, still cut to her shoulders. I forgot she has freckles too, and she looks a lot like my father. Her brown eyes are wide with shock, and I catch a whiff of alcohol. She's been drinking.

"Hi."

"Sanaa, what the hell are you doing here?"

I can already tell this is not going to go well. No "it's good to see you" or "how have you been?"

"Can we come in?"

Her eyes glance from me to Jiro to Usagi, but I smile at her. She sighs and opens the door all the way.

"Thanks," I say, grabbing Jiro's hand and pulling him in with me. "Usagi, can you...?"

"Yes, miss." He nods. He would probably rather stay outside anyway.

Sharon closes the door behind Jiro and waits while I take a quick glance around at her apartment. The space is bright and modern, and all the furniture is new. She has a good job working for someone high up in the consulate, so I'm not surprised she's doing well for herself. I was also not surprised to learn from Usagi that she lives alone.

Along one whole wall of her apartment are stacks of moving boxes, and I eye them suspiciously.

"Sanaa, why are you here? And who is this?" she asks pointing to Jiro.

"This is my husband, Jiro Itō." I give away this information with the attitude this is something she should already know, would know, if she were a part of my life.

Her eyes fall down to my left hand, and Jiro follows her line of sight with a satisfied smile on his face. It's petty, but I want to wave the thing in her face. Look at what you've missed of my life, Aunt Sharon.

"Mariko and Koichi's boy? You're *married* to Mariko and Koichi's child?" The way she spits out "married" I get the distinct feeling she's both jealous and angry, and I can't help but smirk at her unhappy laugh. I'm a little evil and unforgiving tonight. I relax my posture, and a small smile creeps across my lips. Jiro makes eye contact with me and straightens his shoulders. My family is screwed up, but he loves me regardless. He's proud I'm not going to take shit from anyone.

"Yes, and I know everything now. I know why you left, why you won't talk to me. I know about Aunt Charlotte and the real Sanaa and that my real name is Hanako. There are a lot of things, though, I just don't understand. I was hoping we could talk about this now."

"I don't want to talk about this. I don't want to talk to you, to be honest. I told this to Kimie when I cut off communication. I can't look at you and not think of Junko."

"What happened? Why would you ignore me like that?"

Rage boils over on her face, and she walks forward with her finger out and pointed at me.

"Your mother..."

She doesn't get very far because Jiro steps in front of me and pushes me back. I was too much in shock to do anything.

"Don't," Jiro says. She takes one look at him and our swords on his back and steps away from me.

"Your mother was a whore."

The comment slaps me across the face. It stings so much I close my eyes and a tear leaks out. When I examine my heart and mind again, I'm not sad. I'm angry. This is the perfect opportunity for me to put on my passive face. Deep breaths, dark blue sky, dunes.

"She slept with Max. She slept with Mark. I think she even slept with Tadao." Sharon's face is serious, eyes widened in judgment.

Anger works its way up from my stomach, warming my chest. I'm standing perfectly still. If I move, I might kill her.

"I'm glad to see there's a little of Max in you because for the longest time I doubted you were even his child. Kimie refused to have your DNA tested because she was so afraid of being found out. She was afraid of the clans finding out you were Hanako and not Sanaa. She was so self-centered and selfish. That was our last and final argument."

Wait just a minute. Insulting my dead mother is one thing, my aunts is a completely different story.

"Aunt Kimie is the most caring and loving person on this wretched planet. If you're looking for someone self-centered and selfish, you should look in the mirror. How can you say these things about me? About my mother?" Just past her on the breakfast bar of her kitchen counter is a bottle of wine almost gone and a glass half-full. She stormed out of so many holidays and birthdays when I was a kid because she was drunk and not getting enough attention.

"Because it's true. Even your own father doubted you were his. Your whore of a mother was sleeping with both Mark Sakai and Max when she became pregnant."

I hate where this conversation is going. Time to wrap up. As much as I want to be open and honest with Jiro, I don't want him hearing every bit of dirty laundry my family has. I'm already damaged goods. No need to completely destroy me now.

"Regardless of who my mother slept with, which is none of your business anyway, Max Griffin is definitely my father. I've seen all the DNA records and the family trees in the GDB, and I look nothing like Mark Sakai. If you were involved in my life, you'd know this already."

Sharon shrugs her shoulders, reaching out for her wine glass and almost knocking it over before taking a large gulp. She believes every word she's saying, and from what I know of what happened, her version of events is not far from the truth. But just the fact that she is using "whore" to describe my own mother reminds me she was hospitalized for mental instability after my parents were killed.

"You changed your name." She waves her glass at me, and I step back as some wine hits the floor between us.

"I don't want to be a Griffin anymore, and it's time I owned my family heritage." I glance at Jiro as I amble over to the wall of boxes. "I'm aware you've been talking to people, about me, about my family." I run my hand along the boxes and take a quick count, around fifty.

"How do you know that?" she asks, fear inching its way into her voice.

"A very stupid and shallow young lady called my mother a whore earlier today." I fake shock and then laugh. Revenge is at hand. "Now, imagine our surprise when it came flying out of her mouth, and no one has spoken of my mother in public in ages."

"You know," Jiro starts, and his deep voice surprises me for a moment. He's been taking this all in and not saying a word otherwise. "Sanaa is a brilliant detective. Nothing gets past her."

I fold my arms across my chest and lean my back on the wall of boxes.

"So, you've been talking to Risa Yamamoto, and, hmmm, possibly her parents, Nobu and Yukio. Selling the family secrets. Dolling out all the gossip, and for what? This?" I tap the boxes behind me with my foot. "Why would you be packing up to leave Nishikyō when you're on third wave?"

I had Sakai make sure that all of my closest family and friends were on first wave with us, and I never mentioned my other family. When I investigated Sharon in the GDB months ago, she had been assigned to third wave, and I didn't think twice, because I didn't care.

That's right. I don't care. Maybe I should, and maybe I would if I had come here, and we had worked things out. Instead, I've come here and found my parents' past rotting the soul of my aunt. She's not someone I want to introduce around, not someone I want my children to associate with.

Her face has paled a shocking white, her hand holding her wine glass shaking with fear. She's probably a fine employee and saves the drinking for when she's off the clock, but I've caught her in a moment of weakness. This is when my instincts tell me to go for the kill.

"You thought that by betraying me and my family, your own brother and sister-in-law, that you could buy your way onto first wave. You've even secured a hibernation spot that someone had to give up for you. Do you have a job lined up for when we arrive? Wait. You do."

With each statement, I know I'm right, and these arrangements must have happened recently because Lucy and Sakai would have caught on eventually. Sharon gulps and sets her glass down.

"I... I'm not sure what you mean."

Jiro laughs and pulls his tablet out of my bag. With a few strokes of his long fingers across the keypad, he types out a message and waits.

"I came here tonight to make peace with you, to get you to understand that what you've been doing is hurtful to me and to our entire family. Mark Sakai suggested I clear the air. Let me make something abundantly clear. Unpack your boxes because you'll be lucky if you leave this planet alive. Keep your mouth shut if you want to keep your job. Get help for yourself now before I make you get it."

Jiro's tablet pings, and he nods at me.

"You're crazy!" Sharon says, incredulous. "What makes you think that I'm going to take orders from you? A little girl?"

"It's already done, Sharon." I wave at Jiro, and he puts his tablet away. "You're more than aware of my heritage and why my parents never married. Much to my own surprise, I'm going to be in charge on Yūsei. Not you. Not the Yamamotos and whomever else they're working with. Me. If you wanted special consideration, you should have showed me you cared. Instead you made me feel abandoned and lonely for most of my life until you made me angry."

I never wanted any of the power of being an empress, and here I am, using my influence to destroy what's left of my family. I hate myself sometimes.

"Come on, Sanaa. I think we got what we came here for." Jiro has his arm out, and I want badly to just sink into him and forget this, but I'm still pissed off.

"I am not my mother. You didn't have to disown me."

"You still look exactly like her. I can't trust you," she replies, and she's right. She can't trust me, and I can't trust her.

"Don't bother. You'll never see me again."

I walk from the apartment with Jiro at my side and don't look back. I let my feet carry me all the way down the stairs and right outside to the sidewalk, and for a moment, I'm not sure whether to blow up or cry. What's easier?

An empty plastic crate sits on the ground out front, and I kick it. It flies off to the right hitting the wall of the next building over and bouncing into the alley. I turn the corner into the alley, the heat of my rage burning my insides, pick the crate up, and slam it against the unforgiving concrete wall while Jiro and Usagi watch.

"Think it's that easy, ne?" Slam! The plastic hits the wall so hard my hands throb.

"You can betray your family and buy yourself a spot anywhere?" Kick! The crate actually cracks this time, but I pick it up, and wind back with my whole body before aiming at the wall again.

"Wanna just talk and talk and tell lies with no consequences?" I throw the crate all the way down the alley, it hits a metal door, and cracks again. My breathing is so heavy, I'm starting to hyperventilate.

The metal door opens and a man sticks his head out. "Oy! What's going on out here?"

Usagi steps forward, his hand moving to his sword. "Get back inside and mind your own business." The man quickly closes the door.

"Awesome, Sanaa. Let's get something else for you to break." Jiro looks around eagerly, and I let one laughing sob escape my mouth before clamping my hand down on it.

Gods, sometimes it really feels good to beat the crap out of something, a conduit for my smoking dragon instead of just letting the anger die out. It's much more gratifying.

"Aw, you're done already?" Jiro enfolds me in a strong hug, and I let a few tears out of my eyes onto his shoulder. "Oh well. It's always fun while it lasts."

"Let's get out of here before that guy calls the police," Usagi says. "Shall we go for a drink? I watched this neighborhood a lot during the summer, and there's a pub around the corner with a personable staff. I'll test your beer myself." He winks and smiles at me, putting his hand on my shoulder, and I'm doubly relieved. I've dealt with Sharon and received a rare smile from Usagi.

"Yes. Let's get drinks and forget about this." I put my arms around both boys, and Usagi leads us away.

The next day when I check the GDB on Sharon Griffin, she's

voluntarily checked into Ku 2 for psychiatric evaluation and her Colonization Status has been moved to "Tenth Wave - Pending."

Good riddance.

Chapter Thirty-Eight

I spend the weeks all the way through the middle of October packing, packing, packing. Once we're all settled on Yūsei, I swear I'm never moving again. Jiro and I don't have many belongings so he attends meetings all day every day, and I deal with the apartment. I'm definitely not pleased with this job. I'm careful about packing the first five crates then I find myself chucking things in boxes randomly because I'm so sick of being home. Every day, I ask Beni to come and help, but she's helping Mariko.

Now that I know they're home, I climb the stairs each morning for a week to help out. Mariko can't turn me away with Beni around, and I'm sure to smile and be as pleasant as possible while I'm in her apartment. The time I spend there is pleasant for no one, though. Everything reminds her of Koichi, and after about ten different breakdowns, we send her off to visit with her brother and sister-in-law while Beni and I pack instead. I feel awful sending her away, but we were getting nowhere.

Jiro is dealing with more of my imperial duties each day as we get closer to leaving. He has meetings with Minamoto and Maeda often and details still to be worked out concerning Miura's family and crew. They have stayed silent and respectful since the fight, but we don't expect the peace to last long once we land. Jiro and I will have our work cut out for us.

The city is cool all of the time, and I'm in the dōjō a few times per week again with Kentaro. This morning, after putting me through the paces for two hours, Kentaro and I sit down for a break and a glass of water on the mats.

"Jiro hasn't been here in at least a week," Kentaro says, looking around the silent room. "I thought, in the beginning, he'd be here every day, worried I'd steal you away or something."

"He trusts me. He's also pretty sure I can kick your ass if you try anything," I say, laughing and setting my water down before I spill it with giggles. "Besides, he's grateful someone is around to teach me." Sighing, I lie back on the mats. "I'm disappointed I didn't learn more this summer. I had such high hopes to learn every thing about being a ninja before we left for Yūsei, but so much of life got in the way."

"The past few months have been crazy, Sanaa-san, and ninjutsu is a life-long pursuit. You can't learn all the skills in one summer despite how hard you try. Don't forget that the people who hurt Helena and tried to poison us are still out there. You need to stay safe."

I roll onto my side so I can see Kentaro better. He smiles and nods his head at me, fatherly in a way. Maybe there is something attractive about him when he's nice. "How's Kevin? I haven't heard or seen much of him in the past weeks."

"We broke up."

"Oh, no. I'm sorry," I say, waving my hand at him and sitting up, cross-legged. "I shouldn't have mentioned it."

"It's fine. He's a nice bloke but can't make up his mind for shit." Kentaro shrugs. "One minute he wanted to come on the first wave and be with me. Another he couldn't deal with leaving. He loves his job as a pediatrician and doesn't want to leave the kids he's been treating for years. I get it. Three weeks ago, he decided to stick to his fifth wave slot, and I doubt we would have survived an interstellar, long distance relationship."

"That sounds like something out of a sci-fi romance novel. Oh well. We'll find you a cute boy on the other side of this whole ordeal."

He helps me up off the mats and shrugs his shoulders again. "Or a cute girl. I haven't given up on either of them yet."

He walks away from me with a wink and a smile. Hmmm, Kentaro. You're more complex the more I get to know you.

When we're done, Kentaro walks me home from the dōjō and straight to my apartment.

"I don't know what you're up to now, but I need groceries or I'm going to die of starvation. If you want to come across the street with me, I'm heading out in thirty minutes after I clean up." Kentaro wants to spend time together before hibernation, and I have trouble not throwing myself at him and thanking him for his constant attention.

"Sure. Meet you downstairs with Oyama in forty-five minutes?" We nod and part ways.

The apartment is empty and silent, the boxes we've packed stacked against one wall. Jiro's not here, and I miss him. I wonder if this is what the rest of our life will be like, barely seeing each other except in bed at night if we're not traveling. Try not to think about it, Sanaa.

I message Oyama, jump in the shower, and then meet the boys downstairs once I'm ready. I love the little grocer across the street from Sakai building. In fact, I love everything about this block: the ramen place right next door to the grocer, the laundromat, the stoop three doors down where old men sit all day and talk, the tea shop on the corner, and all the people I regularly run into around here. I'll miss this place so much when we're gone.

"Sugar snap peas are in season now, Sanaa-san. How about udon with mushrooms and those tonight?" Oyama is running his hand through the basket of peas, grabbing handfuls and bagging them up.

"Sounds delicious."

I don't have much to do here. This is more of an excuse to get out of the house than anything else. I walk along the aisles and browse for things Jiro and I enjoy — eggplants, green peppers, a fresh batch of tofu (though Oyama makes his own) — but I'm most drawn to the fruit section. I say hello to the owner on my way over, bow, and wish him good health. He's a sweet and happy man who will probably never see Yūsei. What will life be like for everyone who's left behind?

An employee stacks oranges into a pyramid, his hair pulled up at the back, streaks of gray following the slope of his head to the knot even though the rest of him is young. My mouth starts to water thinking about orange slices after dinner. I love citrus — can't get enough of it — but I ate oranges sparingly as a kid because they're expensive. Now I can have as many as I want.

"Excuse me. Can you grab me three ripe oranges?" I ask the employee. "My arms are full." I laugh when I look at what I'm carrying. You'd think Jiro and I eat as much as ten people.

"Yes, miss," he says, and then a deathly silence falls on the place.

All the hair on my body stands straight up as the floor under me vibrates, slowly building to a violent trembling.

Earthquake.

The shaking knocks me to the ground, everything I'm holding flying from my arms and rolling in a dozen different directions. I fall down hard on my hip and knock my head against the floor but am spared any major injuries. Produce plummets off the shelves above me and pelting me on my head over and over. Oranges, grapefruits, apples hit me and bounce off down the aisle.

"Sanaa!" Kentaro shouts from the next aisle over. "Stay down!"

I have no choice, Kentaro. My legs wouldn't hold me even if I could stand.

Then it stops just before the warning sirens start. The earthquake only lasted about forty-five seconds, but it was strong. The floor is still vibrating.

"Are you okay?" the employee asks, offering his hand to help me up. I take it and pull myself upright.

"I think so." I rub at my hip and wince. "Gods, that was a big one. I hope everyone around here is okay."

Oyama stands in the doorway, his hand clutched to the doorjamb. I don't think he even moved. His basket is still full of food. Kentaro pops up from the floor right next to me, and we examine each other. He looks uninjured.

"Let me help you pick up all your produce. Hopefully none of it is damaged." The employee squats down in front of me to grab my fruits and vegetables from the floor, and I gasp and nearly pass out.

It's him! The man who poisoned Helena, the one we saw in the alleyway with Risa. I'm looking at him now from the same angle as the cameras, and it's definitely the same face, the same jawline and forehead. He glances up at me, having heard my sharp intake of breath, and he looks completely different from this angle. That's unreal. He's like a Noh mask, unique from every direction.

The perfect spy. Unrecognizable unless you know him well.

"Hello," I say, my voice coming out in a breathless whisper. I can barely hear myself over the sirens. "I don't believe we've been introduced."

A change shifts through his eyes, from shiny to dim. He knows he's been caught. Straightening up in front of me, he smiles and winks, and my insides grow cold. I've seen him not once (the day he knocked into me coming out of Café les pivoines), not twice (in the waiting room in Ku 2 he sat and read on his tablet after I stared him down), but three times previous to this. His smile and wink are disarming, and if he were wearing a suit with a drink in his hand, he'd be the man that tried to hit on me at the casino, too.

How long has he been working here? Has he been following me other places, and I've just not noticed? I never thought anyone would have the guts to infiltrate Sakai territory, especially with all the security I usually have. I didn't even bring Kazenoho because, if I check behind me, my security staff are stationed in the street right outside.

I'm afraid to break eye contact with him, but I glance at Kentaro and the man does too.

Kentaro pales. "Kazuo," he says.

"Hello, cousin," Kazuo replies.

What?

Kazuo bolts, pushing me down and running for the back door. I try to get up and run after him, but I trip on a grapefruit and slide into a shelf of produce, costing me precious seconds. Kentaro is in the lead, through the door behind Kazuo, but a loud crash at the back of the store happens before he runs back out.

"Argh!" Kentaro screams. "He blocked the door. Out the front!"

I turn and sprint past Oyama yelling at him to get Jiro and Sakai quickly. Kentaro is right behind me, and I take a chance on direction and head towards the end of the nearest block to the alley that leads behind the grocery store. Kentaro and I round the corner, but the alleyway is deserted.

"Up," Kentaro says, and when I look up, I realize Kazuo could have climbed any of the nearby buildings' fire escapes. "Let's go."

We sprint to the nearest ladder, and Kentaro boosts me up. I swing my legs up on the platform and bump my hip again, blinking away the stars of pain in my vision. We climb to the roof, but the area is empty, just the dome stretching up above us and off into the distance. Kazuo probably climbed up and then climbed right back down on the side of another building. That's what I would do.

"Kazuo!" Kentaro screams, his head tilting back and voice echoing across the neighborhood. "Come back here you coward!"

"Cousin, Ken-chan?" I bend over and try to catch my breath.

This must mean Minamoto is almost certainly involved in Helena's poisoning and subsequent attacks on my family.

"*Cousins,*" he corrects me. "Kazuo and Sachi Uchiyama. Twins. My half second-cousins and two of the most skilled assassins in Nishikyō."

Chapter Thirty-Nine

Everyone pours out of buildings to the streets, reuniting with loved ones, looking for people they can't find, and trading stories of what fell over inside. Kentaro and I run for Sakai building and meet everyone on the sidewalk.

"Are you okay?" Jiro grabs me and hugs me tight, his body tense with worry. The last earthquake was something we both barely lived through, and I'll never think of the earth shaking again without picturing the crumbling theater and Tadao Matsuda's headless body.

"I'm fine. Just my hip is bruised. Kentaro tell them." I wave to him, but he shakes his head.

"We should wait to go inside." He turns around and scans the crowd on the sidewalks. "I don't trust the streets right now."

"Sanaa-san, you had me worried. I got everything you were carrying." Oyama indicates his bags, and I give him a hug. It's more for me than anything else. Oyama was like a port in the storm, immovable and calm. Next time there's an earthquake, I'm holding onto him.

The building is cleared for re-entry, and once everyone is in our apartment, Kentaro asks for my tablet, and I pluck it from my bag and hand it over.

"Kazuo and Sachi Uchiyama —" he starts but I immediately cut him off with my outstretched hand.

Wait a second here. What is this... thing... on my bag strap?

Everyone but Beni and Mariko stop talking. I don't silence them because they're chatting about going to the theater tomorrow to catch a movie. A millimeter-thin piece of flat plastic is stuck to the inside of the strap of my bag. It could be the remnants of a price tag, but I've had this bag now for two years.

Sakai peers over my shoulder, and his eyes narrow.

Shit. This is a bug.

I immediately know how long this has been here, since the day of Helena's poisoning when Kazuo bumped into me outside Café les pivoines. I remember he grabbed me by my shoulders and looked into my eyes for a moment, no doubt distracting me from his hand planting the bug. I always sling my bag over one shoulder and carry it across my body so he had access to this part of the strap. Wow. He must have poisoned Helena, met up with Risa at Café les pivoines, planted the bug, heard everything of us finding Helena, and then went to Ku 2 to spy on us.

My mouth dries. If I could move, I'd get some water, but I'm at once horrified and awed. I'm sickened that he's after me and my family, but secretly I can't help but admire him. What has become of me?

Sakai pulls the bug off my bag and holds it up in the light while Jiro, Usagi, and Kentaro peer into it.

"Huh," Jiro says. His eyes are focused far out in space before he blushes slightly around his temples. Jiro is very rarely embarrassed by anything, but now Kazuo has heard everything of our lives together. My bag is with me everywhere, even in the bedroom where I'm intimate with Jiro. I tell him things in bed late at night I would tell no other person.

Sakai takes the bug over to the bathroom, drops it in the toilet, and flushes it away.

"Do you think there are any more?" he asks when he comes back out.

"No, at least I don't think so?"

"That's not very reassuring." He crosses his arms, and I try to recall all of the random places or contact with strangers I've had which is not much since I spend a lot of time here. Kazuo never got close to me at the casino, so no opportunity there. My bag goes with me everywhere unless I'm popping across the street. I haven't worn a coat in months (too hot). I haven't taken off my shoes in public places (no okiya visits). I've worn plenty of clothes, but they've all been washed frequently, and I doubt the bug would survive in the auto-hamper.

I dump my bag out on the couch and inspect everything in it. Every item looks normal. Then I turn my bag inside out and inspect it.

"I think we're okay."

"Regardless, I'll get someone to come in later and sweep everyone's apartments. Kentaro?"

"Right," he says, watching me sink onto the couch. My hip hurts. I'm starving, tired, and sweaty from running and climbing.

I'm a mess. "Kazuo and Sachi Uchiyama. My second half-cousins. They're on the family tree over here." He points on the tablet and everyone but me leans in. Even Mariko and Beni are paying attention now.

Jiro gets his tablet and accesses the GDB. "They're twenty-five-years old? There's no data on them for the past twelve years! Even their photos don't look right." Jiro tips his tablet to me to show me Kazuo and Sachi side-by-side, thirteen-years old. They're both young and innocent, though Sachi's expression is vacant of personality. Kazuo has a small smile, a twinkle in his eye. He's a charmer, I'm sure.

"The missing waitress," Kentaro says, pointing to Sachi. "I haven't seen these two in almost fifteen years. I thought Sachi looked familiar but couldn't place her. Ah, well, they're sort of legendary in my family for being smart and dangerous. They work together as a team because they figured out a long time ago they could get away with anything by doing deeds in pairs. They often cover for each other."

"And we can't track them?" Jiro asks. He's despondent — technology has finally failed him for the first time ever.

"You mean tracking their transactions? Don't bother. You'll never find them that way. They're ghosts in the machine. Kazuo was always especially good with computers. He's been hacking the GDB for at least ten years now. Besides their official birth records, these two don't really exist. They've been living under pseudonyms by re-keying their palm prints to either the deceased or people they make up. They steal tablets and identities like little kids steal candy from stores. It's no big deal to them."

He sighs and sets down the tablet. "They're skilled assassins, both trained in weaponry. Sachi is heartless. Kazuo? I'm not sure. He's curious, used to poke the fish in the pond at Shōfū-an, take apart tablets and see how they worked. Stuff like that. Sachi used to beat other kids up."

I glance up and Kentaro is watching me, a little sad, a little pitying, but overall concerned.

"Kentaro," Sakai asks, his hand on his chin, "how do you know so much about them?"

He smiles sadly. "Eavesdrop on enough meetings, enough private conversations, and whisperings at family gatherings, and you can learn anything. Besides, I've sat in on official meetings where someone has come to my father asking how to contact the twins for their services. We've always flat-out denied their existence."

"Well, I think with the combination of Risa, her parents, Emiko Matsuda, and these twins, it's pretty evident your father is up to something."

"I'm not denying it, but I bet Emiko is the biggest offender here. She's only twenty-eight and now a widow. She's probably still upset you killed her husband, even though I know for sure the two of them never consummated their marriage." His whole body shakes. "Gross."

I try not to think of my mother. Too late.

I'm detached from this conversation, panic welling in my chest like a teapot about to boil. Nothing is going well, I'm injured, and I just want to lie down and fall asleep for a million years, but I can't. I'll never sleep peacefully again wondering if these twins are right outside my door.

"Everyone, I need a minute." Getting up from the couch, I head straight to the bedroom, closing the door behind me and turning on the light.

I get exactly two minutes to freak out. That's it. That's all I'll allow.

Oh my gods, my entire life has been invaded! When I look at our bedroom, I can picture Jiro and me in bed, on the rare nights when we're both home and not already asleep, and we're either talking or being intimate with each other, and my damned bag is sitting right there on the floor or on the chair at the foot of the bed.

I like privacy. I like that there are things I've only ever told Jiro, things I've only ever done with him, that nobody knows about. Just us. Now it's all tainted and corrupt. Some stranger who has caused harm to my family has heard my secrets. He's probably been working across the street because he comes to spy on me.

The hair on the back of my neck stands up, and I rub it before scanning the room. Does anything look out of place? Kentaro said Kazuo hacks the GDB. What if he hacked me? Hacked my palm print and allowed himself access to my apartment. What if he managed to get past security downstairs? Are there cameras here?

I have to check. I have to know I'm not being watched before I can relax. The little voice inside of my head, the one that tells me what to do when I ask it, is saying I'm paranoid, but I'll never not be again. I may hate being alone all the time, but I need my privacy.

Need it.

I work my way methodically from right to left across the room, starting at the door. There's not much left here I haven't packed, but I pick up every knickknack, every piece of paper, every last framed photo and examine them until Jiro opens the door a minute later. He gave me two and a half minutes.

"Sanaa," he says, closing the door behind him on the voices in the living room, "what are you doing?"

"What if he was here? In our private space? Planting listening devices or cameras? What if he's seen you and me together?" I'm starting to feel frantic, picking up everything. Everything is suspicious. "I didn't want this. I wanted a little space, just this little room that was ours and no one else's, and I feel sick thinking of the things I said to you and he heard."

"Like what? Come on. Tell me now."

"No! No. It's done. How can I ever open up again and not think I'm being overheard?"

"Sanaa..." Jiro comes to me as I'm tearing apart our desk and wraps his arms around my chest, pinning mine down. "You can't let them have power over us. This is just another way of controlling you. Kazuo and whoever has hired him are trying to show us they can get to us —"

"They can!"

"They can't. Nothing I've said to you in here I wouldn't say in public."

I burst into a laugh that dissolves into tears. Why? Why did they have to take my privacy from me? It was the only thing I had left. The only thing that was mine.

"I'd even have sex with you in public, Sanaa."

"Well, I certainly would not. You'd be out there doing it *alone*."

"Now, where's the fun in that?" He presses his cheek into mine, and against my better judgement, I relax a little. "You shouldn't be ashamed of anything you've said in here. You've always been honest and loving."

"It feels cheap knowing I've shared those things with someone else."

"Well, it's not like you did it willingly. Try to be calm."

I'm wound up so tight, I could explode at any moment.

There's a soft knock on the door, and I sniff up my tears and turn myself into him. I'm safe at home. I'm safe at home. "I'm safe at home" is my new mantra. I'm beginning to hate mantras.

"Come in," Jiro says, and Sakai opens the door. He sees us, Jiro's arms around me, the knickknacks in my hand, and nods.

"No sign of them, and with the earthquake, the whole city is in chaos. Now we wait. Again."

Chapter Forty

Nishikyō lays low the next day while the city shakes with aftershocks, some strong enough to knock things over and shut down the transitway once more. Sakai sends security to scan our apartment, but they find no other bugs. When they leave, I break into sobs in the bathroom while trying to clean myself up. I'm so tired of all the stress, of my life being invaded again and again. Maybe it wasn't a good idea for Jiro to be so involved in my job. I really do need him more than I've needed anyone.

After I get myself together, I climb the stairs to Mariko's apartment for a scheduled luncheon and pray to the gods she doesn't turn me away today. I don't think I could take the rejection. I need to be around other people now or else I'm going to lose it.

"Sanaa-chan, come in." She opens the door with barely a smile, and I tense up another notch. "How are you feeling?"

"Fine, Mariko-san." I bow to her at the door. I'm sick of constantly wondering about my place in this family. If she's not going to let me in, I'm going to widen the circle around us. I stiffly walk to the couch and sit down.

Beni comes out of the kitchen with bowls of food for us and sits down across from me on a chair, not noticing Mariko still standing at the door.

"Sanaa-san, you have a full week ahead." She grabs her tablet and gets down to business. "You have your final doctor appointment before hibernation in two days. Miko was wondering if you and Jiro could help them pack up the rest of the izakaya?" I nod in response. Sure. Might as well stay busy. "Jiro sent on a request from Minamoto. He'd like to meet at Shōfū-an again. And your aunts write to say they miss you."

My aunts are so understanding. I've barely seen them since the summer. As much as I love living with Jiro, I miss spending time with them in the mornings or snuggling with them on the couch after work. I've always thought of myself as a solitary person with a small circle of friends, but with Helena gone and Miko married, Jiro busy morning, noon, and night, Sakai and Lucy married, and my aunts in Ku 5, I've been really lonely.

Really.

Mariko sits down next to me. "What's the matter?"

My head snaps at her with a flash of anger. What do you mean, what's the matter? I shake my head to clear it. Be strong, Sanaa.

"Tell my aunts I miss them. Can I see them soon?"

"Let me make room on the calendar," she says, smiling at my eager expression.

"What are you two doing this afternoon?" I eat to distract myself. Don't cry, Sanaa.

"We were going to go visit my brother, Matsuo, and have dinner at his place," Mariko says, grabbing her own bowl of rice from the table. "They're not coming on first wave with us, so I wanted to be with them as much as I can before we go."

"That sounds nice." Do I sound disappointed? I meant to sound happy for them.

"What are you doing, Sanaa-chan?"

"Well, usually we go to the dōjō in the afternoon, but Jiro is busy with Mark and Lucy in Ku 1, and I think they'll be gone through dinner. Kentaro is off enjoying his free time. And with Kazuo and Sachi on the loose, I need Usagi with me when I leave the building, so I usually don't. I will probably stay home."

What I want to do is yell, *"Why have you been ignoring me?"* But her eyes are soft and focused at a family photo on the wall before she turns back to me, her hand to her mouth.

"Why don't you come with us tonight?" Her voice shakes, and if I didn't know any better, I'd think she was going to cry. But no tears appear. "It sounds like you'll be alone in your apartment."

Fear, that's what I see. Sadness laced heavily with fear.

"No, no. It's okay. I don't want to intrude. I'm trying to be fine with being alone. I don't have a lot of control over my life, and it's best if I just accept it."

Mariko pauses, and we stare at each other for a moment. Do I detect a small amount of panic? Her pupils widen, and her mouth pinches together. Beni is watching the two of us. Here's a chance to show my humility.

"I'd like to offer my sincerest apologies, Mariko-san." I back away from her on the couch and bow my head low from my seated position. "I've been too informal with you on too many occasions. I have disgraced myself and disgraced this family with my familiarity."

I'm a failure of a daughter-in-law. I will do my best to correct my behavior in the future." I can't see her face, but air escapes the room as both she and Beni gasp.

"Nonsense, Sanaa-chan." Her shaky hand pats the top of mine, the first time she's touched me in months. I think, maybe, finally, she understands. "You have a big family now, and I've been remiss to invite you along. It's my fault. You should spend more time with us. Beni will get Usagi and Oyama."

"But..." I straighten up from my bow and look between them. "No. I couldn't possibly come. I don't want to get in the way." I can only imagine how Matsuo and his wife will feel with three extra people to entertain on such short notice, one of them hovering over everything in the kitchen.

Honestly, this sudden invitation is too little too late. For months, I've been trying to foster a life with her, hell, with anyone in the building, and there's been nothing.

"No objections. In fact, any time you're just sitting at home alone, you should let me know. If you want company, I'd be happy to spend time with you." She glances nervously at Beni, but Beni's eyebrows are pulled together in confusion. I expressed my suspicions about Mariko to Beni before Miko's wedding. Is she now remembering all the dinners and outings I wasn't along for in the intervening months?

My confession is a mistake. I should have confronted Mariko ages ago or never said a word. Now, too many incidents exist to show her at fault, and Beni is witness to them all. Mariko's honor is at stake, and I'm burning with shame that it's all my doing.

Both Beni and Mariko shift in their seats, unable to speak.

"Well," I say, breaking the uncomfortable silence. "I'll be going home then." I stand up to leave, but Beni grabs my hand.

"You'll do no such thing, Sanaa-san. Here..." She leads me over to the large recliner in the corner and hands me a soft blanket. "Sit here. Read. Take a nap. Make yourself at home in *my* home until it's time to leave."

Mariko does not say a word. She stands up from the couch, walks to her room, and closes the door behind her.

I feel incredibly awkward showing up at Matsuo's apartment uninvited, but his wife, Fumiko, smiles and invites me in. They have a large, loft space similar to Sakai's with plenty of room for us all. Oyama helps with dinner, and I sit on the couch, talk, and smile, and just try to be comfortable, but it's hard. I like Matsuo and Fumiko, but I don't know them, so I can't participate in a lot of the conversations.

My thoughts keep drifting as my sake cup is filled over and over. Why couldn't my own family treat me like this? Wait a minute, why haven't these new people in my life, my new family, treated me like this before? Why is it only now, a few weeks before hibernation, that I'm finally invited along to meet members of my new family that I will probably not see for ten years?

Anger wells up in my chest before depression overtakes it, and I admit it. I'm alone even when I'm with other people. They'll never not think I'm an empress, and it changes everything. I'll never know if I'm being humored because of who I am or genuinely liked.

I'm a block from home when I can't stop the tears from flooding my eyes.

"Are you all right?" Usagi's hand lands on my shoulder, and without thinking about what's proper or right, I throw myself at him and hug him around his neck, crying into his shirt. Gods love Usagi, he doesn't hesitate to hug me back. I've had way too much to drink, and I cling to him hard like I would have done to Helena if she had been here. He's my only link to her now.

"I'm sorry. Sorry sorry..."

"Shhh, it's fine. Cry all you want. I'll carry you home."

"I don't wanna go home. Jiro's not there. Don't want to be alone anymore." I lift up my legs and wrap myself around him. Way too familiar but I'm too drunk to care. "Jiro's never home. My aunt hates me. I can't visit my other aunts without an escort. Helena is gone. Miko has Yoichi..." The sobs overtake me, and I can't speak anymore. I want to run on and on about all the times I tried to talk to him or Mariko or Beni, but I don't.

And holy hell, I now feel horrible for laying this on everyone outside in public. I couldn't have waited until we were in our own building? I blame it all on myself. Everything. It's all my fault.

"Bring her up to my apartment, Akio." Mariko's voice is sweet and soft, right at my ear, but she doesn't touch me. There is more distance between us now than there ever was.

Usagi carries me all the way up to Mariko's apartment and sets me on the couch, but I can't look up at him. My eyes swim, and my head is clouded with sake. I'm ashamed for being so emotional, but Usagi squats down in front of me and grabs my hands.

"I'm so sorry I've ignored your messages or been unable to drop work to come and spend time with you."

I glance from him to Mariko, and she turns away, not wanting to make eye contact with me.

"I know it's my job to watch out for you, but I keep forgetting that you like to go out too... That you miss Helena as much as I do, and we could have missed her together."

I nod because I don't want to argue. Usagi and I could have been closer. So much has driven us apart, driven me apart from everyone.

I don't remember falling asleep on the couch, but it's dark when the door chimes, pulling me up to consciousness again. Mariko answers the door in her robe, and Jiro peers into the dark, looking for me.

"I've never come home and found her gone, not since she was away. Thanks for messaging me," he says, kissing his mother on the cheek.

Jiro comes to the edge of the couch and sits, his hand touching my head and my tear-stained cheek before leaning over and kissing my temple. "So I guess you miss me?"

"Yes. So, so much. I never see you anymore, and you're my only friend. I'm so lonely."

He kisses me again, but this time it's wet with my tears.

"I'm sorry. You should have told me. I would have stayed home with you."

"I don't want to make you feel guilty for having to do your job."

"Well, I certainly don't have to show up to every meeting personally and leave you at home all the time." I close my eyes and nod into the couch. "We only have a few weeks left. From now on, I'll either deal with correspondence electronically or you should come with me if we have to attend. Let me take you home."

Jiro reaches down and picks me up like I weigh nothing.

"I'll call on you in the morning," Mariko says, and then Jiro takes me home and puts me to bed.

Chapter Forty-One

I wake in the middle of the night in my own bed, curled into the fetal position, facing the wall, with Jiro wrapped around me. He's so solid and warm that I go back to sleep, and, the next time I wake, the light is on, and Jiro sits next to me with his tablet on.

"Hey," he says, putting his tablet down.

I sit up and look around, rubbing my face with my hands. I blink my eyes slowly, the lids swollen and sticky, and my hair is sticking up in a hundred different directions. Pulling my legs up, I rest my head face-down on my knees. I'm so ashamed of the way I acted yesterday.

"I'm so sorry, Sanaa. I feel like an ass for leaving you here in this building over and over again. Every time I left, I figured you were doing things here with my mother or Beni and asking Usagi to take you out."

"I tried, but he was always busy." I stop for a minute, letting silence sit while I recover my voice. "Usagi's a grown man with a life of his own. There were a few nights when I thought I'd like to go out, but he wasn't home. I messaged him, but I never heard back."

"But, that's his *job*. That's why you pay him."

I have no idea what to say. Should I be mad with Usagi? Threaten to fire him? He's technically family now, and, if he doesn't want to spend time with me, I can't make him. Maybe I should consider hiring someone else for my personal protection.

"So you've been here spending time alone or with my mother and Beni?"

I slowly shake my head. "I only see your mother for the lunches you schedule. That's it. I only see Beni for business matters."

"What have you been doing here all the time I've been gone?" His voice rises higher in octave, completely surprised.

"Um, nothing." I shrug my shoulders. "Sometimes I watch old movies, read..."

"The security staff says you pace the halls and climb the stairs."

He must have investigated while I was sleeping.

"Yes, I do that too. I go to everyone's apartment to see if they're home. They're usually not."

"But I left you in a building full of people!"

"No. Not as much as you think. Miko and Yoichi have their own life now, and though Yoichi apologized, when I spend time with them, I'm a danger to them. Usagi and Oyama have their own lives. Beni is great, but she and your mother spend time together with family out of the building. My aunts work double shifts all the time, and I can't go see them without security. Mark and Lucy are busy, usually with you. Helena is gone..."

Jiro stares at me, not saying a word.

"I finally became friends with the security guards a few weeks ago. I have gifts for Akira's children before we leave." I pluck at the covers and pull them up farther to my chin. "And, I've been talking with Chad, and I haven't told you."

"Okay..." He's waiting for more, but there is no more.

"He's been dating someone, and we've been chatting about her. I've told him all about you and the sword fighting and everything but this imperial business."

Jiro's shoulders soften. "Why haven't you told him?"

"I don't want him to know. Everyone treats me strange because of it. They're all stiff and fake smiles, and I can't tell if they're just being nice to me or what. I doubt I'll ever make genuine friends again."

"Have you gone to see Chad or asked him here? I would hope you did." This breaks me. Jiro trusts me, and I've let him down by not trusting in him to fix this situation ages ago. I wanted to handle this problem myself, but I screwed it up.

"No. We've only chatted or messaged online. Like I said, he has someone he spends all his time with. He asked me to come out a few times, but I always turned him down. You're not around, and if I brought Usagi, I'd have to explain."

The door chimes in the other room, and Jiro huffs, glances at his tablet to see who it is, narrows his eyes at the screen, and gets out of bed. Mariko is here.

I pull on a pair of pants in the bedroom and try to smooth out my hair in the mirror when Jiro's voice filters in from the living room.

"I asked you to watch after her, and now I find she's been

coming to see you, coming to your door, and you haven't been home or answering."

"Don't get angry with me, Jiro-kun." Shit. There's a fight starting in my living room over me.

"What's going on?" Double shit. Sakai is here too. I back away from the door in our bedroom, unwilling to go out and face them.

"She's all alone here," Jiro shouts, "and I thought I could depend on you to spend time with her when I couldn't."

"I'm sorry. I wasn't always around. I missed... I miss your father and spending time with my family has given me peace."

"That's no excuse. Why didn't you bring her with you? I would have loved for my aunts, uncles, and grandmother to get to know her before we left."

"What? Jiro? What are you saying?" Lucy's voice rings above all the others as I hear the door to the hallway close. Goosebumps race up my arms. A confrontation is looming, a huge family fight, and I'm hiding like a coward in the bedroom. I grab a knit sweater, pull it on quickly, and open the door.

Silence descends on everyone as they all turn to look at me.

Mariko is an unhealthy shade of white. "I have a confession to make. All of the nights I said I was taking Sanaa and Miko to my brother's house, I was only taking Miko. There were many nights when Sanaa came to me for company, and I didn't answer the door." Her voice is monotone, like someone who has practiced their confession enough times to not feel anything. My heart is so broken, it's numb. The family dinners Miko referred to at the casino were real, and I wasn't invited.

"I'm sorry..." I start but Jiro's head whips around, and he points straight at me.

"Don't you dare apologize," he snaps, his voice cold.

"Don't you talk to her like that!" Mariko yells.

"Stop yelling! Everyone!" I yell back, and once they're all silent, I sink to my knees and bring my forehead to the floor. "I'm so sorry for everything. I haven't properly apologized to everyone so I need to say it now. Please don't interrupt me. Jiro, I'm sorry your father was killed because everyone at the theater was coming to kill me. I'm sorry you now have to deal with clan politics and can't enjoy your life before you have to take over Sakai family. I'm sorry that, because of me, the Uchiyama twins poisoned Helena, took away my best friend, and Usagi's girlfriend. I'm sorry they tried to kill us all at Izakaya Tanaka... also because of me." I keep my head down. If Jiro sees my face he's going to say it isn't my fault, when everything clearly is. Just because I didn't want these horrible things to happen doesn't mean they're not my fault.

"I owe you all so much, and I feel awful for putting such huge burdens on you. I thought I'd make Sakai clan my family, and it's clearly not working out despite trying my hardest with Mariko-san and Yoichi. It makes it even worse that I know we're married, and I'll never be able to take care of the family someday like Mariko-san does. I take and take from you all, and I don't give enough back. I could never give enough back to replace your father."

"I'm sorry," Mariko blurts out, the apology bursting from her mouth. "Sanaa-chan, I'm sorry for ignoring you all these months. I let you be alone, and I realize what a foolish thing that was to do."

I sit up to seiza in time to see a ripple of pure anger flow over Sakai's face before he becomes passive. "Why on earth would you do such a thing... and then lie about it? You told me months ago you were happy to have her here."

"Be... Because spending time with Sanaa only made me think of Koichi, and it was easier to not spend time with her than to face... face the person connected to his death." She blames me for his death. I don't think I'll ever win back her trust now. "I have damaged this relationship in an irrevocable manner. It kills me to know you've sat alone for months and worried about my family when I have done the complete opposite. You're my family too, and I should have considered your feelings instead of just thinking of my own."

"I just wanted to be your friend." My lower lip quivers, and I bite down on it to make it stop. "I thought maybe we could be close the way Jiro is close with my aunts. You know he goes and visits them once per week? He thought we were doing that and more. Instead I only saw you every other week, if you didn't cancel on me."

"Mother, you canceled the lunches I planned? How could you?" I've never seen Jiro so shocked about anything, not even the day I found out everything about my heritage.

"Jiro..." Mariko reaches out a hand to him, but he steps back towards me.

"It's not her fault!" Jiro screams, his face lifted to the ceiling, attempting to tell the whole world once and for all. "Sanaa, get off your knees, please." He offers me a hand and gently pulls me up.

"So you've been trying to have a life and been denied?" he asks me, and I look at my feet. "Tell me now."

Ugh, I wish Mariko, Sakai, and Lucy weren't here, but I have to tell Jiro the truth or he'll know that I'm lying to protect other people's feelings. I nod my head and slowly make eye contact with him again, watching his anger dissolve into sadness.

"Every day or night I've wanted to see people, I've tried. Last night was the first night I was successful."

"What?" Sakai is fuming, unable to hold his passivity.

"You're serious?" Lucy glances from me to Mariko. Mariko is denying nothing.

Jiro's eyes widen as he paces into the kitchen. "But I've been working most evenings for the past couple of months. Since July!" He closes his eyes and shakes his head. "I wish you had said something sooner."

"How could I? You were working on my behalf, and it's not fair to make everyone here bend over backwards for me. I messaged people constantly for company, and I received nothing but excuses in return. Besides, they all knew I was here alone yet nobody came back to the building during the day or night to see if I needed anything. No one but Oyama, and without him I would have starved. I had to accept that if they wanted to spend time with me they would. That's it."

He takes three strides across the room to me, and he's so intense I shrink back, but at the last moment, he slows his approach. "You are not only the most important person in my life, you are the most important person in this city. The most important person in the colonization. It's inexcusable that people would ignore you. I have been meeting with influential people and garnering your support, and I thought I left you in capable hands at home. Shit. I promised you I would never leave you alone again. I promised on our unborn children!"

He heads straight for the door. Oh no. Where is he going? It's not even eight in the morning.

"Jiro," I start but my voice cracks immediately, and Mariko, Sakai, and Lucy stand and watch. Don't sound desperate, Sanaa. "Won't you stay and have breakfast with me this morning? It's been ages since we last had breakfast together." I try as hard as I can to smile and convince him, though my lungs are light, and I'm unable to breathe. I hate the mornings I wake up and he's already gone.

He pauses for a moment, both shoes on, and clutches his hand to his chest. "Gods, you just broke my heart. Make coffee and tea. I'll be back with breakfast soon, and I'll stay with you all day. Mother, you should go home."

"No," Sakai says, his arms crossed over his chest, "Mariko, you should come upstairs with me and Lucy. We have much to discuss."

Jiro opens the door for her, giving Mariko a deathly stare, one I'm actually frightened by. Mariko dips her head at me at the door and leaves with Sakai and Lucy following close behind.

I'm alone again.

Chapter Forty-Two

Jiro comes back forty minutes later bearing crepes filled with fresh berries and whipped soy creme on the side.

"This is such a lovely breakfast. Thank you." I sit down and wait as he puts a plate in front of me, fills up my coffee, and sits down across from me.

I stop and stare, drink him in. He's here, with me, for breakfast. It's been so long, I've forgotten how fresh and alive he looks in the morning. I want to eat all of this food and snuggle up to him on the couch. That would be the perfect antidote to all the drama this morning, drama I want to forget.

Slicing into the crepes, I get started on this decadent breakfast.

"Sanaa, can I... access your tablet, please?"

"Of course. Did you leave yours someplace?" I gently set down my knife and fork and grab my tablet from the couch.

"No, my tablet's in the bedroom, remember?" I nod and hand mine over before sitting back down. "You know I trust you, right?"

"Yes..." That's not a good way to start a conversation.

"I'm going to look through all your messages. Usagi's not at home, and Beni swears she had no idea my mother was keeping you from spending time with them. You understand, right?"

I suppose I'm not going to easily forget the drama. I nod my head, slow and deliberate. I have nothing to hide. I told him about Chad — I'm not lying about any of this — but letting him have access to all of my correspondence is terrifying. I guard my privacy closely.

I eat while he taps through my inbox, his face progressively getting sadder and angrier the longer he stays on my tablet.

"This is ridiculous. I count over fifty messages to my mother alone since July that have gone unanswered. Usagi, at least, wrote you back most times to tell you he was working but doesn't say on what. Oyama always responds to your requests for food. Beni responded to all of your business requests, but any time you asked her to come over, she said my mother needed her. Miko was working but you could have seen her if only Usagi had taken you. Yoichi never responded once to your messages. You even wrote

Kentaro."

"He's the only one who responded to get together. We've gone to the dōjō when you couldn't and the grocery store on the day of the earthquake. I wasn't sure if it was proper to socialize with him otherwise, just the two of us. I was afraid rumors would spread or something."

He taps on the screen a few more times. "There's this bizarre chain of messages that goes over a span of two weeks where everyone claims they're busy and passes you off to someone else." He sets down the tablet and closes his eyes. "I'm completely horrified. I let people and circumstances separate us. We both did. We can't do that again."

I push my plate away from me, my throat unable to allow food to pass to my stomach anymore.

"You know what kills me about all of this? Your mother actually warned me about you." I laugh, surprised at how bitter it tastes in my mouth, fuzzy and repugnant. "She told me to watch out for you because you always think the best of people. That you're too trusting. And here you were, trusting your mother and me, and we both failed you."

He leans forward, his elbows on the table, and his forehead resting on his hands. His chin-length hair comes loose from behind his ears and covers up the agony on his face. "You haven't failed me. You tried your best with shitty circumstances. I only wish you had talked to me about it."

"I'm sorry," I mumble. I knew he'd be upset, especially with his mother, but I always thought if he found out about this, he would say this is my lot in life, my burden to carry. I would have to accept it, like when Helena told me to accept my fate and just be me.

"I just don't understand. Yoichi told me he has dinner with my mother and Miko all the time. They go to my cousins' together. I keep thinking about those conversations with Yoichi, and it's only now apparent your name was never mentioned. *You* never mentioned those dinners because you didn't attend them, and I always thought you had."

Gods, hearing the depth of my abandonment straight from Jiro's mouth is making my chest seize up. "They all blame me." He doesn't deny my claim, so I press on. "Your mother blames me for your father's death. Your brother blames me for it too, and for Miko's poisoning. Usagi blames me for Helena. Oyama feels bad for Usagi. Miko feels bad for Yoichi and your mother."

At least I'm pretty sure Sakai and Lucy don't blame me for anything, but they're far too busy to provide me with company. My new family, though, has shunned me, as did my old one. How has my life come to this?

"I tried to work things out with Yoichi, honestly. I knew things were not right between me and your mother, but I thought I was reading her wrong especially after our conversation at the house."

"I know."

"We had a few lunches when I thought things were going well between us, but then she would just break into tears. One day she was crying, and I tried to comfort her, but she was violent with me. Practically flung me away. But then other times, she was normal, even caring, though she's not touched or hugged me in months."

"Was Beni there the times she was nicer?"

"Yes."

"My mother is excellent at saving face. She would never have acted unkind to you with other people around." Jiro rubs his face, sighing and growling.

It's all been an act? I believed she was dealing with her own issues and grief privately. But no, she's been blaming me from the beginning.

I square up my shoulders and lift my head. "I'll admit I'm upset and disappointed..." And as soon as I say it, the tears start rolling, but I keep going. "Because I've missed my aunts so much, and I really wanted to be a part of your family since I have very little family of my own." I quickly wipe off my face and take a weak and trembling breath. "I was hoping your mother could be like a mother to me."

Jiro's eyes are focused on me but past me. There are many days when I can't read him, because his emotions run so deep. My guess is he's either so sad he's trying not to cry or so vindictive he's trying not to kill someone. Either way, he's holding himself together just for me.

"You *are* a part of my family, Sanaa. You *are* my family. I can't help but think that if my father were still alive, none of this would have happened. He loved you. There's no way he would have stood for this. There's no way I'm standing for this now that I know."

His chest heaves, anger rising in his voice.

"Jiro, please calm down. If your mother doesn't want to

associate with me, we have to accept her decision. Not every girl gets along with her mother-in-law." I've reached a level of numbness where my mind can't process what's happened to me. I've been ignored. Shunned on purpose. I did nothing to deserve this.

Red, hot anger wells up from my stomach. She's allowed me to be alone for months when we could have comforted each other and been friends. How will we ever fix this? Because right now I want to scream at her, yell at her and tell her how foolish she's been because I'll never forget this.

I can't yell at her if I want to salvage our relationship. And I should try to salvage it somehow because I can't avoid her for the rest of my life.

Where does this energy go? Jiro's right in front of me, his eyes rich with emotion, his tattoos cresting above the low collar of his shirt, his strong hands curled into angry fists. I want those hands on me. Now.

"Jiro, I've missed you like crazy. I want you to take me, on this table, right now."

His eyes widen, realization forming so quick, and he jumps up from his seat, sweeps his hand across our plates, and sends them straight to the floor, my soggy crepes landing in a heap right next to my slippers. I launch myself across the table at him, kissing him hard enough to knock my forehead into his. He doesn't flinch. I pull my clothes off as fast as possible coming to the edge of the table and wrapping my legs around him.

Dominant Jiro pins me down, alternately being hard on me, then slowing down and telling me how much he loves me and missed me. I dig my nails into his back until he winces and kisses me. I want to hit him, hit myself, for being so damned stupid these past few months. We trusted his family blindly, and I let him down by not saying anything. He let me down by never asking, only assuming. We've both been fools. Been fooled.

I may have been fooled, but I'm not broken. I know where everyone stands now, and it'll be that much easier to trust the right people from here on out. Dammit, people will have to earn my trust. I will not indiscriminately put my faith in anyone again.

"Stop, Jiro."

He pulls back quickly. "What?"

"No more anger. I just want to enjoy you." I smile at him, one of the few people now who deserve my love and respect. "Take me to the couch."

We're so good to each other, and the sex is so all-consuming, I actually black out after coming, spent to completeness and unable to function. When I open my eyes, Jiro is sitting over me on the couch. His eyes run me over from my head, down my neck, and over my body to my hips. Then he leans down and runs his hand back up my body where his eyes just were, over my stomach, around my breasts, into the space under my arm, and up to my left hand.

"Jiro..."

"Shhh, I'm storing this away for later."

Chapter Forty-Three

Jiro takes me out for more food since our lovely breakfast ended up on the floor. We have an early lunch at the ramen place across the street with Oyama in the kitchen.

"You haven't been eating. I can tell. You can barely finish your bowl, and you used to eat everything."

I push my lunch away from me and lean back to let my belly expand. "Well, this was actually a lot of food for me. I ate almost the whole bowl." I look up from the few noodles floating in the broth to find Usagi crossing the street and heading straight for us.

"Sanaa-san, Jiro. May I sit?"

"Of course, Usagi." I pull out the chair next to me, and he sits down.

"I've come to apologize. I didn't want to interrupt you earlier when you were home." He smiles, and I blush. "I've missed Helena, and I know it's not your fault she was poisoned. I don't blame you, I promise. All the nights I didn't come to take you out when you asked were spent working. I spent every day, every night, wandering the neighborhoods where Kazuo and Sachi were last seen. I followed Emiko Matsuda, Risa, and her parents. I've even watched Minamoto."

He sighs and nods at Jiro. "I'm sorry. I was so obsessed with this, with finding them, I didn't tell Jiro or Sakai-san. I didn't want them to know I was neglecting you to do this. Because I knew my actions were wrong, but I couldn't stop."

Usagi is looking me straight in the eyes, not avoiding me like I would expect a liar to. Obsession is something I understand. He's the same way I am when I'm latched onto an idea I can't stop thinking about. I believe him.

"You hurt me. I like you a lot and trusted you. I was crushed that you, of all people, ignored me."

"I'm so sorry, Sanaa-san. I feel terrible. If Helena were here, she'd probably break up with me for treating you this way."

He's right, but I hope we both see her again. As mad as I am at him, I'm more angry with Mariko. She abandoned me for all the wrong reasons.

"I forgive you, but you should know it'll take me a long time to forget."

He winces. Good. I don't want to be mean, but I want to make it clear I'm not someone who can be wronged and then immediately forget.

"Also, at Jiro's behest, I'm going to have to insist you always come when I ask you to. No more excuses."

"Yes, Sanaa-san. I understand."

To show I'm not completely heartless, I reach over, take his hand, and squeeze it.

"Thank you for not firing me," he says, and I laugh.

"Usagi, you'll never be fired. We have to work some things out. I was naive to believe everything would be perfect from the get-go."

I was naive to believe Mariko would love me because she loved my mother, naive to believe we could be happy with each other right from the very start because Jiro loved us both. What was I thinking? I can only blame it on my hopefulness and the fact that she lied to me. I can't let myself be that gullible again.

"I have other news," he says, pulling my thoughts back to the present. "Kentaro found Kazuo, and he's on the move today, maybe finding his way to Sachi. We should follow."

I nod eagerly at Jiro. I've been dying to get out and chasing down Kazuo is just what I need.

"Let's go get dressed."

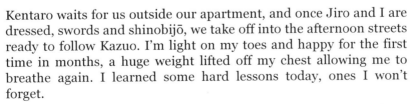

Kentaro waits for us outside our apartment, and once Jiro and I are dressed, swords and shinobijō, we take off into the afternoon streets ready to follow Kazuo. I'm light on my toes and happy for the first time in months, a huge weight lifted off my chest allowing me to breathe again. I learned some hard lessons today, ones I won't forget.

We pick up the trail on Kazuo deep in Minamoto territory bordering Little Kyoto. He's been traveling around, in and out of restaurants and apartment buildings, with a giant bag on his back which gets more full each time he stops. He must be picking up his belongings from all of the places he's lived over the years. But why? Following him all over Ku 6 is tiring. We're constantly ducking in storefronts, out of sight so we're not caught. We take turns checking around corners, watching alleyways, and splitting up to sneak around buildings, picking up his trail when he disappears. At 7:00pm, he finally slows down and ends his journey in a familiar udon shop. It's the same restaurant he met Sachi and Risa at after Sachi tried to poison us all at Izakaya Tanaka.

Jiro, Kentaro, Usagi, and I peel off half a block away and observe him through the window as he seats himself near the back of the restaurant and orders food.

"Thank the gods, he's stopped. My feet are beginning to ache," Kentaro says, leaning against the building.

"This is an izakaya." Usagi leans out and examines the restaurant's storefront. "Let's go in and get something to eat."

I bounce from one foot to the next, stretching out my ankles. I'm glad I've spent my alone time in Sakai building running the stairs.

"Can't. No Oyama." They all sink in disappointment. This is why I never get invited out. "No matter. Let's go in anyway. I need to rest. You can eat."

"That's it! I've had it," Jiro growls, his hands curling into fists shaken upward at the domes. "This is the worst day on record."

"What, Jiro? What have I done now?" I pull back from him because he's all fiery, heaving breaths, and though I usually love it when he's like this, I do not like it when these emotions are directed at me. "I'm sick of this all being my fault."

"It's not. That's not what I mean." He grabs me by my shoulders, looking me in the eyes. "Sanaa, I know this was my idea, and Mark's, to keep you safe at home, but I'm tired of all these restrictions on your life. You're tired of them. Do you want to live like this?"

"No."

"Then eat what you want, when you want. Drink what you want. Go places. Without anyone else. I trust you. You're more than capable of defending yourself. I feel sick knowing I've cooped you up for months."

"Really? Real freedom?"

"Yes. I'll be devastated if something happens to you, but this life you're living is worse than death."

"That would be... amazing." It seems stupid to be overwhelmed by the idea of getting my life back, but I'd rather do what I want and be struck down tomorrow than live a long life held captive like this.

"Use your judgment. We've been all over the ward today. No one is going to know you're here. I think you can eat in peace. If you were at Izakaya Tanaka, that would be a time to have Oyama since you're always there."

"You only have a few weeks left," Kentaro butts in. "Access the cameras outside first if you want to go out and no one is around to escort you."

"And never leave without your sword," Usagi follows up with a nod.

I could cry from joy. I'm going to enjoy every last moment until we leave. I'll figure out how to live on Yūsei when we get there.

We eat dinner in the izakaya, checking the cameras out front with Kentaro's tablet every now and then, and Kazuo stays put. The dome lights dim around 7:30, and, half an hour later, Kazuo grabs his bag and exits the udon restaurant out back. Time to go.

Jiro and I pick a spot across the street from the entrance, in the shadows of an alley, where we can stand side-by-side and not be seen. Kentaro will sneak around to the back. Usagi will watch the alley.

"Don't lock your knees. Keep them loose or you may faint."

I nod at him, and we both wait. After ten minutes, I reach over and grab Jiro's hand. I'm nervous and want his reassurance we're doing the right thing. He rubs his fingers along my left hand and plays with my ring.

Kazuo and Sachi emerge from the end of the alley. He must have met up with her in back of the restaurant. Kazuo's hair is shoulder length and tied back. This must be his normal hair because it's the most popular of all the styles I've seen on him. Sachi's hair is long and tied into pigtails.

We hold completely still in the shadows. The twins scan left and right, and after a moment's hesitation, they take off in the same direction together, matching their long strides.

We give them a one-block lead before Jiro peeks his head out and gestures to Usagi to walk on the opposite side. Staying on our side of the street, Jiro and I match our strides like the twins.

Kentaro emerges from behind the udon restaurant and starts walking a half a block ahead of us.

Kazuo and Sachi don't slow their pace. When they make a right turn, Jiro and I slip into another alley behind them and wait. The twins don't double back. They keep going, cross the street, and head straight for an open community playground nestled between two buildings ahead.

We're way off the main streets now, so far from the neighborhood business district I can almost see the edge of this dome. It slopes down low overhead only two blocks away.

Jiro points to Usagi and gestures to him to come at the playground from the same direction as the twins. Jiro points to Kentaro and swoops his hand around towards the left indicating he should come around from the other side. Then he points to us both and motions that we'll come in over the top. Over the top?

Jiro and I quietly approach the building next to the playground, and as we close in, three other people are heading this way from a few blocks off. The fire escape is on the opposite side of the building so it shouldn't be hard to climb up and get to the roof, but the ladder doesn't lead all the way to the ground. We'll have to boost up.

I stand in position underneath because I think Jiro is going to need me to help him, but he stops. He stops dead, his hands cradling my face, his thumb gently stroking my cheek. I've lost my breath. His expression is so loving and so full of concern for me I can't look away.

Really, I shouldn't be here at all. I'm the last in my line, and if I die, no one else can do the job I have to do. This will be the test of my new life. If I live through tonight, will it be enough to convince everyone I can do this forever?

Quickly, he pulls me to him and kisses me hard, passionately. This could easily be the end for us. After everything we've gone through today, I'm happy to be here with him despite the danger. It's just the two of us, an unbreakable team. I support Jiro and he's supporting me, sticking by me even with everything happening in his family. I want to tell him how important he is to me, but he breaks off the kiss and leans forward to whisper, "I love you," into my ear, and I say it right back. If these are our final last words to each other, I can die content.

I point up. "You first."

Cupping my hands together, I give Jiro a small boost up. He lies down on his stomach and hangs through the opening, and I jump up, lock my hands with his, and climb up next to him. We ascend the stairs being careful not to make any noise, cross the roof of the building, and peek over the top.

Kazuo and Sachi are waiting down below with their bags next to them and Risa is there.

"But you can stay with me, if you like, Kazuo. There's no reason for you to go now." Risa strokes her hand along Kazuo's upper arm, and he backs off. I can see Risa's pout all the way up on the roof. Gods, she's detestable.

"She recognizes me now. They all do, I think. Time to go."

"I'm not done here yet," Sachi whines and stomps her foot, and I clamp my hand over my mouth to stop a laugh. Jiro rolls his eyes at her.

"You wanna stay? Fine. Be my guest. I'm leaving." Kazuo opens his bag and pulls out a sword, placing the long katana on his back.

The three people coming from the opposite direction approach the playground from the street. Risa's parents, Nobu and Yukio Yamamoto, and Emiko Matsuda step up to Risa, Kazuo, and Sachi.

"Are you ready to go?" Emiko asks.

The twins look at each other. "I am," Kazuo says, "but Sachi has unfinished business."

They're about to leave. It's now or never.

"Jiro, what should we do? It sounds like the twins are dividing up. We may never be able to track them again if they leave now."

He nods his head. "We should stop them. Are you up for it?"

"Absolutely. We have to try and stop them now before they do more damage to our family."

I'm crazy, but I don't care. My new family may not want much to do with me, but I'd still do just about anything to protect them.

Chapter Forty-Four

We climb back down the fire escape quickly and motion to Usagi. Hopefully Kentaro figures out we're about to attack.

Jiro and I walk into the street. This area is quiet, and no one is around, being so far on the outskirts of the ward. The hour is late, and people are already in bed. In ten hours, this playground will be filled with kids running and playing on the equipment. Now, the outdoor space is cold and vacant.

Do I draw my sword? Jiro is just standing and waiting. He could be waiting for a train, for all I'd know, he's so calm and alert. I choose to keep Kazenoho on my back.

Our adversaries exit the playground to the street. We are far outnumbered, but I believe Nobu and Yukio are worthless in this exchange, and I'm certain Risa can't fight worth a damn.

"Hello, cousins," Jiro says, and they all stop. Usagi creeps out of the shadows and corners them from behind. "You know, I really don't think you'll be taking the Uchiyamas anywhere tonight. They have a lot to answer for."

Kazuo actually sighs and rolls his eyes. Paired with the annoyance in his voice from earlier, I get the feeling he's sick of all of this. Isn't he a trained assassin? Maybe he needs a career change.

Sachi acts quickly. From out of her pocket, she takes a small canister, pops the end, and throws it between us. Smoke billows out of the tiny plastic bomb, and shit, I can't see anything. Drawing my sword right now would definitely be too dangerous. Before I can reach up to grab my shinobijō, Jiro's hand is on mine and pulling me off to the side. Footsteps run in each direction.

Risa screams, "Nobody kill me! I'm not ready to die!" Then sobs.

"How she ever thought I'd find her attractive is beyond me. Get your staff out, Sanaa," Jiro whispers. If we can't see anyone, then they can't see us either. Might as well not give up our location if we don't have to. I draw out the staff and keep it vertical by my side like Kentaro taught me.

From the right, the *shiiiiing* of a sword being drawn and

striking echoes towards us. Usagi? I let Jiro lead through the smoke towards the grunts and clashes of swords. He slowly pulls Oninoten out, his hands flexed and arms tense, and a chill runs up my spine. Watching Jiro use his sword is my favorite thing on earth.

Someone runs past us on our left, another smoke bomb hits the ground with a clink, hissing and spitting out acrid fog. Sachi is doing a good job of keeping us disoriented. Now it sounds like sword fighting is coming from straight ahead, so Jiro and I stop for a moment to reorient ourselves.

Five footsteps and a yell rings out before I turn and block Sachi who comes straight down on me from the smoke with a staff. We block left, right, left, right. She sweeps, and I jump back and knock into Jiro who didn't want to strike because I was in the way. I duck down, and he lunges over me with a stab that would have hit Sachi squarely in the chest if she hadn't jumped back. She runs off into the smoke with a high pitched squeal and cackle. I didn't even get a chance to use any of the weapons in my shinobijō.

"*Nantekotta?* She is seriously off her meds," I whisper at Jiro, and he laughs lightly.

"Have you been studying Japanese swear words at home?"

"*Kusokurae.*" I smirk at him, and he laughs quietly again.

"Coming from the girl who won't even say fuck in English, that's adorable."

The smoke is creepy and disorienting. My eyes burn, and I try not to breathe deeply so I don't cough. It won't be long before the smoke is detected and fire crews arrive on the scene. The dome fans are already kicking to high speed, the smoke whipping past me at a swift rate. We don't have much time.

I draw out Kazenoho with my right hand. I've never fought with a weapon in each hand before and something tells me this is not the time to try out that technique.

"Back to back," Jiro whispers, and I press my back up against his. His hand comes down on my staff, takes the weapon from me, and puts it away.

"What do we do?"

"We wait right here until we can be sure where to go next."

Jiro's words are cut off by Kazuo running straight for us, and with his scream and his eyes wide, he is terrifying. He's on my side so I stab for his chest, twisting out of the way as his sword descends.

Jiro turns, kicking out at Kazuo's feet. Kazuo slashes at me while jumping over Jiro, and I block him. He came within a centimeter of getting me.

Jiro battles Kazuo, and I'm stunned by how fast they are. Jiro is up, down, up, side, stab, back, lunge... and all the time Kazuo is on defense. I keep looking left and right and wondering if Sachi will show up. Where is Usagi? Kentaro?

Kazuo may be tiring. His sword is late to every one of Jiro's moves, so I run at him from behind. He thinks I'm going to stab, but instead I jump and kick for his head.

No one expects you to fight hand-to-hand when you have a sword drawn. Surprising my opponents has always been my strong suit.

He had his eyes on my sword which I kept in my left hand off to the side. He didn't see my kick coming from the right until it was too late. Kazuo reels, his head snapping to the side, before coming back to the center.

Kazenoho dips in my weaker left hand, hits the ground and bounces back up, slicing my leg.

"Ouch!" Shit! I injured myself. Did that really just happen? I'm flying so high on adrenaline the cut doesn't even hurt.

Jiro jumps in front of me, Oninoten out, ready to defend me against Kazuo.

"Fantastic!" Kazuo says, letting out a bark of a laugh. "You're better than I thought you were, Sanaa."

"Are you all right?" Jiro asks without turning his head.

I straighten up with Kazenoho out. It's not a deep cut, but it is bleeding pretty heavily.

"I'll be fine." Inching forward, I force Kazuo back one step while Jiro circles him to the right. Jiro's eyes are laughing. He's alive and excited, and I have to stop myself from getting distracted by how astonishing he becomes when he fights.

"Come on, Kazuo." I wag Kazenoho's tip at him, ignoring my leg. "Let's fight. I've been cooped up for weeks, and I'm eager for swordplay."

Kazuo smirks at me. "No, no. I'm just not feeling it tonight. We'll meet again, I'm sure."

"Don't disappoint her, Kazuo." Jiro edges in a little more. "She'll be all sulky tomorrow if she doesn't clash swords tonight."

Kazuo laughs, never taking his eyes off me. "Seems as though it's your own fault, Jiro, if she's sulky. You leave her at home enough."

Jiro tenses, and his stare turns cold.

"Can't tell you how many times I've watched Sanaa pace the front hall of your building, chat with your security staff, and gaze longingly out the window. You should have seen her cling to Usagi the other night. She cried about how you leave her home alone all the time. You should be more attentive to your wife."

My skin crawls, and I suck in a quick breath to halt my tears. I've let my enemies see me weak. See me lonely. I've been far too careless.

It's deathly quiet for a moment before I hear footsteps running from my right. Sachi laughs but the clash of two staff weapons echoes into the smoke for about a dozen hits before she grunts and retreats.

"Later, Mr. and Mrs. Itō." Kazuo quickly bows to us both and runs off before either of us can strike at him.

My katana dips low. Kazuo knows what I've been going through. He has sat and watched me while Jiro has been gone. Jiro pulls me aside because I'm too dazed to defend myself now. He places his back against the wall of the apartment building next to us, grabs the back of my head and pulls me to his chest.

"I'm so sorry."

My chest heaves, prelude to a huge crying fit, but Jiro squeezes me even tighter.

"Shhh, don't cry now. We're not in the clear yet. You may need to fight again."

"Oh-oh-oh-okay," I stammer out, my lower lip unwilling to obey and shaking. I close my eyes against his chest, and listen to his steady breathing and heartbeat until my eyes dry. When I pull away from him, he looks deep into my eyes before down at my leg.

"Gods, you're bleeding all over the place."

We both freeze to listen as footsteps come flying past us but no one stops. Jiro lifts his shirt in the back and pulls out a knife.

"Bye bye, sex pants. I loved these things on you." He slices into my pants above the knee, cuts the leg off them, and binds up my injury. "It's not deep. We'll get the doctor to come tonight."

I nod and hold back the tears again. I was worried Kazuo was watching me in my home. No. He was just listening to me there but watching me through the front door windows into the lobby. When I think of all the days I spent down in the lobby, reading on the couch, looking out the front doors and waiting for someone to come home, or talking to the security staff, I cringe knowing Kazuo was observing every emotion on my face.

"I owe you... for so much," Jiro says, tipping my face up to him, but I shake my head as footsteps approach us again. Owe me for fighting? Owe me for putting up with being alone for months? He doesn't owe me anything.

"Kentaro!" I whisper as loudly as I can, and out of the fog, he appears with his jō out and a smile on his face.

"I forgot Sachi is good at the staff, but I got a hit on her."

"Thank the gods you're okay, Ken-chan." I reach my arm out and pull him to us, and we all back up to the building.

"Usagi?" he asks.

"He's here somewhere," Jiro says, scanning the retreating fog. "We heard him sword fighting a few minutes ago."

Footsteps approach us from the left. The smoke is clearing so I can tell it's Usagi right away by his bald head, but his sword is not right.

"I'm here, and I'm fine, but my sword is not."

"Oh no." I groan and pull Usagi's sword close. About ten centimeters from the tip down are gone. "Where's the rest of it?"

"In the street somewhere. I almost got Kazuo but then he came at me from behind. When I struck out at him, he jumped out of the way, and I hit a lamppost I didn't know was there. Damned smoke."

"We should go find the tip. Maybe it can be repaired?" Jiro steps away and sheathes Oninoten. "I think they're gone now. The smoke is clearing."

Kentaro slips his jō into the carrier on his back and sighs. "I shooed off your cousins and Emiko right at the beginning of the fight. They were standing paralyzed in the playground. Emiko saw me. I have no idea what she'll tell my father. And then Risa..." He breaks into snorts of laughter. "I think she may have peed her pants."

The sound of sirens erupts from about ten blocks off, and a window squeaks open in the building above us. "Is something on fire down there?" a man's voice shouts down.

I put my finger to my mouth. "We should get out of here before anyone finds us. Let's fan out that way and see if we can find the rest of Usagi's sword."

We all walk in the direction of Usagi's last fight, and not far in front of me, a long section of metal catches the light of a lamp.

"Here! I found it." I strip off my outer shirt and use it to wrap up the broken segment of Usagi's sword.

We all stand and look at the bundle in my hands. I feel like I'm carrying a dead member of my family, and I hand it solemnly to Usagi who clutches it to his chest.

"I'm sorry, Usagi."

Jiro pulls on me. "Come on everyone. Let's go before we get caught."

Chapter Forty-Five

Over the course of five days, the glue stitches I received after the fight slowly dissolve every time I take a shower, and my wound starts to heal. The cut was not very big, but it will most likely leave a scar. My first sword fighting scar. I'm stupidly proud of it, especially since I gave it to myself.

Beni and Mariko come by every morning to check in on us and bring breakfast, and though I love Beni and have never felt uncomfortable with her, I'm struggling with Mariko. I do my best to smile and make small talk, but I construct a bubble of personal space around her I don't intrude on. I can see the physical strain at the corners of her eyes and mouth as she strives to be pleasant with me. I give her credit for even trying. I almost wish I never knew about her betrayal because I have a hard time faking it, hard time smiling even though I'm sad, hard time talking even though I want to sulk.

Fake it till you make it, Sanaa. I've been in this position before, and it got easier. I still breathe a huge sigh of relief every time she leaves.

I take Jiro's advice and leave the building unattended for the first time ever, throwing Kazenoho over my shoulder, waving to the frozen security guards downstairs who have never seen me walk out the door alone, and cross the street to the grocery store.

"Itami-sama!" The owner, a little man named Kawabata, hurriedly runs to me while looking around. "Where is Itō-san? Oyama?"

"I'm alone, Kawabata-san. It's fine." I squeeze his shoulder and smile, letting him know it's okay I'm on my own.

I'm sure Kawabata would relax if I slipped into easy Japanese with him. He's part of the older crowd in Ku 6 who have reverted back to using just Japanese unless dealing with non-Japanese. But they all think of me as "half" regardless of my heritage. I didn't grow up here, and they all know it, so I stick to English. I try not to cross too many lines with them.

"I came by to ask you about the young man you had working here."

"He's gone, Itami-sama. Never came back after the earthquake."

"I figured as much. No one ever came to visit him?"

Kawabata shakes his head. "No. Never. He was very quiet, often standing at the front of the store and staring into space. He liked to listen to music."

"Music?"

"He had headphones he would wear while stacking the shelves. It never bothered me or anyone else so I let it go."

He was watching my building from across the street, observing me in my home, and I'd bet even money he wasn't listening to music, he was listening to the bug in our apartment.

"Did he ever mention anyone? Family? Friends?"

Kawabata stops arranging some produce and taps his cheek, thinking. "He said he had a young lady he was interested in but that she was unavailable. He also mentioned a sister, but I got the feeling the sister was gone or estranged."

Hmmm, interesting. Risa was ready and waiting, definitely available, so I don't think she was the object of his affection. I need to try and find him again on surveillance. There may be a girl he's had his eye on I can go to and interview. As for Sachi, I suspect they aren't as close as I originally thought.

Chapter Forty-Six

It's time to say goodbye to Nishikyō even though our newest enemies are still on the loose. For the past week, Jiro and I have been traveling around to all our old haunts, drinking in the sights and sounds of a city we'll leave far behind. We went back to the alley behind Izakaya Tanaka — it's been closed a few weeks now — where we had our first kiss and to the tempura restaurant where we had our third date. Jiro said goodbye to everyone including Asa, the flirtatious waitress. She was disappointed to see us still together especially when she caught sight of my ring. Sorry, Asa-chan.

We visit Jiro's grandmother and all of his young cousins who are not coming until third and fifth wave because the kids have growing to do before hibernating. We don't even tell Mariko we're visiting her family members. I don't want to punish her for these past few months, but Jiro does. I've never seen him so cold to his mother. They don't have the same easiness they used to have, and it makes me sick, especially when we visit my aunts and he's relaxed with them. Aunt Lomo fawns over Jiro, and he smiles and softens so sweetly when she hugs him. The whole dynamic has changed.

Then it's time to meet with Minamoto and Tamiko who will be on first wave with us. The visit is cool but vaguely pleasant with Tamiko being the more hospitable host of the two. Minamoto stays tight-lipped. Maybe he's cursing the fact I'm still alive? I try not to let the hate show in my eyes. How this man ever donated DNA to Kentaro is a mystery.

Kentaro's all ready to go too. His bags and belongings are being sent with his family, though, and they are leaving for the space elevator two days after us.

"The building will be lonely without you guys, so I'm going to go to Kevin's in the intervening days. We broke up, but whatever. He's been asking me to come."

"He misses you," I say with a little laugh. I can understand why.

"Maybe," he says, cocking a crooked smile at me. "I don't think I can sleep with him again, though." He sighs and stares off into space, and I sit in agonizingly excited silence. Kentaro is actually talking about his sex life, and I'm extremely curious. Come on! Spill it!

"Sanaa-san, I just don't know... Don't know..." He stammers off, shaking his head.

"Don't know what?" Oh, I hate myself for prying.

He sighs, slaps his knees, and stands up to leave our apartment. Jiro was gone, and he came by to chat.

"Don't know what I'm doing. I'm hoping, when we get to Yūsei, everything will be clearer. Anyway, I'll see you later," he says, waving at the door after slipping on his shoes at lightning speed.

Argh. Kentaro. Really, once he started smiling and being less of an idiot boy, he was actually quite enjoyable, and now I want to know more. I guess I have to wait.

Finally, our tour of Nishikyō brings us to the dōjō where I sit on the mats and weep openly. I love this place and everything it symbolizes for me, my awakening into adulthood, my passions and reasons for living. Who will practice here when we're gone? Probably no one. Almost the entire Itō and Sakai family are going in the first wave. No one will be left to pound on the mats and clash swords in this space every day.

Today is Jiro's twenty-third birthday, and in five more days, we'll all be gone, heading to the space elevator and up to orbit. Everything but two boxes and two bags have been picked up and shipped to the space elevator, but I can't help but gift him something.

"Can I give you your birthday present now?"

We've had our tea and coffee while snuggling on the couch, lazing about and enjoying a peaceful morning for once. Every day has been filled until now. The fifteenth of November has brought a cool wind, and the city is comfortable, as is our apartment. I do not miss summer.

Jiro kisses my temple and laughs. "You didn't have to get me anything."

"I know, but I've wanted to give you this one thing."

Throwing off our blanket, I run into the bedroom and pull the long box out from under the bed where I've been hiding it for a few weeks. "Close your eyes."

He's sitting with his eyes closed when I exit the bedroom. "You can probably tell what it is before you even open it but... Happy twenty-third birthday."

He opens his eyes and smiles at the box as I set it on his lap.

"You're not the only one who can give weapons as gifts."

He pulls out one of my family wakizashi I had Beni retrieve from the storage space in Ku 9 before everything was taken away. This short sword has always been one of my favorites, and I remember Jiro eyeing it when we were in the storage space the first time. The blade is forged in the same manner as Oninoten and Kazenoho with the same signature stamp on the side. The blade and grip needed a lot of work though. Beni took it to Masa, Jiro's distant cousin who made my shinobijō, and had the sword taken care of.

"It's beautiful. You had it repaired? But, I can't take your family heirlooms."

"Jiro," I say, wrapping my arms around him, "have you forgotten that we're married now? They're yours as much as mine. Besides, I don't want this sitting in some box never being used. When I look at this sword, I know it was meant to be in your hands right next to Oninoten." I let go but not before giving him a kiss. "Even if you never truly believe that all of those things in storage are yours as well, which they are, you should at least believe they are mine to be given away as I please. So there. Happy birthday."

He sets down the sword and smiles at it for a moment.

"Thank you, love. I've always wanted my own wakizashi." He reaches over to his tablet. "But, I think it's entirely unfair you don't get a birthday."

I wave my hand at him and pick up my coffee. "It's not a big deal. We'll celebrate some other time."

"Nope. You didn't know this but I arranged the big dinner party tonight for you as well. Not just my birthday but *our* birthdays."

"Jiro, you didn't have to do that. I would have been fine without all the fuss."

"Well, you can't change it now, and I invited Chad and his girlfriend."

"What?" I choke on my coffee, and Jiro laughs while pounding on my back. "I haven't seen him since January."

"You talk online all the time," he murmurs straight into my ear before kissing my cheek. "I want to meet him before we go."

He hands me his tablet. "So this is for you. I've worked on these for the last six months."

My pulse pounds in my ears. I've seen Jiro on his tablet during quiet times or when I would come home from visiting with Sakai or Lucy or Mariko, and he would always turn it off and set it down. I knew he was drawing — that he would never stop drawing, of course. But, especially after Tanabata when I got the most excellent and happiest surprise of my life, I didn't want to pry into his secrets. I didn't think he was hiding things from me. He would show me eventually. I had to be patient. Patience is not something I'm good at, though. It has taken a lot of willpower not to sneak his tablet away and look for myself.

The first drawing is the one he did of the main room at the house in the desert, the one with me curled up on the couch sleeping. I sometimes feel like that was the beginning of our life together, not the first time we ever clashed swords or the first time we saw each other on New Year's Eve. Our time in the house changed us both.

"Swipe through. There are more."

The next drawing is one of our apartment, the main room we're sitting in now that shares space with the kitchen, our couch with my blanket on it, the coffee table with two steaming mugs, the drawing Jiro first gave me on the wall. He even included my slippers I like to wear when the city temps dip low in the winter. I'm going to miss this apartment.

I start to cry looking at the third sketch of Izakaya Tanaka. It's just how I remember with the maneki-neko along the walls, the hand-painted signs, and Miko stands at the bar with her cute short hair cut, her chin propped on her hand and smiling at Jiro. Did she pose for this or is this all from Jiro's head?

I especially love the next one. Jiro must have spent a lot of time watching Kentaro and me fight with each other in the dōjō because the drawing is of me, with my back turned, tattoos facing Jiro. My staff is raised, and I'm blocking Kentaro who is striking down on me from above with determination on his face. I tilt the tablet to show Jiro, and he smiles.

"I never thought I'd draw Ken-chan, but he's become such a major part of our lives. Do you regret asking him to join us?"

I shake my head and wipe away my tears. "No. Not for a moment."

"Me neither."

The next sketch is of our bedroom. All of the things on our desk, our belongings on the shelves, and our rumpled bed which we never make. I have to stop looking because my tears are dropping on the tablet.

"Just two more, Sanaa."

I let out a little laugh on the next one. I should have known that moment at the casino, when Jiro and I were leaving and he looked me over before calling a taxi, was being stored away for future use. I never checked myself in a mirror that whole night, and if this is what Jiro sees when I wear the little black dress, then I will definitely wear it more often. I especially love the expression on my face. It has that hint of evil Jiro says I get when I'm sexy, the same look I used to call him away from the poker table when I wanted to go home.

"That's my favorite," Jiro says, leaning forward.

"I gathered."

"One more. I wanted to draw even more but, well, time has been short."

I expect the sketch to be of us somehow, but it's not. In all of the drawings Jiro has ever shown me, he's never drawn himself. I will have to push him to draw self-portraits. Instead, the drawing is of me and Sakai, sitting at the table during Miko's wedding. When I walked around the table to talk to him, I thought Jiro leaned over to chat with Usagi who was on his other side. No, he must have watched me the entire time. My hand is on the sake cup on the table, and Sakai and I are in deep conversation.

"This one feels especially personal."

"Mark is important to you. He's important to us all, but I think the two of you need each other, just as much as you and I do."

"*Almost* as much," I say, reaching out and holding his hand. "I don't think I could go on without you."

He shakes his head. "Me neither. We're like two halves of the same person. I wasn't whole until I met you." He lifts my hand and presses it to his lips. "Happy twenty-first birthday, Sanaa."

Chapter Forty-Seven

"I don't know what I'll do without a sword." Usagi sits forward and puts his head in his hands on the transitway to Ku 4 from Ku 6, so I get up and sit next to him, hug his arm and rest my head on his shoulder.

"Don't worry. As long as we're together, I'll always make sure you have one. We'll figure it out when we get to Yūsei."

Jiro, Usagi, and I are arriving in Ku 4 for dinner fashionably late. After Jiro and I spent the morning together celebrating our birthdays, we accompanied Usagi to Ku 5 to retrieve his broken sword, but Masa and his shop were unable to fix the tip. Poor Usagi. He's so depressed. He's lost so much this year. First, Helena and now his sword. If only we had caught Kazuo, he would feel like the months he neglected me were worth it. He still apologizes all the time.

"Let's go drink and try to forget about it for tonight," Jiro says, patting him on the back.

"You're right." Usagi sits up and rubs his bald head. "It's time to celebrate birthdays." He smiles weakly at us both, but the effort is lost, even if it is valiant.

A few weeks ago, Jiro asked me what we should do for his birthday, so I suggested we have a big party in Little Italy. When we enter Oyama's pick for a restaurant, the space is filled to capacity. The establishment is spacious with a long bar serving beer and liquor surrounded by four-top tables. The entire front is packed with people eating, drinking, and talking.

Jiro opens the door for me and smiles down at my bare legs. I decided to wear the sweet little gray silk shirt Aunt Lomo made for me and pair it with a black, short skirt I picked up last week. Ever since I wore that dress to the casino, Jiro keeps saying I should wear skirts more often. What he really means is I should wear skirts without underwear more often. He mentions it at least once per week, so today's his birthday, and I happily oblige him.

We arrive in the back room, and a chorus of happy birthdays and otanjōbi omedetōs greet us from all of our family and friends. Even Aunt Kimie and Lomo are here as well. This is another moment when I know Jiro misses Koichi, and I miss him and Helena.

The sea of people part, and I spot Chad and a small Japanese girl our age talking to Sakai in the back. My past and present lives are colliding in one big room. I pull Jiro with me to talk to Chad and the way he's smiling at his girlfriend I immediately know they're in love. All of the time we've spent apart this year dissolves away, and it feels like yesterday that I walked into work and handled the changes Emiko Matsuda had brought upon us.

My smile falters a moment when I remember everything that happened that day — alterations to the ship specs, to the housing designs I was assigned, new astral coordinates. Something big and significant changed right then. Why? Did it have something to do with me? Or was it a coincidence I was taken from my job the same day?

Chad turns and we smile at each other, all nagging thoughts of the colonization washed from my mind. His normally dark, African skin is bright and cheery, happier than I've ever seen him. I introduce Jiro, and I'm so pleased Chad and Jiro get along right off the bat. Chad's girlfriend, Izumi, works in my old department at the Colonization Committee. She's smart and petite much like me. I try not to smile when I realize I was more Chad's type than he was mine.

"The short hair is nice, Sanaa. I almost didn't recognize you when you walked in."

"It may seem like I've changed a lot, but really, I'm the same old me."

After dinner, Jiro and I split up for a while and make our way around the room, talking to everyone, trying every last appetizer left on the table, and drinking a whole ton of wine which is not as bad as I originally thought it was. My palate is expanding due to Oyama. I take extra time to sit and reminisce with Chad and get to know Izumi a little better. They can't stay late because they both have early shifts the next day.

I've definitely had too much to drink when I go to Oyama and give him a huge hug to thank him for making Jiro's birthday a success.

"It's your birthday too, Sanaa-san. Happy twenty-first," he says, his voice soft-spoken and kind. I'm too close to him, but I don't care. I've always thought of him as being huggable, but he's on my staff, and I pay his salary, so besides the kiss I gave him for the cake,

I have barely touched him. Times change.

"Oyama, I want beer next, I think. Can I go to the bar and get it from the bartender?"

"Sure. Just watch him pour for other people first, and then watch and make sure he pulls your glass from the same stack as everyone else's glasses."

"Is that how it works?"

"That's my procedure. Then I usually taste the drink as well, but tonight, I think you'll be fine." He smiles and pats me on the shoulder. "I'm glad you're taking an interest. I know you want to be more independent. I hope I can help."

I love Oyama. I'm such a lovable drunk. Love, love, love.

The main dining area has quieted, almost everyone left is finishing up or having another drink before heading home. The lights are low, intimate and romantic with candles lit along the length of the dark bar. I perch myself on a chair and am diligently watching the bartender draw my beer from the tap when someone comes and sits right next to me.

I turn to smile because I'm sure it's Jiro. He's awfully romantic tonight, his hand always on my waist or hugging me when I least expect it.

It's not Jiro.

"Good evening, Sanaa. I hear birthday wishes are appropriate tonight."

Kazuo. He smiles warmly at me, but I'm frozen inside, my instincts blurred by the amount of liquor sloshing around in my system. What should I do? Yell? Scream? I'm paralyzed.

The bartender sets two drinks down in front of us, and Kazuo jerks his chin at them.

"Let's have a drink together, and then I'll go." He picks up his own beer and takes a long swig from the glass. His hair is pulled back — jet black this time, no gray — and his ease is so disarming I pick up my beer and sip. I'm way too drunk to be dealing with Kazuo. Is he going to kill me? I have nothing to defend myself with, and Jiro is in another room.

I swear these things only happen when I'm three sheets to the wind. I'd give up drinking too if I thought I'd be safer, but I don't think it'd make a difference.

"I'm obviously not alone. Don't try anything."

"I know." He smiles and laughs. "Trust me, I'm very observant. But I'm here for a reason, and I'm pretty sure you will not be alone for long." He drinks again and drains at least half the pint in one go. "I've interrupted your night to tell you Sachi and I are leaving tomorrow."

"What? Why?"

"It was difficult, but I convinced her to leave now before she completely loses her mind on you. She's been angry for months. I don't think you even had any idea."

I twist my beer in my hand and take another sip. "I've never met her before recently, so, no, I have no idea what you're talking about."

"I know." His face melts into a sympathetic expression and the back of my neck tingles in response. This is wrong, very wrong. "Anyway, I'm having a change of heart, warmed by your compassion for your friends and family. Enjoy your last few days before you go. We won't be around."

He stands up from his chair, smooths out his button down shirt, and unexpectedly leans in to kiss me on the cheek. My whole body snaps back, and I brace myself on the bar as I meet his eyes in a cold stare. How dare he?

But he only smiles and shakes his head.

"Otanjōbi omedetō, Sanaa. See you in another life, on another world." He turns and strides straight for the front of the restaurant, his black boots pounding on the floor.

"Wait!" I call after him, stumbling from my chair, but thankfully, not falling over. "What did you mean, I made Sachi angry? Where are you going? And why are you being nice to me?"

He doesn't answer. The door swings shut behind him, and through the front picture window, his shadow trails off down the street, fading away light years before my fear does.

Chapter Forty-Eight

Kazuo told me to enjoy my last five days, and I just can't. I drunkenly reported to Jiro and Sakai about our confrontation, but all we could do was shrug our shoulders and move on. There's no time left to track him. No time to figure out their plans. Five days is at once the longest and the shortest of time periods. Before I know it, we're saying goodbye to our apartment, to Nishikyō, to our continent, and flying halfway around the world before getting on a train and going straight out to the space elevator.

My life has become surreal and panic-inducing and exciting. My last journey on Earth is not at all how I thought it would be, and yet being back at the base and glimpsing the cliffs in the distance where I lived for several weeks is familiar. Really, I just want to curl up in a ball and go to sleep. I want to shut down. This is too much change.

Jiro and I split up for the ride up to orbit. He wants to be in the observation lounge, but I'm sure I'll panic and completely lose my mind if I'm surrounded by that much blue sky. I tell him to go, and I sit with Beni and my aunts instead. Then a nurse comes by, sees my white knuckles, and offers me meds, and by gods, I take them. Everyone breathes a huge sigh of relief, too, I know it.

The only thing I regret is not seeing the look of joy on Jiro's face as we ascend into orbit.

I'm happy I've taken the drugs. Once the elevator has come to a halt, and the shuttle is docked with us, I float from my spot, giddy and giggling at Beni whose hair surrounds her head like a halo. Tons of people have made this trip before me, and I'm sure I'm not the first nor last silly and drugged-up girl to be pushed along the corridor from the elevator to the shuttle. Zero gravity is a lot of fun, but I doubt I'll remember much of it later. Everything is hazy and soft, and everyone is hilarious, but nothing in my brain is sticking permanently.

Once we're aboard the shuttle, Jiro is seated back next to me, and I grin at him like a lunatic.

"You took the meds?" he asks with a smile.

"Yes. I'm much happier now." I pat his hand a few times and promptly pass out.

I'm woken up at spacedock and feel marginally less drugged, but still very calm, sleepy, and complacent, which is the whole reason why they gave me the drugs in the first place. Now that everything is no longer hilarious, I can't believe how much of a bother zero gravity is. There's no up or down. Everyone is floating, and I'm disoriented. I heard a woman about twenty people behind me panicking five minutes ago. Her voice got progressively higher and higher and higher, and then she was silent. They probably forced the meds on her and good for them. If it were my job to deal with panicking people, I would want them all drugged too.

I am the only one in our party that took them. We wait in line, each of us strapped to the wall in this corridor, and I push to the length of my strap so I can look down the hall at all of my family and friends. Miko is a little green, but she smiles at me when I smile at her. Her parents behind her are bored. Everyone else is doing well, even Aunt Kimie and Lomo. They both take Aunt Lomo's hair out of her clips and play with it. They're funny, those two.

"You seem realllllly happy," Jiro says, poking me in the ribs.

"I am," I say, giving him an exaggerated wink and some finger guns. He lets out a laugh, and Sakai glances over at me with a smile. "Though the bureaucracy is a little tiring, ne?"

"I hate waiting in line. Even in space." He sighs before grabbing my hand and squeezing.

The admitting doctors can only take six people at a time so we wait. Eventually, I'm unstrapped from the wall by an assistant, pulled into a small room, and strapped to the wall again so I don't float away. A young female doctor scans my hand and types into her tablet.

"Okay, Ms. Itami. Your birth control implant has been deactivated and won't be reactivated until you're awake. Of course, this doesn't mean you are immediately ripe for impregnation, but still, sexual intercourse on the ship and before hibernation is strictly prohibited."

Damn.

"If you've had sex in the last twenty-four hours, please indicate so right now."

"I have."

"Then we will give you an extra spermicide as a precaution. The hibernation drugs will pick up where the birth control implant left off but the twelve-hour fasting period before hibernation gives some doctors pause. The spermicide is not necessary, but it's also very important that no one becomes pregnant on the flight. Now, looking over your records from your Nishikyō doctor, everything else is in order. You took the meds on the way up?"

"I did indeed," I say with a wide smile, and she smiles back.

"You did indeed. They'll wear off soon. From here, you'll be shuttled to your ship with the rest of your hibernation class. You'll be given a tour, meet the crew, put in flight jump suits, and then hooked up to an IV for nutrition to begin your twelve-hour fast. You are to empty your bladder and bowels as many times as possible, but in general, you won't do much during the twelve hours. Rest, visit with your friends and family, look out the window, read, and try to relax. When the fast is over, we'll get you in your hibernation suit, and you can work with your hibernation techs on who goes to sleep first. It's different for every class."

"And then?"

"You go to sleep, and we'll see you in seven point four-five years."

Seven point four-five years.

I'm glad I'm on the meds because I smile and nod and move out into the back hall with everyone else without breaking into tears.

We're all loaded into another shuttle with no windows. Only about ten minutes pass before the doors open again, and we're at the ship. I didn't even know we were moving. I like that they kept the stars and open space hidden for these transitions. I would've been overwhelmed by it.

Once we're off the shuttle and floating into the ship, I feel a little more like myself and, thankfully, less anxious. The process has been going smoothly, and I'm not as worried anymore. Our class is greeted by a young Japanese man with a military-style buzz cut and wearing a flight suit.

"Hello and konnichiwa. Welcome aboard *The Murasaki*. Your home for the next seven and a half years asleep. I am Flight Supervisor Hoshi Endo, and I will be your flight class coordinator."

I am secretly pleased our ship is named after the author of *The Tales of Genji*. I love that book.

Behind Hoshi Endo, the corridor is bright white and simple. All the metal we salvaged from Earth was hauled up here to make these ships, and seeing it now, I'm impressed. Everything looks brand-new and not the least bit recycled. The whole ship is not metal, of course. I didn't babysit all of those composite labs for nothing. I know the windows are made of super strong transparent composite material we developed a few years ago.

"Your tour before fasting will be short, but you'll be guided through the main areas. We'll float past the flight deck where you can meet the first-leg Captain. There are eight crews for this flight that will rotate in and out of hibernation. We do this to conserve resources and to make it fair for the crews who still want to see their families again someday. Hibernation technicians operate on a one-year rotation as well but they are woken up twice during the trip and hence there are only four crews."

I'm fascinated by all the information coming at me, and my eyes are locked on Hoshi as he gives his prepared speech. I'm glad to hear the Committee thought about the crews' families.

"After the flight deck, we'll float past the short-stay quarters, then the crew quarters, and then the multi-purpose room which is where you will spend the majority of your time here. Tours of the engine room are not provided, sorry. Please don't ask for one. Crews are triple-checking the hyperdrives and calculations and cannot be disturbed. I can tell you we're expecting the trip to take a little less than seven and a half years, and approximately thirty individual jumps with downtime in between."

We didn't see the ship from the outside, but I get the impression it's huge. Corridors stretch down into pinpoints, and we pass doors upon doors upon doors. We float through at least five airlocks, pushing off from walls and climbing along hand-over-hand. Jiro is absolutely tickled the entire time, and I can't help but smile at him especially with his long hair floating around his head. When I'm up next to him, I tuck the strands back and laugh when they refuse to stay put.

After our tour of the flight deck which is a room filled with panels and buttons, we float past the quarters Hoshi Endo spoke about.

"Here are the short-stay quarters where you will bunk after the trip is over and before you are moved planet-side. Our hibernation technicians will also live here during the flight. The next corridor contains all of the crew quarters... And here is the multi-purpose room."

In the large multi-purpose room, opposite the door, is the biggest window I've seen yet, and it provides us with a breathtaking view. We're in orbit over Earth. I knew this, of course, but seeing it with my own eyes is just...

"Amazing." Jiro grabs my hand, and we shoot past everyone else straight for the window. Pressed against the limitless vacuum of space, I feel like I'm falling for a moment, so I close my eyes and take a deep breath before opening them again.

Earth is still beautiful in spite of everything we've done to it. The globe below is steeped in brown and beige, with pockets of tea-colored ocean left in several places. Searching the surface, I spot oases on the mainland and a few of the radioactive fossilized forests. I wonder what future humans will think of Earth if they ever come back here.

Hoshi comes up next to us. "We're pretty far north, and when we hit the dark side, you can see Nishikyō off in the distance." He smiles at us. "It's been a while since I was there."

"It's still the same," I say. "I think it always will be."

Jiro pulls me into a hug, and I look up at his face watching the world turn underneath us.

You're right, Jiro. It is amazing.

Chapter Forty-Nine

Turns out that twelve hours of fasting, even in space with an amazing view, is pretty boring. We're all changed into one-piece flight suits with short sleeves so IVs can be inserted with the bags snaked up and strapped to our backs. Then we hang around the multi-purpose room for hours on end.

At first, we have fun playing in zero gravity. But after spinning in place, throwing objects across the room, and playing pranks on each other for an hour, everyone calms down and lazes about. Near the window are plenty of chairs so we can strap in and rest. Aunt Kimie, Lomo, Miko's parents, Mariko, and Beni all sit down and take a nap.

"I'm pretty tired, but I don't want to go to sleep. I think sleeping for seven years is enough."

On the "floor" are footholds in front of the window, so you can "stand" and look out instead of floating. Jiro cruises over and sticks his feet in, and I maneuver myself into his arms being careful of our IVs. Sakai and Lucy do the same thing all the way on the other end of the window. Miko and Yoichi are off in a corner together. Usagi and Oyama are reading on their tablets, strapped in at a table. I wish more individual rooms existed for some privacy, but at least we all know each other enough to not care about witnessing intimate last moments.

"I'm so glad we had time together before we left," Jiro whispers into my ear. "I want to make sure you're the last person I see before I go to sleep."

The tears start, and I can't stop them, but they're so strange. They break away from my face and float up in and amongst Jiro's hair. He backs up for a moment and laughs.

Gods. Everything is funny in zero gravity, even my sadness.

I take the opportunity to spend time with everyone during the twelve hours. We float around and switch with each other every hour. I talk with Miko about what she and Yoichi did before we left. They spent their time together much the same as Jiro and I did, especially since her birthday is two days after Jiro's. Yoichi and Jiro stare out the window, murmuring quietly to each other. I sit and hold hands with both my aunts and chat about things we did when I was younger, but we fall silent after a while once Aunt Lomo starts to cry. Then I sit with Mariko and Beni and we discuss the first foods we'll eat when we're finally on Yūsei. We have our priorities.

Hibernation technicians come back in around the seven-hour mark and change everyone's IV bags. Usagi is escorted away by a hibernation tech after they have a whispered discussion. I wonder where he's off to?

Despite not wanting to sleep, I can't help but tire. It's been an exhausting day. I yawn so hard my body shakes. Jiro floats me over to a chair and the two of us strap in next to each other and fall asleep for two hours holding each other's hands. Sleeping in zero gravity is very comfortable.

At the eleven-hour mark, the lead hibernation tech comes in and asks to speak with us all. The time has come to decide who wants to sleep first and who wants to be with whom when they go to sleep.

Sakai and Lucy offer to go first.

"I think we'll be fine on our own. Right, Mark?"

My heart skips a beat. Don't cry anymore, Sanaa.

Aunt Kimie and Lomo offer to go next, and I will be with them both. Miko's parents are after them. Usagi and Oyama, then Miko and Yoichi. Mariko and Beni will stay with Miko and Yoichi, and Jiro and I will stay with Mariko and Beni. And finally, Jiro and I will sleep. We'll be the last awake.

Sakai and Lucy leave with a wave of their hands. I want to throw myself after them, hug and kiss, and make a scene like some old Italian grandmother sobbing over the casket of a loved one, but instead I smile and wave back. This is hard enough without added drama.

After ten minutes, Aunt Kimie and Lomo are next, and I float down the hall behind them to Hibernation Chamber 2-1.

"This ship can hold four thousand people in hibernation for the trip," the technician says, leading us through a door to a small room where two suits are waiting for Aunt Kimie and Lomo.

"Wow! Four thousand people? What about the other ships?" I ask. So many people in here, already asleep.

"They're all the same design except for the cargo ship which is, well, just cargo. All of your belongings. But the new ships will carry six thousand people per ship, and the hyperdrives can perform longer jumps, so they will make it to Yūsei faster than we will. We expect second wave to arrive only one year behind us."

"Then do you turn around and go back?"

"Yes, the crew that does the last leg will go back with an empty ship. They expect the trip back to take less time due to course adjustments."

There's so much I never knew about colonization.

Aunt Kimie and Lomo strip down naked after having their IVs unhooked, and I haven't seen either of them like this in a long time so I avert my eyes. They're each given special underwear to wear which the technician explains is similar to a diaper and is changed frequently the first couple of weeks, then a catheter is inserted while we sleep.

To aid in this, the hibernation suits (which we were all measured for before we left) slip over the head, down the arms (there's a cutout for the IV), then the suit is pulled down your body and has a zipper up and down the legs so the lower half of the body can be accessed. This all makes me nervous for a minute that my lower body will be out for everyone to see but the technician smiles and seems really sweet. I guess we have to trust some people.

While my aunts get dressed, I remember I forgot to ask about Helena.

"Oh, yes! Our nanotech superwoman? She's doing great already. Sleeping peacefully three decks down. Her doctor is bunking down with us for a few months before going into hibernation herself. Remarkable stuff. Mr. Harada went to visit her earlier."

So that's where Usagi took off to! He saw Helena with his own eyes. I'm sure he would have said something if she were not right.

The hibernation pods area is astonishingly large, ten units high and hundreds of units long. They do remind me eerily of the morgue but everything is bright and warm and each pod is clear so we can see into it. To the right of Aunt Kimie and Lomo's beds, which are extracted from the wall, Sakai and Lucy are already asleep. It happens so fast. They were awake not ten minutes ago!

Sakai's face is peaceful, his hair undone. I've grown to love that face over this year — it could be stern or happy, sad or loving. And Lucy, she is the best kind of person. I'm lucky to have them both in my life.

All of these goodbyes are making me mushy.

"Sanaa-chan, it's our big moment. For the longest time, I never believed we'd be here, but we are." Aunt Kimie pulls me to her, and Aunt Lomo sandwiches me between them. I love my aunts so much.

"We didn't get to see enough of each other these past few months," I mumble into Aunt Kimie's shoulder. "I want us to live close on Yūsei. Please..."

"Of course. Whatever you want." Aunt Lomo kisses the top of my head, just like when I was a little girl. "We'll see you on the other side."

"Okay, ladies. Climb into your pods, strap in your feet, and lie down. I'll strap down your chest."

My aunts float into their pods, the technician straps them down, hooks up their IVs, and nods to me.

I grab a hand from each of them. "Sweet dreams, you two."

"And you'll be asleep in three, two, one."

Everyone is asleep but Jiro and me. Once we're into our hibernation suits, the technician leaves us alone in the room so we can privately say goodbye to each other. She probably has to do this all the time.

Our final kiss before sleep makes me ache and cry. It reminds me of our first kisses, our lips pressed tightly to each other, my hands clutched to Jiro's strong back. My heart won't stop fluttering, and it's threatening to halt my lungs from breathing. The contact between us is electrifying, energy flowing from Jiro straight into my soul. I wonder if he understands the effect he has on me. I don't like to *need* or rely on anyone, but I do love being in love. I just don't want it to end right now.

Panic seeps into my chest. I want to abandon this idea of sleeping apart for seven years and go back home. I know I can't.

Jiro pulls away from me, holds my face, and searches my eyes. "We'll be fine. No worries," he says, enfolding me in a hug.

"Jiro," I whisper in his ear, "I never made out a will, but I'll tell you what I want if I don't make it."

"Shhh. Don't say such things." His voice cracks, and no, I don't want to go on. Don't want to say these things aloud.

"You never know. Just listen to me. I want to be cremated, and my ashes spread over grass wherever our family settles. Lay me someplace green under the sky I'm so afraid of. And you should marry and have a big family but never forget me."

He hugs me even tighter. "I could never forget you."

I press the side of my head against his, and we both exhale at the same time.

"What do you want, Jiro?"

"Cremated, and I hope there'll be forests there."

"Like your tattoos?"

His head nods next to mine.

"Okay. Remember how much I love you."

"And I you. You're my one and only."

I want to show him I'm strong, I can do this, so I pull away and smile at him. I take in every detail of his dark eyes, his eyebrows that only curve the slightest amount, his powerful chin, his lips I want to kiss again but don't. If everything goes all right, I'll feel like no time has passed.

Jiro turns and knocks on the door.

At our beds, I strap my feet down and lay back as the technician reaches into Jiro's pod and secures him across the chest before securing me. I have a fleeting moment of panic, imagining Kazuo above me, watching me sleep. Where did he go? Don't think about it, Sanaa.

I'm glad I'm across from Jiro so I can see him, just like I wanted, and his smile puts my fears at rest.

"Okay, you two. You'll be asleep in three, two, one."

The last thing I see is my love looking back at me.

Chapter Fifty

"Sanaa, it's time to wake up."

What?

"Sanaa, open your eyes slowly and try not to move too much."

"Jiro?"

Open my eyes? Is he kidding me? I just went to sleep. But I can't follow directions anyway because nothing about my body wants to work.

Wait. I can move my mouth. Did I move my mouth? Did I actually say Jiro's name out loud?

"Yes, love. It's me. I'm right next to you."

I manage to crack my left eye a little bit — just a little — and my bed is not as bright as I remember it being a moment ago when I fell asleep. I did fall asleep a moment ago, right? Something must have gone wrong.

"My... eyes... stuck." My eyelids are gummy and frozen in place, and my mouth is dry, my lips slow, my voice a whisper.

"Hold on a second," says a voice I've not heard before. A warm, wet cloth is placed on my eyes and gently wipes away the sleep from them. Jiro chuckles as I sigh with relief.

"Oh my gods. Your hair is so long."

"It is?"

I slowly open my eyes, and Jiro is over me. He's clean-shaven, but wow, his hair is long, too. He braided it down, the white streak in his hair snaking in and out of the bumps. His face is softer and a little older. I can hardly believe it but he's even more like Sakai than before.

"Jiro, did... we... make it?"

He smiles and nods at me. I want to jump up and get out of here right now.

"Sanaa Itami, welcome back," says the voice I don't know again. "I'm right behind you. My name is Cathy, and I've been your technician for this last year of flight. It's nice to meet you." Whoever this Cathy is I love her already. She has a sweet, British accent that reminds me of Lucy. "Now, I've been pumping you full of fluids for the past hour and removed your catheter. Pretty soon, you're going to want to go to the bathroom, and your first time will be a little painful. It's completely normal. You should be fine within twelve hours. Jiro here tells me he's your husband?"

"Yes, though, I guess... not on official documents." My voice is so slow. It hasn't been used in seven years?

"Good enough for me. He's been awake now for twenty-four hours and knows what you'll be going through. You both are in remarkable shape, though. Whatever you did before you left, it was a good idea."

Jiro leans down and kisses me on the cheek. Warmth bursts there as he presses his lips to me before he pulls away to whisper, "See? I told you it would be fine."

I can't turn my head and meet his eyes because a strap is across my forehead, holding my head in one spot. Wow, hibernation works. No dreams, no awareness of time passing. Just unconscious one moment, awake the next.

Cathy unstraps my head, and Jiro unstraps my chest.

"You should be able to sit up, but it may take some effort. Your muscle mass is still pretty dense, though. I suspect you'll be fast to recover much like your husband."

"I'm as weak as a baby," Jiro says. His voice is deeper than it used to be, and he's the same, but, yeah, older. It's crazy.

I get my arms next to me, and because my legs are strapped down, I can use my hips as leverage to push myself up. Sitting requires a lot of effort though. I'm definitely weak.

My hair drifts up to me, and I gasp, completely startled. It's so long, back past my shoulders again with a small brown patch on the tips near the front of my face where my hair was red.

"Here, Jiro," Cathy says. Her hand drifts in from my peripheral vision holding out a hair elastic to Jiro. He gently pulls my hair back and secures it at my neck. Mmmm, his touch is warm and sends an involuntary shiver up my spine.

"Your face has changed a little, Sanaa. Not too much."

"Same for you." My voice and lips are still so slow, it comes out like, "Saaaammmme foooooor yooooou."

He cocks his head and smiles at me. "I think you could use some coffee."

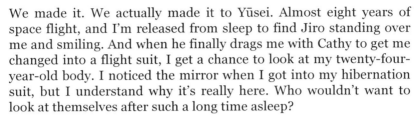

We made it. We actually made it to Yūsei. Almost eight years of space flight, and I'm released from sleep to find Jiro standing over me and smiling. And when he finally drags me with Cathy to get me changed into a flight suit, I get a chance to look at my twenty-four-year-old body. I noticed the mirror when I got into my hibernation suit, but I understand why it's really here. Who wouldn't want to look at themselves after such a long time asleep?

I've never had much in the way of body hair so at least that's not a problem. My arms and legs are supple, but I can tell where the muscles were. I glance back at my tattoos, and they're still gorgeous. My gaze falls down across my chest, and wow, my breasts have grown at least a size — probably due to the shift in fat on my body.

"I'm a lucky man," Jiro says, laughing, and I roll my eyes at him and blush while trying to get the suit zipped up over them. I wonder what he's like under his suit. I scan him from his head to his toes, and my blush rockets to flaming red levels.

Jiro leans in after I'm dressed and whispers so Cathy can't hear, "I can still read your mind, and it's as dirty as it ever was."

"You should talk."

He pulls me in and hugs me tight. We're both soft and comforting.

"I feel like no time passed, but I still missed you. How is that?" Jiro's breath tickles my ear. I lean my head against him. "It was strange being awake before you. I watched you for an hour yesterday. Cathy had pulled your hair under your head, and you looked almost the same."

"I missed you, too. Did you dream?"

"No, and I'm glad of it."

"Me, too."

After some practice with Jiro talking about what to expect with my body for the next few hours, my voice speeds back up to normal. Then I have the urge to urinate like Cathy said I would. The first time is indeed painful, and I hate peeing in zero gravity. This vacuum contraption is no fun as far as I'm concerned.

After I'm done in the bathroom, I have some time to be with Jiro alone before he brings me up to the multi-purpose room.

"Have you seen the planet? Are we in orbit over Yūsei?" He nods at me, but his expression lacks the twinkle and smile I expected. "What is it? Something's wrong, I can tell."

"Mark woke me up a day earlier than you so he and I could speak before we woke you up. Yūsei is everything we expected, and, well, more."

My heart is threatening to jump out of my chest, and I think I may up and die. My body is too weak for this kind of excitement.

"What? You're going to give me a heart attack. Just tell me already."

He shakes his head. "No. This will be better if you see it for yourself, and we woke you now because now is the right time to see it. Remember. I like to surprise you."

He pulls my hand, but my vision starts to darken. "Jiro, I'm going to pass out."

"It's okay. Don't panic. Trust me." He pulls me from under my arm and pushes me up from behind.

When we get to the multi-purpose room, Sakai and Lucy are waiting for us. I float straight to Sakai for a hug. He's the same except for his longer hair and shadow of a beard. I wonder how often the men are able to shave in space? Lucy's hair is ridiculously long, and she has a few extra lines around her eyes but her smile is the same.

"Sanaa-chan, wow. You look, dare I say it, more like your father this time. And your hair is long again." Sakai's arms tighten around me, and he's softer too. We're all going to have to exercise as soon as possible.

Lucy and I kiss on the cheek. "Sanaa, it's good to see you. Are you ready? Look." She turns me. I put one arm around her and the other around Sakai since their feet are strapped in.

The planet below us is beautiful. Wide oceans in every saturation of color from light aquamarine to deep royal blue stretch out in front of me. And there are clouds in the sky! There haven't been clouds on Earth in at least a hundred years. They swirl and dot all over the ocean like cotton.

The globe is slowly rotating and land comes up from underneath us. One large continent spans the majority of my view from white snowy mountains in the north bordering a wide desert, beige and ochre. The mountains trail south along the center of the continent with forest and farmland on either side. Two large lakes, one white and the other black, dominate the continent with rivers flowing in every direction. A string of smaller islands, each a substantial size, sits off the coast in the south. This is an incredible stretch of land, right before me.

Yūsei is glorious.

But wait... Farmland. Regular farmland.

"Mark, what? What am I seeing?"

"Shhh, Sanaa. It's coming," Jiro says. He and Lucy nod at each other.

"What?" I whisper, my voice retreating.

"Nighttime."

A line of darkness creeps across the globe. The terminator, the line between day and night, makes its way across the vista below, and as nighttime hits the mainland, my stomach sinks.

Lights. I see lights.

My new home?

It already has residents.

END BOOK TWO

Thank You!

Thank you so much for reading *Released*. I hope you don't hate me for that ending. Don't worry. There are more Nogiku Series books!

You can buy the next book in the Nogiku Series, *Reunited*, right now!

Would you like to know when my next book is available?
Get my **Newsletter** at
http://www.spajonas.com/newsletter
or follow me on **Twitter** at
http://www.twitter.com/spajonas
or Like me on **Facebook** at
http://www.facebook.com/SJPajonas

Please consider leaving a review of *Released* on Amazon, Barnes & Noble, Goodreads or wherever you find reviews. Your review can help other readers find books they'll enjoy. I appreciate all reviews, positive or negative.

This is the second book in the Nogiku Series. You can learn more about this series and my other works of fiction at http://www.spajonas.com

Thank you for reading!

A Note About Honorific Suffixes

In Japanese, the most common way of showing respect to another person's social standing is with the use of honorific suffixes that are appended on the end of either first or last names. The most common, -san, means either Mr., Ms., or Mrs. When you are addressing someone who is higher in the chain of command than yourself (i.e. your boss or high elected officials deserving of respect) you should use the suffix -sama. When addressing friends or schoolmates, it's popular to use -chan or -ko for girls (sometimes cutting their first name down to one syllable before appending the suffix) and -chan or -kun for boys.

It's important to note that you should never use a suffix on your own name. If you're introducing yourself, do not call yourself David-san or Smith-san. Just David or David Smith will do.

Glossary

Since Nishikyō is seventy percent Japanese, most of the people speak Japanese as part of their daily life whether they are Japanese or not. It was important, therefore, to keep some of the dialogue Japanese without explaining too much and interrupting the story.

For a list of Japanese Terms used in this book and the entire Nogiku Series, please visit http://www.onigiripress.com/NogikuGlossary

The Structure of Nishikyō

By the time Sanaa's story takes place, Nishikyō has been around for 350 years already. Built in the northern wilderness of remote Canada, it was conceived to house the last of Earth's residents after the Environmental Decline. Japan, always technologically advanced and ready for any natural catastrophe, fared the best of every nation on the planet hence the population of Nishikyō is seventy percent Japanese.

The city is domed for normal habitats due to the heat and decline of atmosphere on Earth, though every ward has distinct buildings to house the residents. Nishikyō has both above-ground and below-ground structures.

Nishikyō is shaped like a clock with Ku 1 directly north at the top, Ku 2, the Medical Services Ward, at the center, and the rest of the city laid out around Ku 2 clockwise. Ku 8, the Extinction Ward, and Ku 10, the Farming Ward, both spiral out from the city farther into the desert than any of the other wards. Most wards are linked by footpaths and street tunnels but the transitway is the easiest way to get anywhere in the city.

Nishikyō is divided into ten wards or kus.

Ku 1 - Administration & Business Ward: This is where all governmental work is done.

Ku 2 - Medical Services Ward: This ward is solely dedicated to Medical and Pharmaceutical services. Geographically, it's in the center of the city so that it can be easily reached in an emergency.

Ku 3 - Multicultural Mix Living Quarters: This ward contains the majority of the Middle East, India, Russia, China, and its surrounding countries' refugees.

Ku 4 - Multicultural Mix Living Quarters: This ward contains the majority of European, Australian, African, and surrounding island nation refugees.

Ku 5 - Multicultural Mix Living Quarters: This is the ward in which Sanaa grew up. Like Kus 3 and 4, it is a mix of residential and businesses and contains the majority of North and South American refugees as well as a high Japanese population since it's located directly next to Ku 6.

Ku 6 - Japanese Living Quarters: This is where Jiro grew up, where the Itō family dōjō is located, and where most of the story takes place.

Ku 7 - Entertainment Ward: Izakaya Tanaka is located here as are most movie theaters, gaming establishments, love hotels, restaurants, and okiyas.

Ku 8 - Extinction Ward: This is where most research is done on plants, animals, and artifacts that have been cataloged and saved after the Environmental Decline. There are no living quarters in Ku 8.

Ku 9 - Science & Engineering Ward: This is where Sanaa lives when the story first begins. It is solely dedicated to Science and Engineering advances, most especially the colonization of Yūsei.

Ku 10 - Farming Ward: By far the largest of all the wards, Ku 10 provides food, beverages, and the majority of textiles to Nishikyō residents. All growing, processing, and distribution of these materials originates here. There are no living quarters in Ku 10.

Acknowledgements

The second book was both harder and easier than the first. The ideas came easy, but they were harder to get into a coherent storyline. The publishing process was easier because I had a lot of knowledge saved away from publishing Removed. But it was a more hectic schedule with Released because I went from my computer to your hands in three months including one last draft edit. I don't regret publishing this one so quickly (it was ready to go) but maybe next time I'll give myself a little more time. Be prepared for more in 2014!

Still, one of my biggest thanks goes out to Jennifer Andrews who helped me shape the Japanese language. She assisted with Removed and Released, and continues to support me and answer my texts. Bless her. She has patience beyond words.

Ladies (and possibly gentlemen), hands off Kentaro. He belongs to Skylar Rudich. I'm not joking about this.

Biggest thanks goes to this long list of earliest readers: Lauren Weinhold, Carli Bandeira, Carrie Coker Bishop, Cathy Rumfelt, Kelly Brock, Aimee Osbourne-Gille, Jessica Fomin, Nicole Kinnunen, Sarah Heath, Amanda Baxter, Mary McKenzie Kelly, Connie Chang Chinchio, Laura Chau, Rebecca Burgess, Laura Taylor, Stephanie Fletcher, Annika Barranti Klein, Cori Wilbur, Pia Bloom Henderson, Karen Clark, Lisa Kelly, Angela Tong, Leah Bear, Katie Benedict, Cathy Bechler, Marie Carney, Michelle Gibbs, Jessie Spressart, Christopher Bechler, Jennifer Wingate Sobolewski, Rangsiwan Fasudhani, Susan Case, Linel Soto, Stephanie Martin, Kristine Monstad, Rachel McElwain, Bertha Crowley, Elizabeth Long, Ingrid D'eon, Elizabeth Lesso, Maya Elson, Yahaira Ferreira, Tien Johnson, and Whitney Gegg-Harrison. These people gave me invaluable feedback and helped craft the end result you just read. I love them all.

Extra thanks goes to Kelly Brock and Sarah LaFleur who helped proofread Released at the last minute.

My SCBWI buddies have been supporting me since Removed with cheering, retweets, and blog posts. Thanks to Kim Sabatini, Jodi Moore, Carli Bandeira, Megan Gilpin, and Katie Carroll.

I continue to be grateful for my family especially my mother and father, Claire and Ray Bush, my brother, Brendan, and his family, my Pajonas side of the family, Vic and Karen, all of my husband's brothers and sisters. Thanks to my girls, C and D, again for letting mommy work while you played with play-doh or stickers. My husband, Keith, must think I'm nuts by now. I woke at 5am every day for over a week to finish this draft, and anyone who knows me knows I am not a morning person. He never once gave me flack for groaning when the alarm went off, and he covered for me on weekends when all I did was edit for eight hours straight. I love him. Thanks, baby.

About the Author

Stephanie (S. J.) is a writer, knitter, amateur astrologer, Capricorn, and Japanophile. She loves foxes, owls, sushi, yoga pants, Evernote, and black tea. When she's not writing, she's thinking about writing or spending time outside, unless it's winter. She hates winter. Someday she'll own a house in both hemispheres so she can avoid the season entirely. She's a mom to two great kids and lives with her husband and family outside NYC. They have no pets. Yet. When it comes to her work, expect the unexpected. She doesn't write anything typical.

Visit her on her website at http://www.spajonas.com/

Made in the USA
San Bernardino, CA
25 October 2018